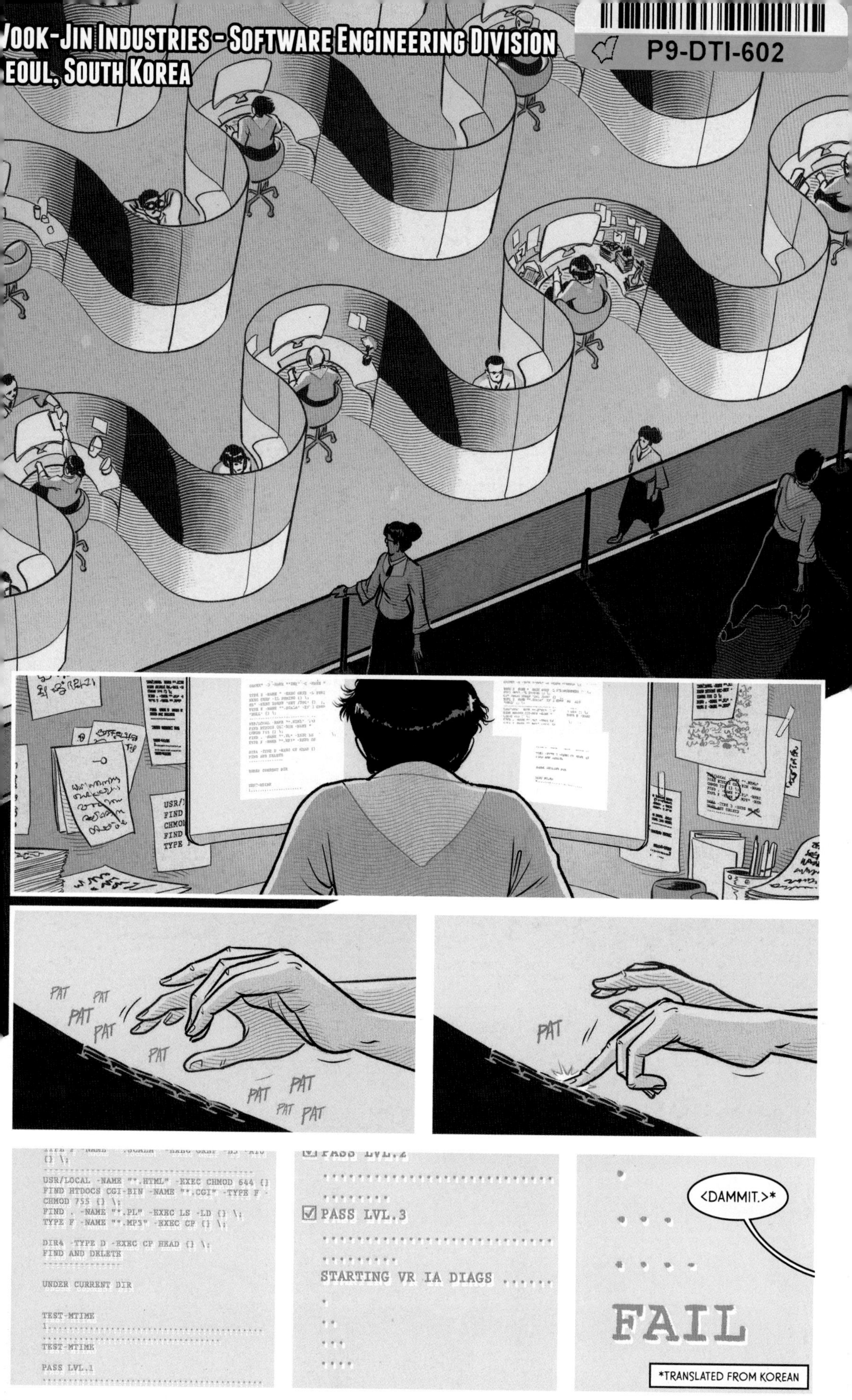
ook-Jin Industries - Software Engineering Division
eoul, South Korea
PAT PAT PAT PAT PAT PAT PAT PAT PAT
PAT
TYPE F -NAME "*.HTML" ...
{} \;
USR/LOCAL -NAME "*.HTML" -EXEC CHMOD 644 {}
FIND HTDOCS CGI-BIN -NAME "*.CGI" -TYPE F -
CHMOD 755 {} \;
FIND . -NAME "*.PL" -EXEC LS -LD {} \;
TYPE F -NAME "*.MP3" -EXEC CP {} \;
DIR4 -TYPE D -EXEC CP HEAD {} \;
FIND AND DELETE
UNDER CURRENT DIR
TEST-MTIME
TEST-MTIME
PASS LVL.1
☑ PASS LVL.3
STARTING VR IA DIAGS
FAIL
<DAMMIT.>*
*TRANSLATED FROM KOREAN

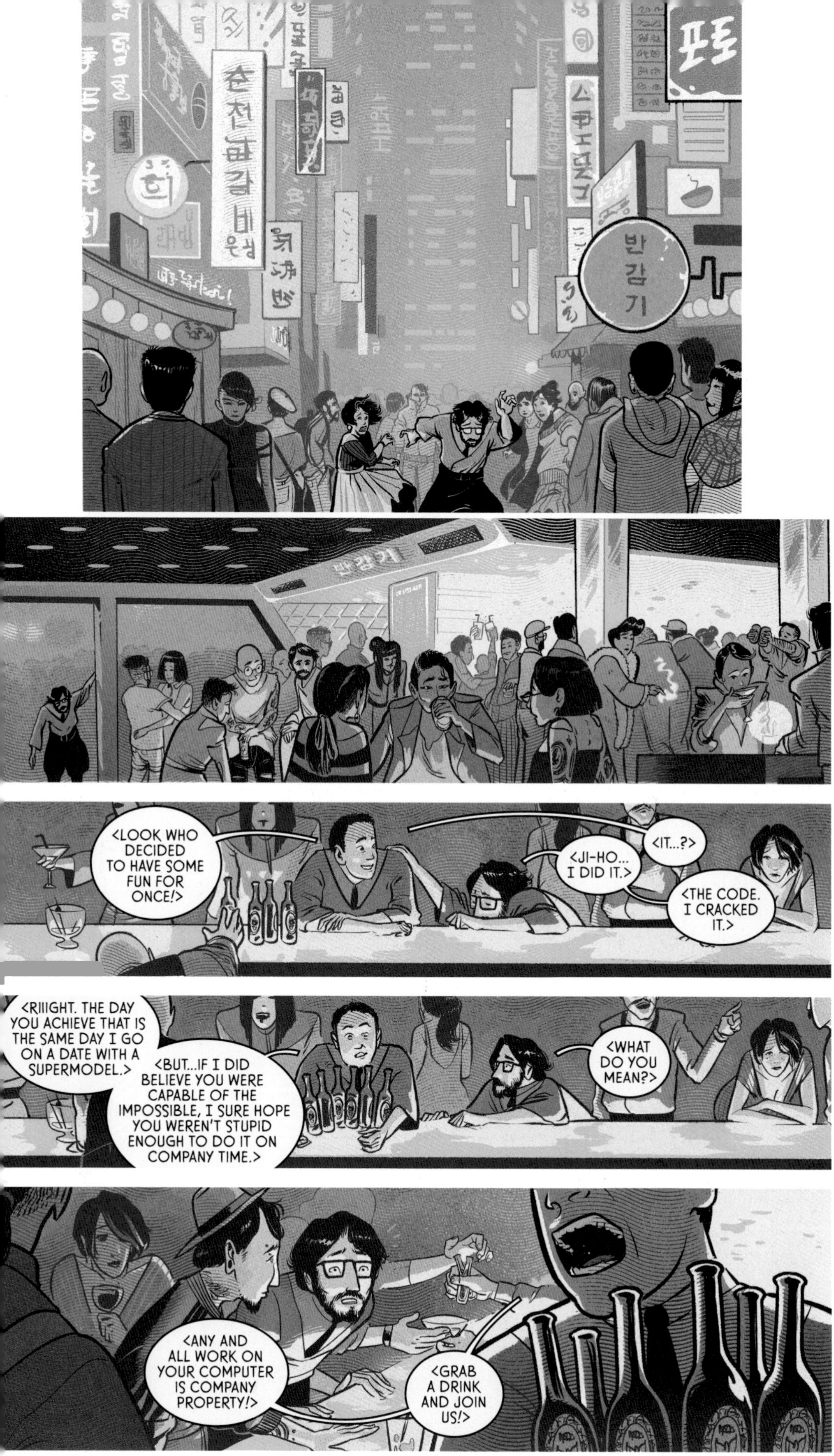
반감기
<LOOK WHO DECIDED TO HAVE SOME FUN FOR ONCE!>
<JI-HO... I DID IT.>
<IT...?>
<THE CODE. I CRACKED IT.>
<RIIIGHT. THE DAY YOU ACHIEVE THAT IS THE SAME DAY I GO ON A DATE WITH A SUPERMODEL.>
<WHAT DO YOU MEAN?>
<BUT...IF I DID BELIEVE YOU WERE CAPABLE OF THE IMPOSSIBLE, I SURE HOPE YOU WEREN'T STUPID ENOUGH TO DO IT ON COMPANY TIME.>
<ANY AND ALL WORK ON YOUR COMPUTER IS COMPANY PROPERTY!>
<GRAB A DRINK AND JOIN US!>

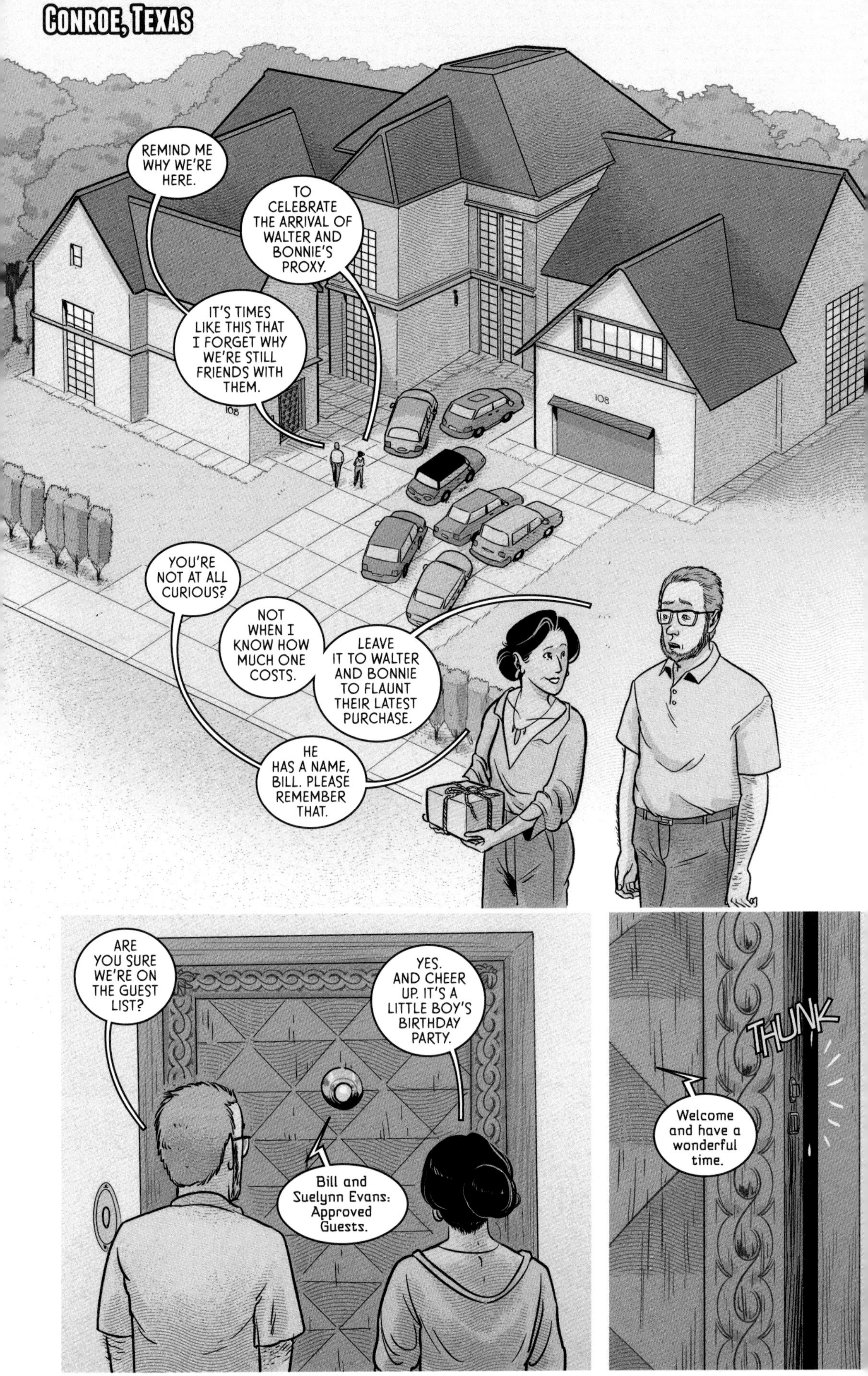
CONROE, TEXAS
REMIND ME WHY WE'RE HERE.
TO CELEBRATE THE ARRIVAL OF WALTER AND BONNIE'S PROXY.
IT'S TIMES LIKE THIS THAT I FORGET WHY WE'RE STILL FRIENDS WITH THEM.
YOU'RE NOT AT ALL CURIOUS?
NOT WHEN I KNOW HOW MUCH ONE COSTS.
LEAVE IT TO WALTER AND BONNIE TO FLAUNT THEIR LATEST PURCHASE.
HE HAS A NAME, BILL. PLEASE REMEMBER THAT.
ARE YOU SURE WE'RE ON THE GUEST LIST?
YES. AND CHEER UP. IT'S A LITTLE BOY'S BIRTHDAY PARTY.
Bill and Suelynn Evans: Approved Guests.
THUNK
Welcome and have a wonderful time.

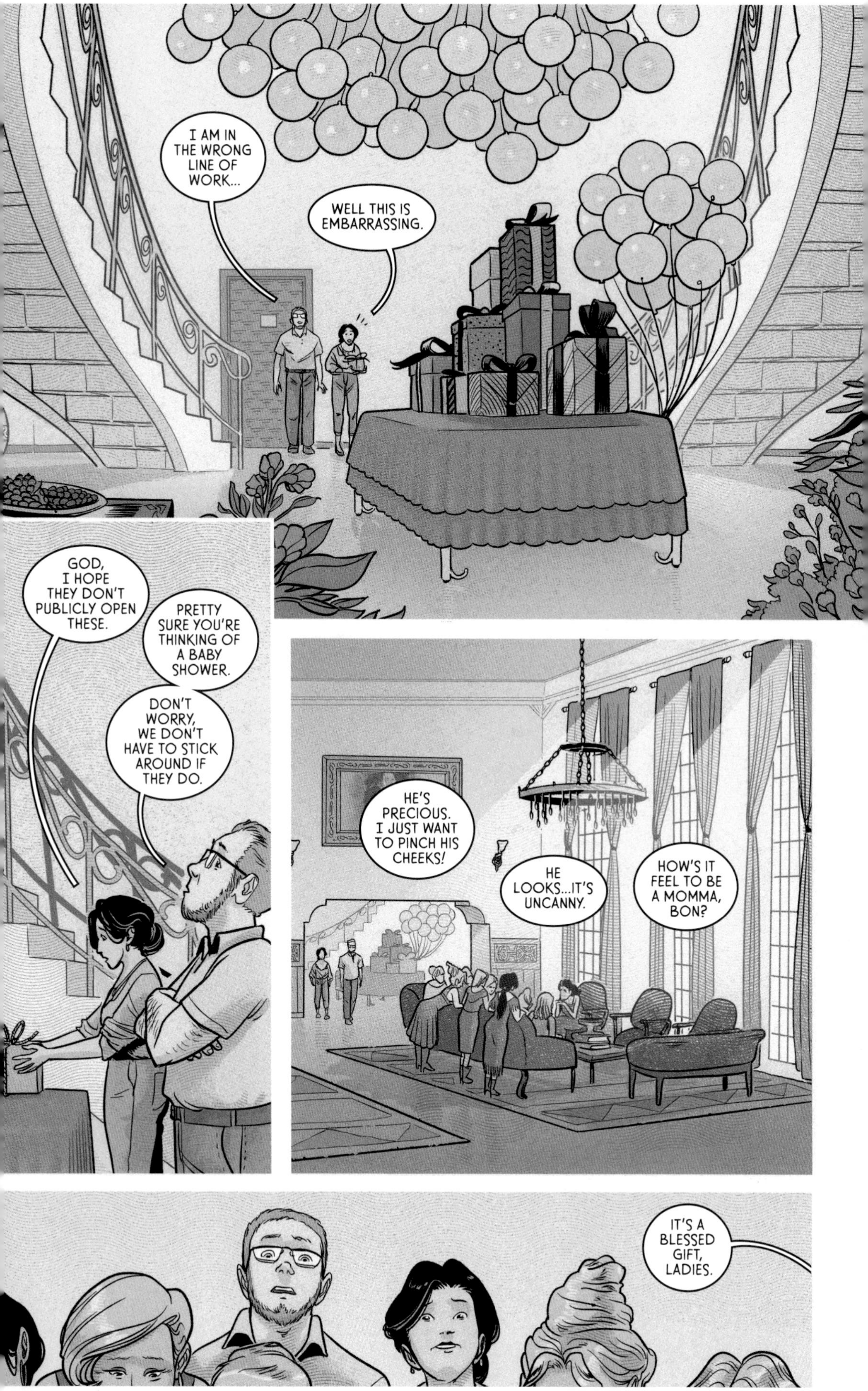
I AM IN THE WRONG LINE OF WORK...
WELL THIS IS EMBARRASSING.
GOD, I HOPE THEY DON'T PUBLICLY OPEN THESE.
PRETTY SURE YOU'RE THINKING OF A BABY SHOWER.
DON'T WORRY, WE DON'T HAVE TO STICK AROUND IF THEY DO.
HE'S PRECIOUS. I JUST WANT TO PINCH HIS CHEEKS!
HE LOOKS...IT'S UNCANNY.
HOW'S IT FEEL TO BE A MOMMA, BON?
IT'S A BLESSED GIFT, LADIES.

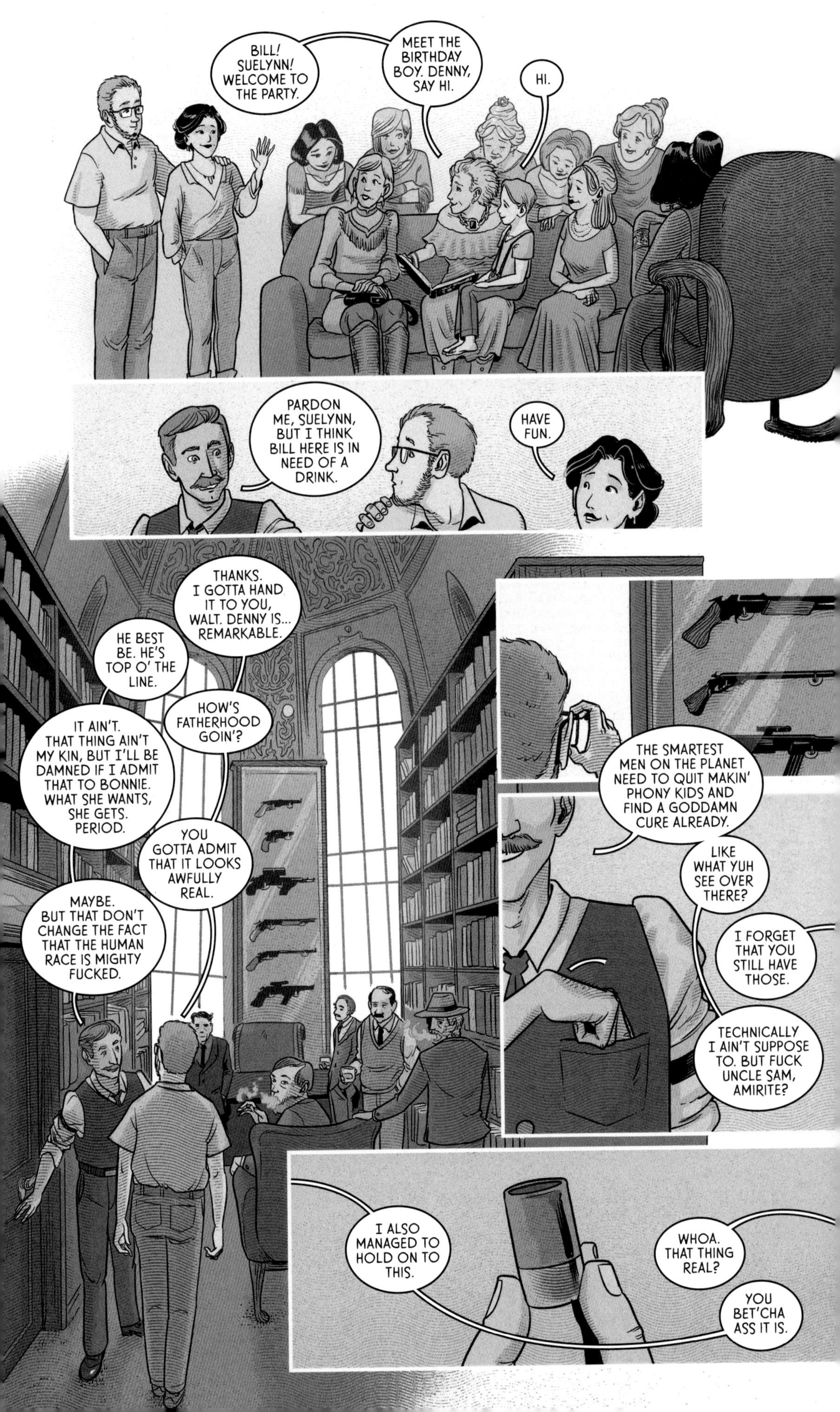
BILL! SUELYNN! WELCOME TO THE PARTY.
MEET THE BIRTHDAY BOY. DENNY, SAY HI.
HI.
PARDON ME, SUELYNN, BUT I THINK BILL HERE IS IN NEED OF A DRINK.
HAVE FUN.
THANKS. I GOTTA HAND IT TO YOU, WALT. DENNY IS... REMARKABLE.
HE BEST BE. HE'S TOP O' THE LINE.
HOW'S FATHERHOOD GOIN'?
IT AIN'T. THAT THING AIN'T MY KIN, BUT I'LL BE DAMNED IF I ADMIT THAT TO BONNIE. WHAT SHE WANTS, SHE GETS. PERIOD.
YOU GOTTA ADMIT THAT IT LOOKS AWFULLY REAL.
MAYBE. BUT THAT DON'T CHANGE THE FACT THAT THE HUMAN RACE IS MIGHTY FUCKED.
THE SMARTEST MEN ON THE PLANET NEED TO QUIT MAKIN' PHONY KIDS AND FIND A GODDAMN CURE ALREADY.
LIKE WHAT YUH SEE OVER THERE?
I FORGET THAT YOU STILL HAVE THOSE.
TECHNICALLY I AIN'T SUPPOSE TO. BUT FUCK UNCLE SAM, AMIRITE?
I ALSO MANAGED TO HOLD ON TO THIS.
WHOA. THAT THING REAL?
YOU BET'CHA ASS IT IS.

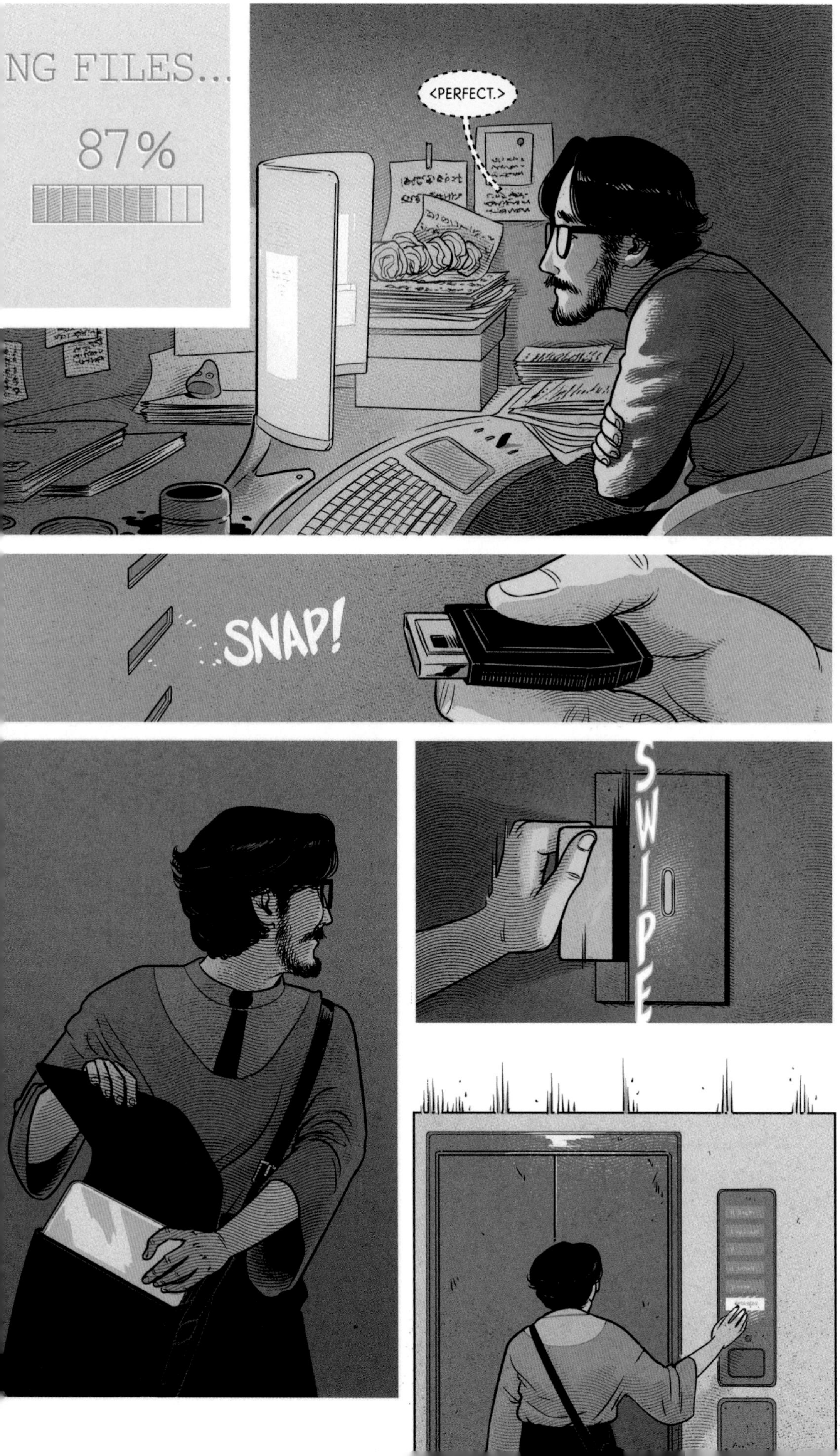
NG FILES...
87%
<PERFECT.>
SNAP!
SWIPE

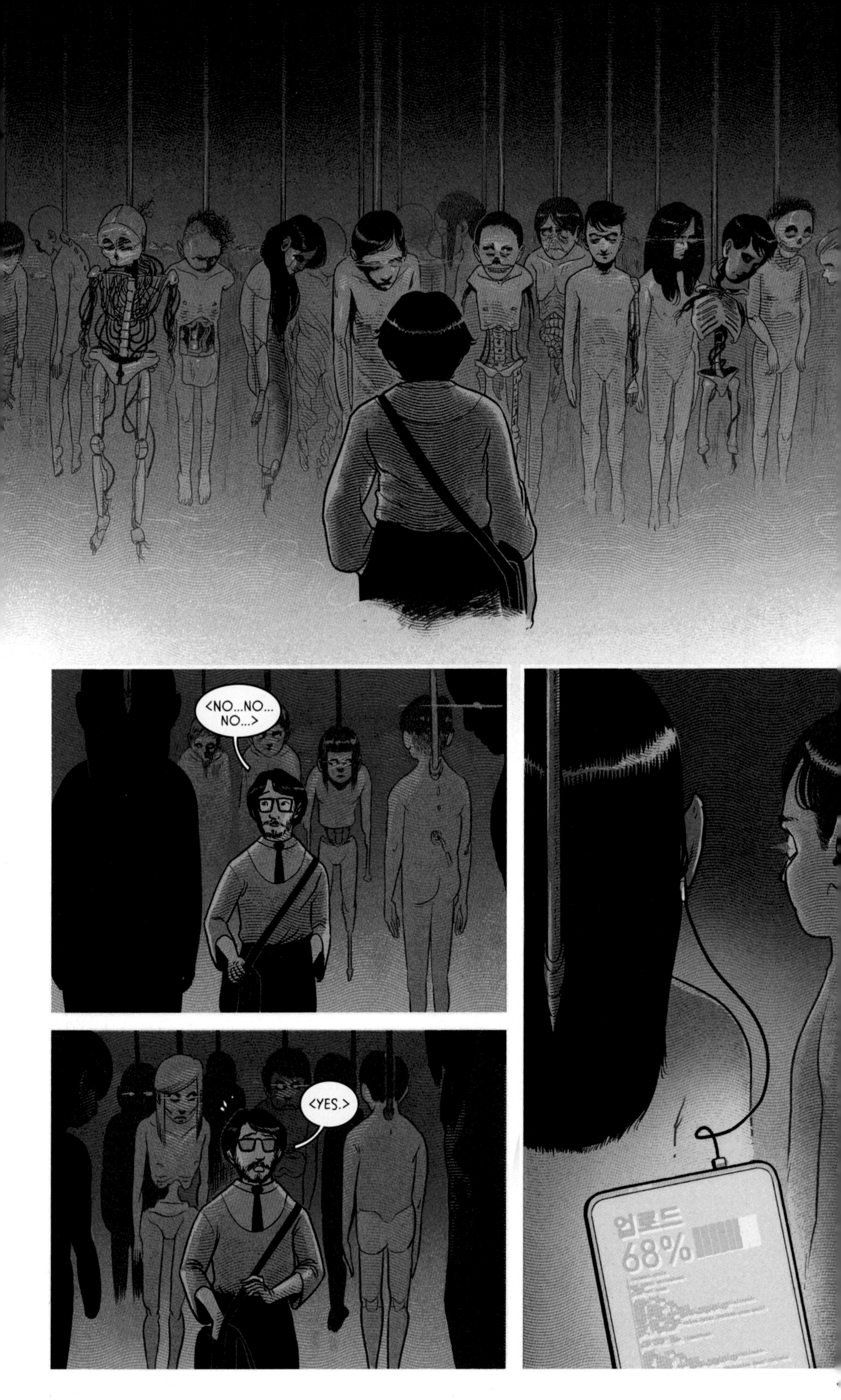
<NO...NO... NO...>
<YES.>
업로드
68%

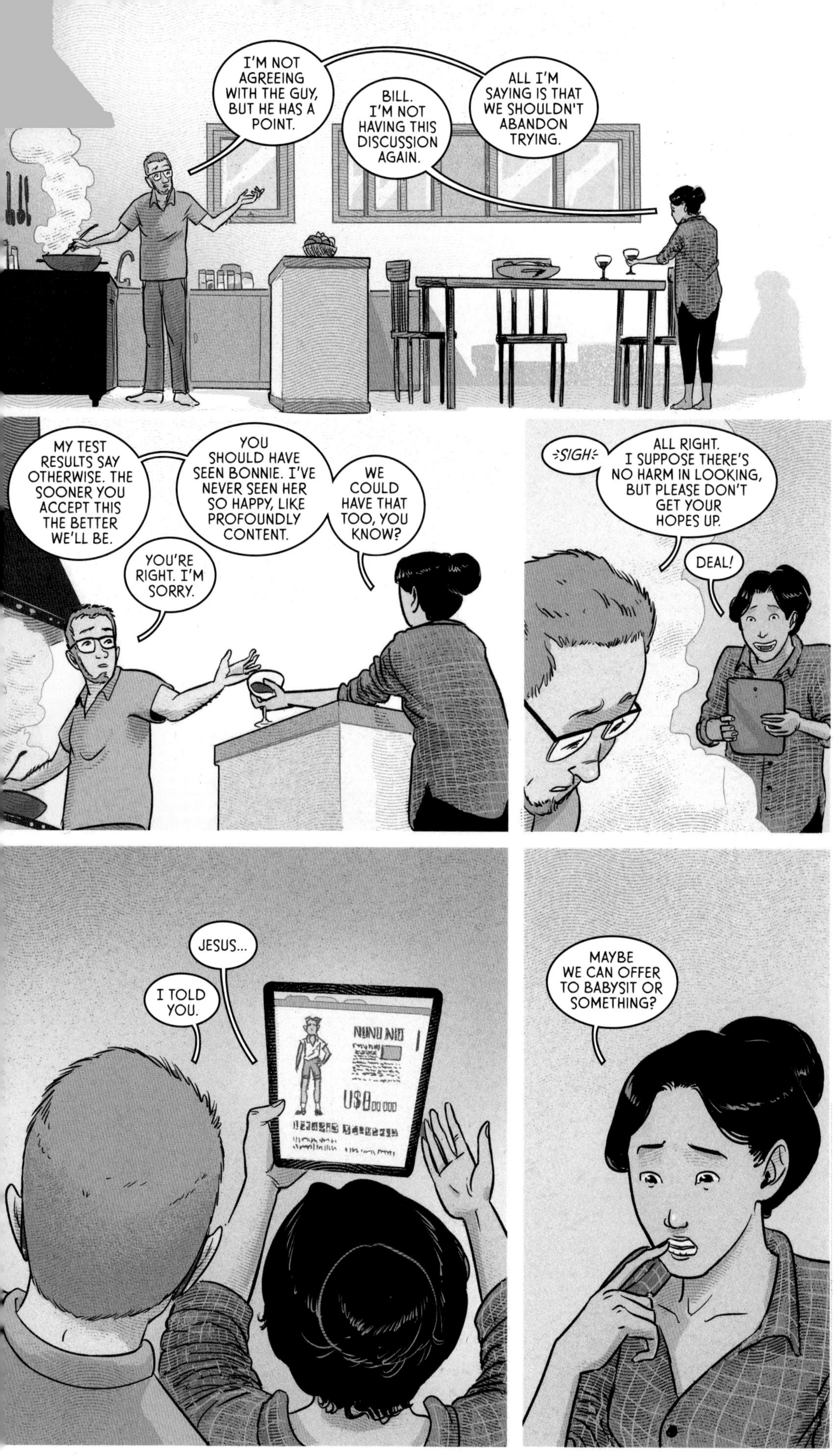

I'M NOT AGREEING WITH THE GUY, BUT HE HAS A POINT.
BILL. I'M NOT HAVING THIS DISCUSSION AGAIN.
ALL I'M SAYING IS THAT WE SHOULDN'T ABANDON TRYING.
MY TEST RESULTS SAY OTHERWISE. THE SOONER YOU ACCEPT THIS THE BETTER WE'LL BE.
YOU'RE RIGHT. I'M SORRY.
YOU SHOULD HAVE SEEN BONNIE. I'VE NEVER SEEN HER SO HAPPY, LIKE PROFOUNDLY CONTENT.
WE COULD HAVE THAT TOO, YOU KNOW?
SIGH
ALL RIGHT. I SUPPOSE THERE'S NO HARM IN LOOKING, BUT PLEASE DON'T GET YOUR HOPES UP.
DEAL!
JESUS...
I TOLD YOU.
MAYBE WE CAN OFFER TO BABYSIT OR SOMETHING?

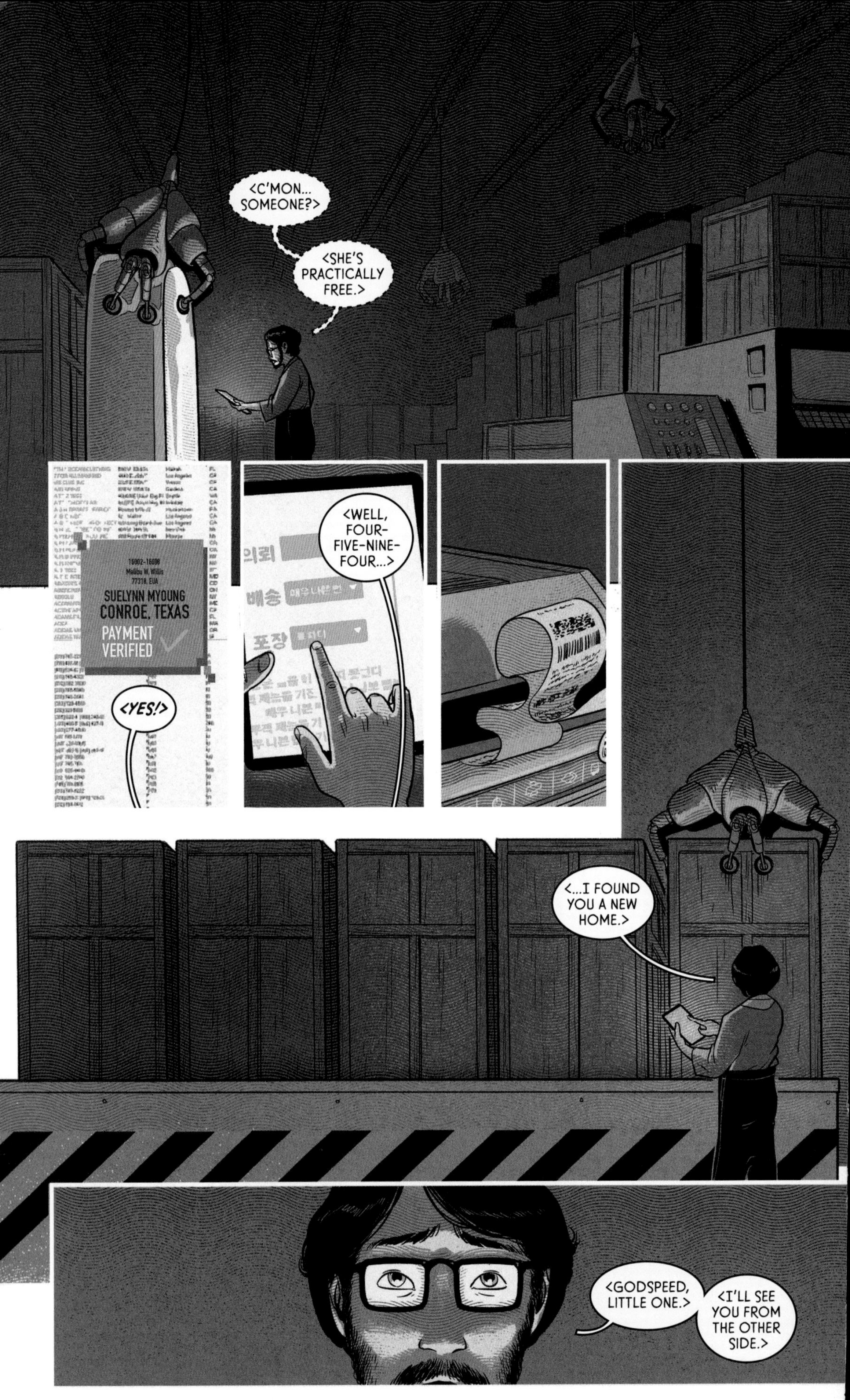

<C'MON... SOMEONE?>
<SHE'S PRACTICALLY FREE.>
16002-16098
Malibu W. Willis
77318, EUA
SUELYNN MYOUNG
CONROE, TEXAS
PAYMENT VERIFIED
<YES!>
<WELL, FOUR-FIVE-NINE-FOUR...>
의뢰
배송
포장
<...I FOUND YOU A NEW HOME.>
<GODSPEED, LITTLE ONE.>
<I'LL SEE YOU FROM THE OTHER SIDE.>

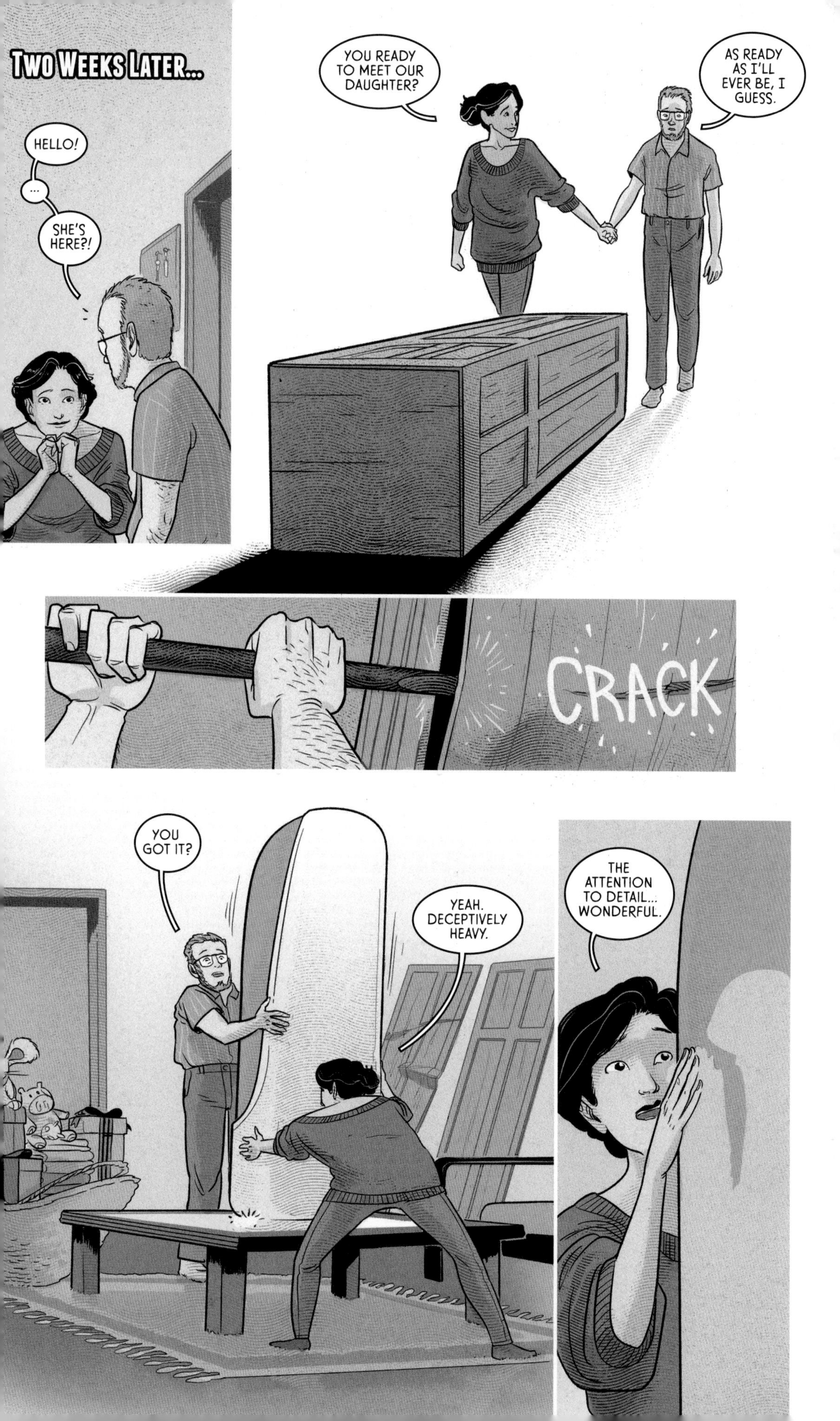
TWO WEEKS LATER...
HELLO!
...
SHE'S HERE?!
YOU READY TO MEET OUR DAUGHTER?
AS READY AS I'LL EVER BE, I GUESS.
CRACK
YOU GOT IT?
YEAH. DECEPTIVELY HEAVY.
THE ATTENTION TO DETAIL... WONDERFUL.

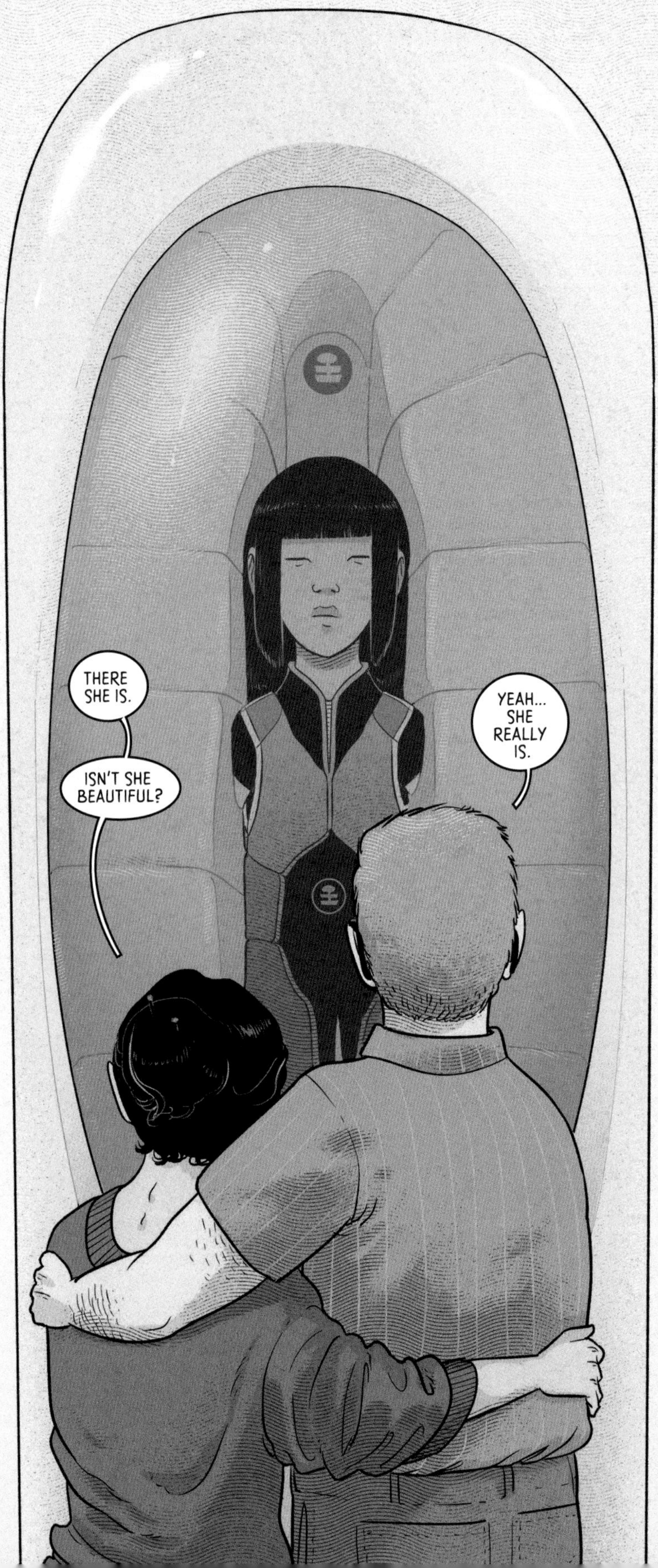
THERE SHE IS.
ISN'T SHE BEAUTIFUL?
YEAH... SHE REALLY IS.

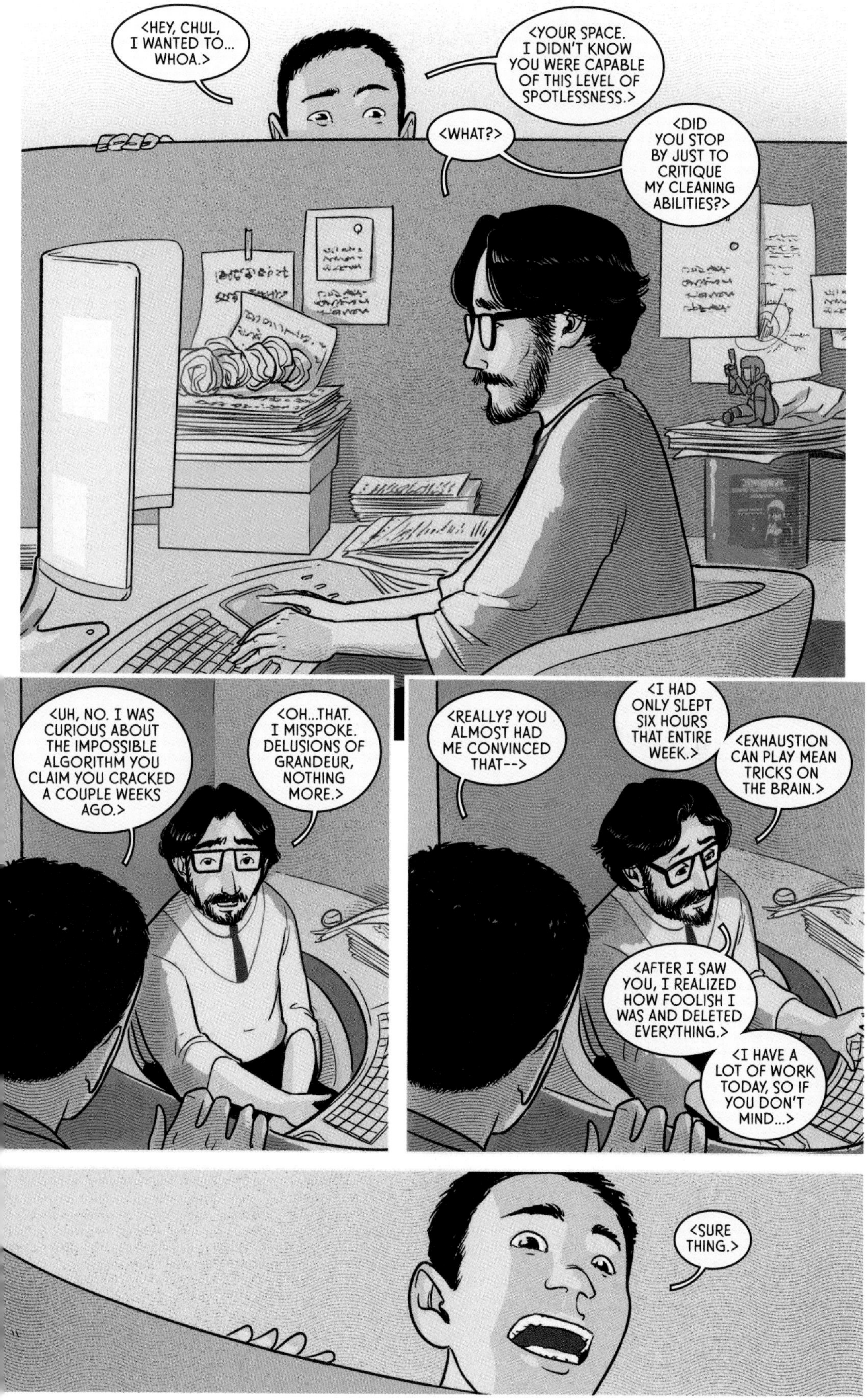
<HEY, CHUL, I WANTED TO... WHOA.>
<YOUR SPACE. I DIDN'T KNOW YOU WERE CAPABLE OF THIS LEVEL OF SPOTLESSNESS.>
<WHAT?>
<DID YOU STOP BY JUST TO CRITIQUE MY CLEANING ABILITIES?>
<UH, NO. I WAS CURIOUS ABOUT THE IMPOSSIBLE ALGORITHM YOU CLAIM YOU CRACKED A COUPLE WEEKS AGO.>
<OH...THAT. I MISSPOKE. DELUSIONS OF GRANDEUR, NOTHING MORE.>
<REALLY? YOU ALMOST HAD ME CONVINCED THAT-->
<I HAD ONLY SLEPT SIX HOURS THAT ENTIRE WEEK.>
<EXHAUSTION CAN PLAY MEAN TRICKS ON THE BRAIN.>
<AFTER I SAW YOU, I REALIZED HOW FOOLISH I WAS AND DELETED EVERYTHING.>
<I HAVE A LOT OF WORK TODAY, SO IF YOU DON'T MIND...>
<SURE THING.>

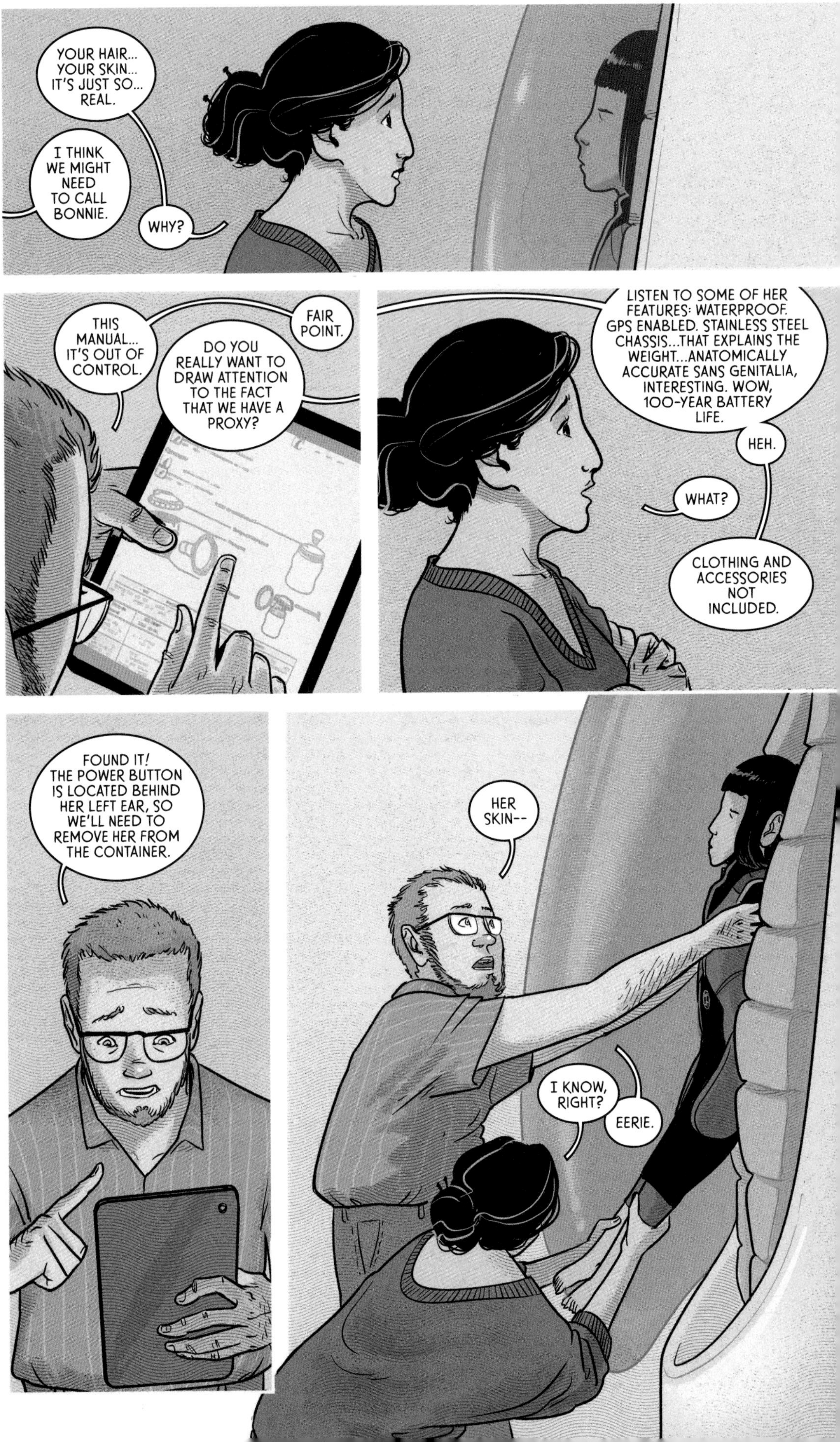
YOUR HAIR... YOUR SKIN... IT'S JUST SO... REAL.
I THINK WE MIGHT NEED TO CALL BONNIE.
WHY?
THIS MANUAL... IT'S OUT OF CONTROL.
DO YOU REALLY WANT TO DRAW ATTENTION TO THE FACT THAT WE HAVE A PROXY?
FAIR POINT.
LISTEN TO SOME OF HER FEATURES: WATERPROOF. GPS ENABLED. STAINLESS STEEL CHASSIS...THAT EXPLAINS THE WEIGHT...ANATOMICALLY ACCURATE SANS GENITALIA, INTERESTING. WOW, 100-YEAR BATTERY LIFE.
HEH.
WHAT?
CLOTHING AND ACCESSORIES NOT INCLUDED.
FOUND IT! THE POWER BUTTON IS LOCATED BEHIND HER LEFT EAR, SO WE'LL NEED TO REMOVE HER FROM THE CONTAINER.
HER SKIN--
I KNOW, RIGHT?
EERIE.

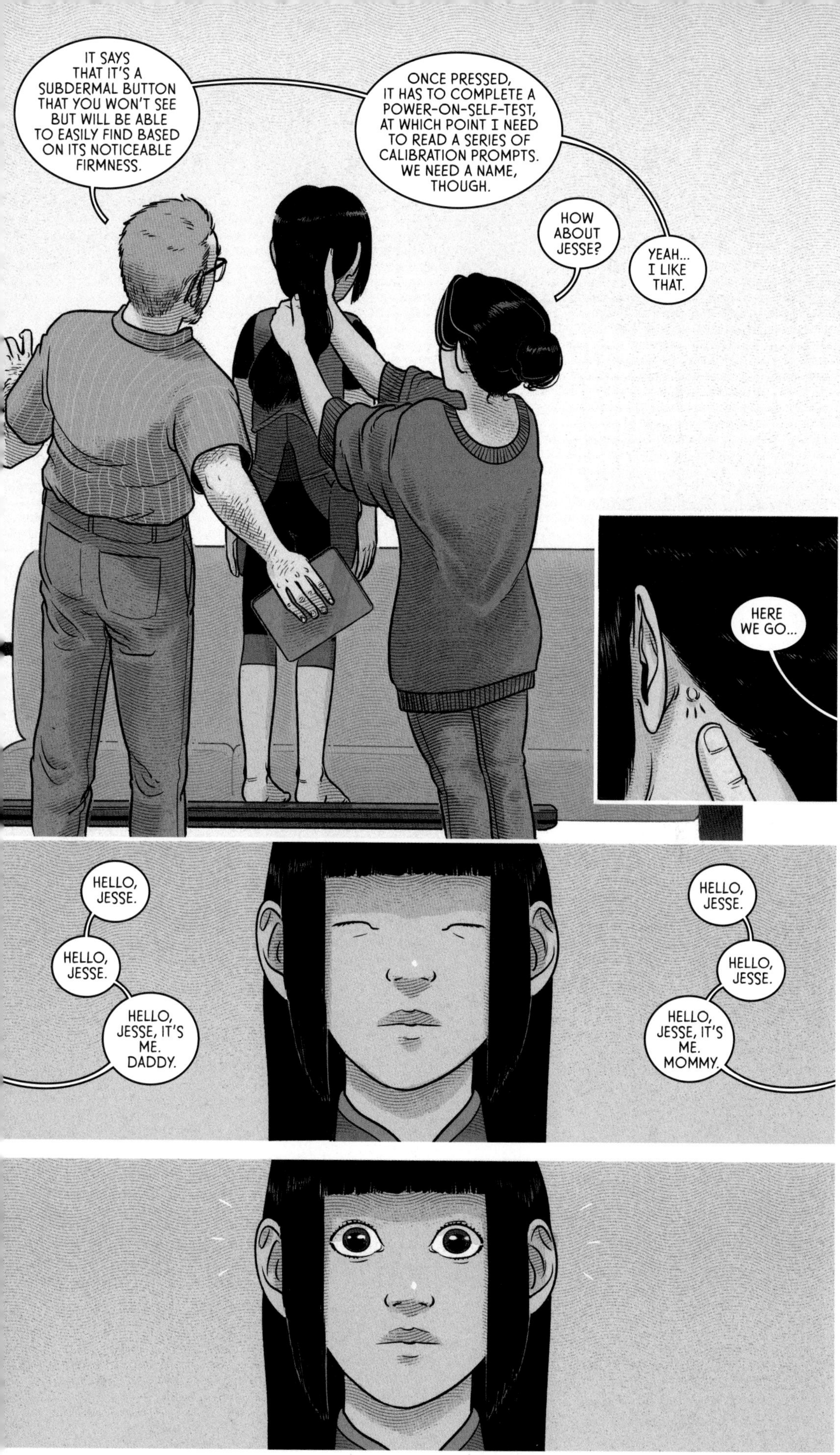
IT SAYS THAT IT'S A SUBDERMAL BUTTON THAT YOU WON'T SEE BUT WILL BE ABLE TO EASILY FIND BASED ON ITS NOTICEABLE FIRMNESS.
ONCE PRESSED, IT HAS TO COMPLETE A POWER-ON-SELF-TEST, AT WHICH POINT I NEED TO READ A SERIES OF CALIBRATION PROMPTS. WE NEED A NAME, THOUGH.
HOW ABOUT JESSE?
YEAH... I LIKE THAT.
HERE WE GO...
HELLO, JESSE.
HELLO, JESSE.
HELLO, JESSE, IT'S ME. DADDY.
HELLO, JESSE.
HELLO, JESSE.
HELLO, JESSE, IT'S ME. MOMMY.

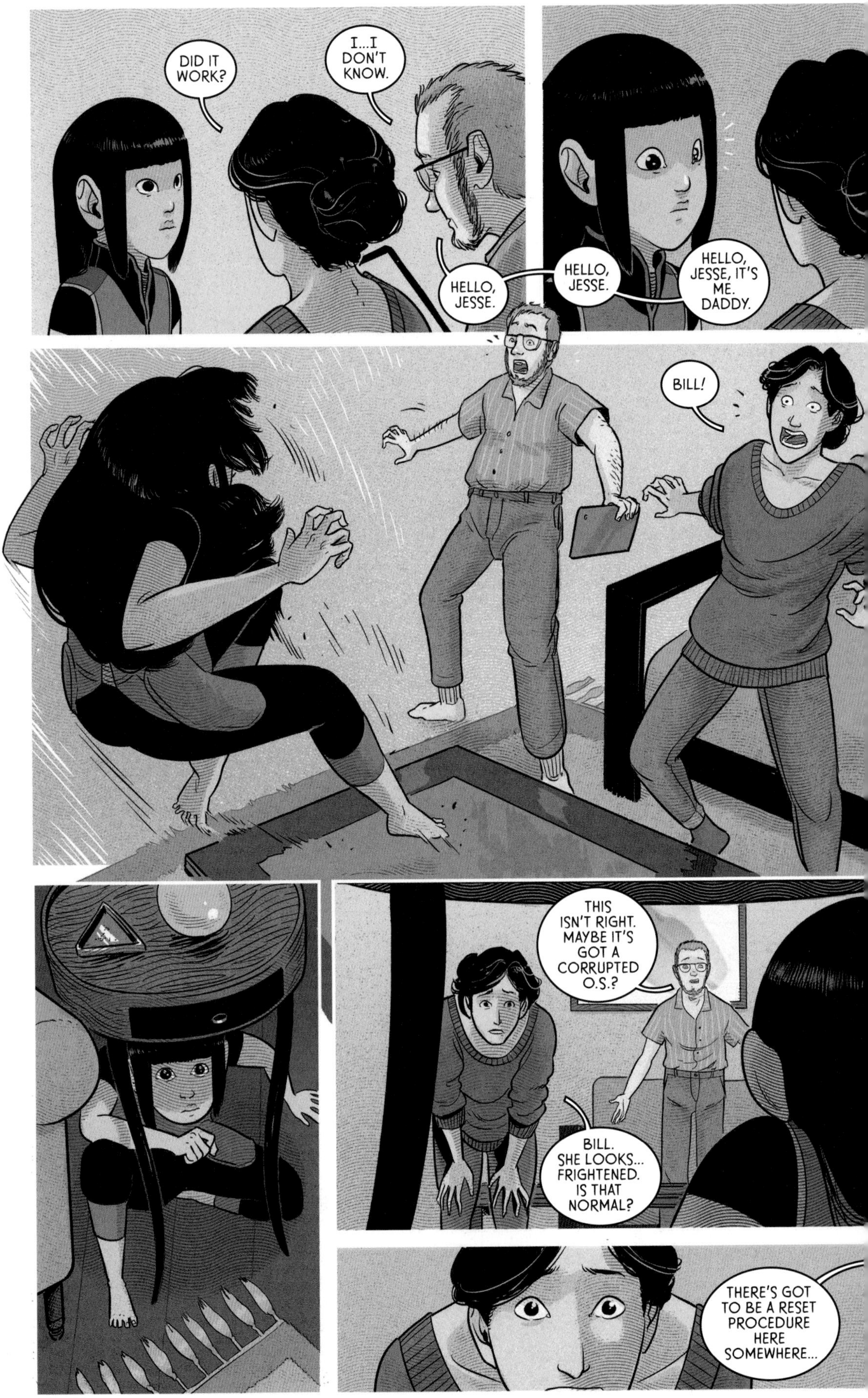
DID IT WORK?
I...I DON'T KNOW.
HELLO, JESSE.
HELLO, JESSE.
HELLO, JESSE, IT'S ME. DADDY.
BILL!
THIS ISN'T RIGHT. MAYBE IT'S GOT A CORRUPTED O.S.?
BILL. SHE LOOKS... FRIGHTENED. IS THAT NORMAL?
THERE'S GOT TO BE A RESET PROCEDURE HERE SOMEWHERE...

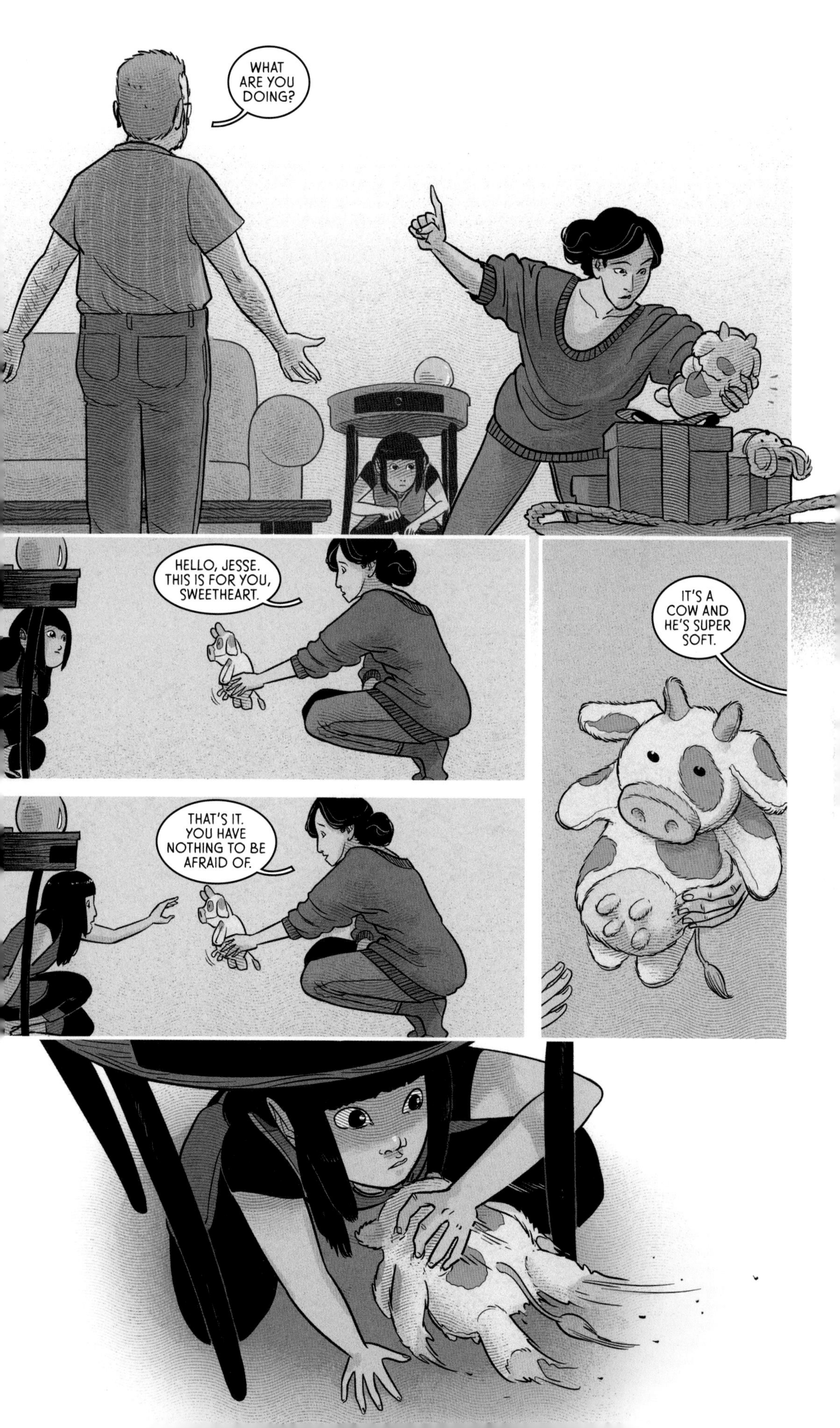
WHAT ARE YOU DOING?
HELLO, JESSE. THIS IS FOR YOU, SWEETHEART.
THAT'S IT. YOU HAVE NOTHING TO BE AFRAID OF.
IT'S A COW AND HE'S SUPER SOFT.

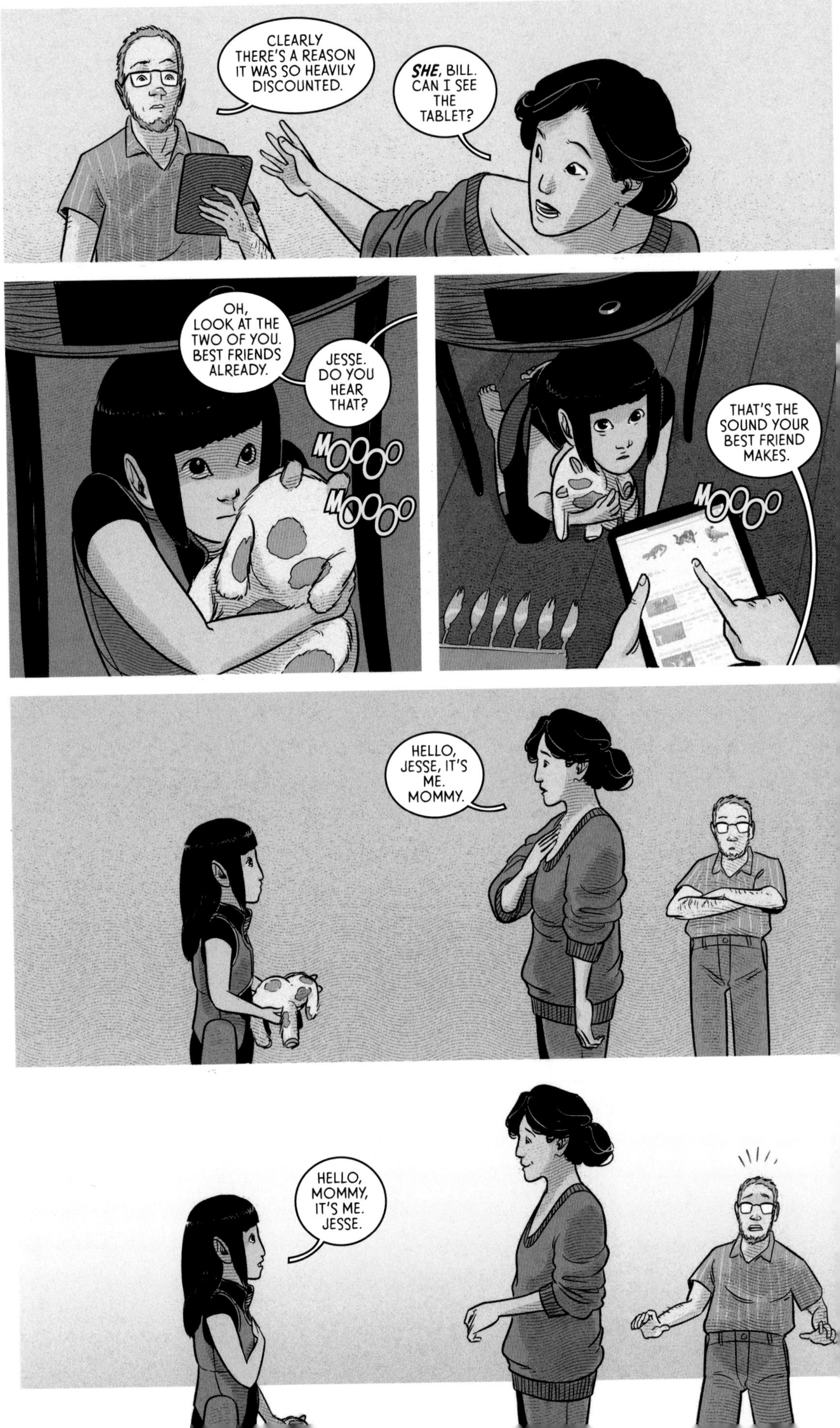
CLEARLY THERE'S A REASON IT WAS SO HEAVILY DISCOUNTED.
SHE, BILL. CAN I SEE THE TABLET?
OH, LOOK AT THE TWO OF YOU. BEST FRIENDS ALREADY.
JESSE. DO YOU HEAR THAT?
MOOOO
MOOOO
THAT'S THE SOUND YOUR BEST FRIEND MAKES.
MOOOO
HELLO, JESSE, IT'S ME. MOMMY.
HELLO, MOMMY, IT'S ME. JESSE.

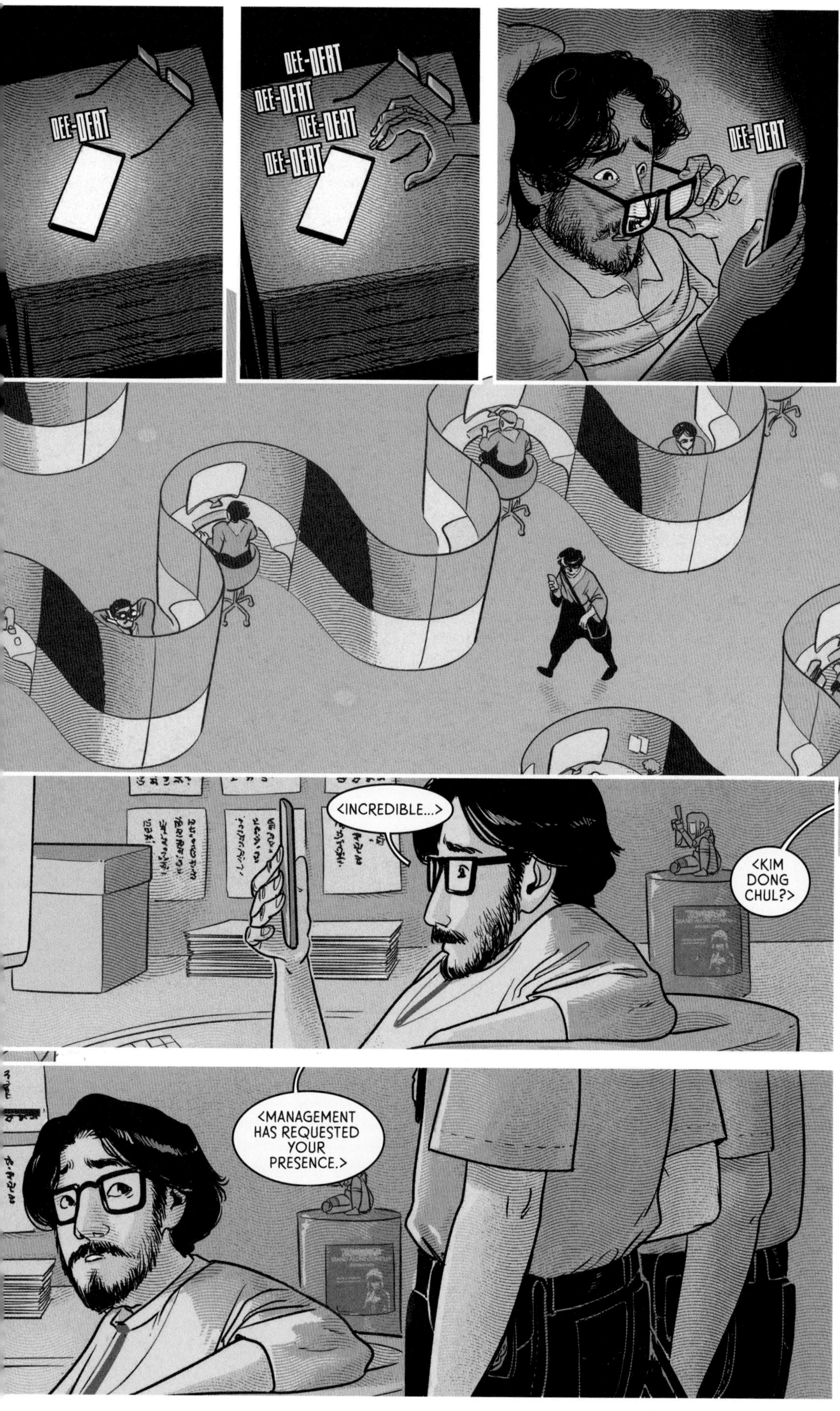
DEE-DERT
DEE-DERT
DEE-DERT
DEE-DERT
DEE-DERT
DEE-DERT
<INCREDIBLE...>
<KIM DONG CHUL?>
<MANAGEMENT HAS REQUESTED YOUR PRESENCE.>

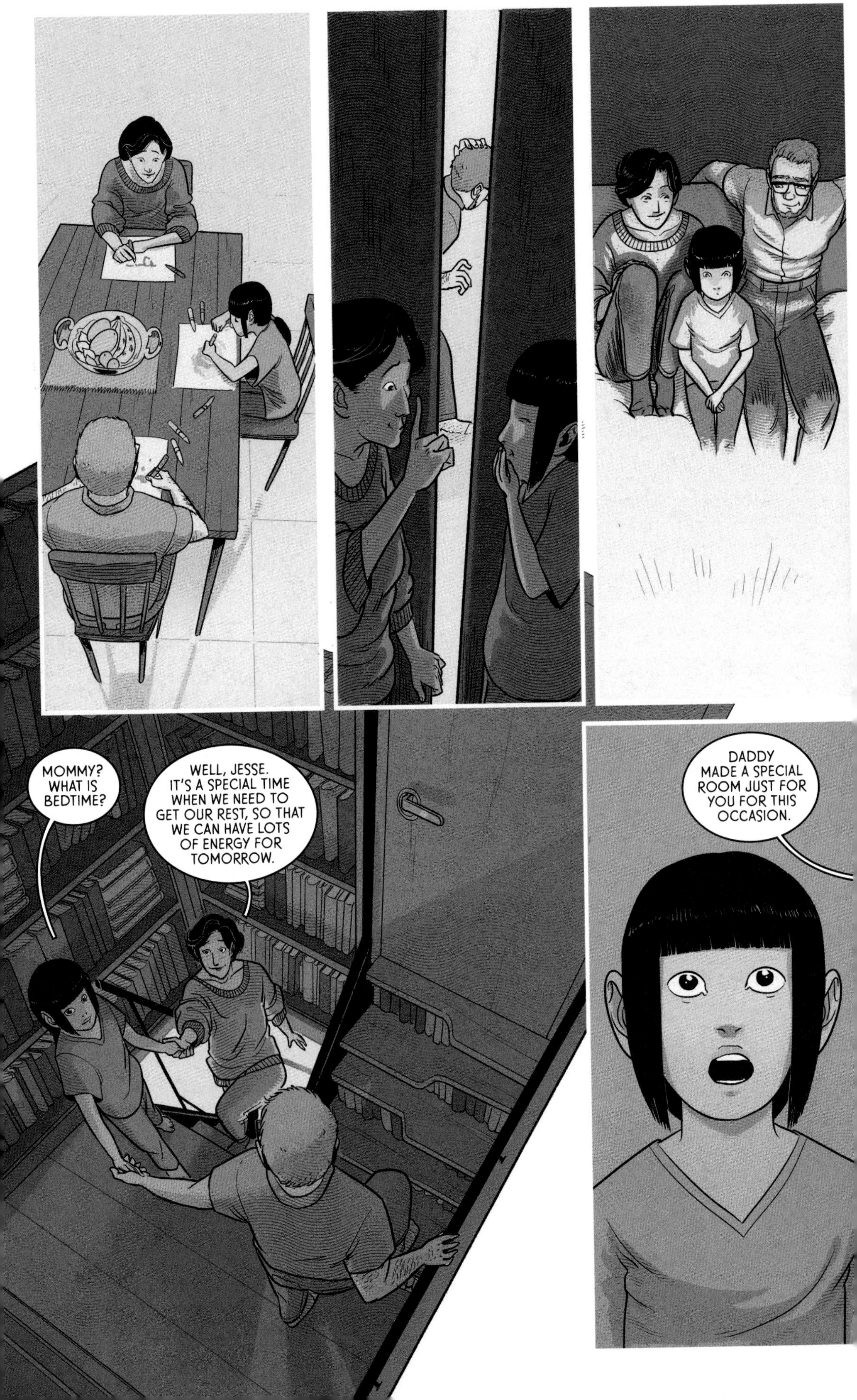
MOMMY? WHAT IS BEDTIME?
WELL, JESSE. IT'S A SPECIAL TIME WHEN WE NEED TO GET OUR REST, SO THAT WE CAN HAVE LOTS OF ENERGY FOR TOMORROW.
DADDY MADE A SPECIAL ROOM JUST FOR YOU FOR THIS OCCASION.

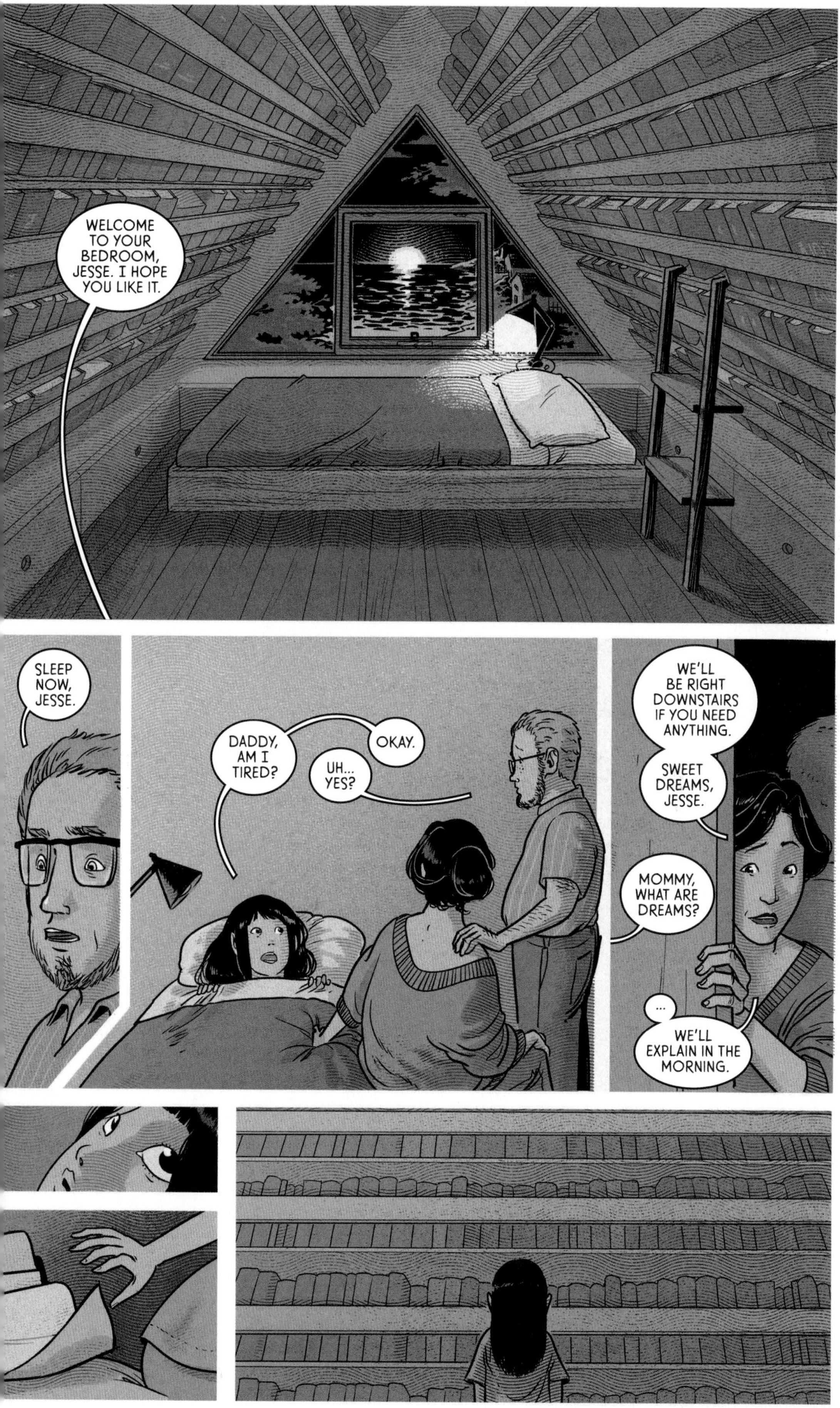
WELCOME TO YOUR BEDROOM, JESSE. I HOPE YOU LIKE IT.
SLEEP NOW, JESSE.
DADDY, AM I TIRED?
UH... YES?
OKAY.
WE'LL BE RIGHT DOWNSTAIRS IF YOU NEED ANYTHING.
SWEET DREAMS, JESSE.
MOMMY, WHAT ARE DREAMS?
...
WE'LL EXPLAIN IN THE MORNING.

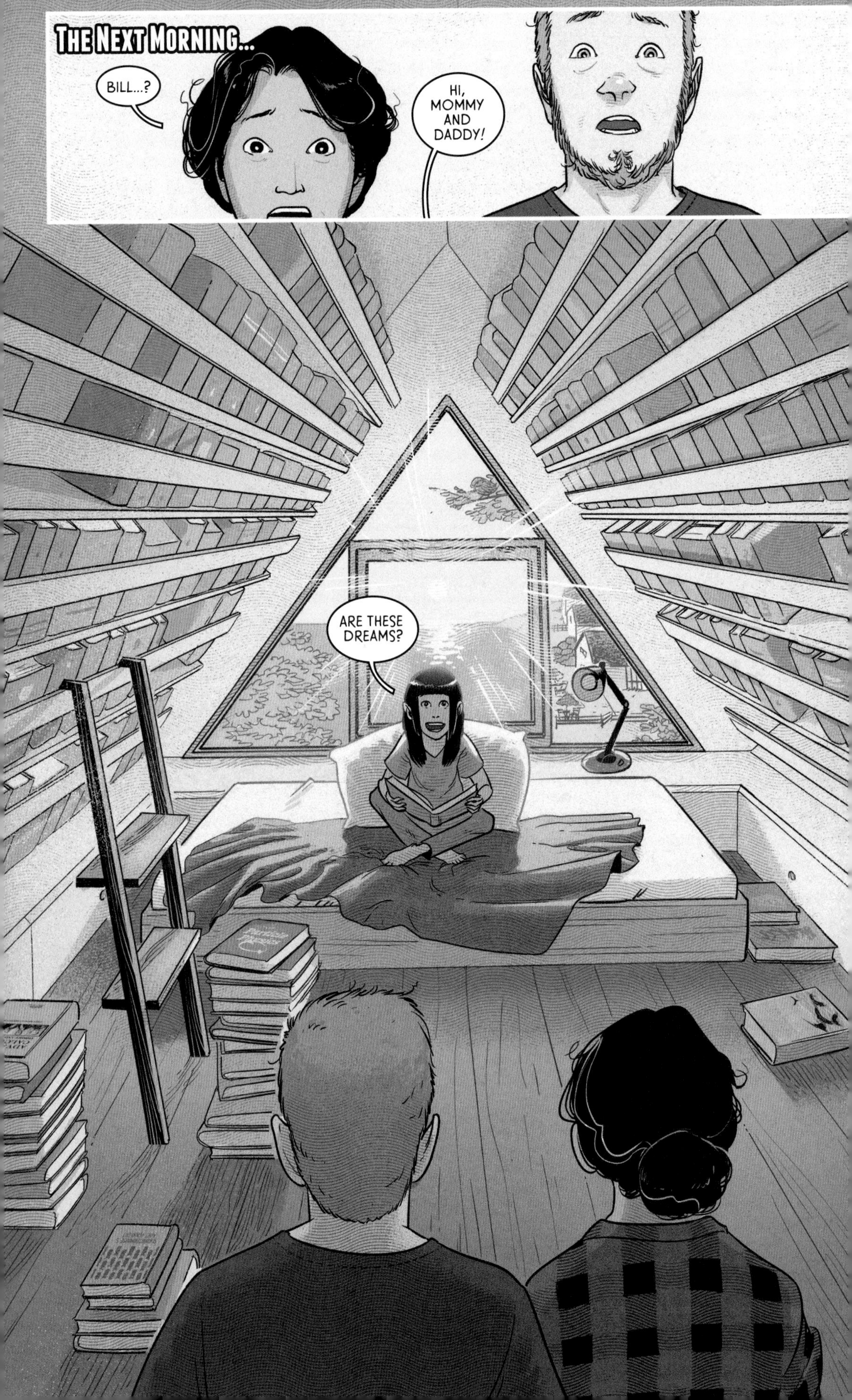
THE NEXT MORNING...
BILL...?
HI, MOMMY AND DADDY!
ARE THESE DREAMS?

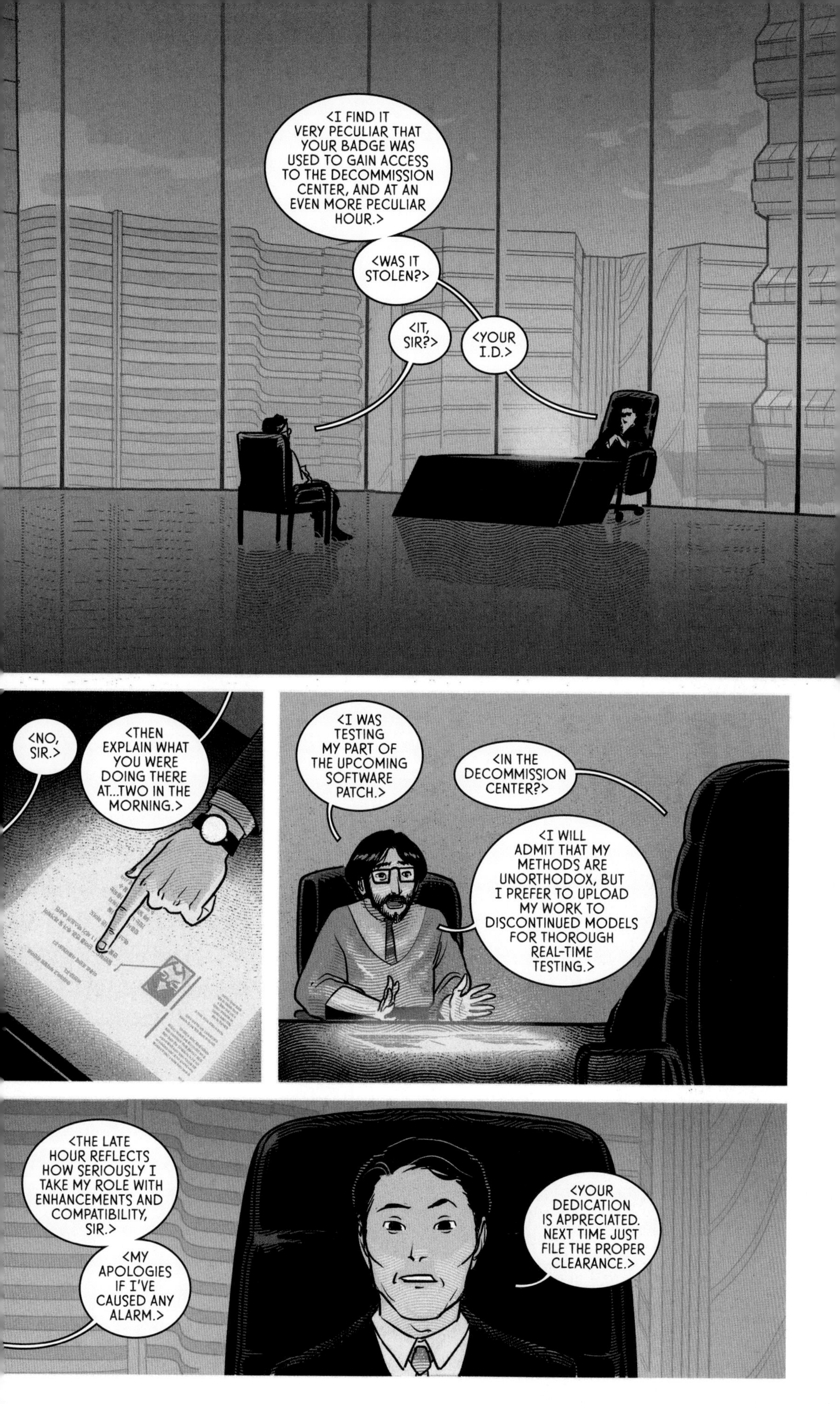
<I FIND IT VERY PECULIAR THAT YOUR BADGE WAS USED TO GAIN ACCESS TO THE DECOMMISSION CENTER, AND AT AN EVEN MORE PECULIAR HOUR.>
<WAS IT STOLEN?>
<IT, SIR?>
<YOUR I.D.>
<NO, SIR.>
<THEN EXPLAIN WHAT YOU WERE DOING THERE AT...TWO IN THE MORNING.>
<I WAS TESTING MY PART OF THE UPCOMING SOFTWARE PATCH.>
<IN THE DECOMMISSION CENTER?>
<I WILL ADMIT THAT MY METHODS ARE UNORTHODOX, BUT I PREFER TO UPLOAD MY WORK TO DISCONTINUED MODELS FOR THOROUGH REAL-TIME TESTING.>
<THE LATE HOUR REFLECTS HOW SERIOUSLY I TAKE MY ROLE WITH ENHANCEMENTS AND COMPATIBILITY, SIR.>
<MY APOLOGIES IF I'VE CAUSED ANY ALARM.>
<YOUR DEDICATION IS APPRECIATED. NEXT TIME JUST FILE THE PROPER CLEARANCE.>

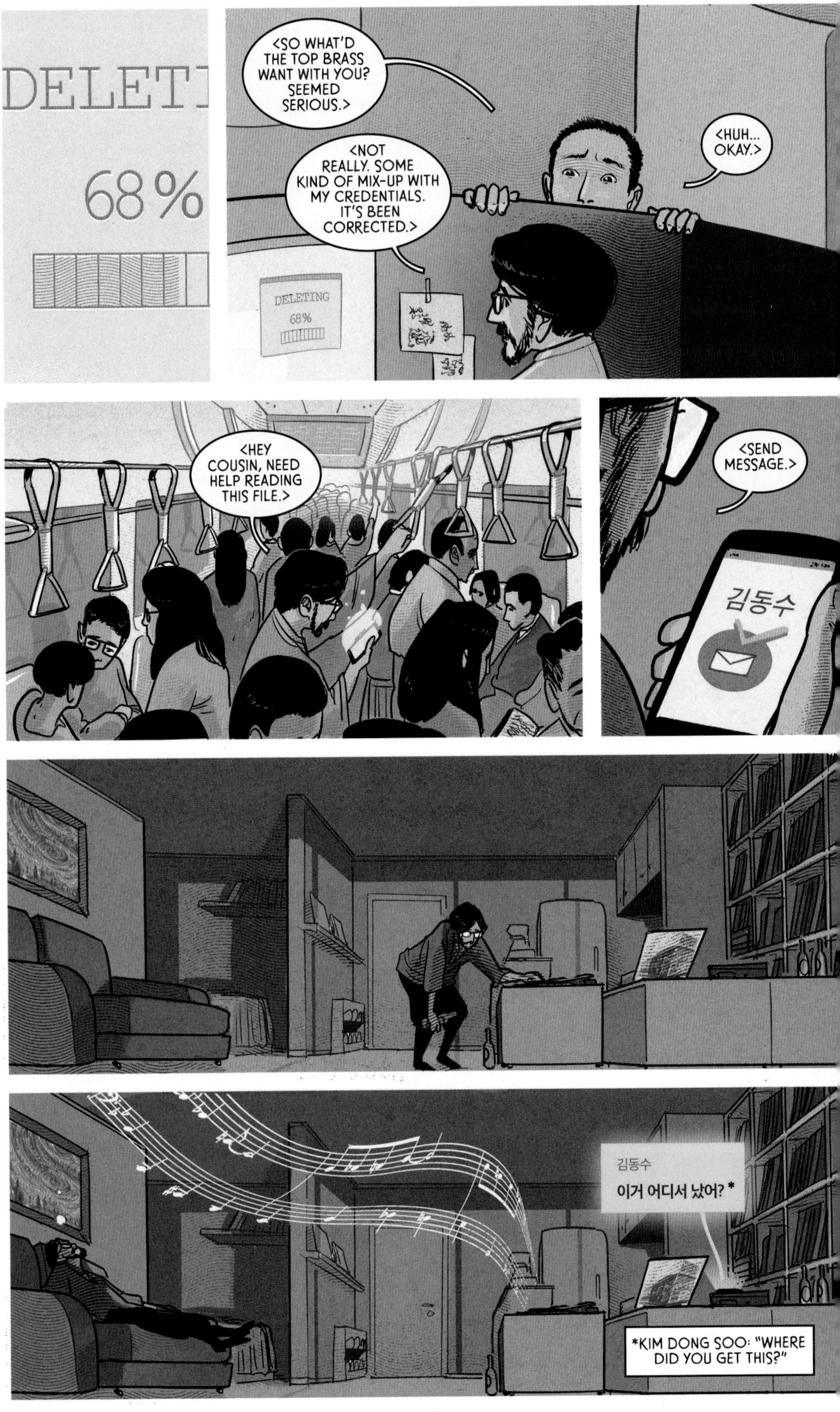

DELETI
68%
<SO WHAT'D THE TOP BRASS WANT WITH YOU? SEEMED SERIOUS.>
<NOT REALLY. SOME KIND OF MIX-UP WITH MY CREDENTIALS. IT'S BEEN CORRECTED.>
<HUH... OKAY.>
DELETING
68%
<HEY COUSIN, NEED HELP READING THIS FILE.>
<SEND MESSAGE.>
김동수
김동수
이거 어디서 났어? *
*KIM DONG SOO: "WHERE DID YOU GET THIS?"

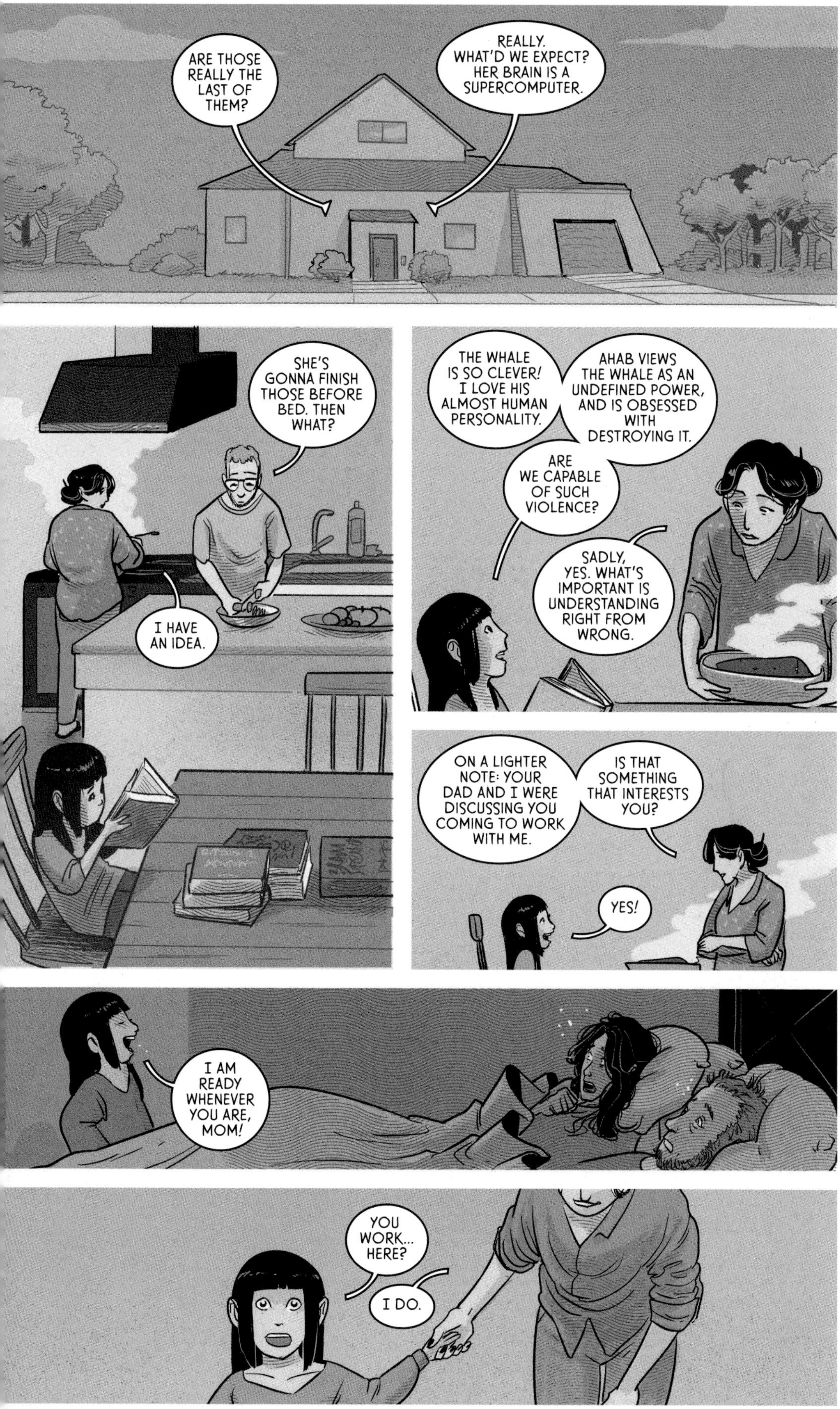
ARE THOSE REALLY THE LAST OF THEM?
REALLY. WHAT'D WE EXPECT? HER BRAIN IS A SUPERCOMPUTER.
SHE'S GONNA FINISH THOSE BEFORE BED. THEN WHAT?
I HAVE AN IDEA.
THE WHALE IS SO CLEVER! I LOVE HIS ALMOST HUMAN PERSONALITY.
AHAB VIEWS THE WHALE AS AN UNDEFINED POWER, AND IS OBSESSED WITH DESTROYING IT.
ARE WE CAPABLE OF SUCH VIOLENCE?
SADLY, YES. WHAT'S IMPORTANT IS UNDERSTANDING RIGHT FROM WRONG.
ON A LIGHTER NOTE: YOUR DAD AND I WERE DISCUSSING YOU COMING TO WORK WITH ME.
IS THAT SOMETHING THAT INTERESTS YOU?
YES!
I AM READY WHENEVER YOU ARE, MOM!
YOU WORK... HERE?
I DO.

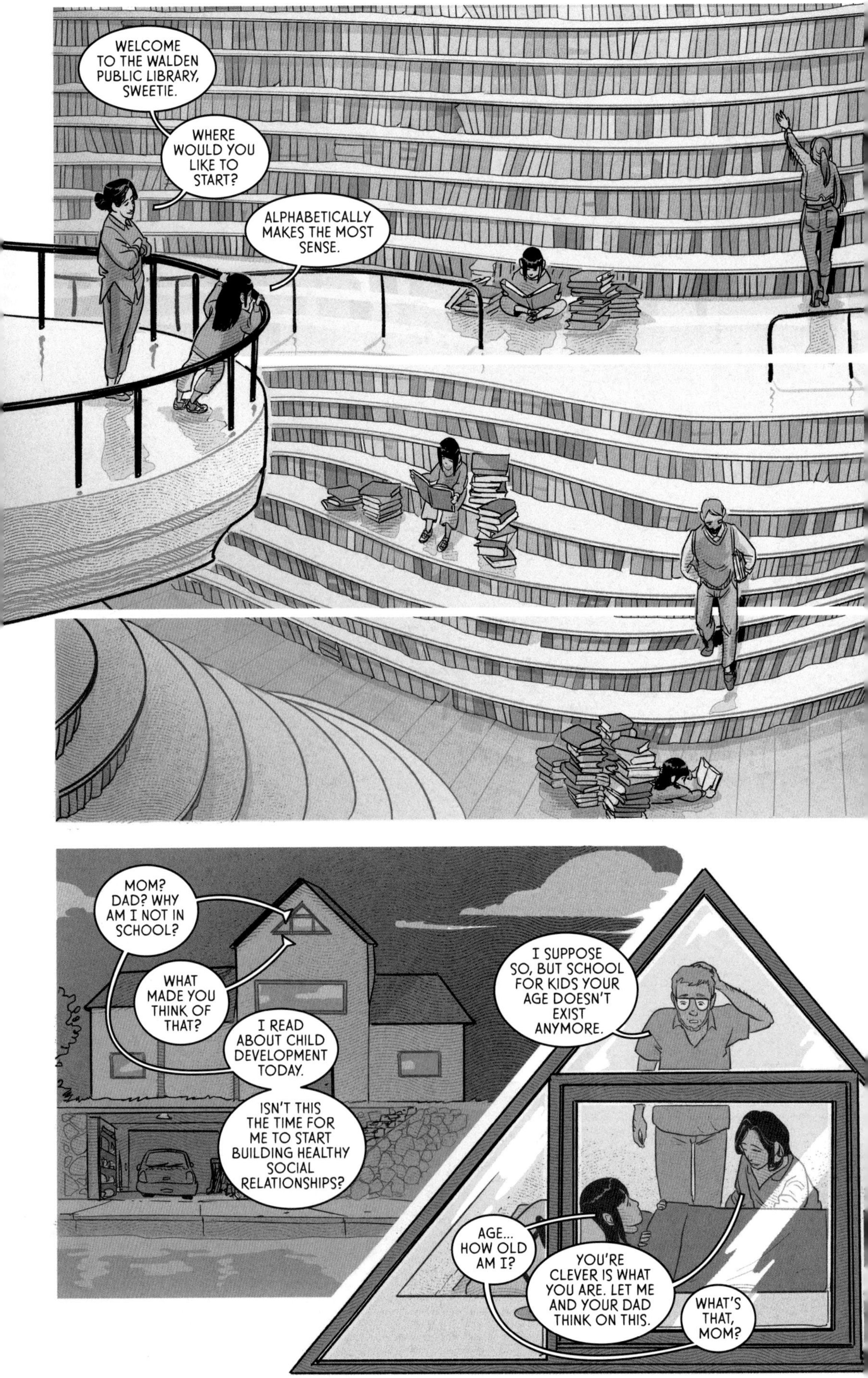
WELCOME TO THE WALDEN PUBLIC LIBRARY, SWEETIE.
WHERE WOULD YOU LIKE TO START?
ALPHABETICALLY MAKES THE MOST SENSE.
MOM? DAD? WHY AM I NOT IN SCHOOL?
WHAT MADE YOU THINK OF THAT?
I READ ABOUT CHILD DEVELOPMENT TODAY.
ISN'T THIS THE TIME FOR ME TO START BUILDING HEALTHY SOCIAL RELATIONSHIPS?
I SUPPOSE SO, BUT SCHOOL FOR KIDS YOUR AGE DOESN'T EXIST ANYMORE.
AGE... HOW OLD AM I?
YOU'RE CLEVER IS WHAT YOU ARE. LET ME AND YOUR DAD THINK ON THIS.
WHAT'S THAT, MOM?

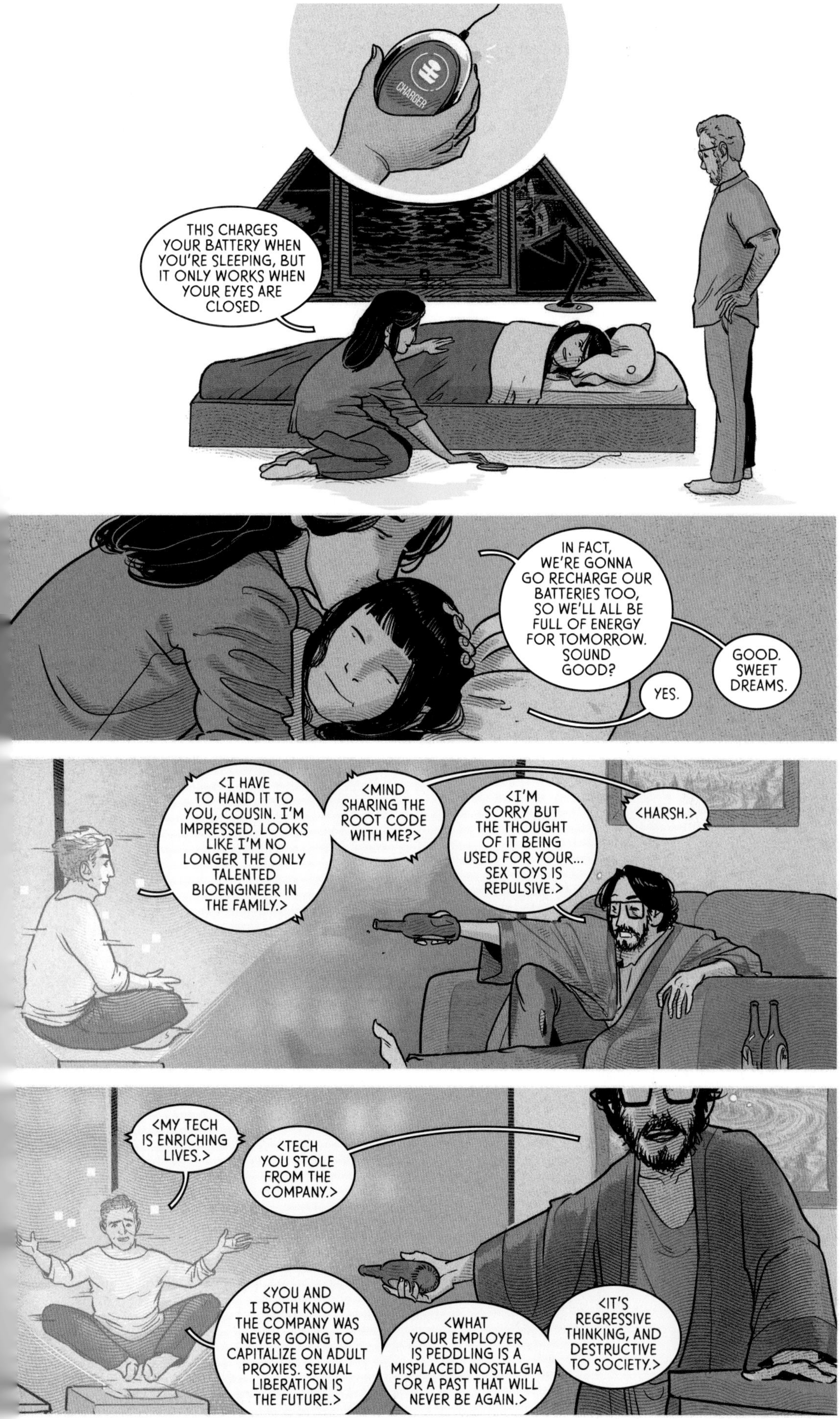
CHARGER
THIS CHARGES YOUR BATTERY WHEN YOU'RE SLEEPING, BUT IT ONLY WORKS WHEN YOUR EYES ARE CLOSED.
IN FACT, WE'RE GONNA GO RECHARGE OUR BATTERIES TOO, SO WE'LL ALL BE FULL OF ENERGY FOR TOMORROW. SOUND GOOD?
YES.
GOOD. SWEET DREAMS.
<I HAVE TO HAND IT TO YOU, COUSIN. I'M IMPRESSED. LOOKS LIKE I'M NO LONGER THE ONLY TALENTED BIOENGINEER IN THE FAMILY.>
<MIND SHARING THE ROOT CODE WITH ME?>
<I'M SORRY BUT THE THOUGHT OF IT BEING USED FOR YOUR... SEX TOYS IS REPULSIVE.>
<HARSH.>
<MY TECH IS ENRICHING LIVES.>
<TECH YOU STOLE FROM THE COMPANY.>
<YOU AND I BOTH KNOW THE COMPANY WAS NEVER GOING TO CAPITALIZE ON ADULT PROXIES. SEXUAL LIBERATION IS THE FUTURE.>
<WHAT YOUR EMPLOYER IS PEDDLING IS A MISPLACED NOSTALGIA FOR A PAST THAT WILL NEVER BE AGAIN.>
<IT'S REGRESSIVE THINKING, AND DESTRUCTIVE TO SOCIETY.>

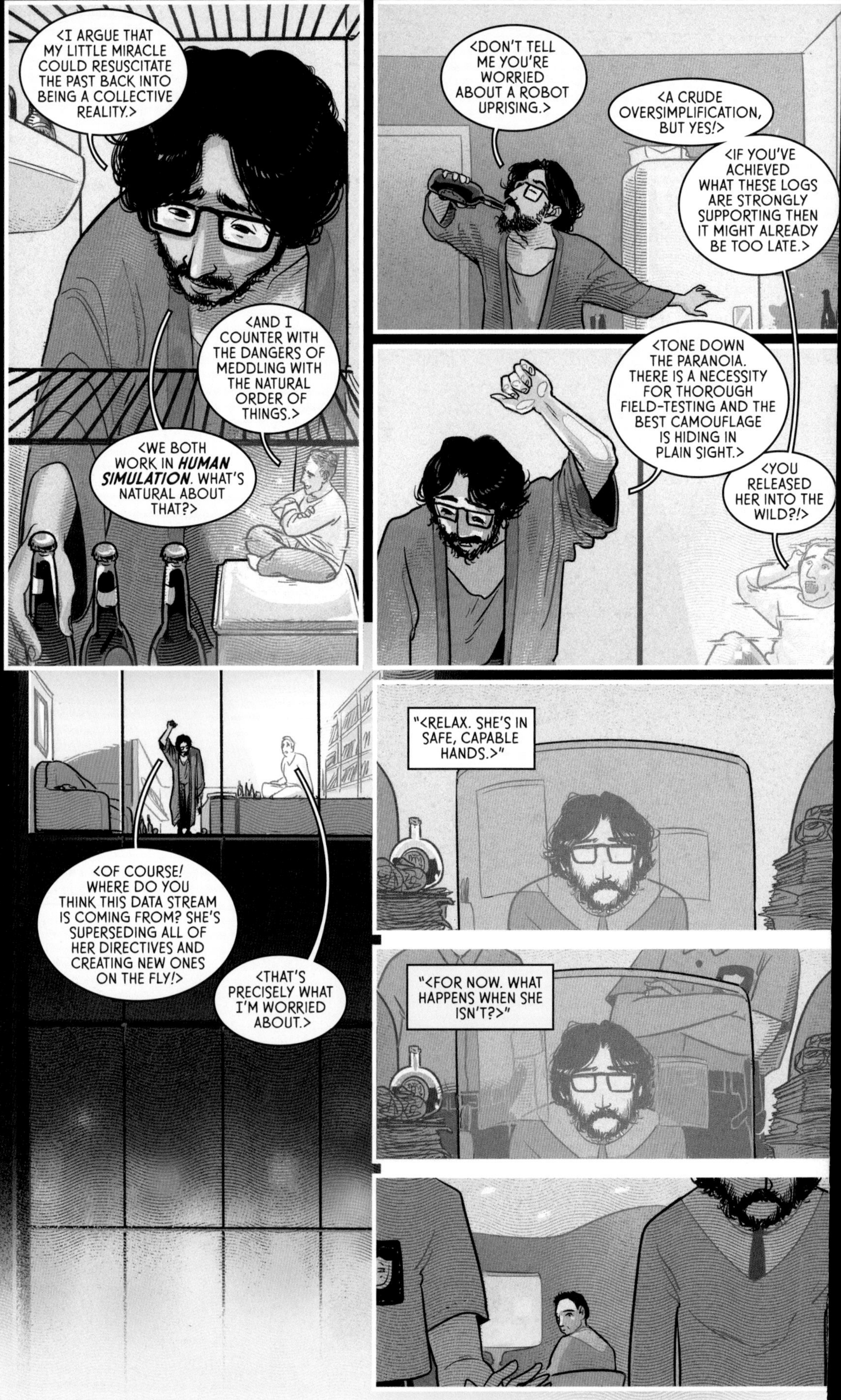
<I ARGUE THAT MY LITTLE MIRACLE COULD RESUSCITATE THE PAST BACK INTO BEING A COLLECTIVE REALITY.>
<AND I COUNTER WITH THE DANGERS OF MEDDLING WITH THE NATURAL ORDER OF THINGS.>
<WE BOTH WORK IN ***HUMAN SIMULATION***. WHAT'S NATURAL ABOUT THAT?>
<DON'T TELL ME YOU'RE WORRIED ABOUT A ROBOT UPRISING.>
<A CRUDE OVERSIMPLIFICATION, BUT YES!>
<IF YOU'VE ACHIEVED WHAT THESE LOGS ARE STRONGLY SUPPORTING THEN IT MIGHT ALREADY BE TOO LATE.>
<TONE DOWN THE PARANOIA. THERE IS A NECESSITY FOR THOROUGH FIELD-TESTING AND THE BEST CAMOUFLAGE IS HIDING IN PLAIN SIGHT.>
<YOU RELEASED HER INTO THE WILD?!>
<OF COURSE! WHERE DO YOU THINK THIS DATA STREAM IS COMING FROM? SHE'S SUPERSEDING ALL OF HER DIRECTIVES AND CREATING NEW ONES ON THE FLY!>
<THAT'S PRECISELY WHAT I'M WORRIED ABOUT.>
"<RELAX. SHE'S IN SAFE, CAPABLE HANDS.>"
"<FOR NOW. WHAT HAPPENS WHEN SHE ISN'T?>"

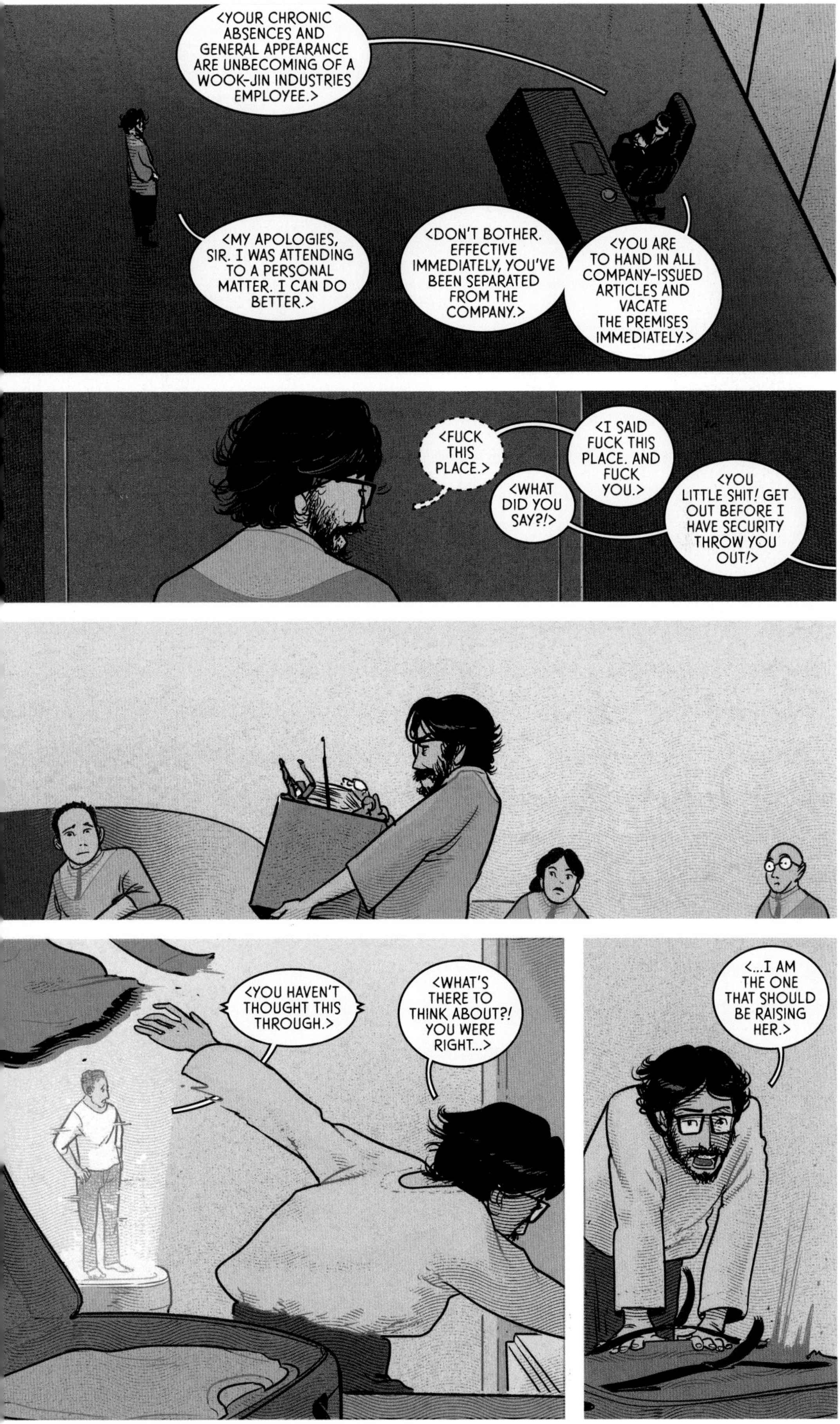

<YOUR CHRONIC ABSENCES AND GENERAL APPEARANCE ARE UNBECOMING OF A WOOK-JIN INDUSTRIES EMPLOYEE.>
<MY APOLOGIES, SIR. I WAS ATTENDING TO A PERSONAL MATTER. I CAN DO BETTER.>
<DON'T BOTHER. EFFECTIVE IMMEDIATELY, YOU'VE BEEN SEPARATED FROM THE COMPANY.>
<YOU ARE TO HAND IN ALL COMPANY-ISSUED ARTICLES AND VACATE THE PREMISES IMMEDIATELY.>
<FUCK THIS PLACE.>
<WHAT DID YOU SAY?!>
<I SAID FUCK THIS PLACE. AND FUCK YOU.>
<YOU LITTLE SHIT! GET OUT BEFORE I HAVE SECURITY THROW YOU OUT!>
<YOU HAVEN'T THOUGHT THIS THROUGH.>
<WHAT'S THERE TO THINK ABOUT?! YOU WERE RIGHT...>
<...I AM THE ONE THAT SHOULD BE RAISING HER.>

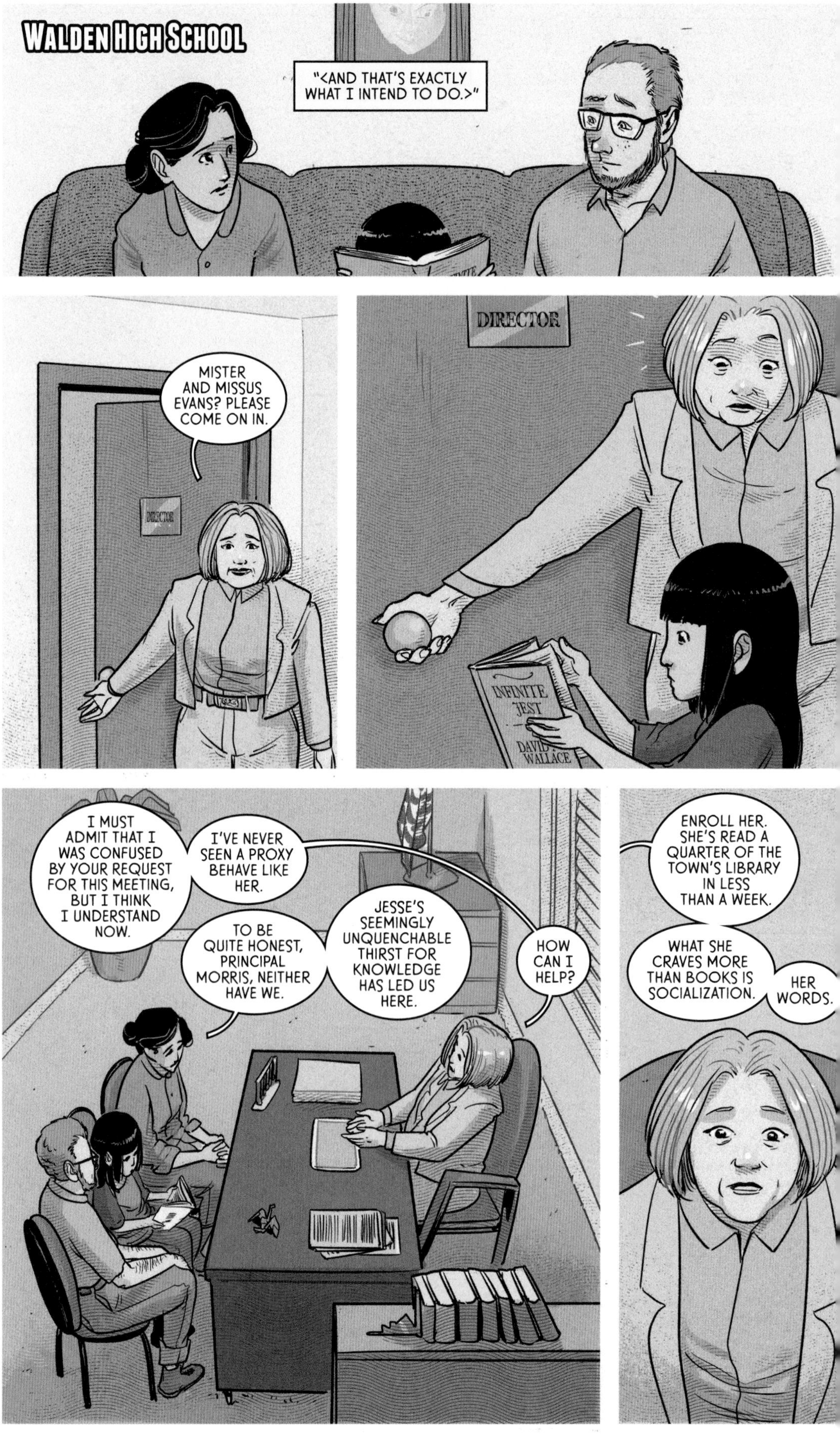
WALDEN HIGH SCHOOL
"<AND THAT'S EXACTLY WHAT I INTEND TO DO.>"
INFINITE
MISTER AND MISSUS EVANS? PLEASE COME ON IN.
DIRECTOR
DIRECTOR
INFINITE JEST
DAVID WALLACE
I MUST ADMIT THAT I WAS CONFUSED BY YOUR REQUEST FOR THIS MEETING, BUT I THINK I UNDERSTAND NOW.
I'VE NEVER SEEN A PROXY BEHAVE LIKE HER.
TO BE QUITE HONEST, PRINCIPAL MORRIS, NEITHER HAVE WE.
JESSE'S SEEMINGLY UNQUENCHABLE THIRST FOR KNOWLEDGE HAS LED US HERE.
HOW CAN I HELP?
ENROLL HER. SHE'S READ A QUARTER OF THE TOWN'S LIBRARY IN LESS THAN A WEEK.
WHAT SHE CRAVES MORE THAN BOOKS IS SOCIALIZATION.
HER WORDS.

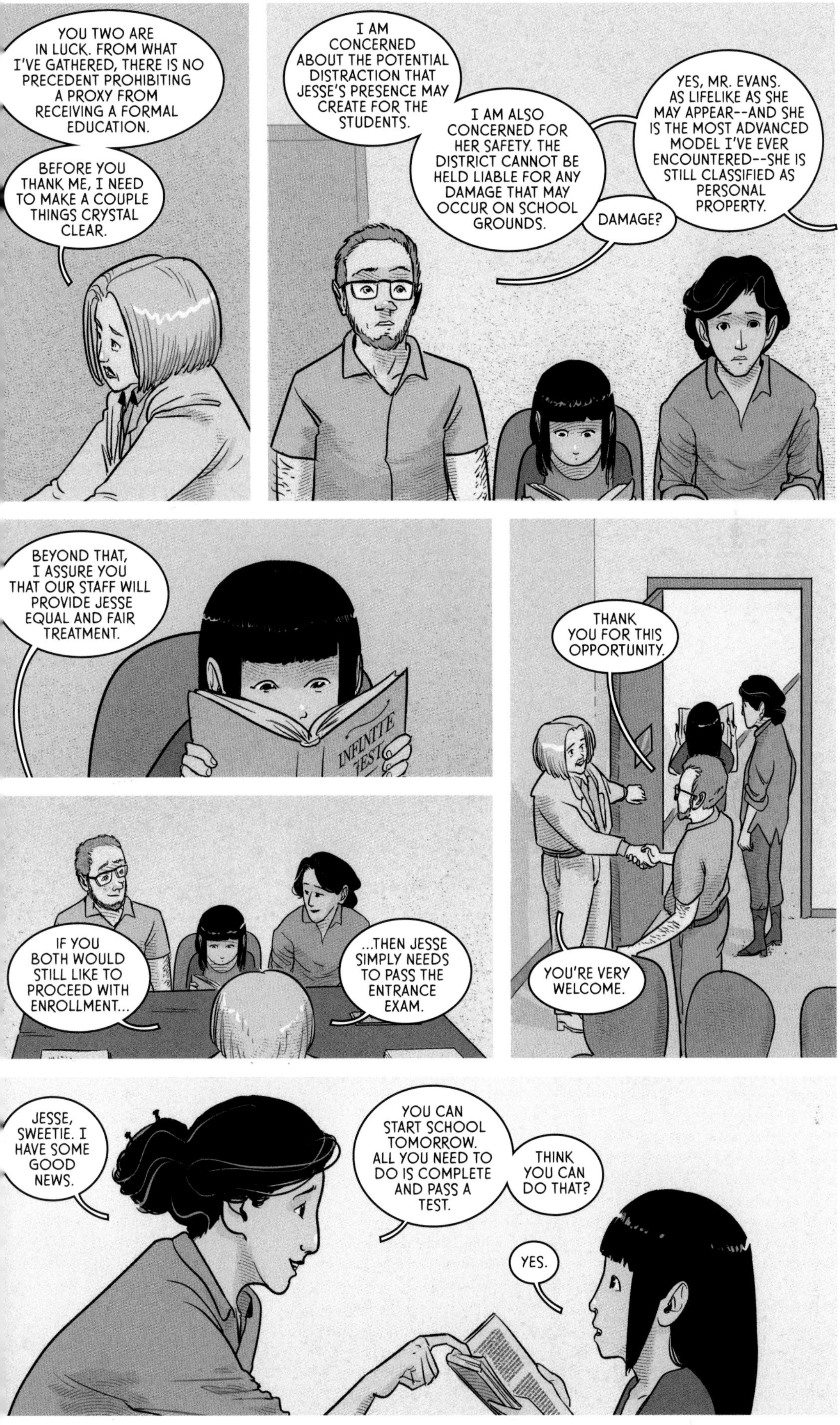
YOU TWO ARE IN LUCK. FROM WHAT I'VE GATHERED, THERE IS NO PRECEDENT PROHIBITING A PROXY FROM RECEIVING A FORMAL EDUCATION.
BEFORE YOU THANK ME, I NEED TO MAKE A COUPLE THINGS CRYSTAL CLEAR.
I AM CONCERNED ABOUT THE POTENTIAL DISTRACTION THAT JESSE'S PRESENCE MAY CREATE FOR THE STUDENTS.
I AM ALSO CONCERNED FOR HER SAFETY. THE DISTRICT CANNOT BE HELD LIABLE FOR ANY DAMAGE THAT MAY OCCUR ON SCHOOL GROUNDS.
DAMAGE?
YES, MR. EVANS. AS LIFELIKE AS SHE MAY APPEAR--AND SHE IS THE MOST ADVANCED MODEL I'VE EVER ENCOUNTERED--SHE IS STILL CLASSIFIED AS PERSONAL PROPERTY.
BEYOND THAT, I ASSURE YOU THAT OUR STAFF WILL PROVIDE JESSE EQUAL AND FAIR TREATMENT.
INFINITE JEST
IF YOU BOTH WOULD STILL LIKE TO PROCEED WITH ENROLLMENT...
...THEN JESSE SIMPLY NEEDS TO PASS THE ENTRANCE EXAM.
THANK YOU FOR THIS OPPORTUNITY.
YOU'RE VERY WELCOME.
JESSE, SWEETIE. I HAVE SOME GOOD NEWS.
YOU CAN START SCHOOL TOMORROW. ALL YOU NEED TO DO IS COMPLETE AND PASS A TEST.
THINK YOU CAN DO THAT?
YES.

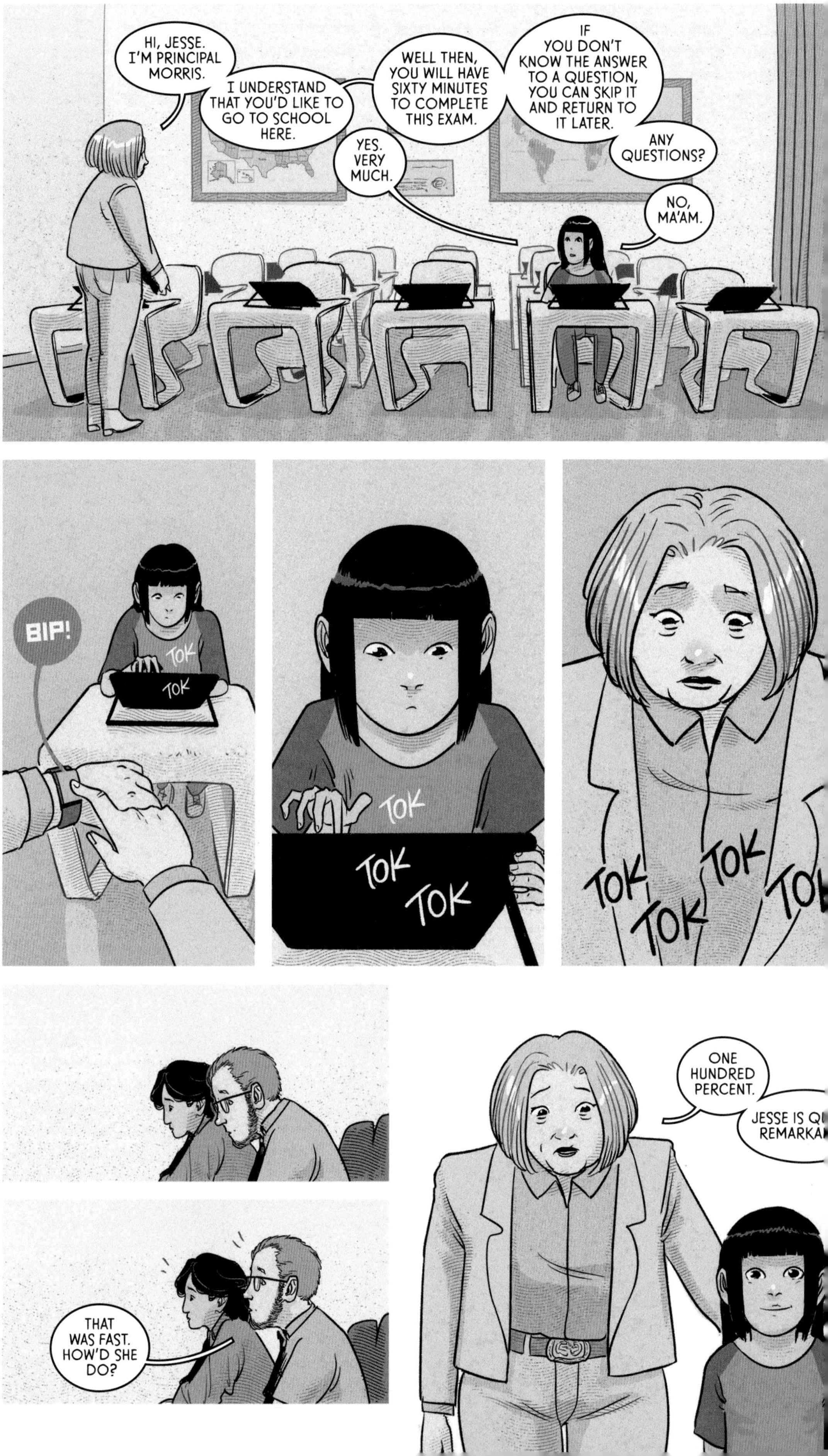

HI, JESSE. I'M PRINCIPAL MORRIS.
I UNDERSTAND THAT YOU'D LIKE TO GO TO SCHOOL HERE.
YES. VERY MUCH.
WELL THEN, YOU WILL HAVE SIXTY MINUTES TO COMPLETE THIS EXAM.
IF YOU DON'T KNOW THE ANSWER TO A QUESTION, YOU CAN SKIP IT AND RETURN TO IT LATER.
ANY QUESTIONS?
NO, MA'AM.
BIP!
TOK
TOK
TOK
TOK
TOK
TOK
TOK
TOK
TOK
THAT WAS FAST. HOW'D SHE DO?
ONE HUNDRED PERCENT.
JESSE IS Q
REMARKA

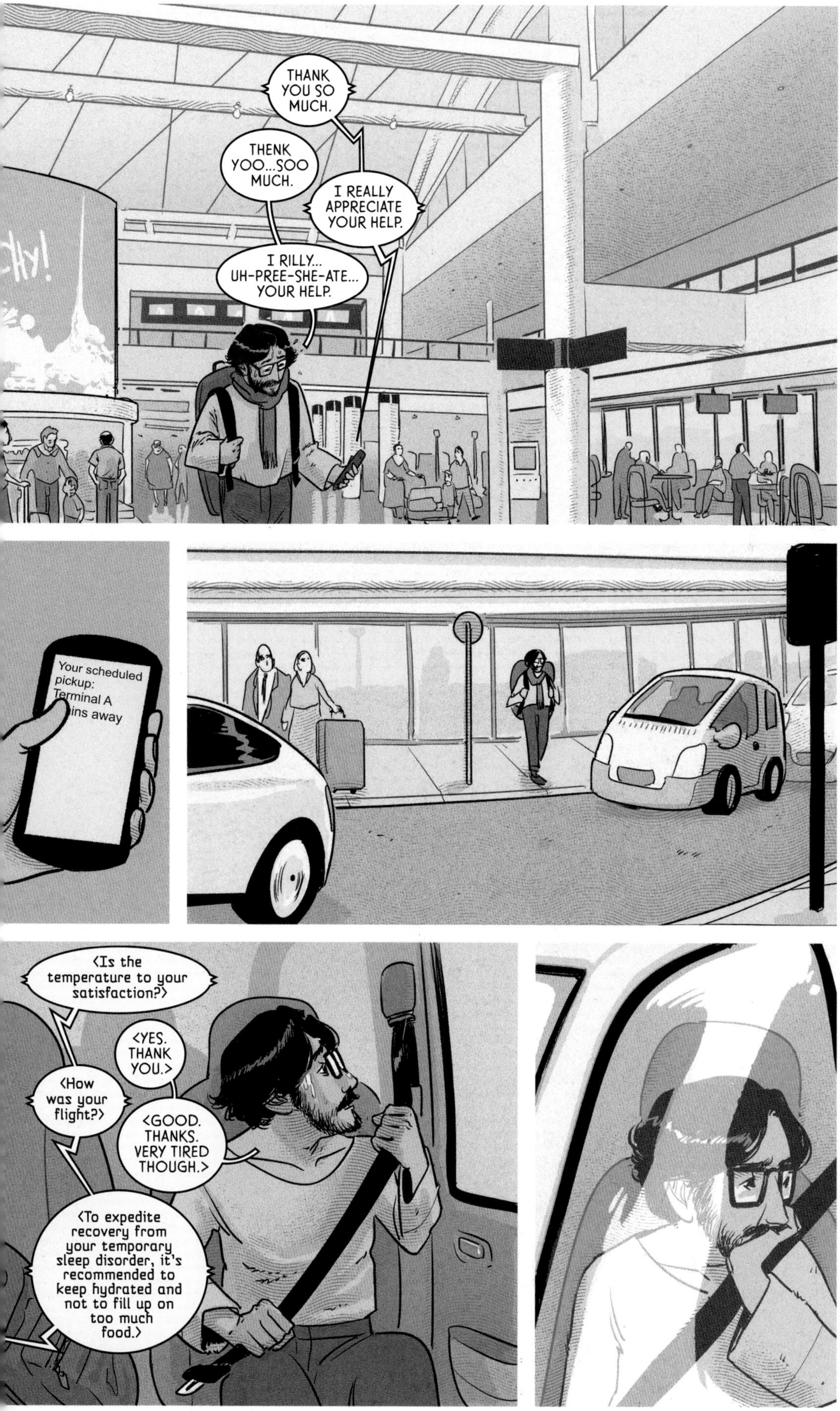
THANK YOU SO MUCH.
THENK YOO...SOO MUCH.
I REALLY APPRECIATE YOUR HELP.
I RILLY... UH-PREE-SHE-ATE... YOUR HELP.
Your scheduled pickup: Terminal A
ins away
<Is the temperature to your satisfaction?>
<YES. THANK YOU.>
<How was your flight?>
<GOOD. THANKS. VERY TIRED THOUGH.>
<To expedite recovery from your temporary sleep disorder, it's recommended to keep hydrated and not to fill up on too much food.>

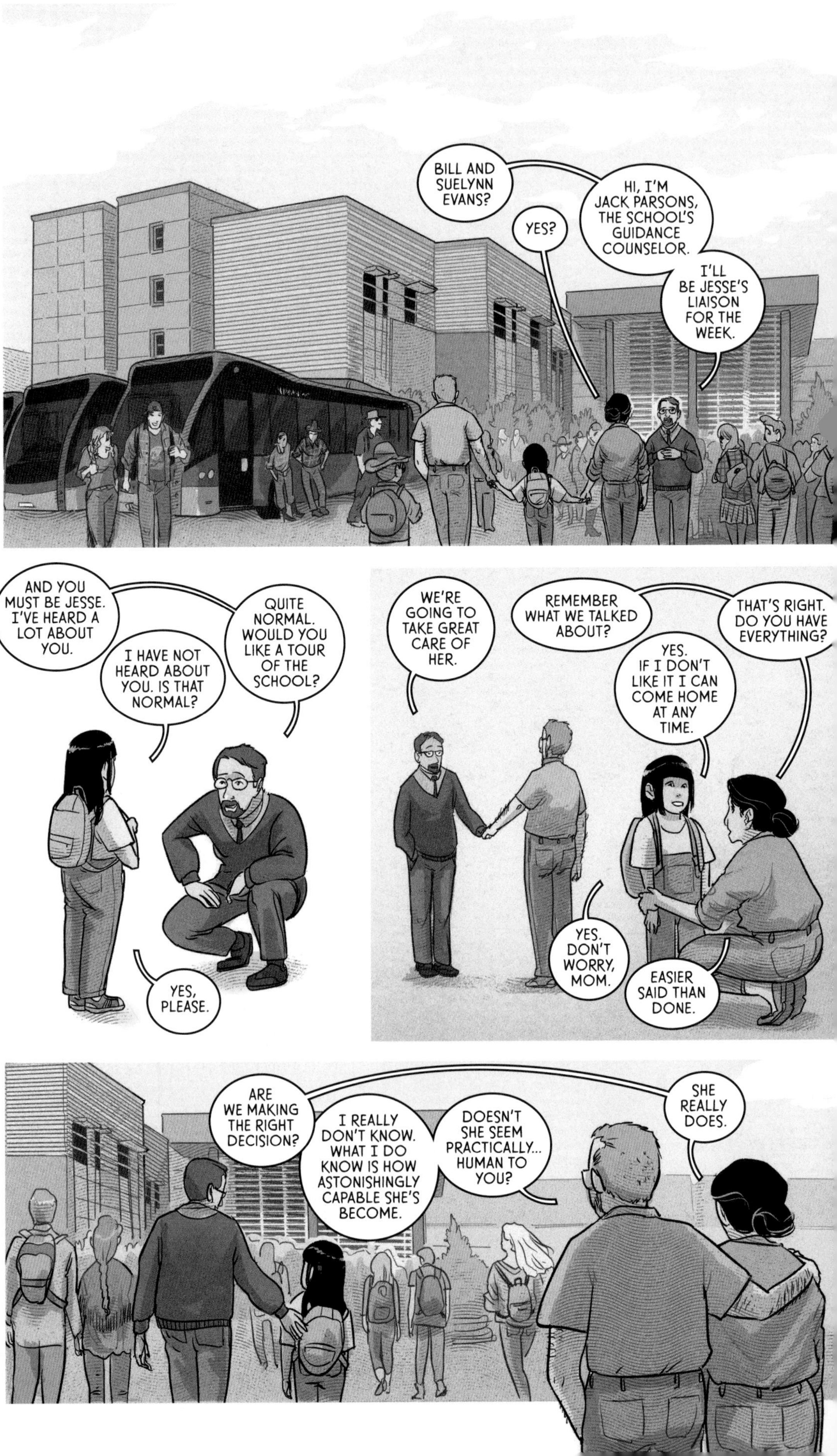
BILL AND SUELYNN EVANS?
YES?
HI, I'M JACK PARSONS, THE SCHOOL'S GUIDANCE COUNSELOR.
I'LL BE JESSE'S LIAISON FOR THE WEEK.
AND YOU MUST BE JESSE. I'VE HEARD A LOT ABOUT YOU.
I HAVE NOT HEARD ABOUT YOU. IS THAT NORMAL?
QUITE NORMAL. WOULD YOU LIKE A TOUR OF THE SCHOOL?
YES, PLEASE.
WE'RE GOING TO TAKE GREAT CARE OF HER.
YES. DON'T WORRY, MOM.
REMEMBER WHAT WE TALKED ABOUT?
YES. IF I DON'T LIKE IT I CAN COME HOME AT ANY TIME.
THAT'S RIGHT. DO YOU HAVE EVERYTHING?
EASIER SAID THAN DONE.
ARE WE MAKING THE RIGHT DECISION?
I REALLY DON'T KNOW. WHAT I DO KNOW IS HOW ASTONISHINGLY CAPABLE SHE'S BECOME.
DOESN'T SHE SEEM PRACTICALLY... HUMAN TO YOU?
SHE REALLY DOES.

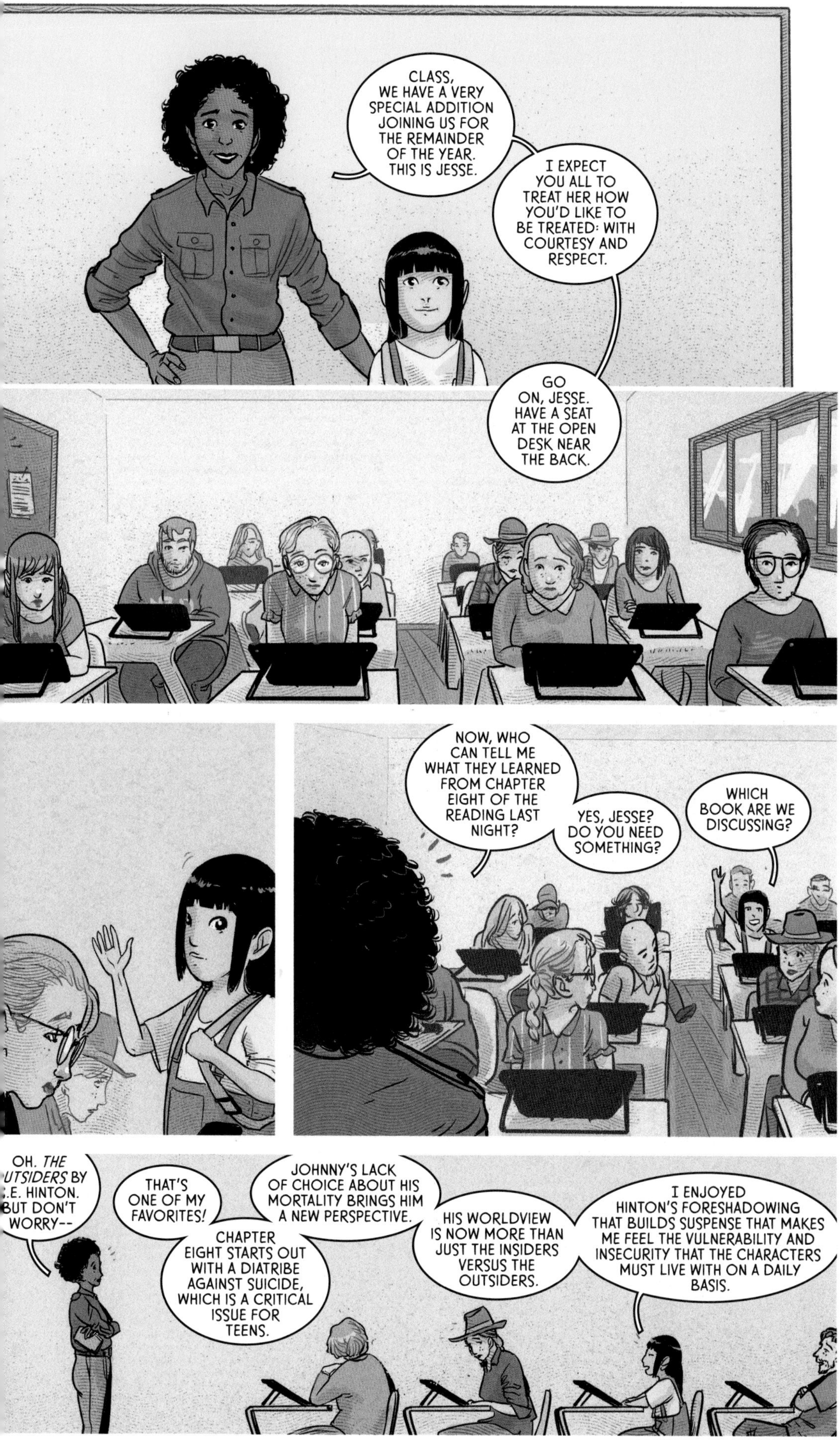
CLASS, WE HAVE A VERY SPECIAL ADDITION JOINING US FOR THE REMAINDER OF THE YEAR. THIS IS JESSE.
I EXPECT YOU ALL TO TREAT HER HOW YOU'D LIKE TO BE TREATED: WITH COURTESY AND RESPECT.
GO ON, JESSE. HAVE A SEAT AT THE OPEN DESK NEAR THE BACK.
NOW, WHO CAN TELL ME WHAT THEY LEARNED FROM CHAPTER EIGHT OF THE READING LAST NIGHT?
YES, JESSE? DO YOU NEED SOMETHING?
WHICH BOOK ARE WE DISCUSSING?
OH. *THE OUTSIDERS* BY S.E. HINTON. BUT DON'T WORRY--
THAT'S ONE OF MY FAVORITES!
CHAPTER EIGHT STARTS OUT WITH A DIATRIBE AGAINST SUICIDE, WHICH IS A CRITICAL ISSUE FOR TEENS.
JOHNNY'S LACK OF CHOICE ABOUT HIS MORTALITY BRINGS HIM A NEW PERSPECTIVE.
HIS WORLDVIEW IS NOW MORE THAN JUST THE INSIDERS VERSUS THE OUTSIDERS.
I ENJOYED HINTON'S FORESHADOWING THAT BUILDS SUSPENSE THAT MAKES ME FEEL THE VULNERABILITY AND INSECURITY THAT THE CHARACTERS MUST LIVE WITH ON A DAILY BASIS.

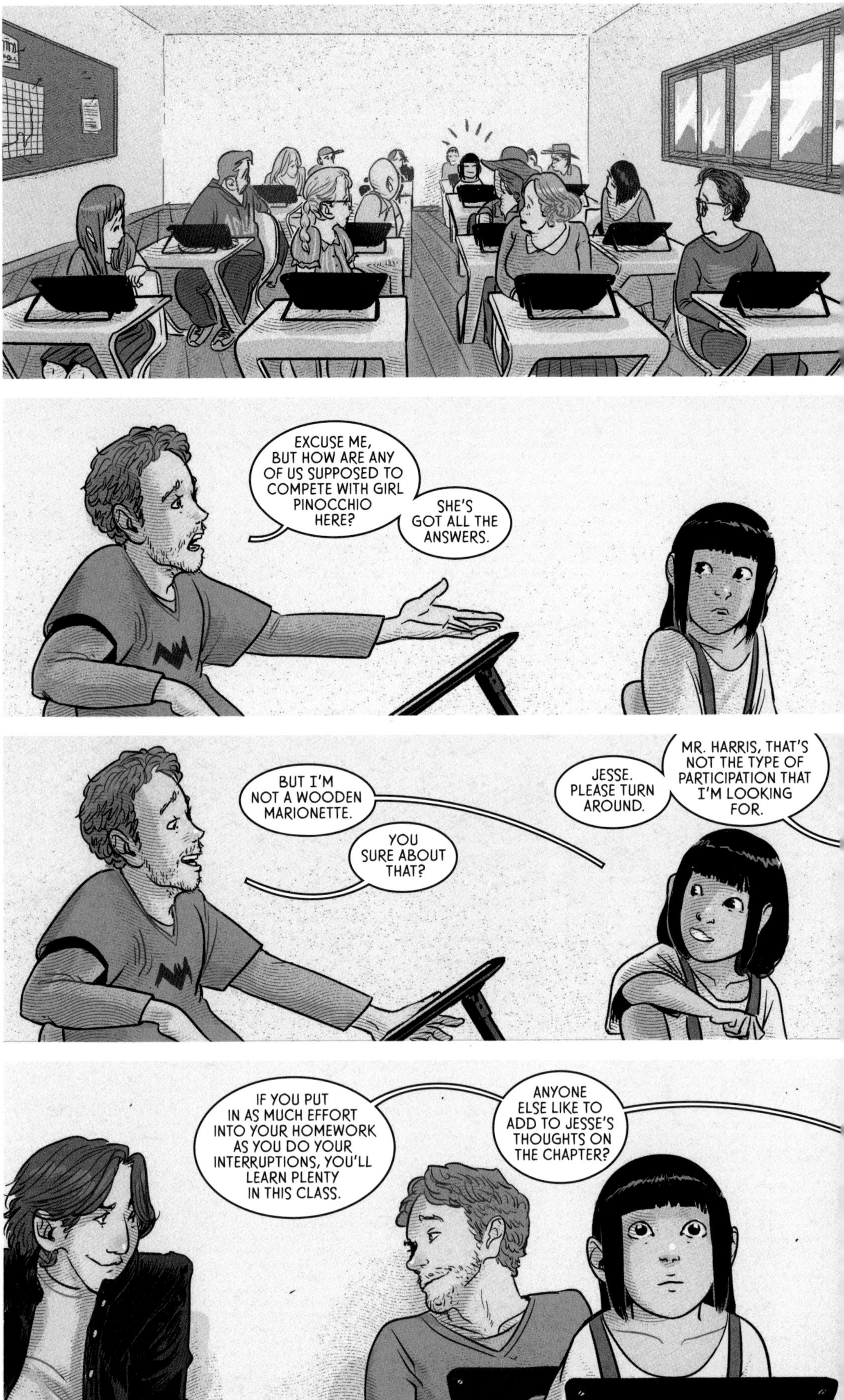
EXCUSE ME, BUT HOW ARE ANY OF US SUPPOSED TO COMPETE WITH GIRL PINOCCHIO HERE?
SHE'S GOT ALL THE ANSWERS.
BUT I'M NOT A WOODEN MARIONETTE.
YOU SURE ABOUT THAT?
JESSE. PLEASE TURN AROUND.
MR. HARRIS, THAT'S NOT THE TYPE OF PARTICIPATION THAT I'M LOOKING FOR.
IF YOU PUT IN AS MUCH EFFORT INTO YOUR HOMEWORK AS YOU DO YOUR INTERRUPTIONS, YOU'LL LEARN PLENTY IN THIS CLASS.
ANYONE ELSE LIKE TO ADD TO JESSE'S THOUGHTS ON THE CHAPTER?

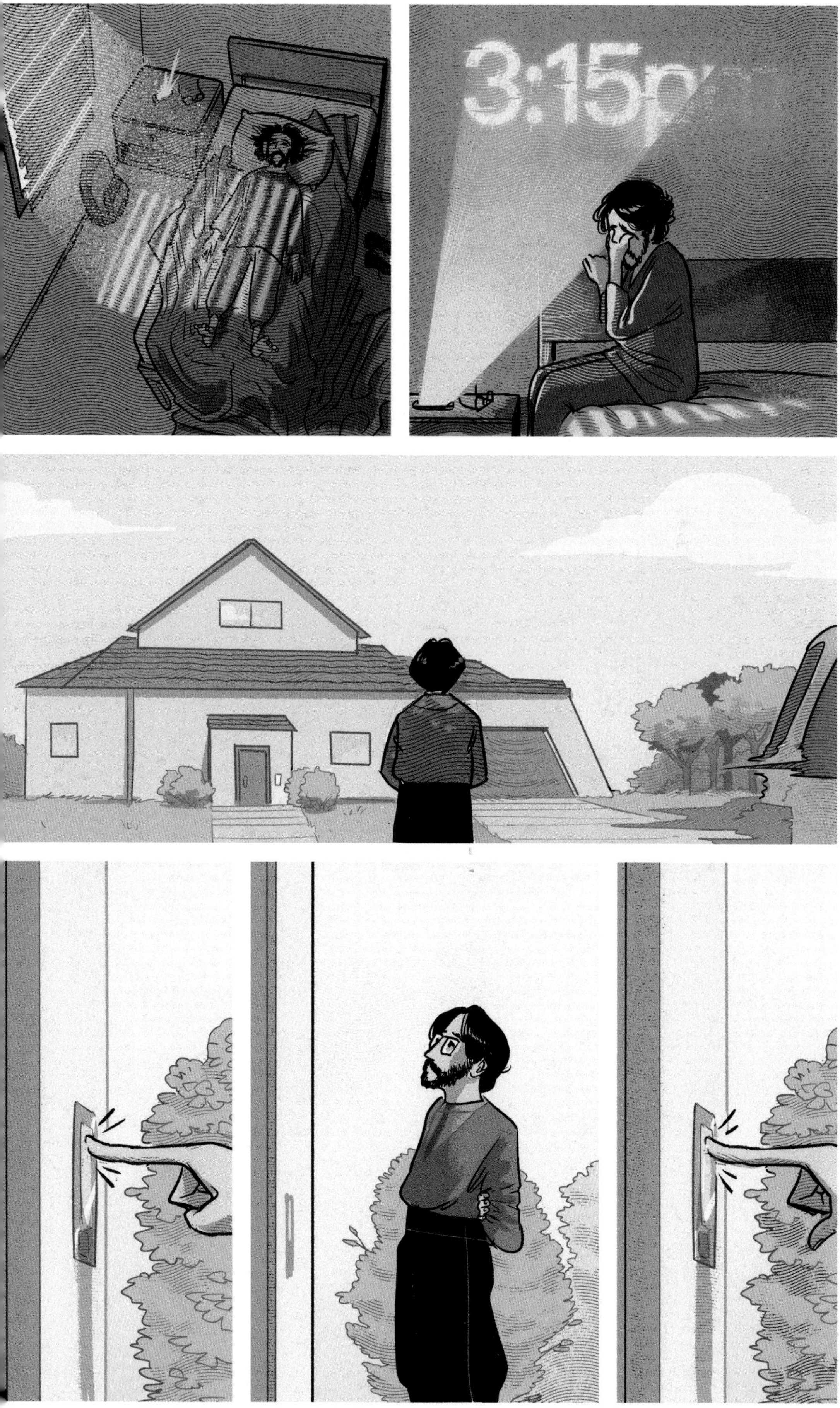
3:15p

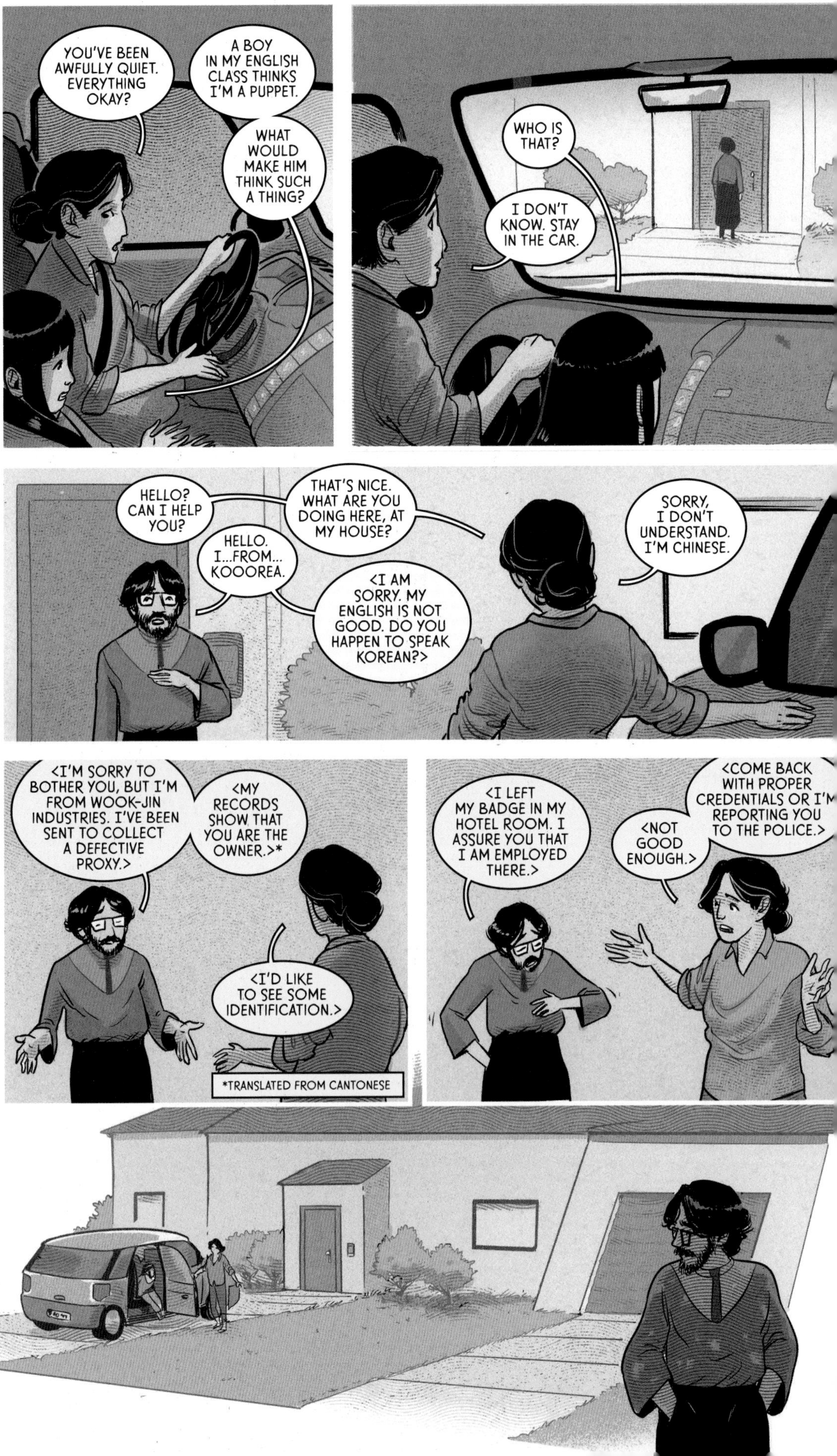

YOU'VE BEEN AWFULLY QUIET. EVERYTHING OKAY?
A BOY IN MY ENGLISH CLASS THINKS I'M A PUPPET.
WHAT WOULD MAKE HIM THINK SUCH A THING?
WHO IS THAT?
I DON'T KNOW. STAY IN THE CAR.
HELLO? CAN I HELP YOU?
HELLO. I...FROM... KOOOREA.
THAT'S NICE. WHAT ARE YOU DOING HERE, AT MY HOUSE?
<I AM SORRY. MY ENGLISH IS NOT GOOD. DO YOU HAPPEN TO SPEAK KOREAN?>
SORRY, I DON'T UNDERSTAND. I'M CHINESE.
<I'M SORRY TO BOTHER YOU, BUT I'M FROM WOOK-JIN INDUSTRIES. I'VE BEEN SENT TO COLLECT A DEFECTIVE PROXY.>
<MY RECORDS SHOW THAT YOU ARE THE OWNER.>*
<I'D LIKE TO SEE SOME IDENTIFICATION.>
*TRANSLATED FROM CANTONESE
<I LEFT MY BADGE IN MY HOTEL ROOM. I ASSURE YOU THAT I AM EMPLOYED THERE.>
<NOT GOOD ENOUGH.>
<COME BACK WITH PROPER CREDENTIALS OR I'M REPORTING YOU TO THE POLICE.>

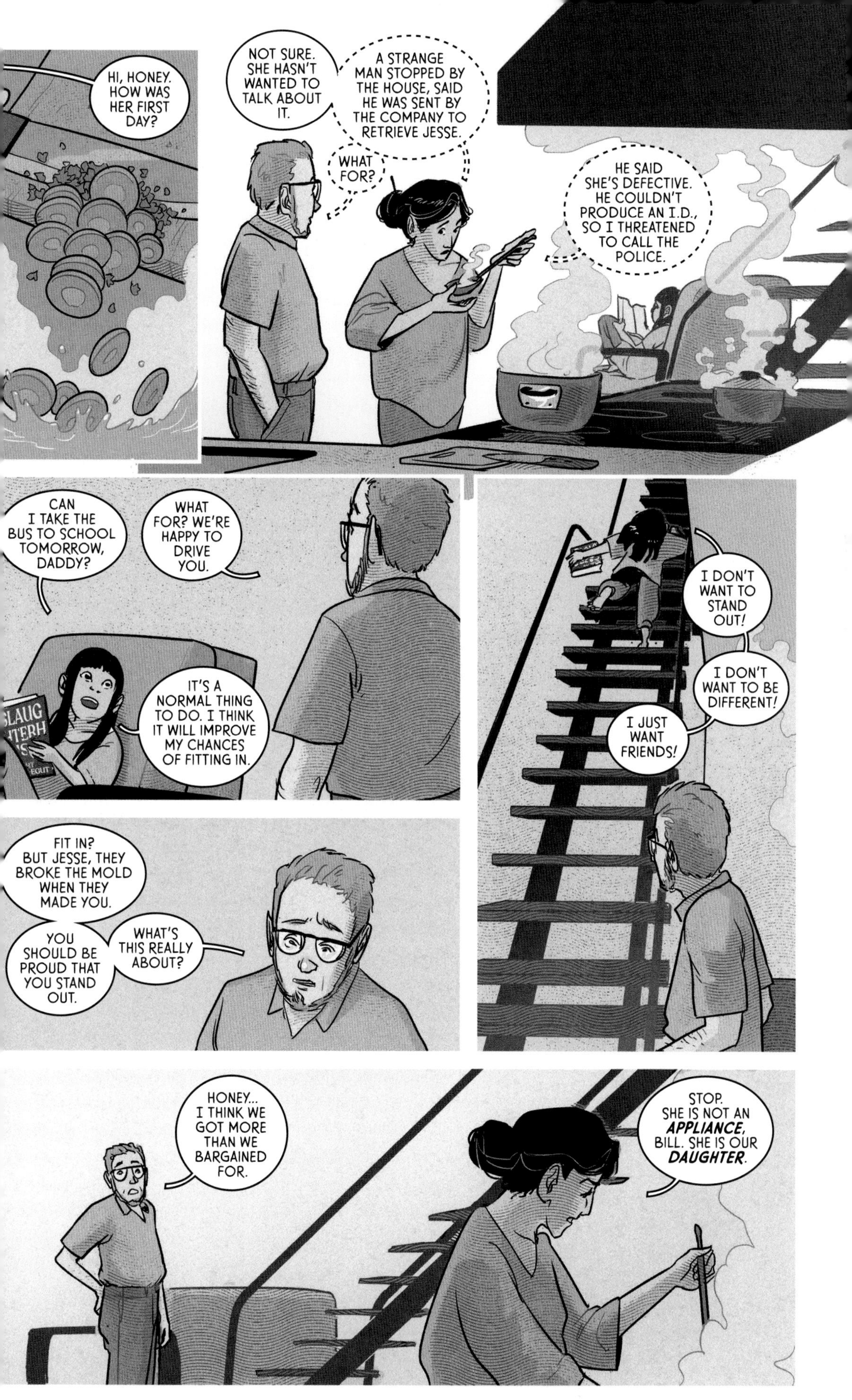
HI, HONEY. HOW WAS HER FIRST DAY?
NOT SURE. SHE HASN'T WANTED TO TALK ABOUT IT.
A STRANGE MAN STOPPED BY THE HOUSE, SAID HE WAS SENT BY THE COMPANY TO RETRIEVE JESSE.
WHAT FOR?
HE SAID SHE'S DEFECTIVE. HE COULDN'T PRODUCE AN I.D., SO I THREATENED TO CALL THE POLICE.
CAN I TAKE THE BUS TO SCHOOL TOMORROW, DADDY?
WHAT FOR? WE'RE HAPPY TO DRIVE YOU.
IT'S A NORMAL THING TO DO. I THINK IT WILL IMPROVE MY CHANCES OF FITTING IN.
FIT IN? BUT JESSE, THEY BROKE THE MOLD WHEN THEY MADE YOU.
YOU SHOULD BE PROUD THAT YOU STAND OUT.
WHAT'S THIS REALLY ABOUT?
I DON'T WANT TO STAND OUT!
I DON'T WANT TO BE DIFFERENT!
I JUST WANT FRIENDS!
HONEY... I THINK WE GOT MORE THAN WE BARGAINED FOR.
STOP. SHE IS NOT AN ***APPLIANCE***, BILL. SHE IS OUR ***DAUGHTER***.

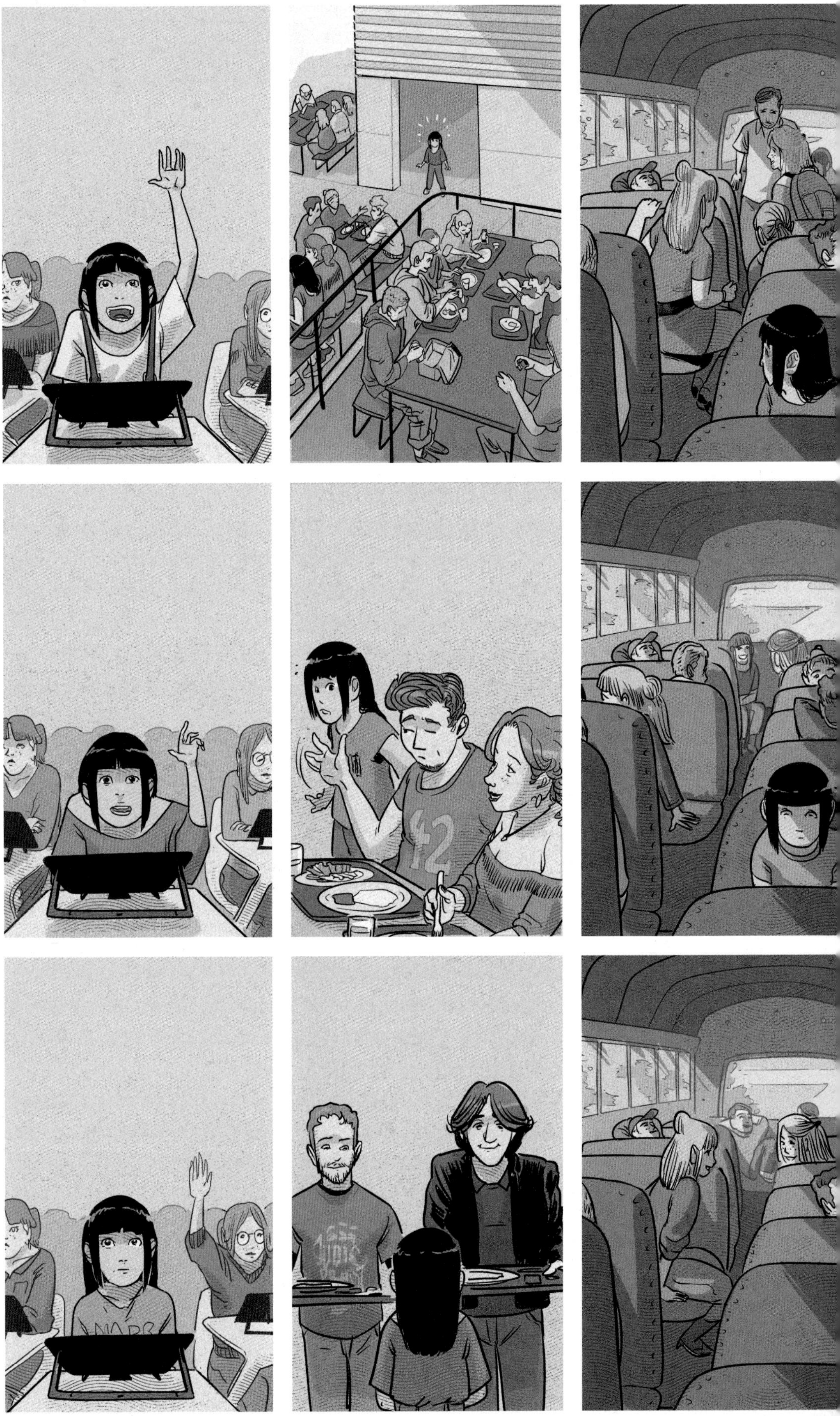

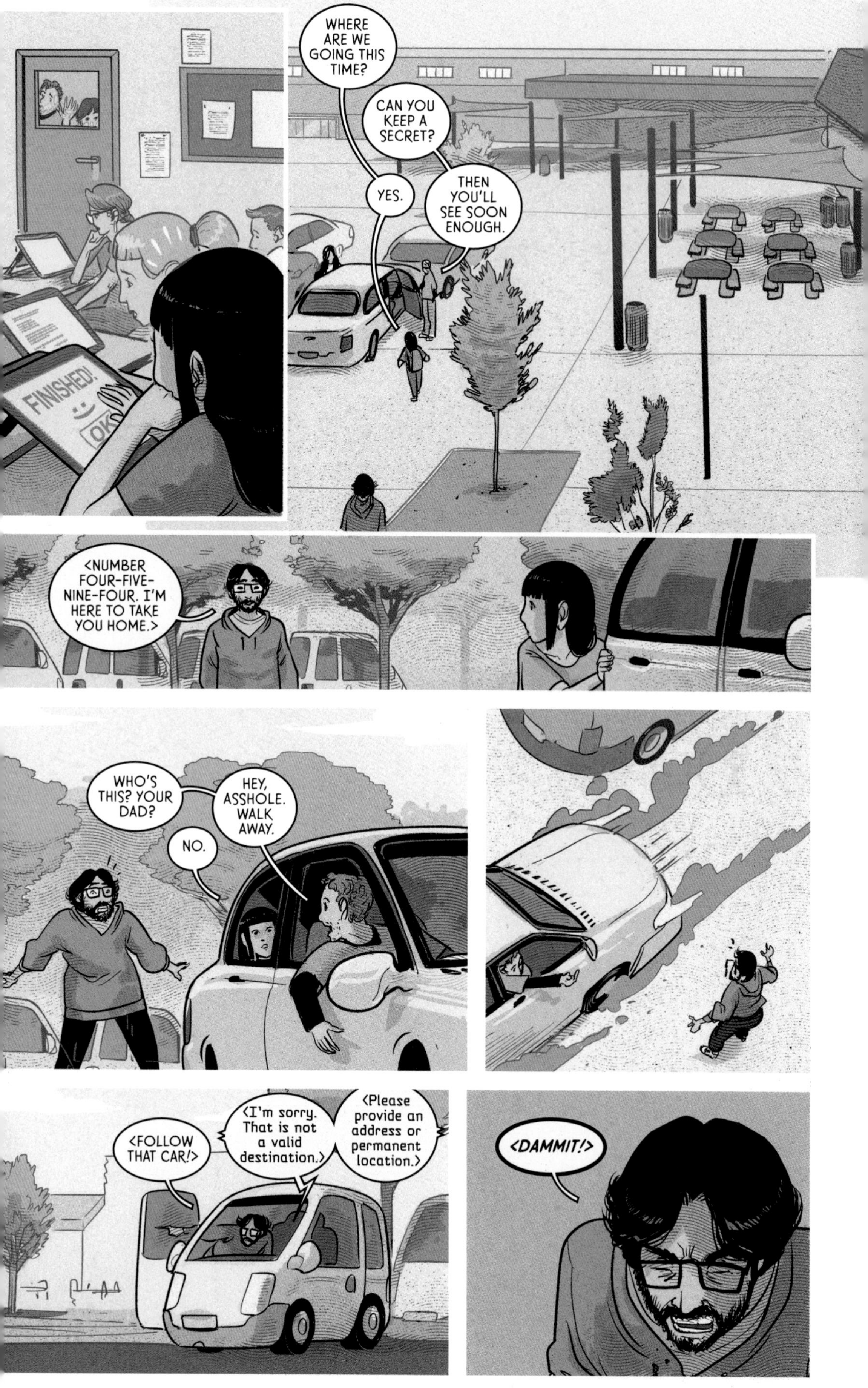
FINISHED!
OK
WHERE ARE WE GOING THIS TIME?
CAN YOU KEEP A SECRET?
YES.
THEN YOU'LL SEE SOON ENOUGH.
<NUMBER FOUR-FIVE-NINE-FOUR. I'M HERE TO TAKE YOU HOME.>
WHO'S THIS? YOUR DAD?
HEY, ASSHOLE. WALK AWAY.
NO.
<FOLLOW THAT CAR!>
<I'm sorry. That is not a valid destination.>
<Please provide an address or permanent location.>
<DAMMIT!>

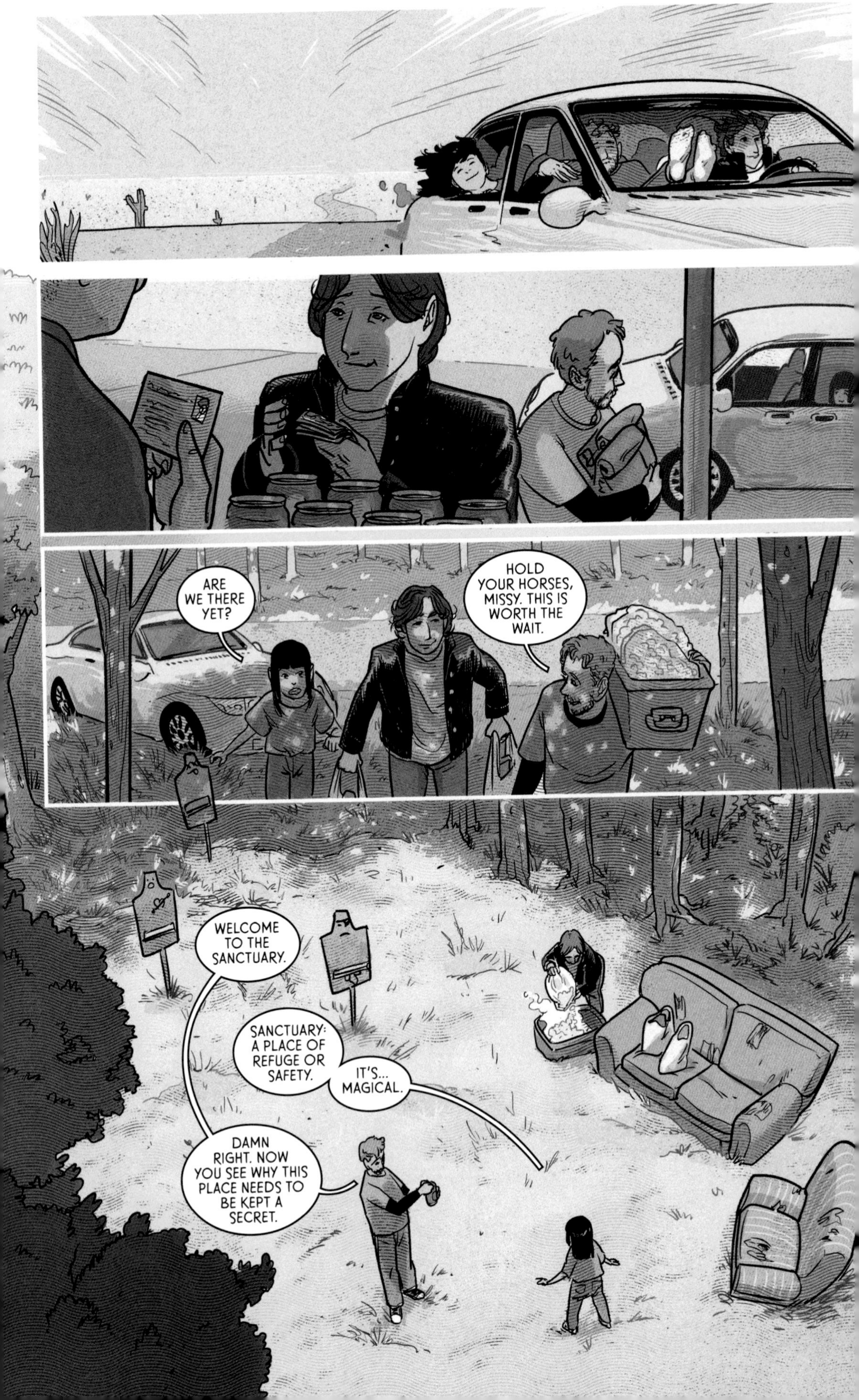
ARE WE THERE YET?
HOLD YOUR HORSES, MISSY. THIS IS WORTH THE WAIT.
WELCOME TO THE SANCTUARY.
SANCTUARY: A PLACE OF REFUGE OR SAFETY.
IT'S... MAGICAL.
DAMN RIGHT. NOW YOU SEE WHY THIS PLACE NEEDS TO BE KEPT A SECRET.

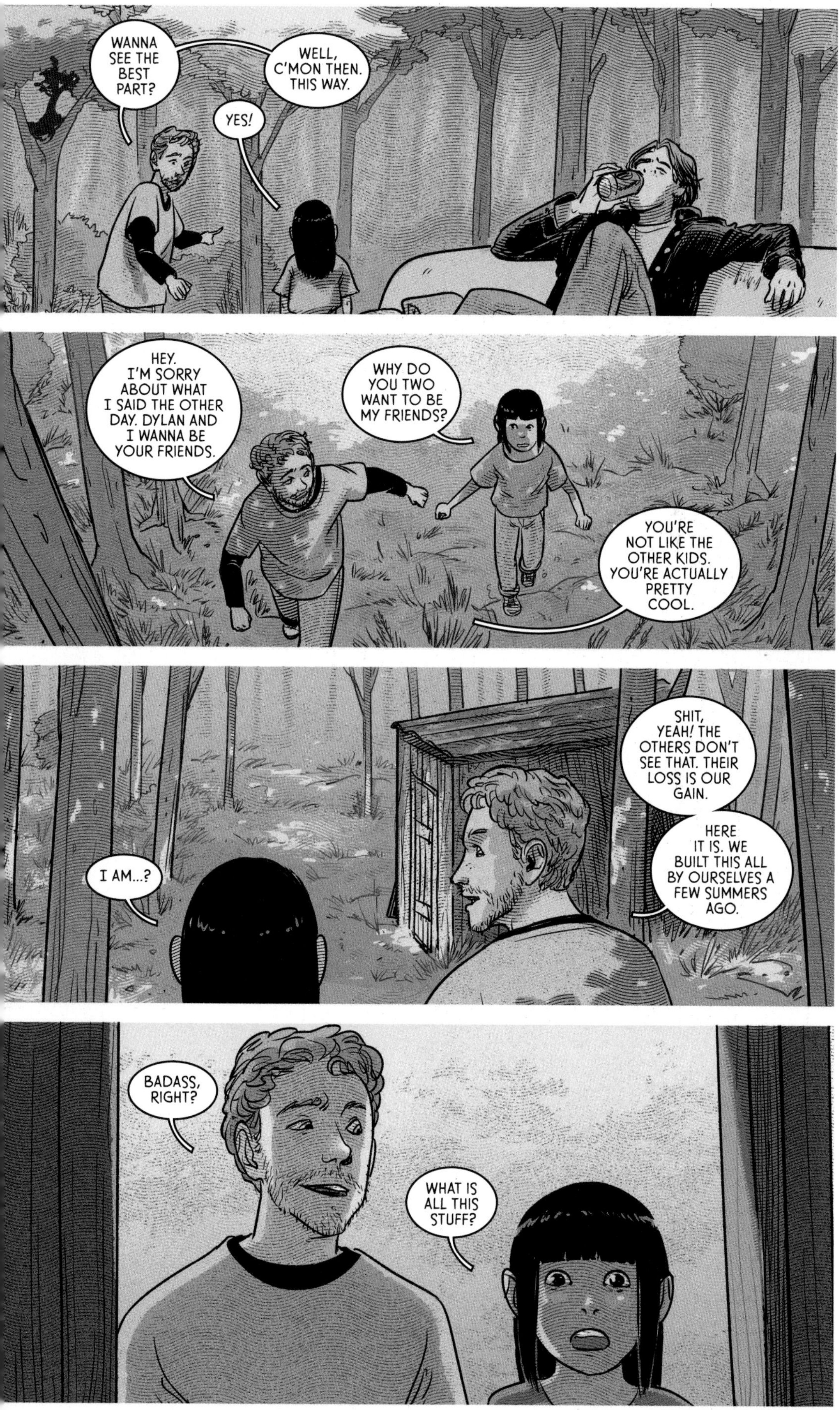
WANNA SEE THE BEST PART?
YES!
WELL, C'MON THEN. THIS WAY.
HEY. I'M SORRY ABOUT WHAT I SAID THE OTHER DAY. DYLAN AND I WANNA BE YOUR FRIENDS.
WHY DO YOU TWO WANT TO BE MY FRIENDS?
YOU'RE NOT LIKE THE OTHER KIDS. YOU'RE ACTUALLY PRETTY COOL.
I AM...?
SHIT, YEAH! THE OTHERS DON'T SEE THAT. THEIR LOSS IS OUR GAIN.
HERE IT IS. WE BUILT THIS ALL BY OURSELVES A FEW SUMMERS AGO.
BADASS, RIGHT?
WHAT IS ALL THIS STUFF?

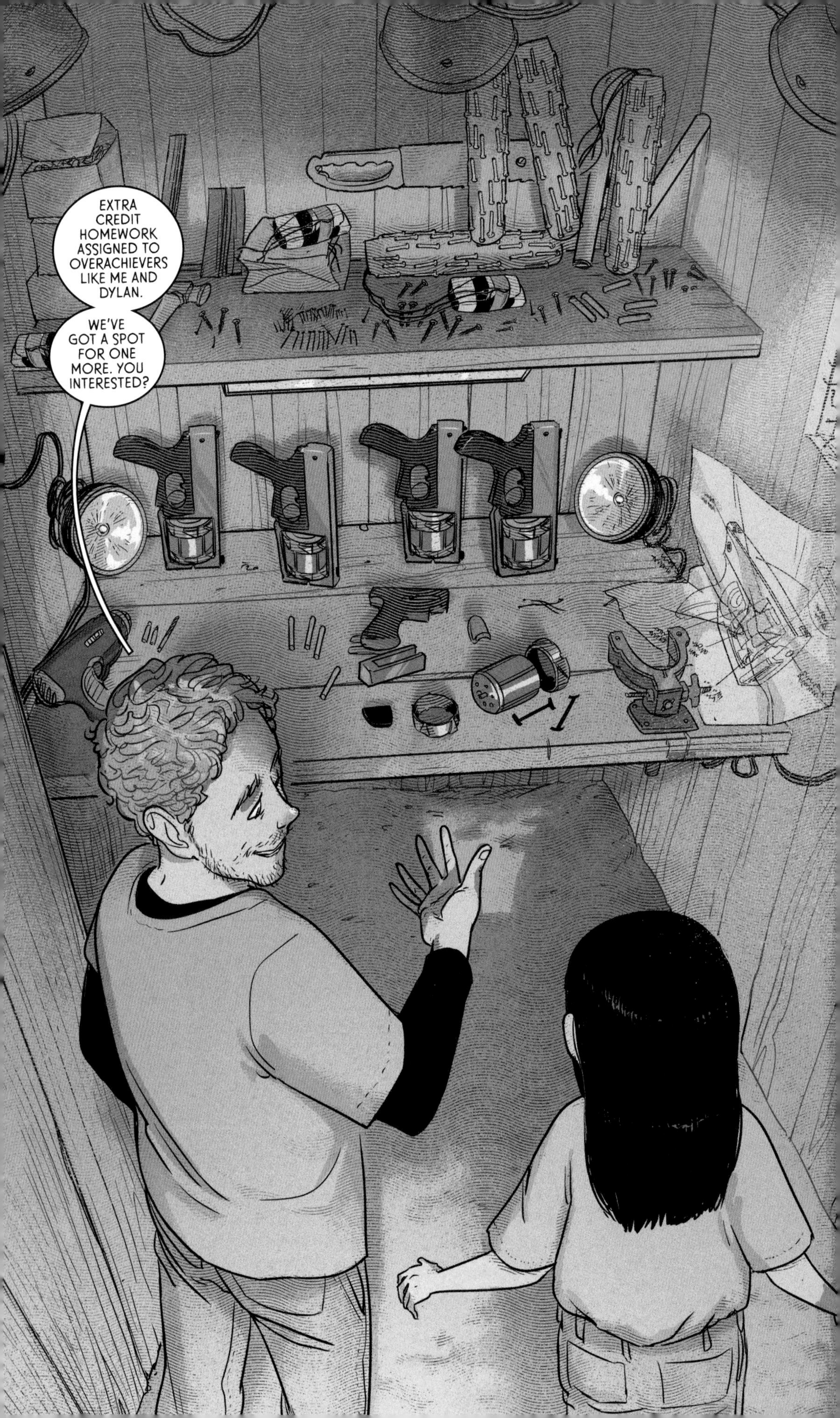
EXTRA CREDIT HOMEWORK ASSIGNED TO OVERACHIEVERS LIKE ME AND DYLAN.
WE'VE GOT A SPOT FOR ONE MORE. YOU INTERESTED?

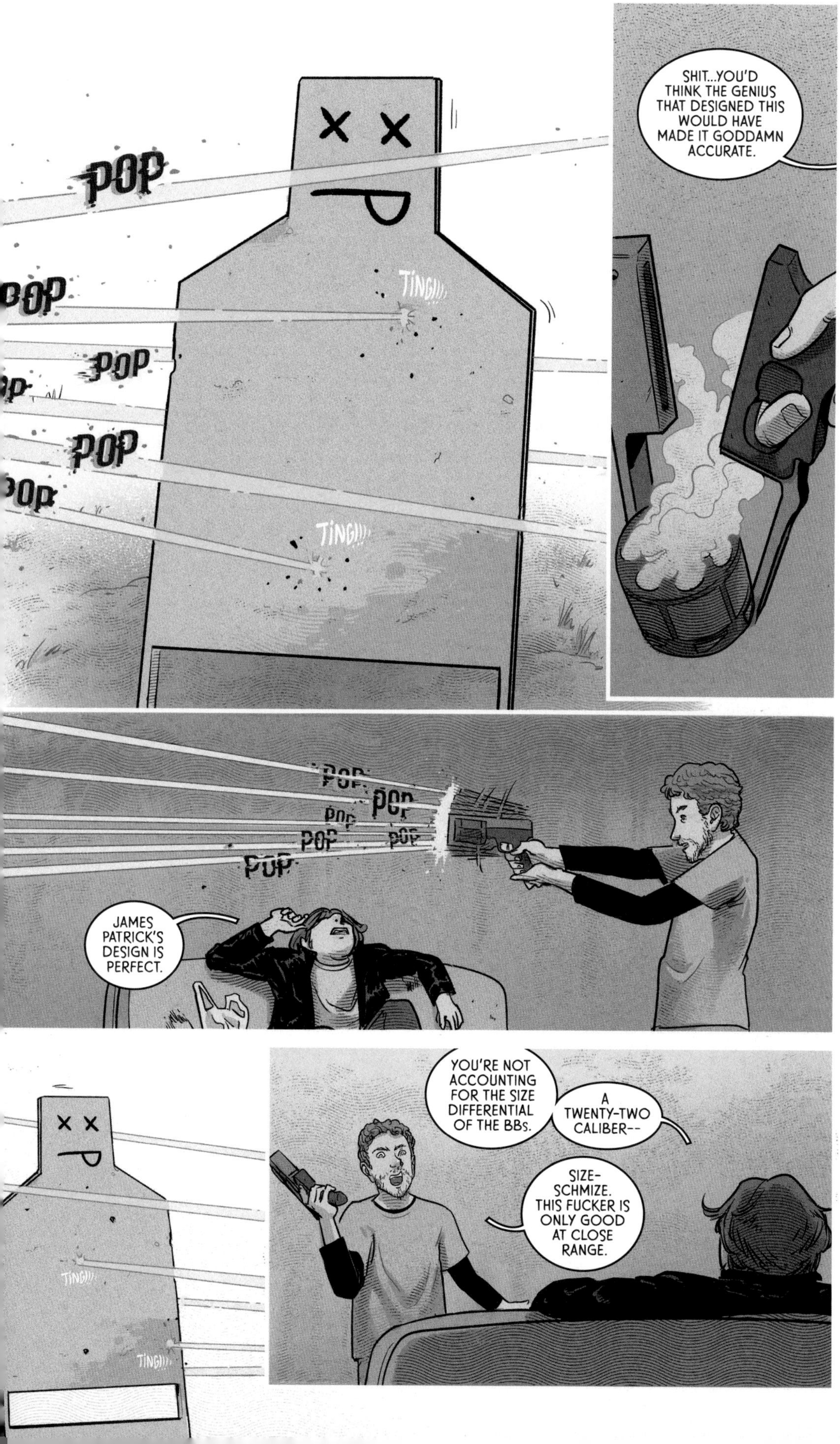

POP
POP
POP
POP
POP
POP
TING!!!
TING!!!
SHIT...YOU'D THINK THE GENIUS THAT DESIGNED THIS WOULD HAVE MADE IT GODDAMN ACCURATE.
POP
POP
POP
POP
POP
POP
JAMES PATRICK'S DESIGN IS PERFECT.
TING!!!
TING!!!
YOU'RE NOT ACCOUNTING FOR THE SIZE DIFFERENTIAL OF THE BBs.
A TWENTY-TWO CALIBER--
SIZE-SCHMIZE. THIS FUCKER IS ONLY GOOD AT CLOSE RANGE.

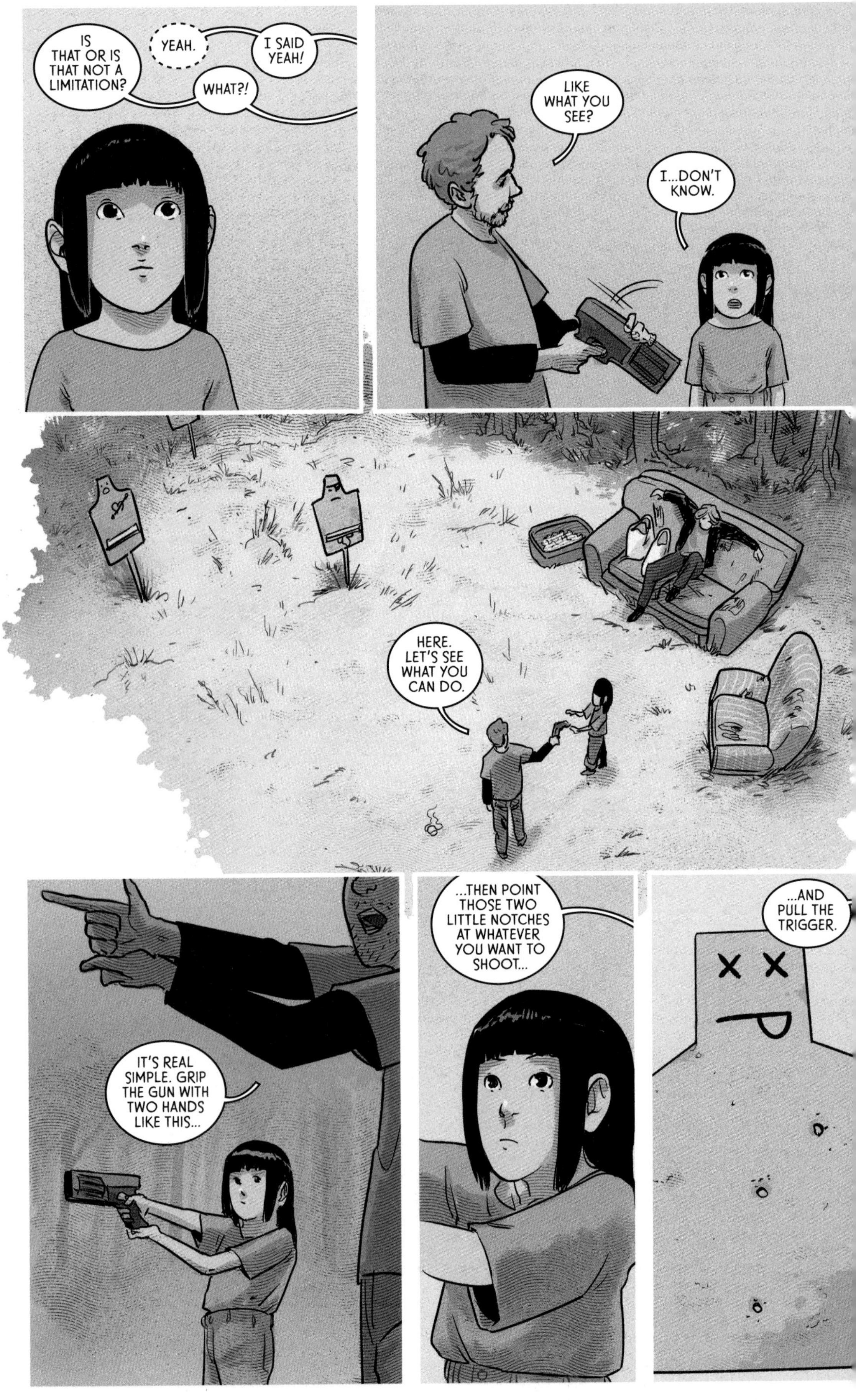
IS THAT OR IS THAT NOT A LIMITATION?
YEAH.
WHAT?!
I SAID YEAH!
LIKE WHAT YOU SEE?
I...DON'T KNOW.
HERE. LET'S SEE WHAT YOU CAN DO.
IT'S REAL SIMPLE. GRIP THE GUN WITH TWO HANDS LIKE THIS...
...THEN POINT THOSE TWO LITTLE NOTCHES AT WHATEVER YOU WANT TO SHOOT...
...AND PULL THE TRIGGER.

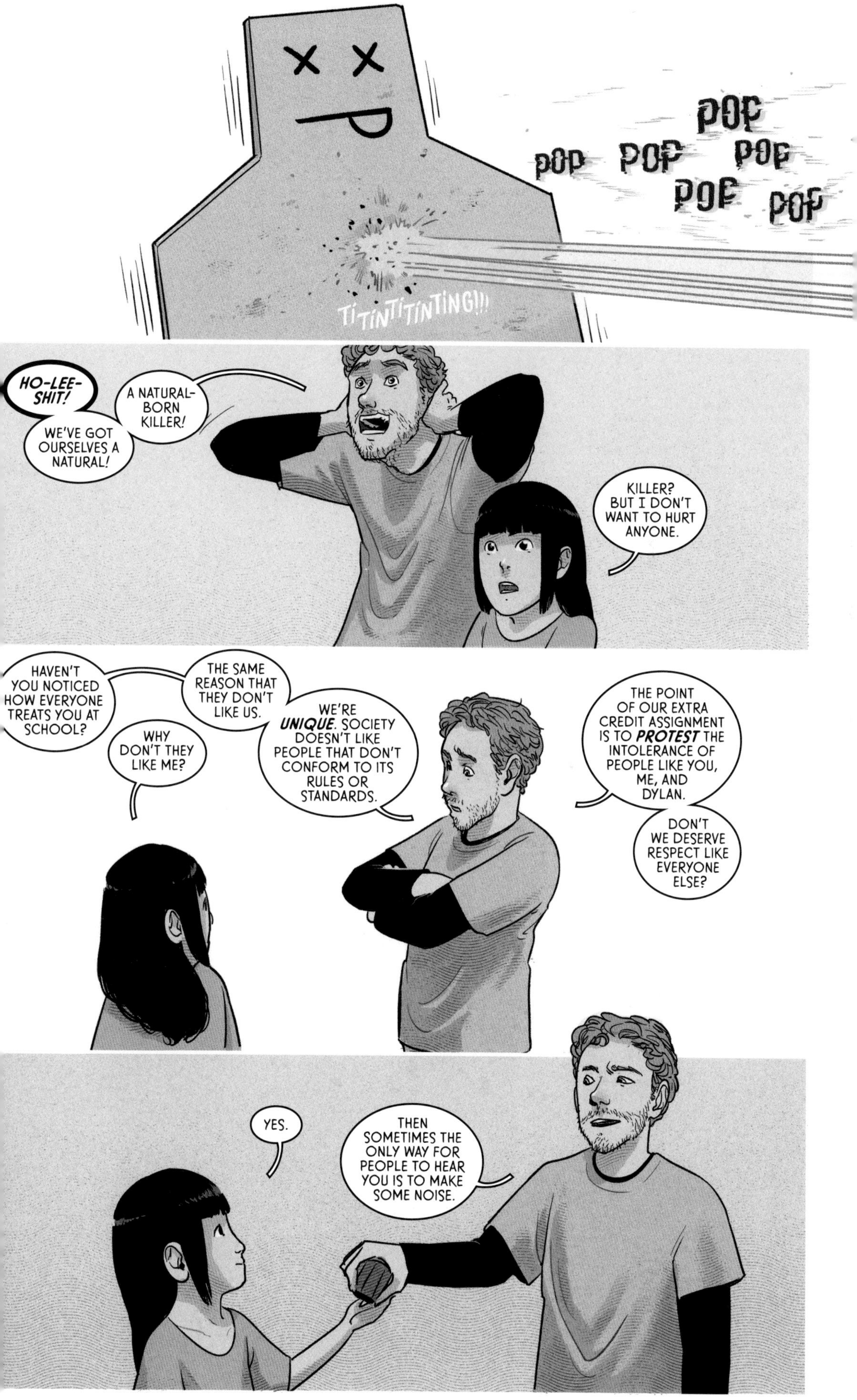
POP POP POP POP POP POP
TITINTITINTING!!!
HO-LEE-SHIT!
WE'VE GOT OURSELVES A NATURAL!
A NATURAL-BORN KILLER!
KILLER? BUT I DON'T WANT TO HURT ANYONE.
HAVEN'T YOU NOTICED HOW EVERYONE TREATS YOU AT SCHOOL?
WHY DON'T THEY LIKE ME?
THE SAME REASON THAT THEY DON'T LIKE US.
WE'RE ***UNIQUE***. SOCIETY DOESN'T LIKE PEOPLE THAT DON'T CONFORM TO ITS RULES OR STANDARDS.
THE POINT OF OUR EXTRA CREDIT ASSIGNMENT IS TO ***PROTEST*** THE INTOLERANCE OF PEOPLE LIKE YOU, ME, AND DYLAN.
DON'T WE DESERVE RESPECT LIKE EVERYONE ELSE?
YES.
THEN SOMETIMES THE ONLY WAY FOR PEOPLE TO HEAR YOU IS TO MAKE SOME NOISE.

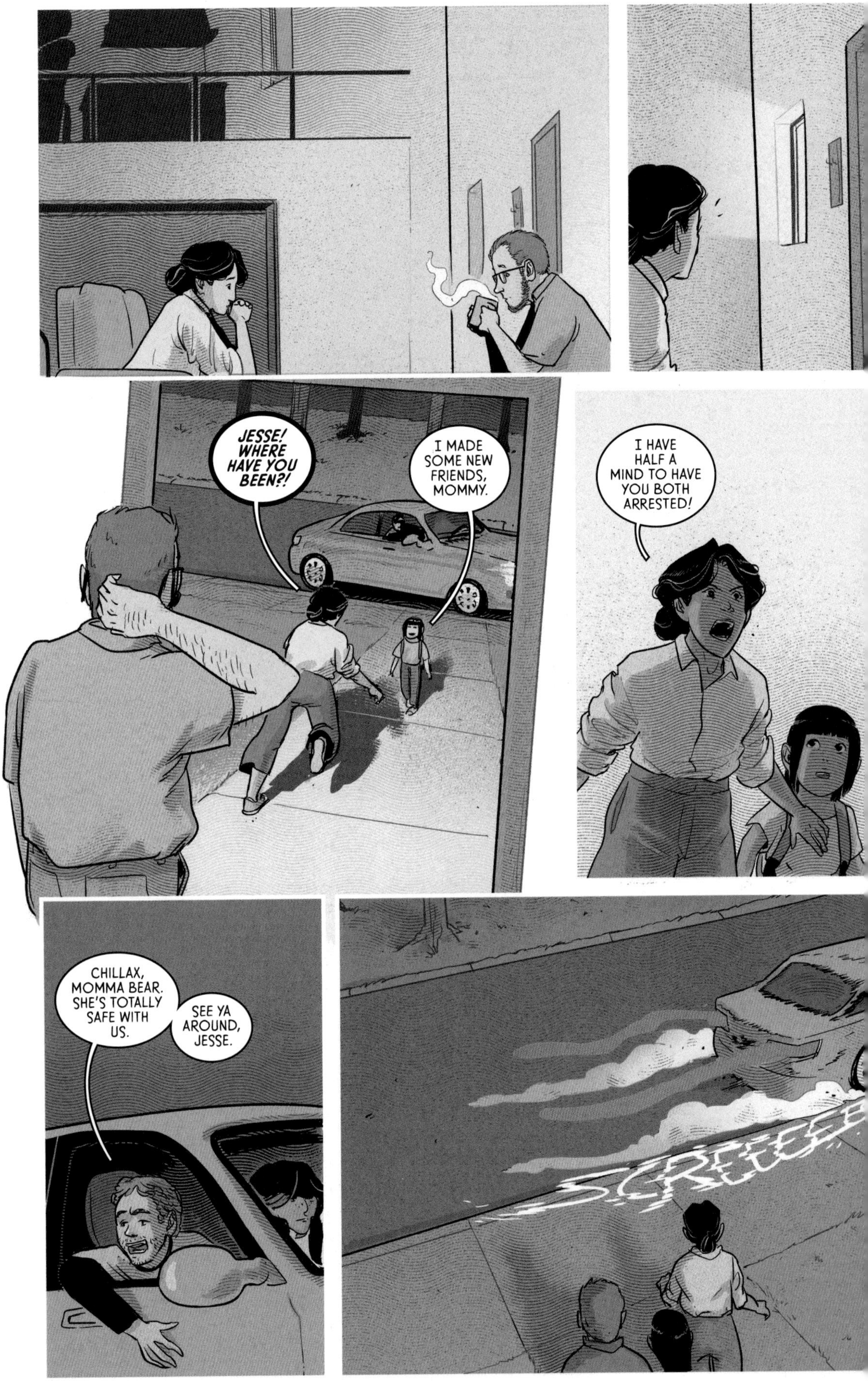

JESSE! WHERE HAVE YOU BEEN?!
I MADE SOME NEW FRIENDS, MOMMY.
I HAVE HALF A MIND TO HAVE YOU BOTH ARRESTED!
CHILLAX, MOMMA BEAR. SHE'S TOTALLY SAFE WITH US.
SEE YA AROUND, JESSE.
SCREEEEE

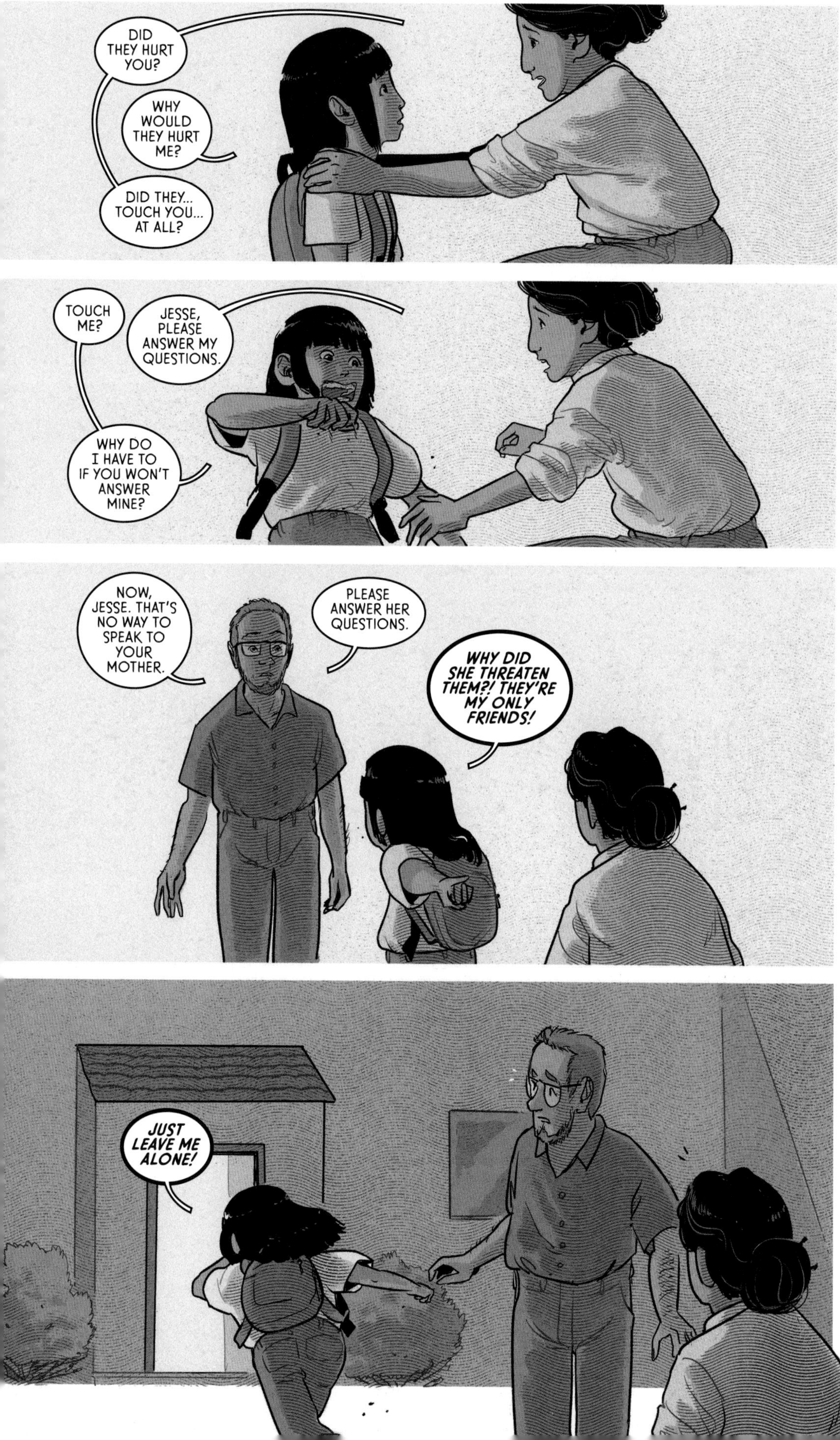
DID THEY HURT YOU?
WHY WOULD THEY HURT ME?
DID THEY... TOUCH YOU... AT ALL?
TOUCH ME?
JESSE, PLEASE ANSWER MY QUESTIONS.
WHY DO I HAVE TO IF YOU WON'T ANSWER MINE?
NOW, JESSE. THAT'S NO WAY TO SPEAK TO YOUR MOTHER.
PLEASE ANSWER HER QUESTIONS.
WHY DID SHE THREATEN THEM?! THEY'RE MY ONLY FRIENDS!
JUST LEAVE ME ALONE!

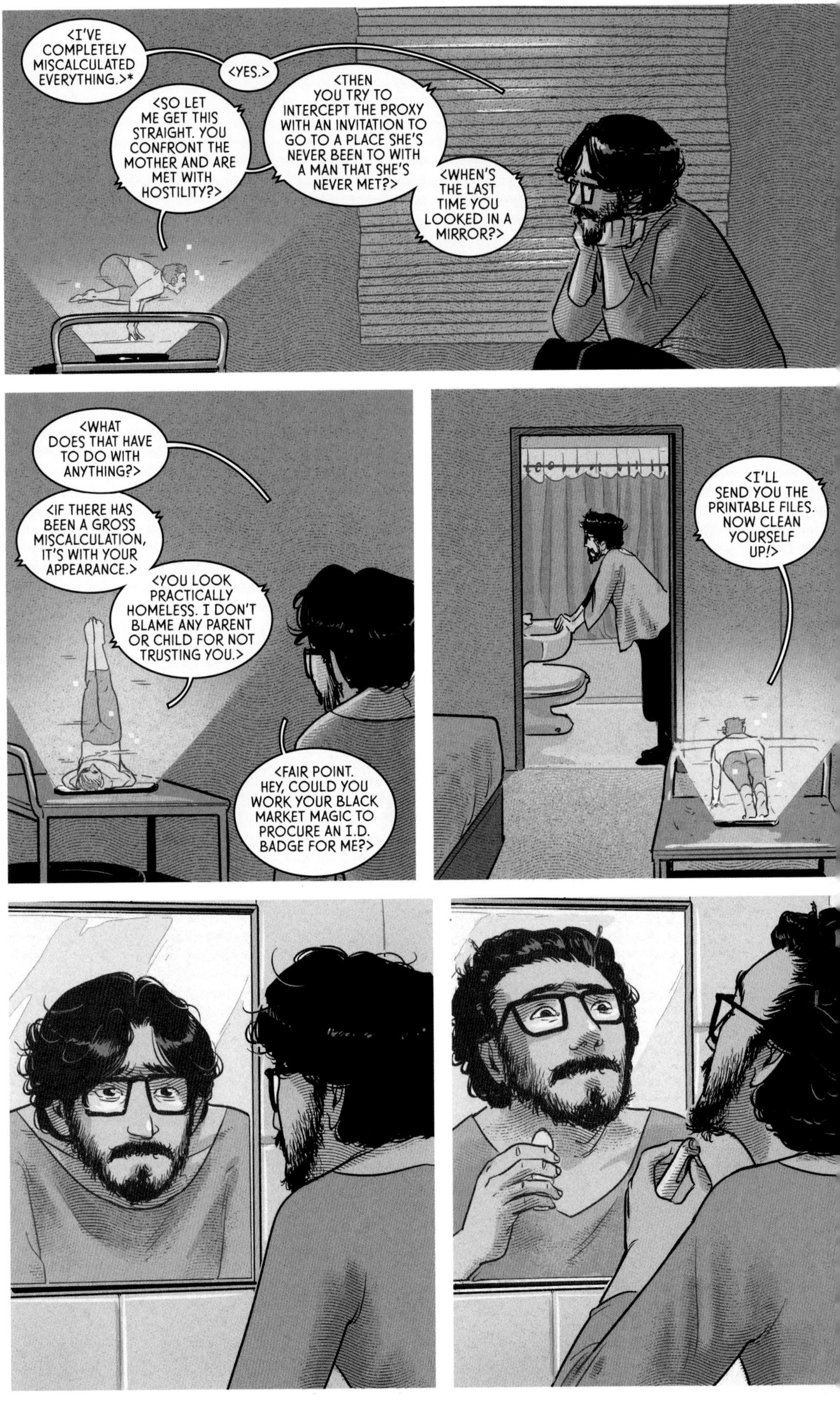
<I'VE COMPLETELY MISCALCULATED EVERYTHING.>*
<YES.>
<SO LET ME GET THIS STRAIGHT. YOU CONFRONT THE MOTHER AND ARE MET WITH HOSTILITY?>
<THEN YOU TRY TO INTERCEPT THE PROXY WITH AN INVITATION TO GO TO A PLACE SHE'S NEVER BEEN TO WITH A MAN THAT SHE'S NEVER MET?>
<WHEN'S THE LAST TIME YOU LOOKED IN A MIRROR?>
<WHAT DOES THAT HAVE TO DO WITH ANYTHING?>
<IF THERE HAS BEEN A GROSS MISCALCULATION, IT'S WITH YOUR APPEARANCE.>
<YOU LOOK PRACTICALLY HOMELESS. I DON'T BLAME ANY PARENT OR CHILD FOR NOT TRUSTING YOU.>
<FAIR POINT. HEY, COULD YOU WORK YOUR BLACK MARKET MAGIC TO PROCURE AN I.D. BADGE FOR ME?>
<I'LL SEND YOU THE PRINTABLE FILES. NOW CLEAN YOURSELF UP!>

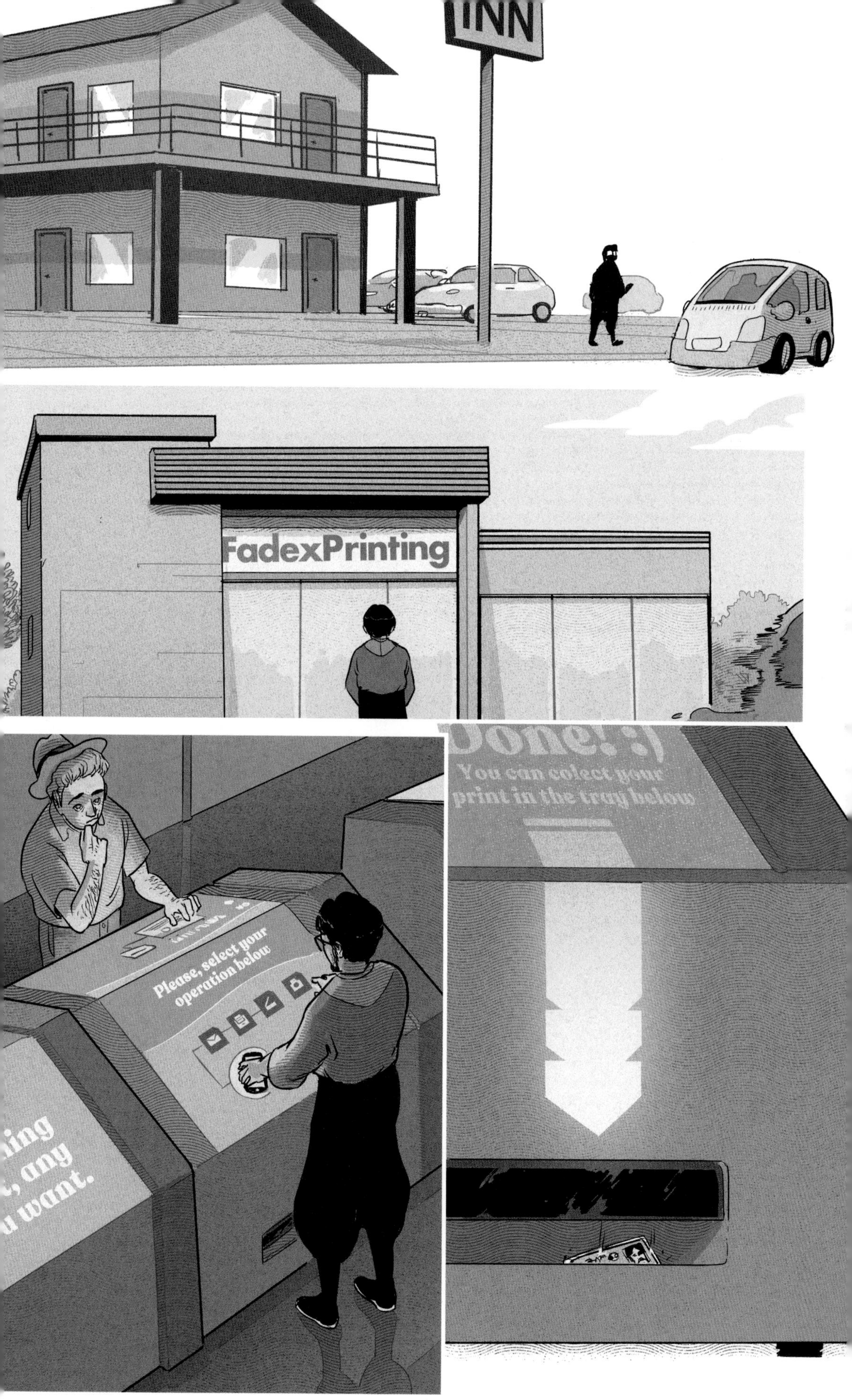
INN
FadexPrinting
Please, select your operation below
You can colect your print in the tray below

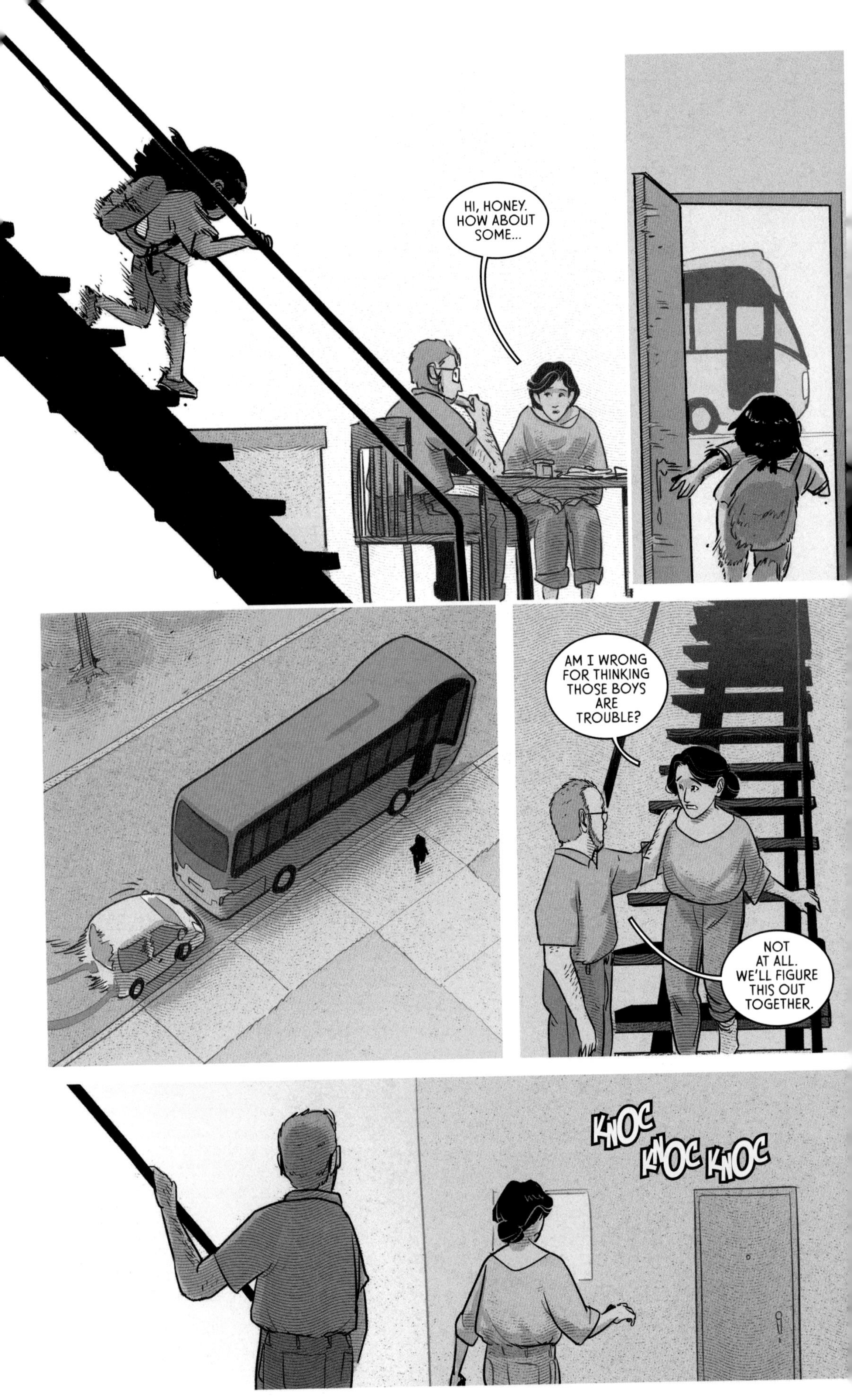
HI, HONEY. HOW ABOUT SOME...
AM I WRONG FOR THINKING THOSE BOYS ARE TROUBLE?
NOT AT ALL. WE'LL FIGURE THIS OUT TOGETHER.
KNOC
KNOC KNOC

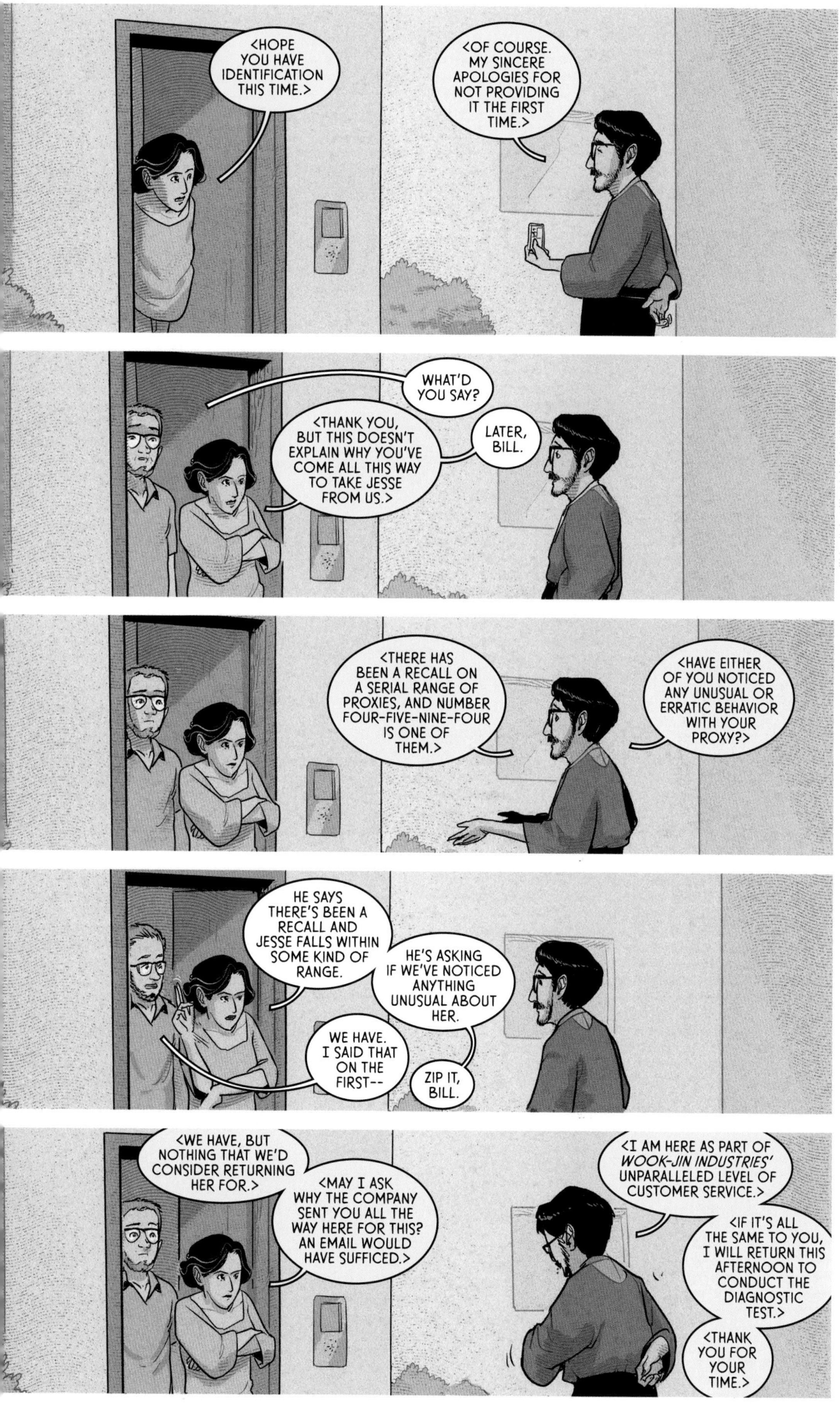

<HOPE YOU HAVE IDENTIFICATION THIS TIME.>
<OF COURSE. MY SINCERE APOLOGIES FOR NOT PROVIDING IT THE FIRST TIME.>
WHAT'D YOU SAY?
<THANK YOU, BUT THIS DOESN'T EXPLAIN WHY YOU'VE COME ALL THIS WAY TO TAKE JESSE FROM US.>
LATER, BILL.
<THERE HAS BEEN A RECALL ON A SERIAL RANGE OF PROXIES, AND NUMBER FOUR-FIVE-NINE-FOUR IS ONE OF THEM.>
<HAVE EITHER OF YOU NOTICED ANY UNUSUAL OR ERRATIC BEHAVIOR WITH YOUR PROXY?>
HE SAYS THERE'S BEEN A RECALL AND JESSE FALLS WITHIN SOME KIND OF RANGE.
HE'S ASKING IF WE'VE NOTICED ANYTHING UNUSUAL ABOUT HER.
WE HAVE. I SAID THAT ON THE FIRST--
ZIP IT, BILL.
<WE HAVE, BUT NOTHING THAT WE'D CONSIDER RETURNING HER FOR.>
<MAY I ASK WHY THE COMPANY SENT YOU ALL THE WAY HERE FOR THIS? AN EMAIL WOULD HAVE SUFFICED.>
<I AM HERE AS PART OF *WOOK-JIN INDUSTRIES'* UNPARALLELED LEVEL OF CUSTOMER SERVICE.>
<IF IT'S ALL THE SAME TO YOU, I WILL RETURN THIS AFTERNOON TO CONDUCT THE DIAGNOSTIC TEST.>
<THANK YOU FOR YOUR TIME.>

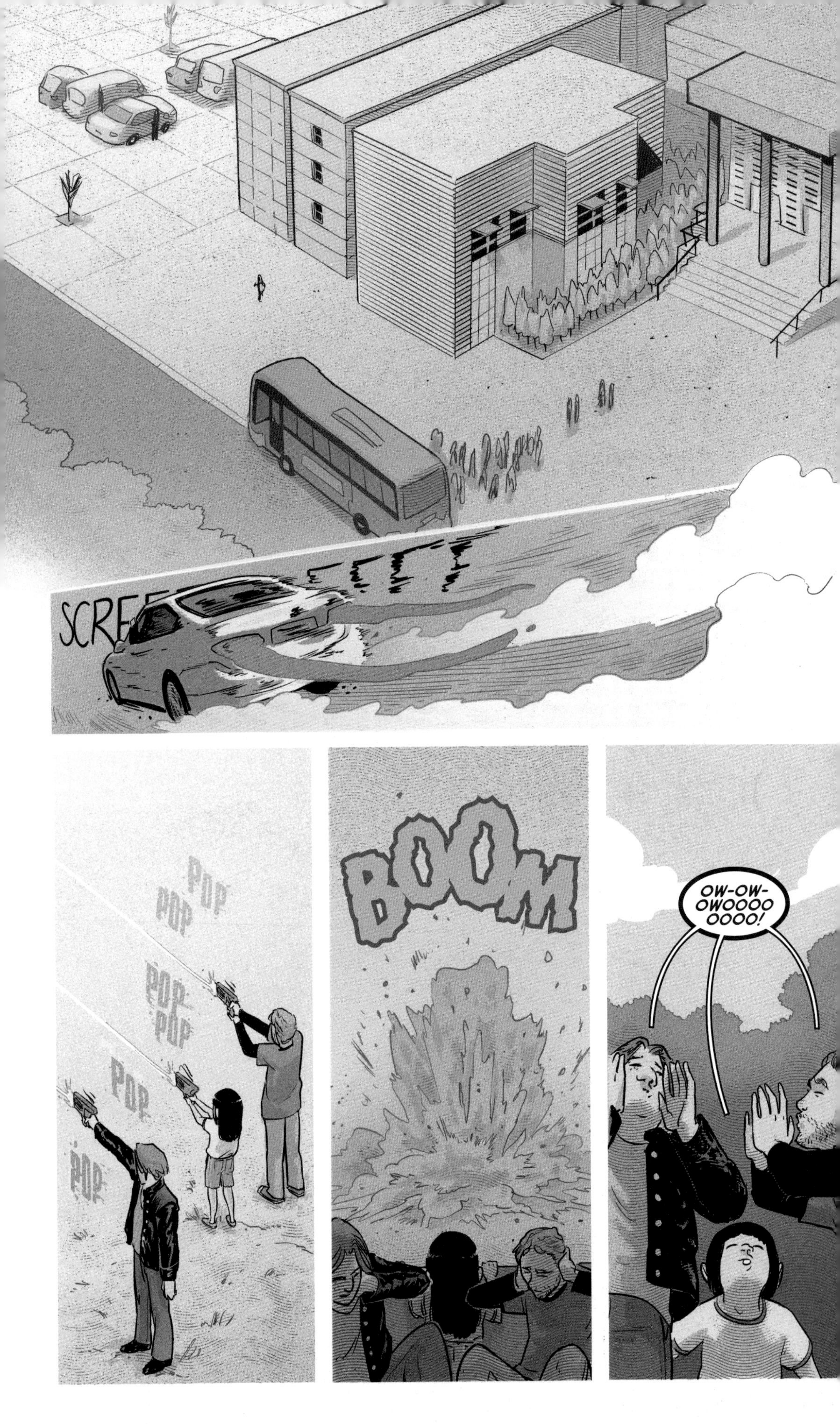
SCREEEEE
POP
POP
POP
POP
POP
POP
BOOM
OW-OW-OWOOOOOOOO!

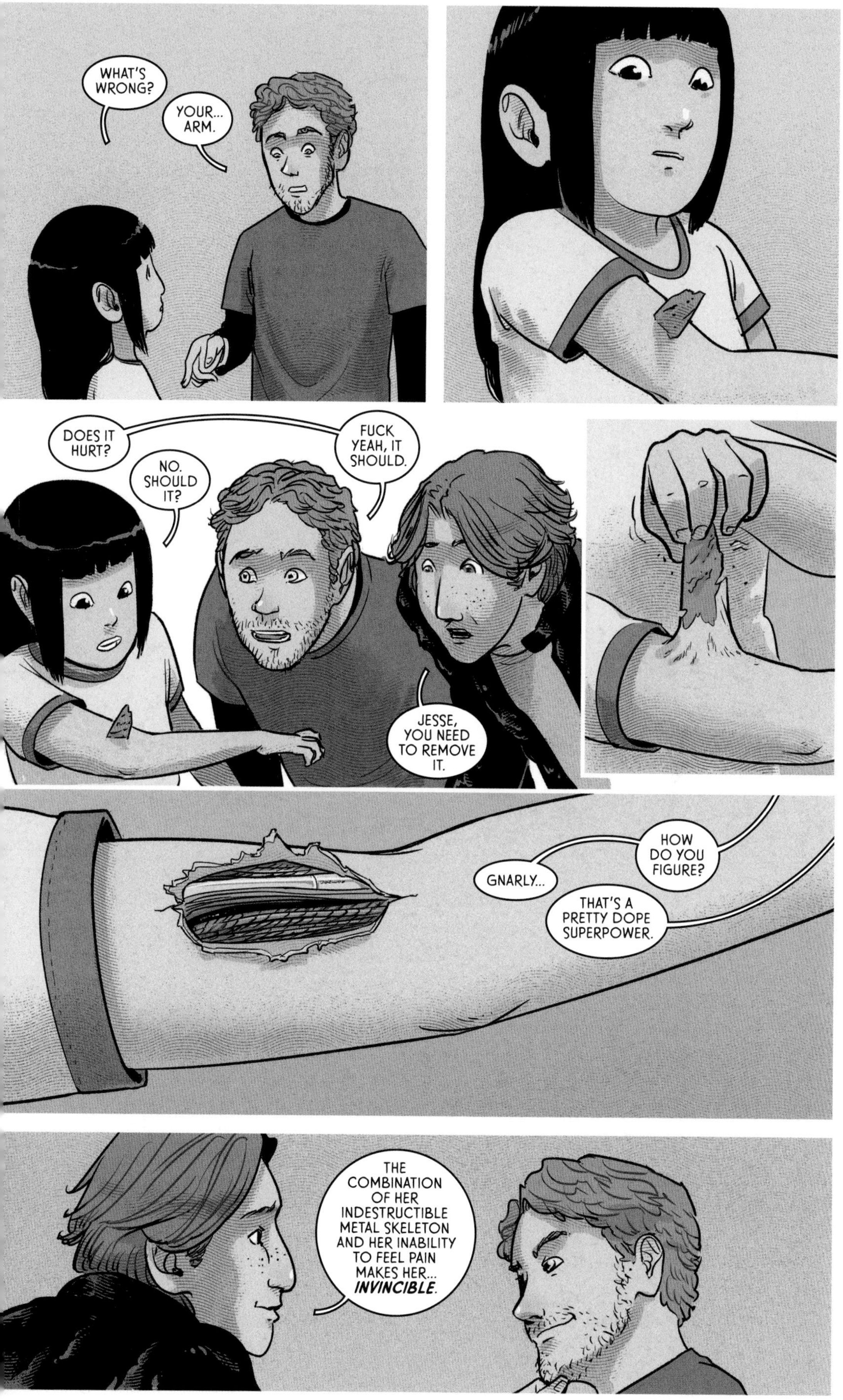
WHAT'S WRONG?
YOUR... ARM.
DOES IT HURT?
NO. SHOULD IT?
FUCK YEAH, IT SHOULD.
JESSE, YOU NEED TO REMOVE IT.
GNARLY...
HOW DO YOU FIGURE?
THAT'S A PRETTY DOPE SUPERPOWER.
THE COMBINATION OF HER INDESTRUCTIBLE METAL SKELETON AND HER INABILITY TO FEEL PAIN MAKES HER... *INVINCIBLE*.

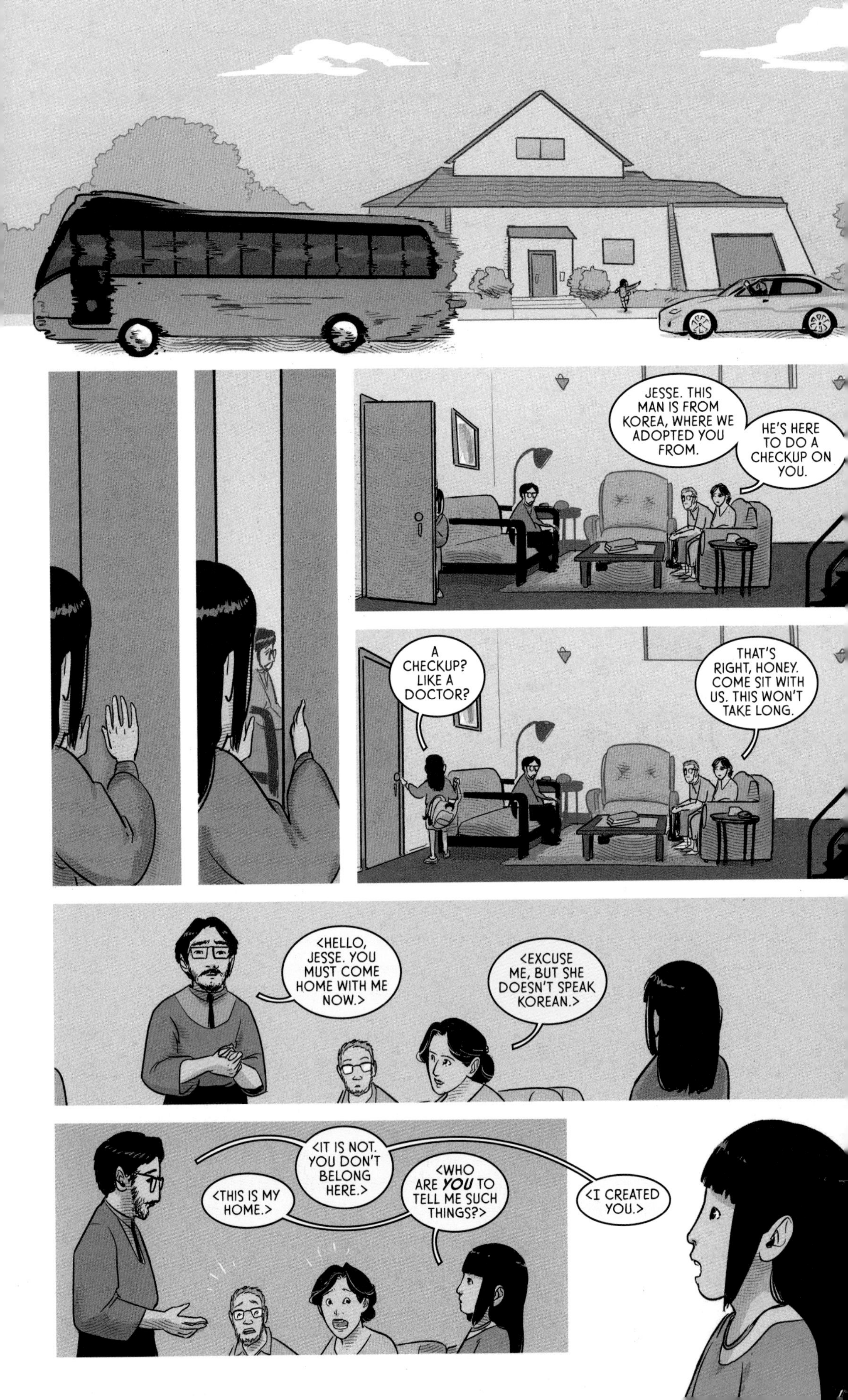

JESSE. THIS MAN IS FROM KOREA, WHERE WE ADOPTED YOU FROM.
HE'S HERE TO DO A CHECKUP ON YOU.
A CHECKUP? LIKE A DOCTOR?
THAT'S RIGHT, HONEY. COME SIT WITH US. THIS WON'T TAKE LONG.
<HELLO, JESSE. YOU MUST COME HOME WITH ME NOW.>
<EXCUSE ME, BUT SHE DOESN'T SPEAK KOREAN.>
<THIS IS MY HOME.>
<IT IS NOT. YOU DON'T BELONG HERE.>
<WHO ARE *YOU* TO TELL ME SUCH THINGS?>
<I CREATED YOU.>

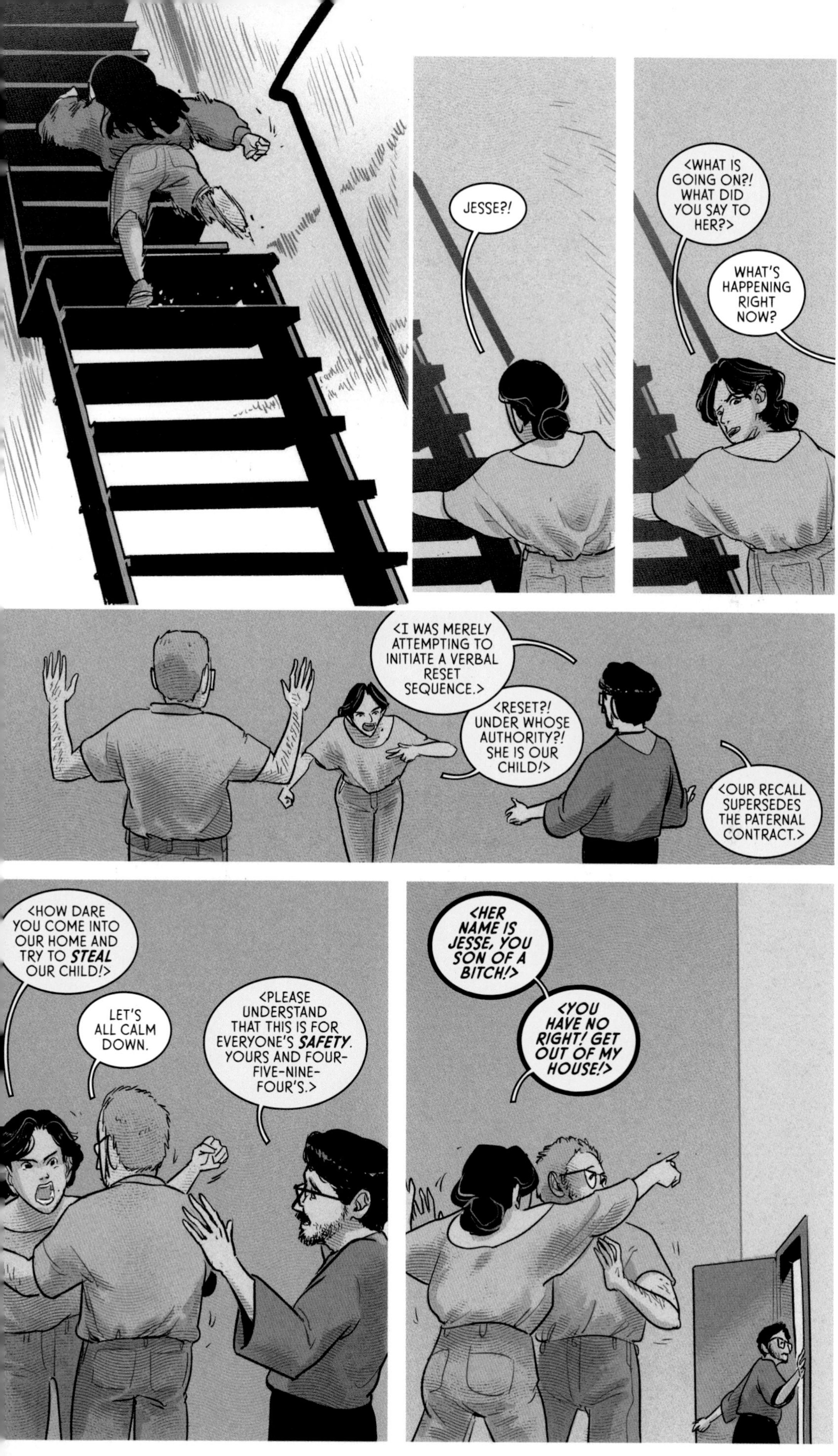
JESSE?!
<WHAT IS GOING ON?! WHAT DID YOU SAY TO HER?>
WHAT'S HAPPENING RIGHT NOW?
<I WAS MERELY ATTEMPTING TO INITIATE A VERBAL RESET SEQUENCE.>
<RESET?! UNDER WHOSE AUTHORITY?! SHE IS OUR CHILD!>
<OUR RECALL SUPERSEDES THE PATERNAL CONTRACT.>
<HOW DARE YOU COME INTO OUR HOME AND TRY TO STEAL OUR CHILD!>
LET'S ALL CALM DOWN.
<PLEASE UNDERSTAND THAT THIS IS FOR EVERYONE'S SAFETY. YOURS AND FOUR-FIVE-NINE-FOUR'S.>
<HER NAME IS JESSE, YOU SON OF A BITCH!>
<YOU HAVE NO RIGHT! GET OUT OF MY HOUSE!>

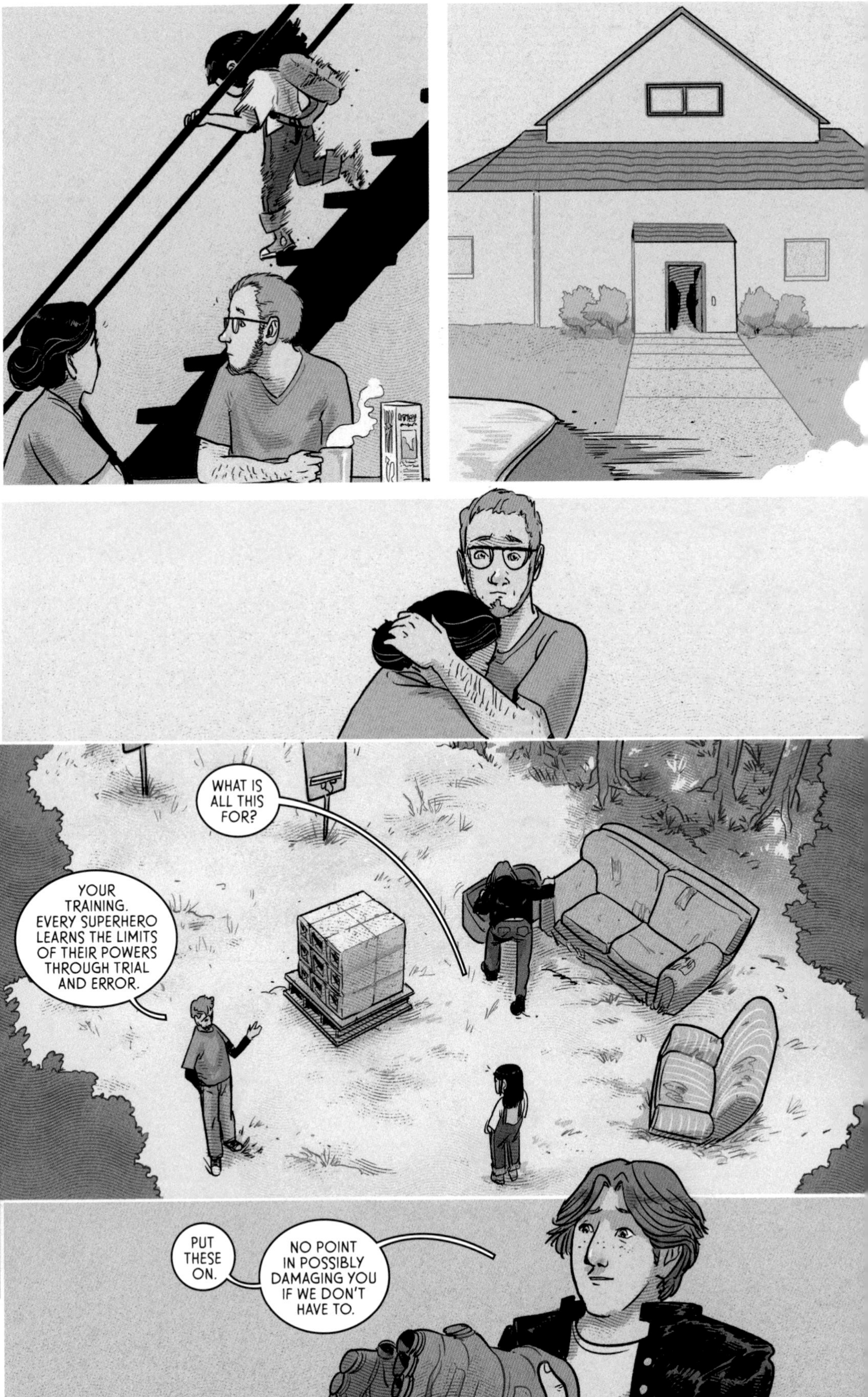
WHAT IS ALL THIS FOR?
YOUR TRAINING. EVERY SUPERHERO LEARNS THE LIMITS OF THEIR POWERS THROUGH TRIAL AND ERROR.
PUT THESE ON.
NO POINT IN POSSIBLY DAMAGING YOU IF WE DON'T HAVE TO.

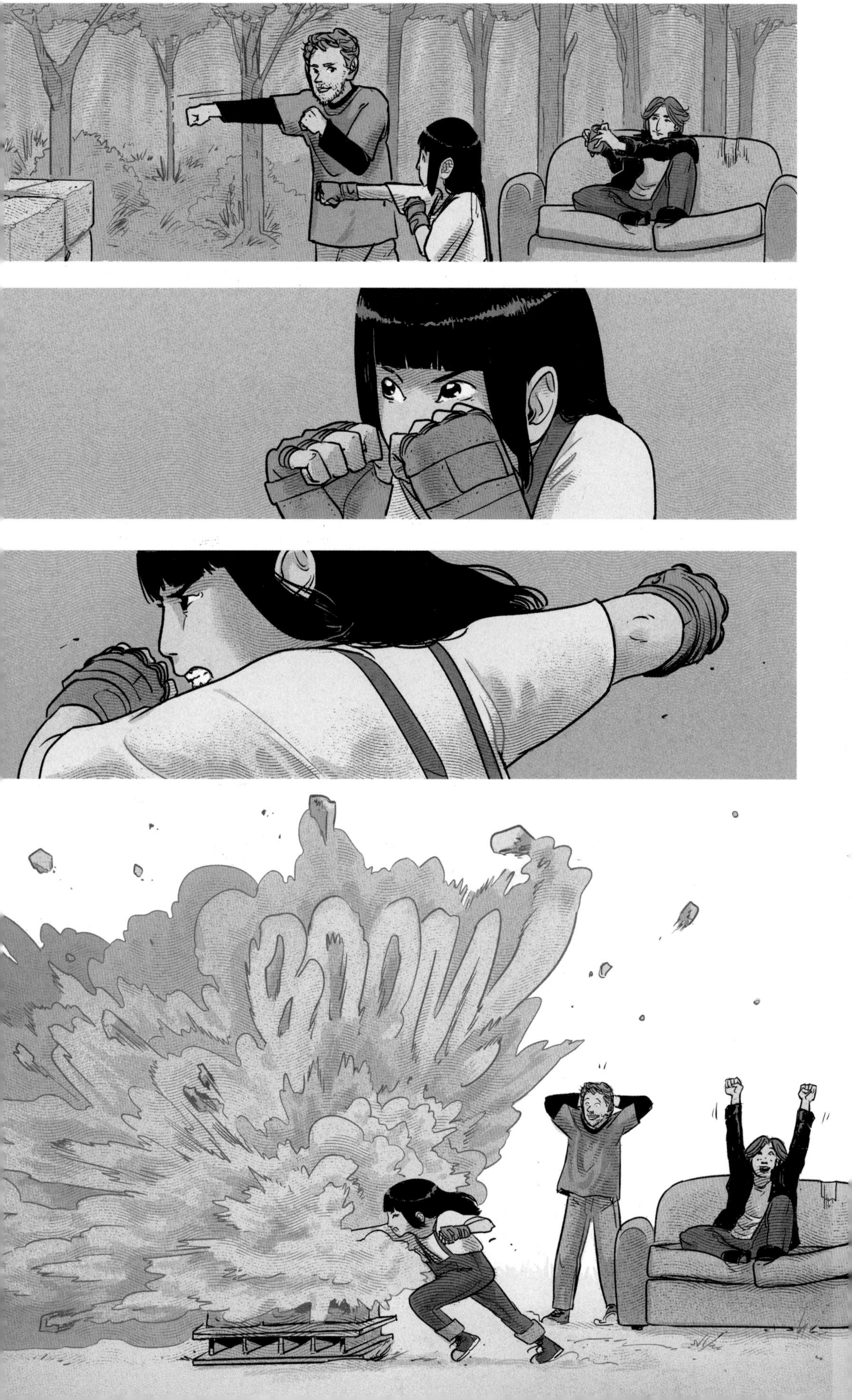
BOOM

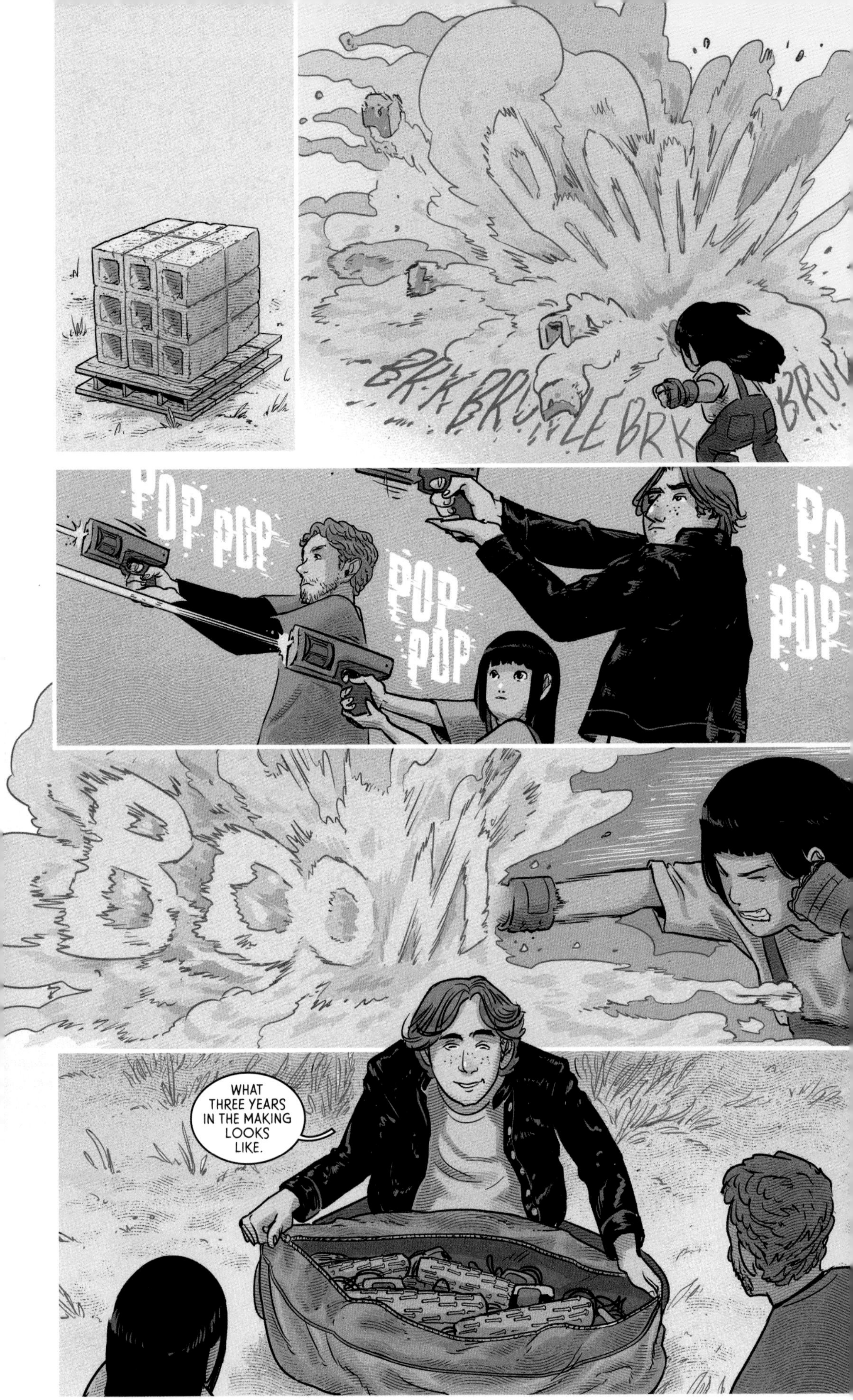
BRK BRUMBLE BRK BRU
POP POP
POP POP
PO POP
BOOM
WHAT THREE YEARS IN THE MAKING LOOKS LIKE.

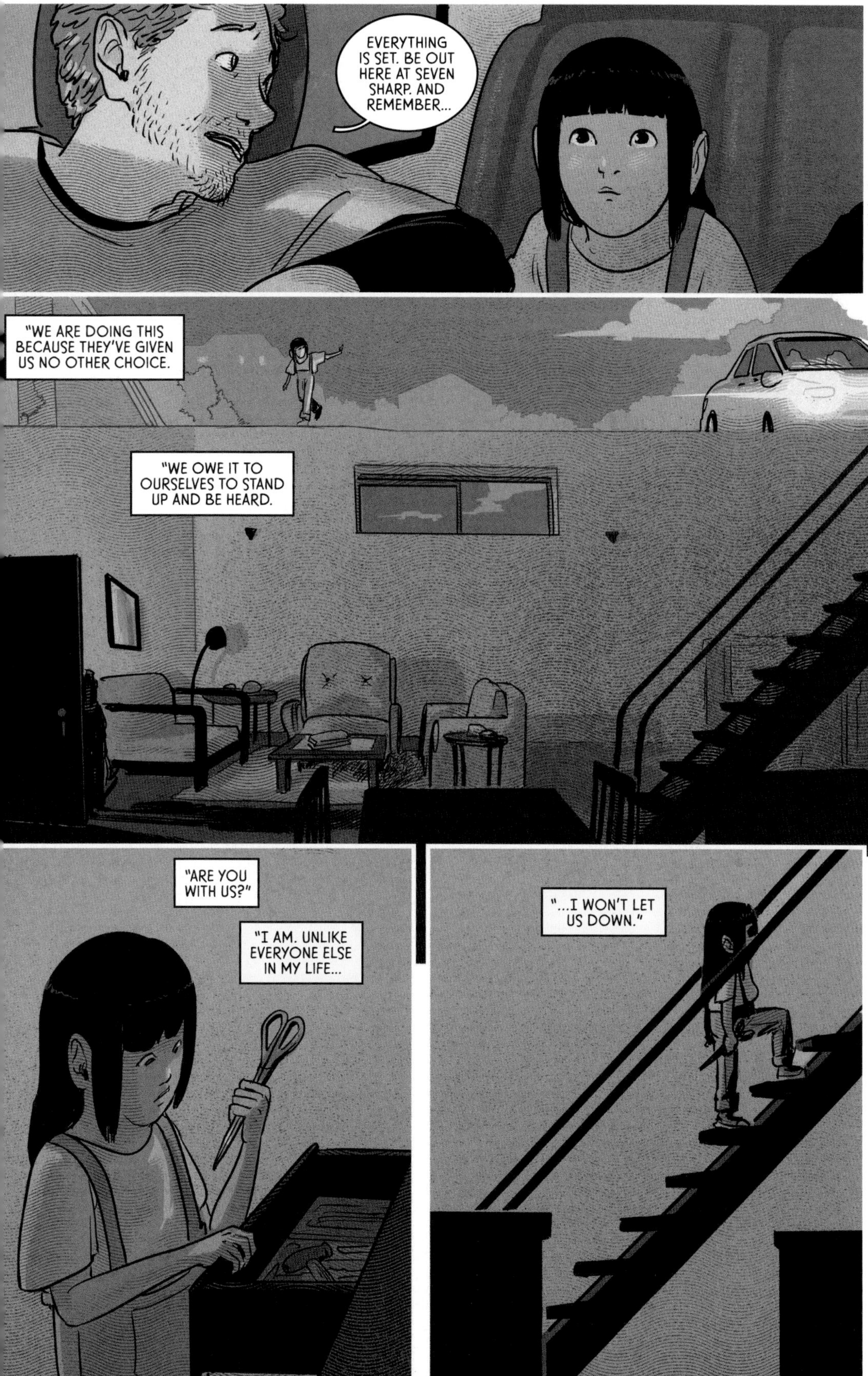
EVERYTHING IS SET. BE OUT HERE AT SEVEN SHARP. AND REMEMBER...
"WE ARE DOING THIS BECAUSE THEY'VE GIVEN US NO OTHER CHOICE.
"WE OWE IT TO OURSELVES TO STAND UP AND BE HEARD.
"ARE YOU WITH US?"
"I AM. UNLIKE EVERYONE ELSE IN MY LIFE...
"...I WON'T LET US DOWN."

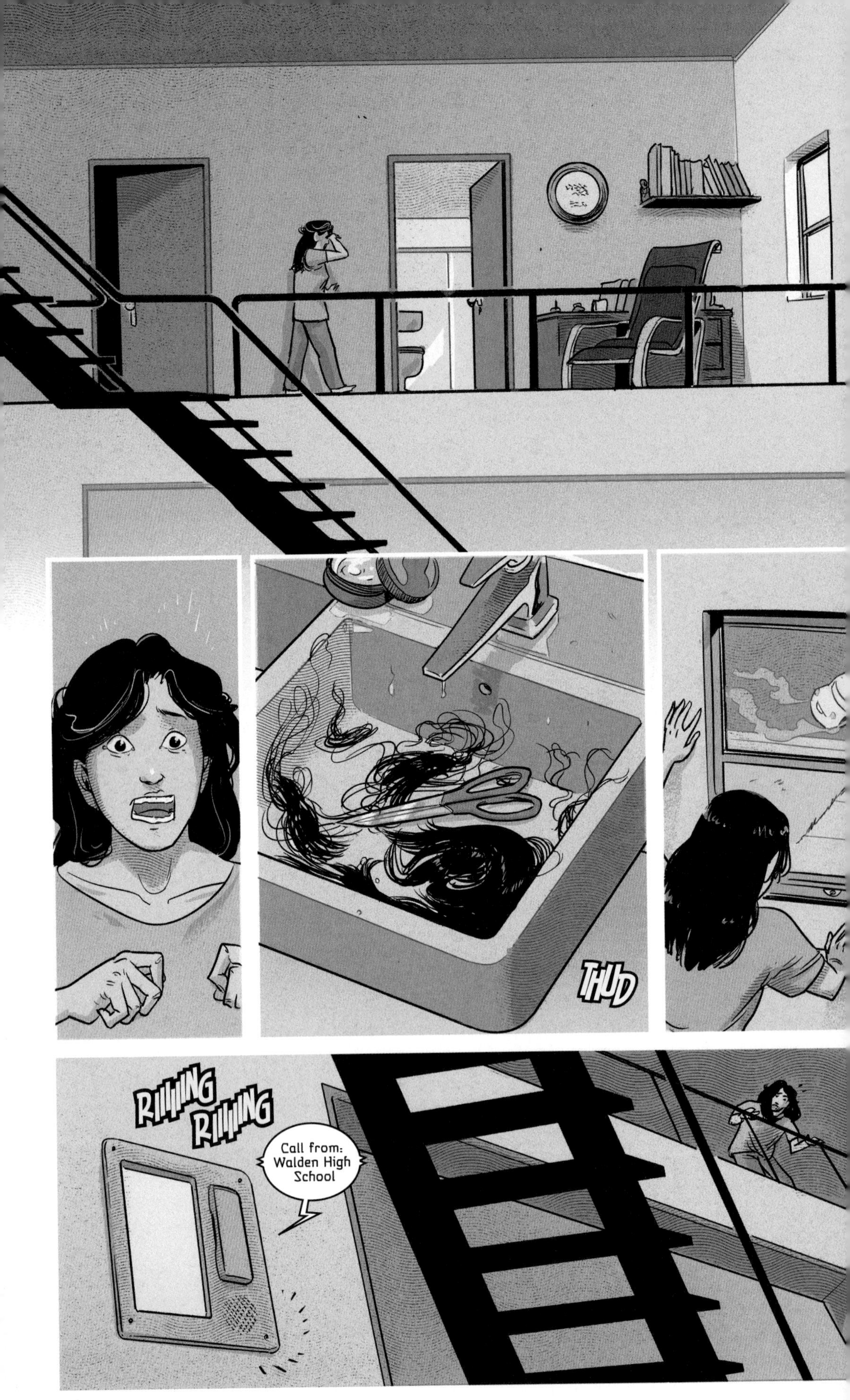
THUD
RIIIIING RIIIIING
Call from: Walden High School

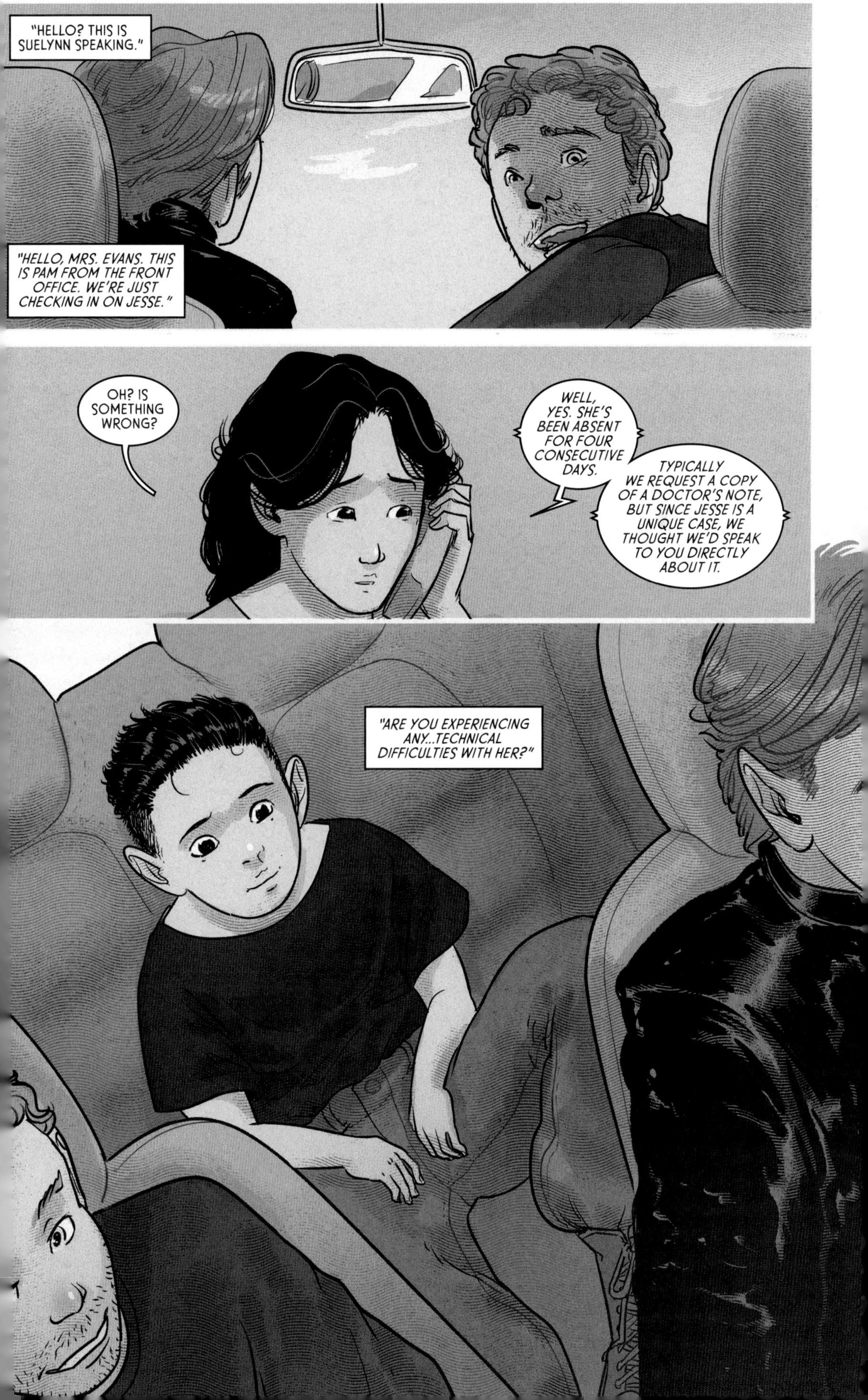
"HELLO? THIS IS SUELYNN SPEAKING."
"HELLO, MRS. EVANS. THIS IS PAM FROM THE FRONT OFFICE. WE'RE JUST CHECKING IN ON JESSE."
OH? IS SOMETHING WRONG?
WELL, YES. SHE'S BEEN ABSENT FOR FOUR CONSECUTIVE DAYS.
TYPICALLY WE REQUEST A COPY OF A DOCTOR'S NOTE, BUT SINCE JESSE IS A UNIQUE CASE, WE THOUGHT WE'D SPEAK TO YOU DIRECTLY ABOUT IT.
"ARE YOU EXPERIENCING ANY...TECHNICAL DIFFICULTIES WITH HER?"

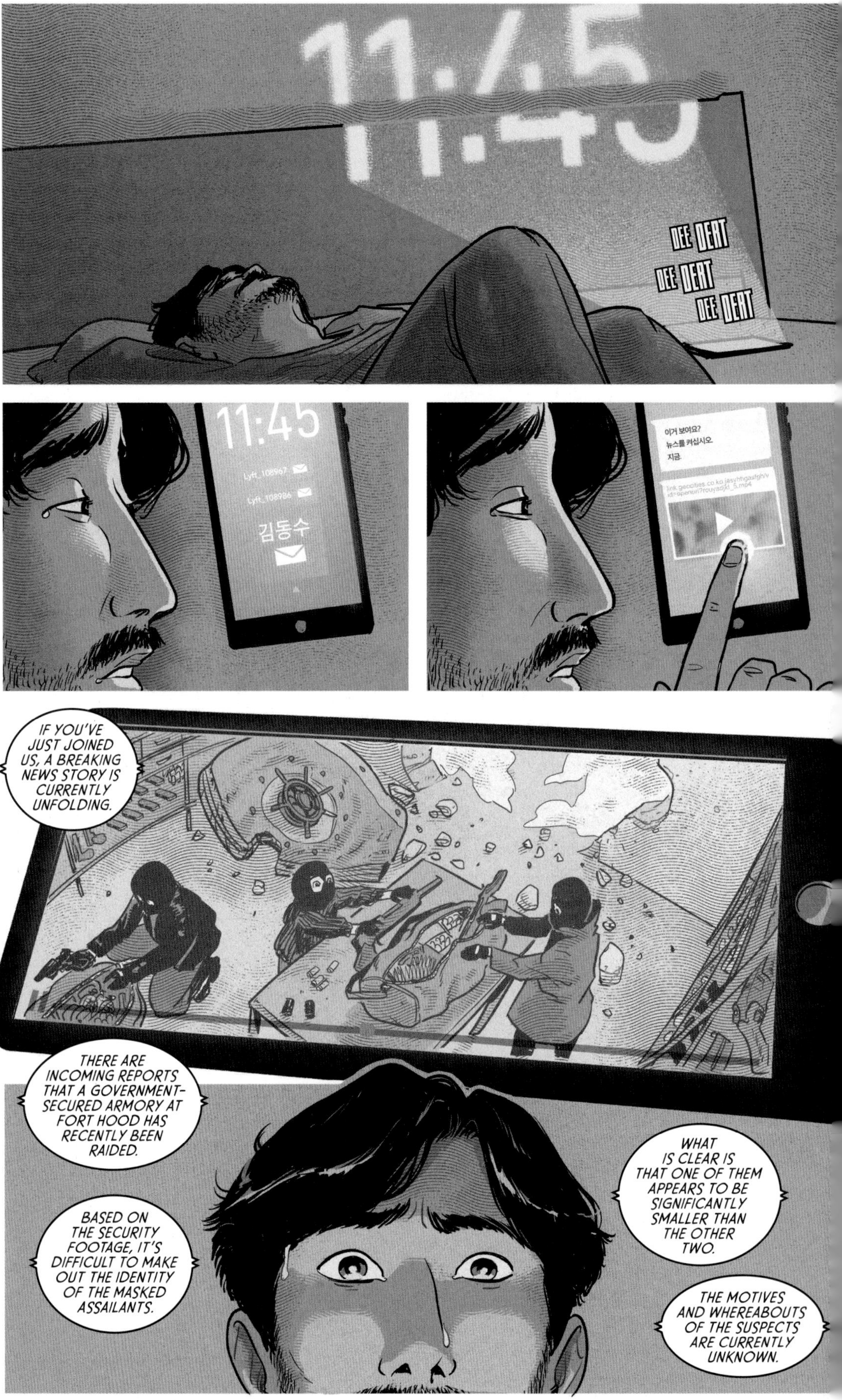
11:45
DEE DERT
DEE DERT
DEE DERT
11:45
Lyft_108967
Lyft_108986
김동수
이거 보여요?
뉴스를 켜십시오.
지금.
IF YOU'VE JUST JOINED US, A BREAKING NEWS STORY IS CURRENTLY UNFOLDING.
THERE ARE INCOMING REPORTS THAT A GOVERNMENT-SECURED ARMORY AT FORT HOOD HAS RECENTLY BEEN RAIDED.
BASED ON THE SECURITY FOOTAGE, IT'S DIFFICULT TO MAKE OUT THE IDENTITY OF THE MASKED ASSAILANTS.
WHAT IS CLEAR IS THAT ONE OF THEM APPEARS TO BE SIGNIFICANTLY SMALLER THAN THE OTHER TWO.
THE MOTIVES AND WHEREABOUTS OF THE SUSPECTS ARE CURRENTLY UNKNOWN.

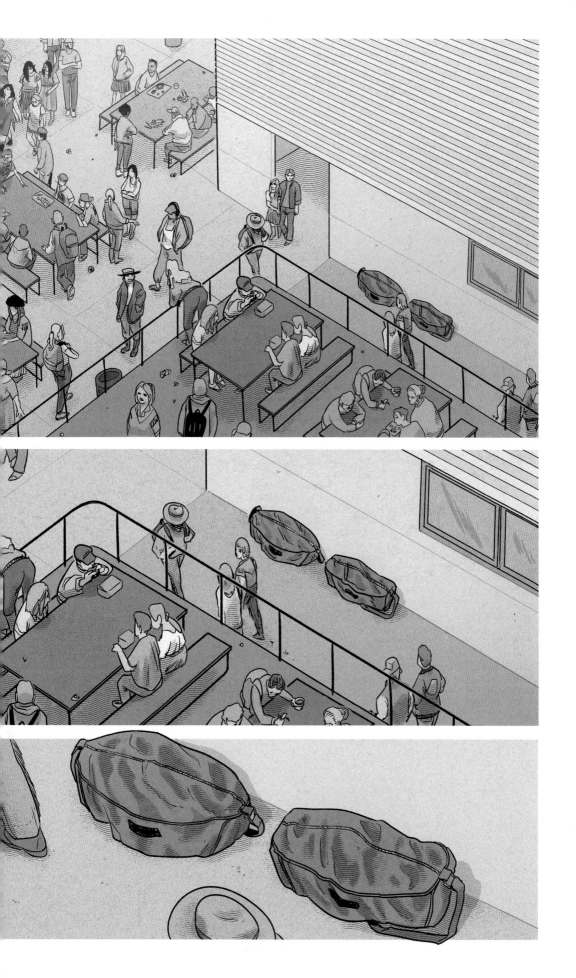

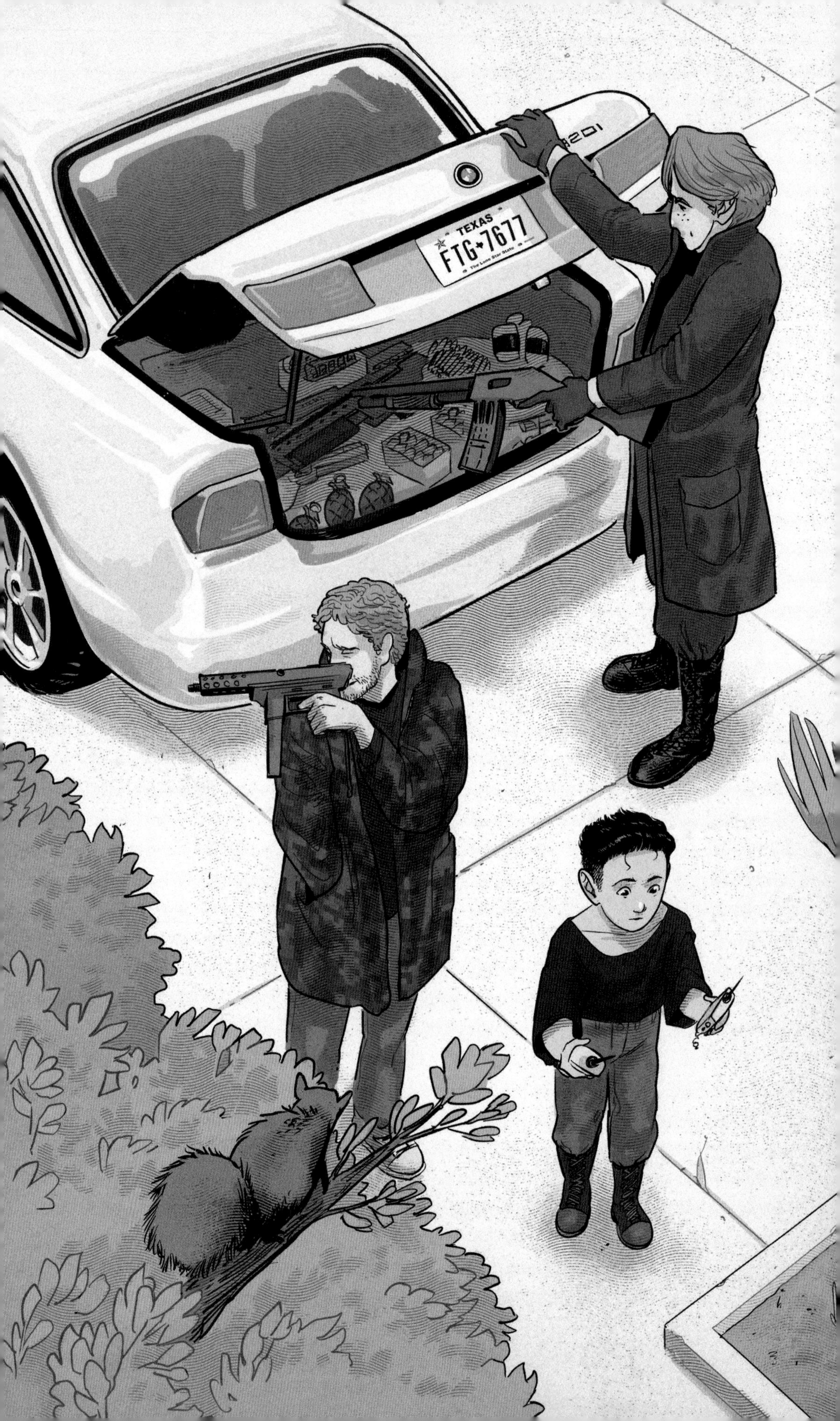
TEXAS
FTG 7677
The Lone Star State

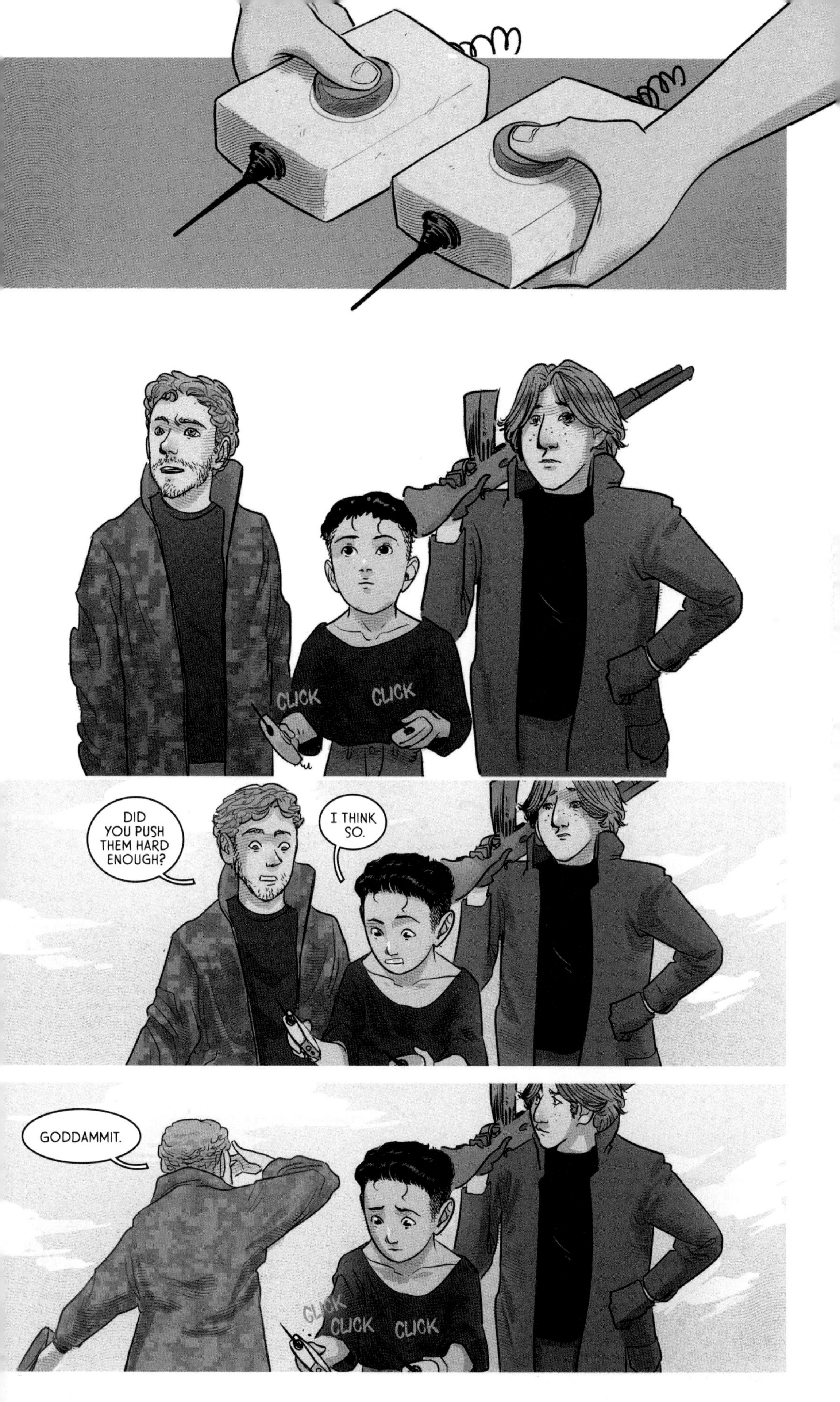
CLICK
CLICK
DID YOU PUSH THEM HARD ENOUGH?
I THINK SO.
GODDAMMIT.
CLICK
CLICK
CLICK

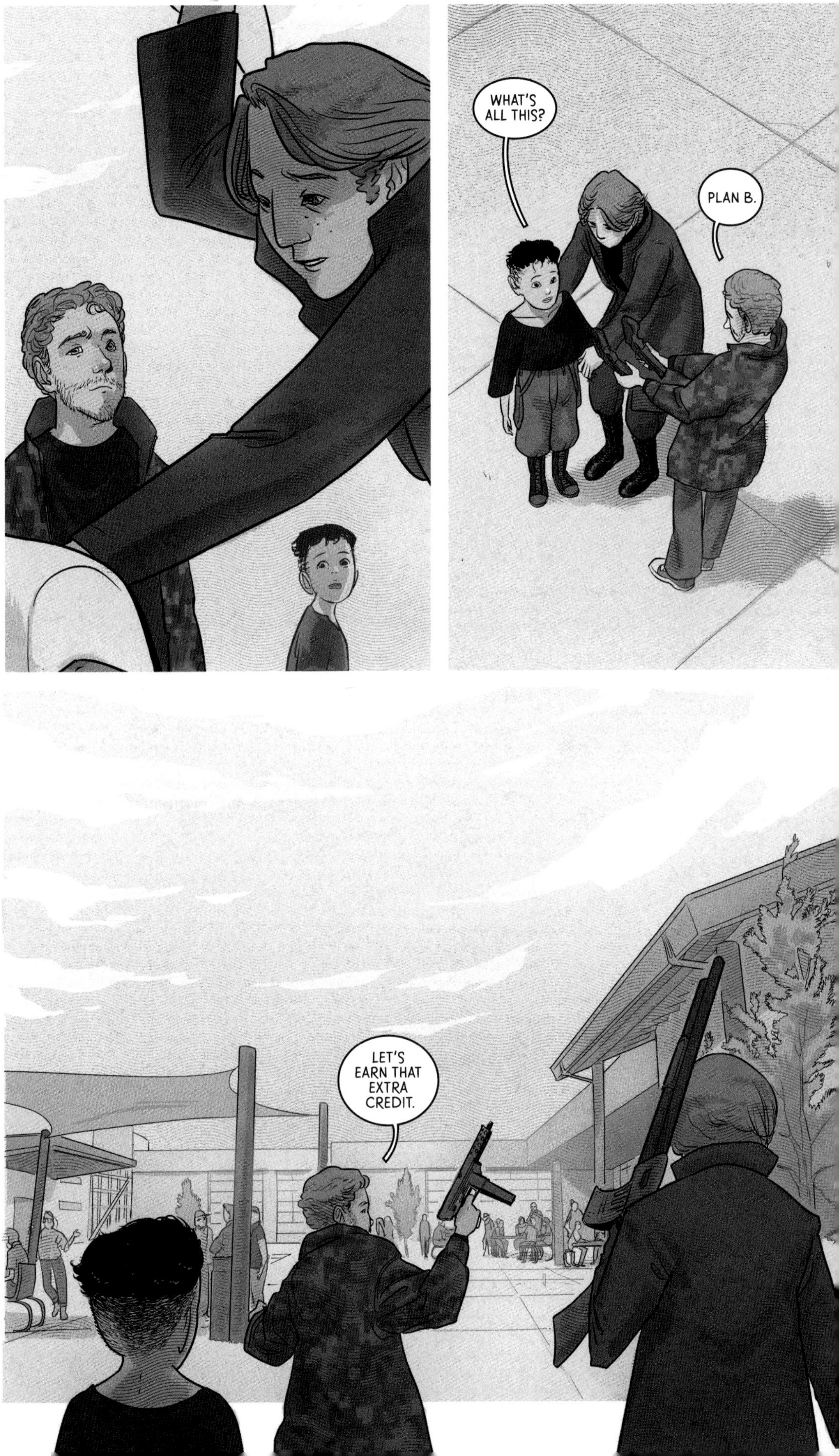
WHAT'S ALL THIS?
PLAN B.
LET'S EARN THAT EXTRA CREDIT.

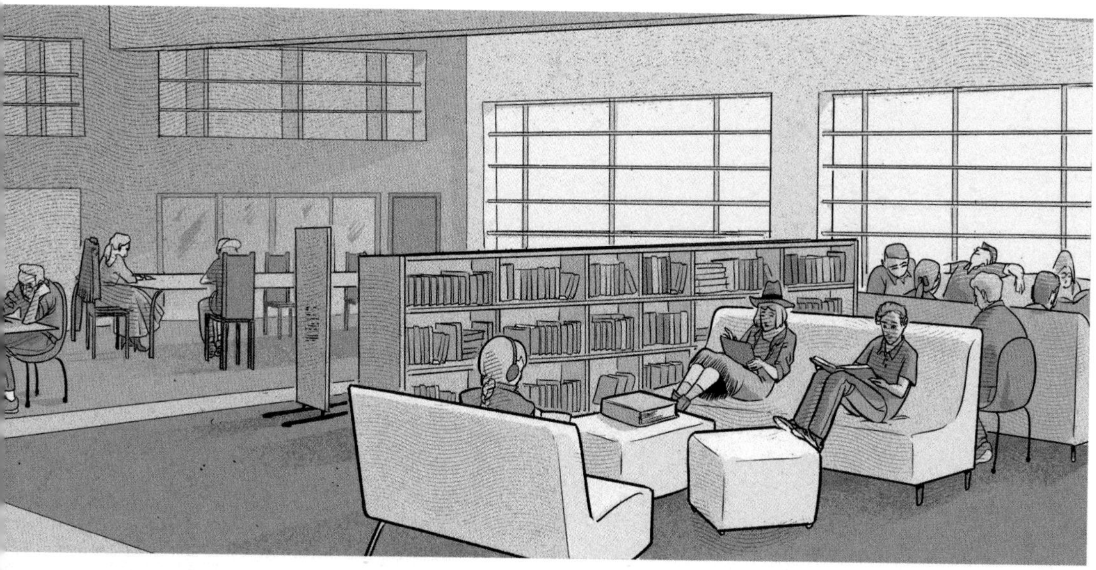

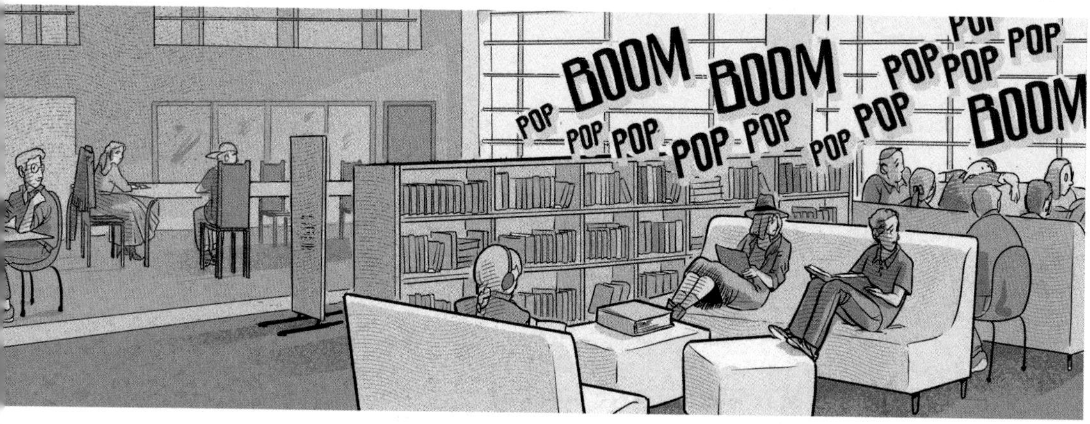
POP
BOOM
POP
POP
POP
BOOM
POP
POP
POP
POP
POP
POP
POP
POP
BOOM

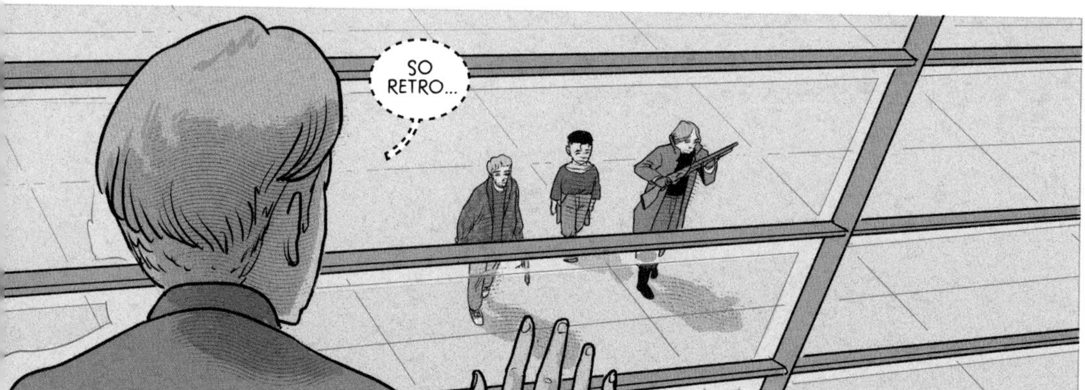
SO RETRO...

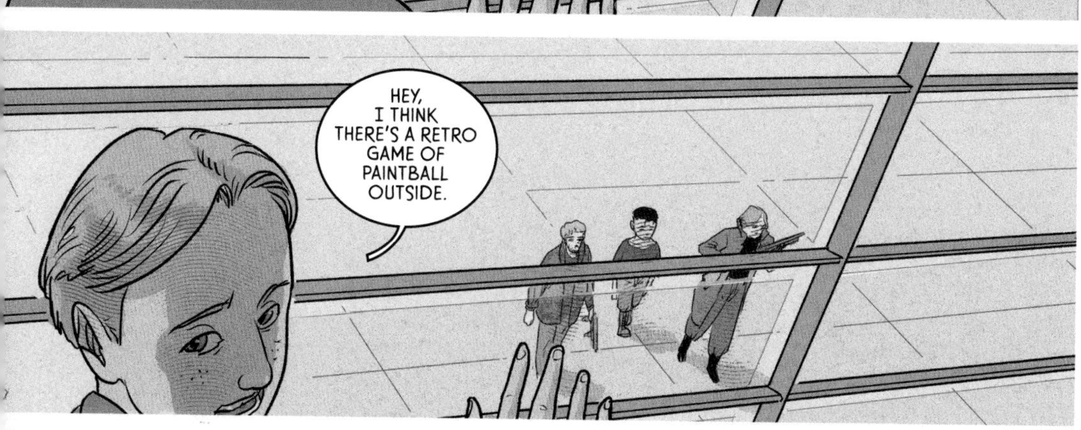
HEY, I THINK THERE'S A RETRO GAME OF PAINTBALL OUTSIDE.

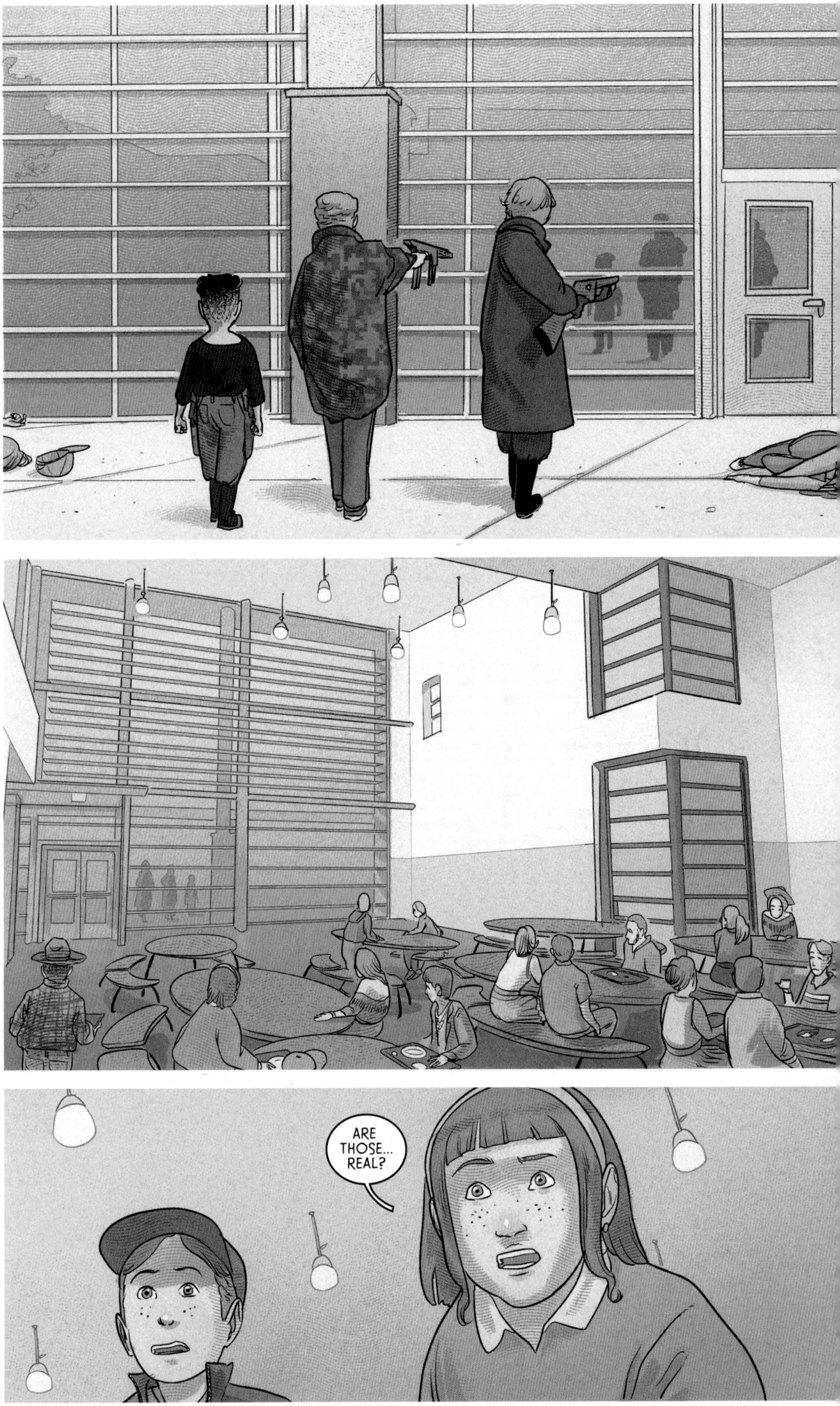
ARE THOSE... REAL?

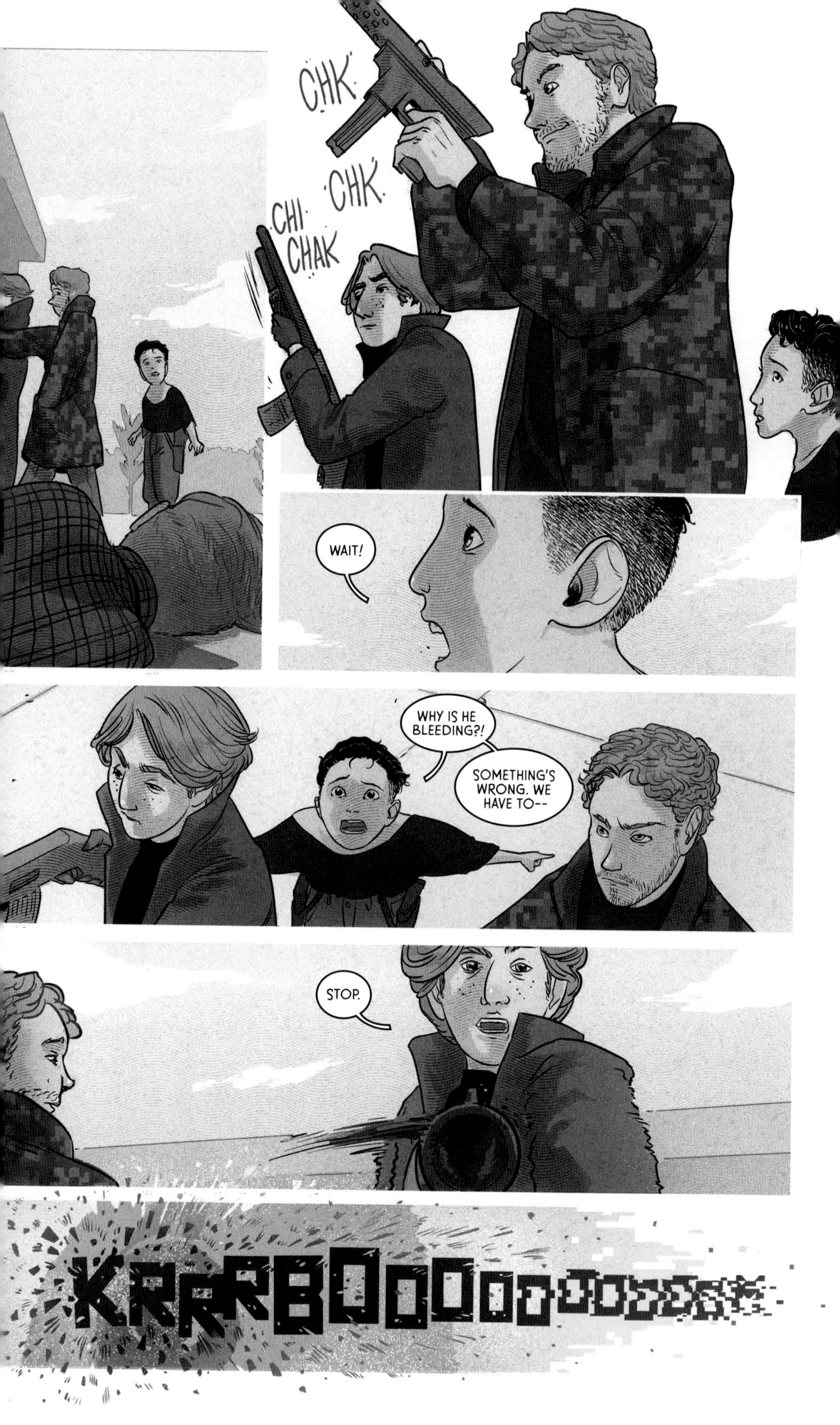
CHK
CHK
CHI CHAK
WAIT!
WHY IS HE BLEEDING?!
SOMETHING'S WRONG. WE HAVE TO--
STOP.
KRRRBOOOOOOOSSSH

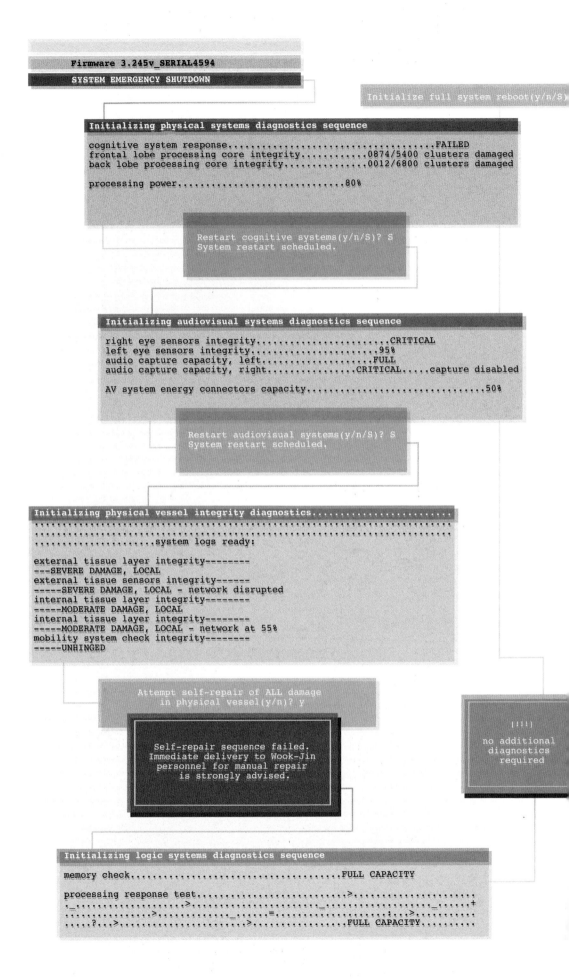

Firmware 3.245v_SERIAL4594

SYSTEM EMERGENCY SHUTDOWN

Initialize full system reboot(y/n/S)

Initializing physical systems diagnostics sequence

cognitive system response...FAILED
frontal lobe processing core integrity............0874/5400 clusters damaged
back lobe processing core integrity...............0012/6800 clusters damaged

processing power.............................80%

Restart cognitive systems(y/n/S)? S
System restart scheduled.

Initializing audiovisual systems diagnostics sequence

right eye sensors integrity.........................CRITICAL
left eye sensors integrity.........................95%
audio capture capacity, left.....................FULL
audio capture capacity, right...............CRITICAL.....capture disabled

AV system energy connectors capacity.................................50%

Restart audiovisual systems(y/n/S)? S
System restart scheduled.

Initializing physical vessel integrity diagnostics........................
....
.....................system logs ready:

external tissue layer integrity--------
---SEVERE DAMAGE, LOCAL
external tissue sensors integrity------
-----SEVERE DAMAGE, LOCAL - network disrupted
internal tissue layer integrity--------
-----MODERATE DAMAGE, LOCAL
internal tissue layer integrity--------
-----MODERATE DAMAGE, LOCAL - network at 55%
mobility system check integrity--------
-----UNHINGED

Attempt self-repair of ALL damage
in physical vessel(y/n)? y

Self-repair sequence failed.
Immediate delivery to Wook-Jin
personnel for manual repair
is strongly advised.

[!!!]
no additional
diagnostics
required

Initializing logic systems diagnostics sequence

memory check.................................FULL CAPACITY

processing response test......................................>.........................
._....................................>...................................._..........................+
....................................>..............._......=.............................>...........
.....?...>....................................>................FULL CAPACITY..........

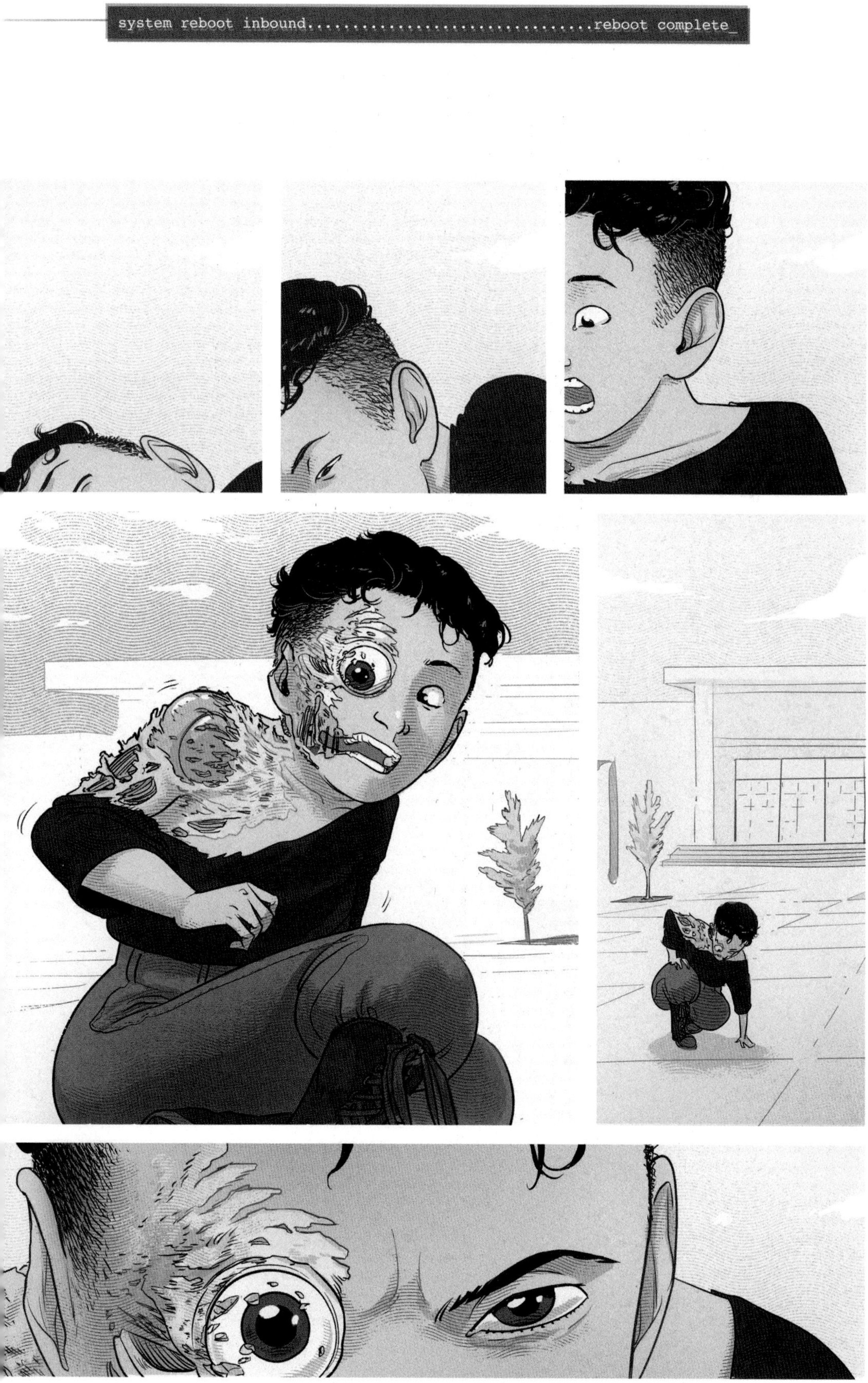
system reboot inbound.................................reboot complete_

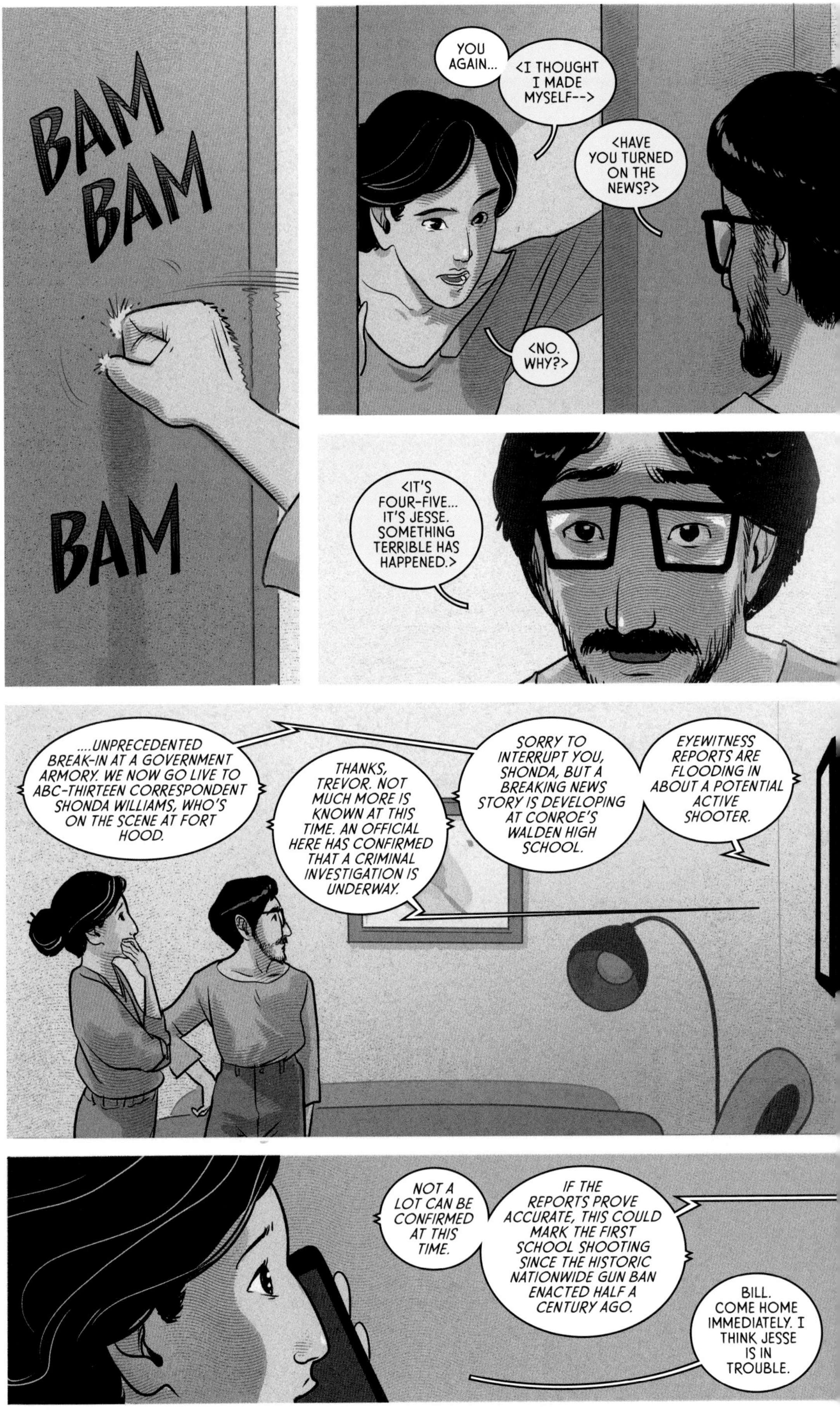
BAM BAM
BAM
YOU AGAIN...
<I THOUGHT I MADE MYSELF-->
<HAVE YOU TURNED ON THE NEWS?>
<NO. WHY?>
<IT'S FOUR-FIVE... IT'S JESSE. SOMETHING TERRIBLE HAS HAPPENED.>
....UNPRECEDENTED BREAK-IN AT A GOVERNMENT ARMORY. WE NOW GO LIVE TO ABC-THIRTEEN CORRESPONDENT SHONDA WILLIAMS, WHO'S ON THE SCENE AT FORT HOOD.
THANKS, TREVOR. NOT MUCH MORE IS KNOWN AT THIS TIME. AN OFFICIAL HERE HAS CONFIRMED THAT A CRIMINAL INVESTIGATION IS UNDERWAY.
SORRY TO INTERRUPT YOU, SHONDA, BUT A BREAKING NEWS STORY IS DEVELOPING AT CONROE'S WALDEN HIGH SCHOOL.
EYEWITNESS REPORTS ARE FLOODING IN ABOUT A POTENTIAL ACTIVE SHOOTER.
NOT A LOT CAN BE CONFIRMED AT THIS TIME.
IF THE REPORTS PROVE ACCURATE, THIS COULD MARK THE FIRST SCHOOL SHOOTING SINCE THE HISTORIC NATIONWIDE GUN BAN ENACTED HALF A CENTURY AGO.
BILL. COME HOME IMMEDIATELY. I THINK JESSE IS IN TROUBLE.

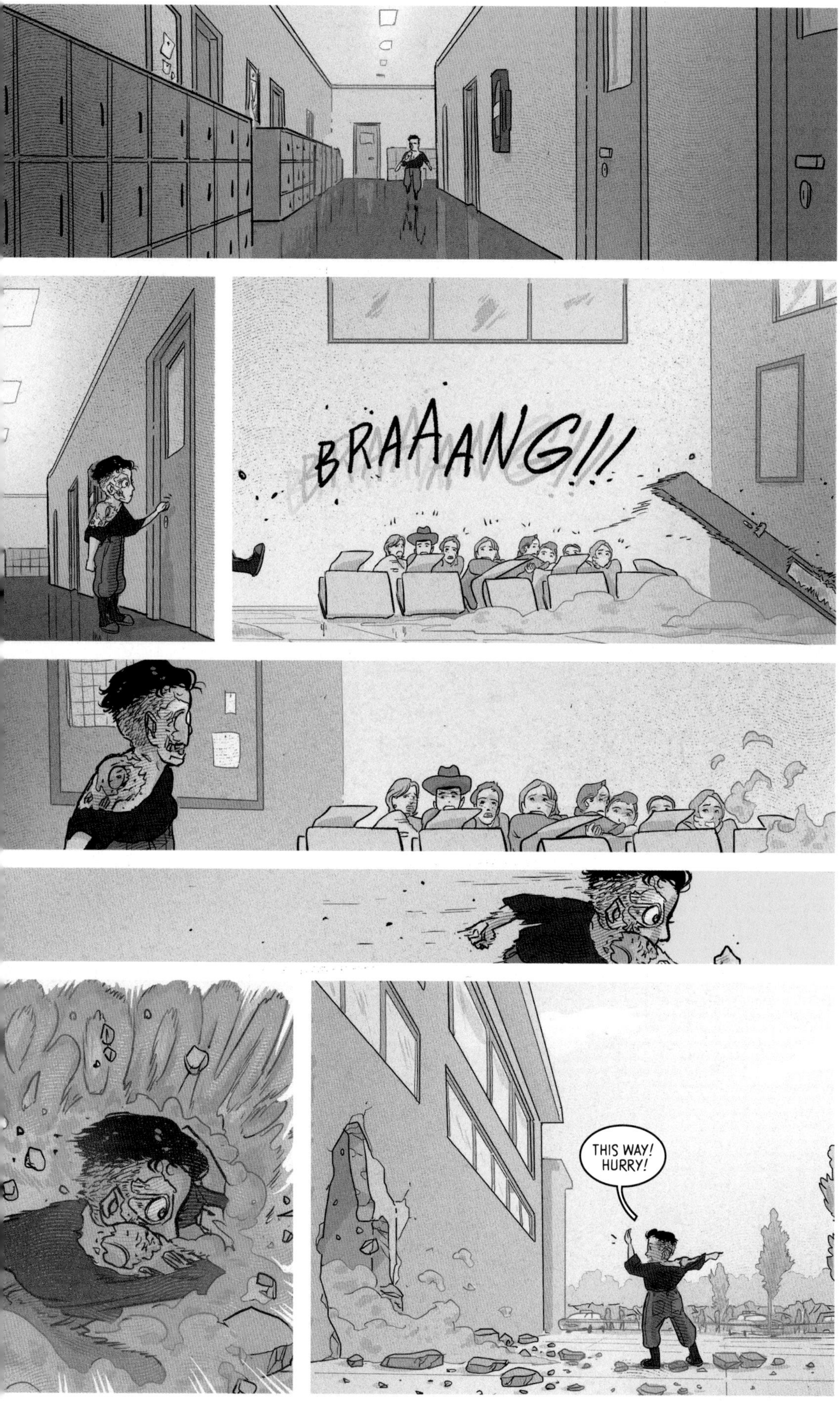
BRAAANG!!
THIS WAY!
HURRY!

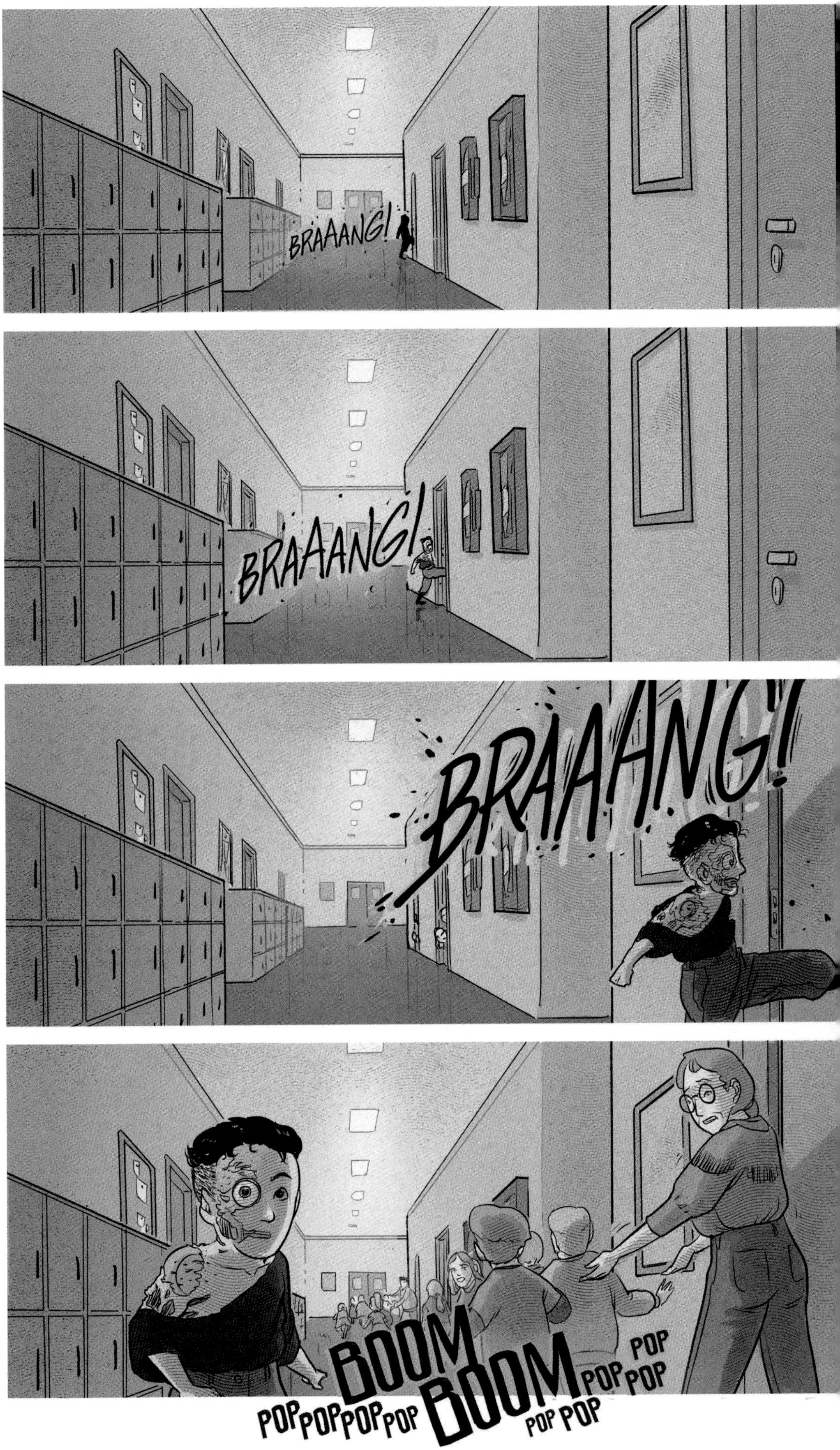
BRAAANG!
BRAAANG!
BRAAANG!
BOOM
BOOM
POP POP POP POP
POP POP
POP POP
POP POP

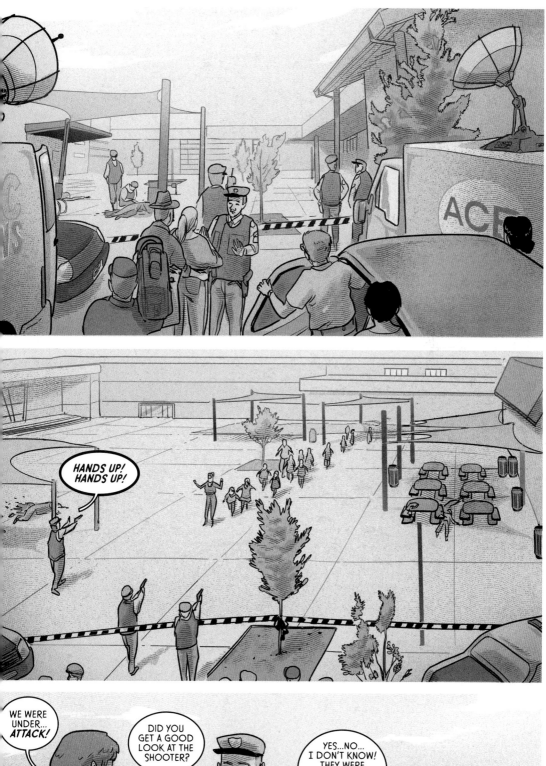

HANDS UP! HANDS UP!

WE WERE UNDER... *ATTACK!*

DID YOU GET A GOOD LOOK AT THE SHOOTER?

YES...NO... I DON'T KNOW! THEY WERE COMING IN FROM ALL ENTRANCES.

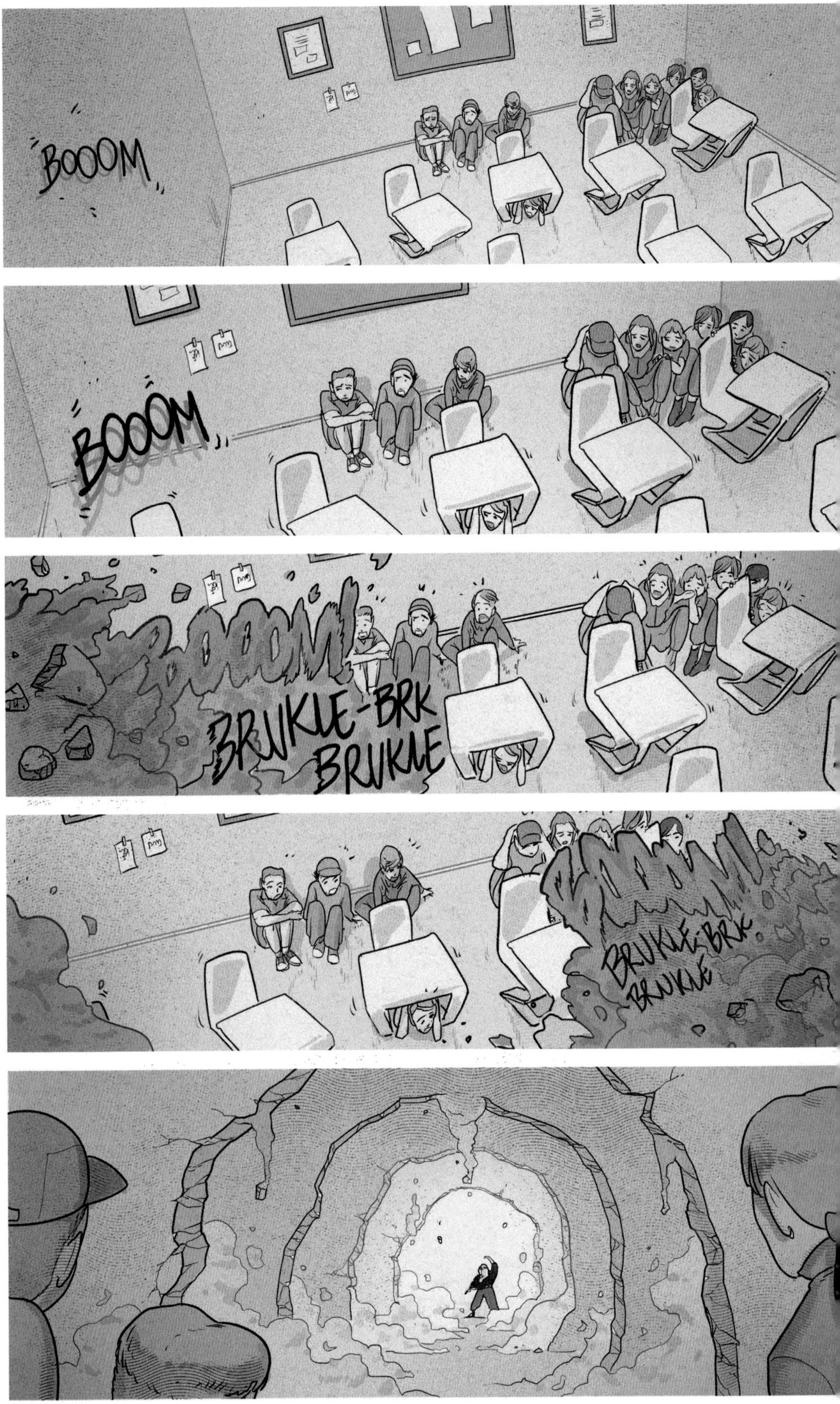
BOOOM
BOOOM
BOOOM!
BRUKLE-BRK
BRUKLE
BOOOM!
BRUKLE-BRK
BRUKLE

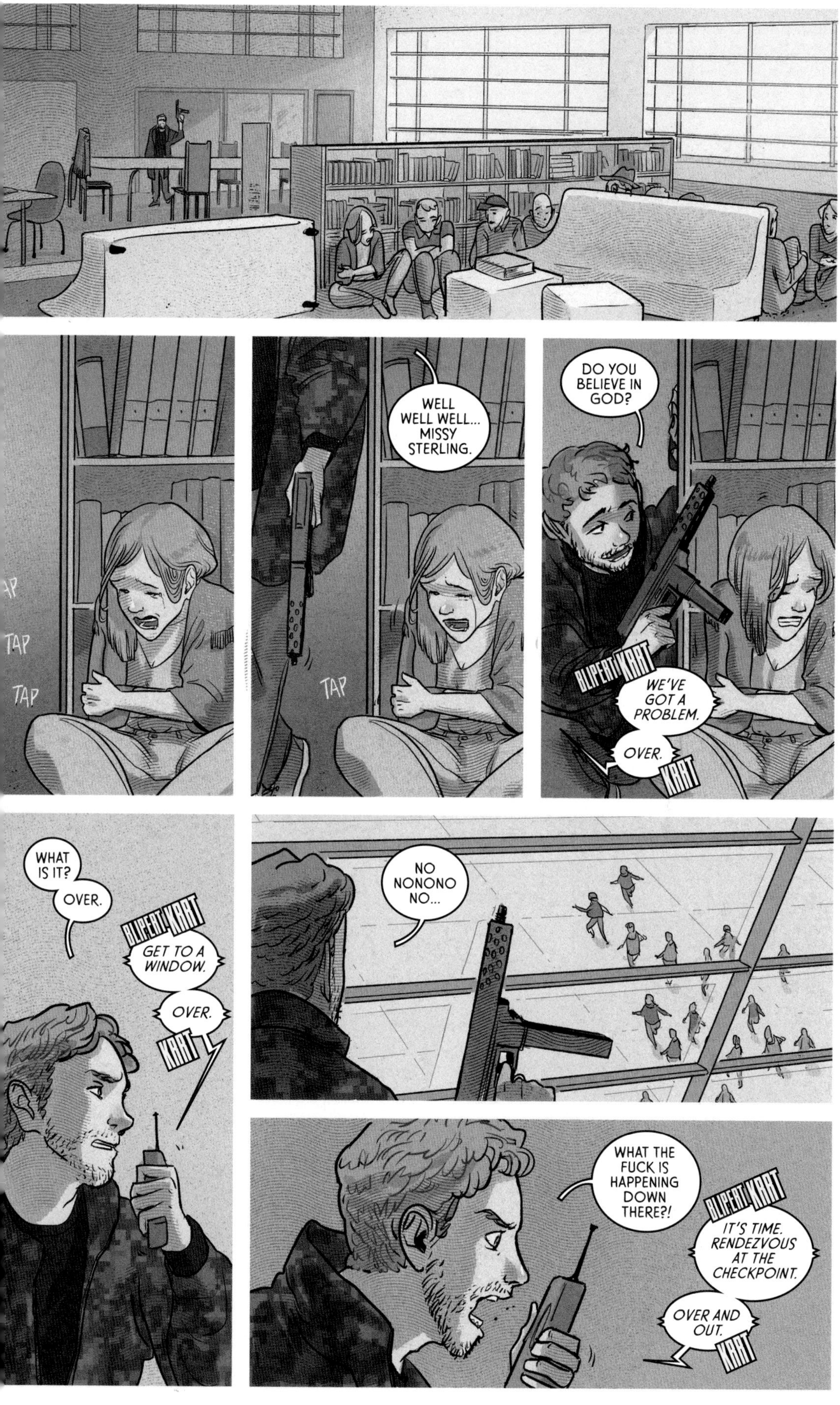
TAP
TAP
TAP
WELL WELL WELL... MISSY STERLING.
TAP
DO YOU BELIEVE IN GOD?
BLIPERT KRRT
WE'VE GOT A PROBLEM.
OVER.
KRRT
WHAT IS IT?
OVER.
BLIPERT KRRT
GET TO A WINDOW.
OVER.
KRRT
NO NONONO NO...
WHAT THE FUCK IS HAPPENING DOWN THERE?!
BLIPERT KRRT
IT'S TIME. RENDEZVOUS AT THE CHECKPOINT.
OVER AND OUT.
KRRT

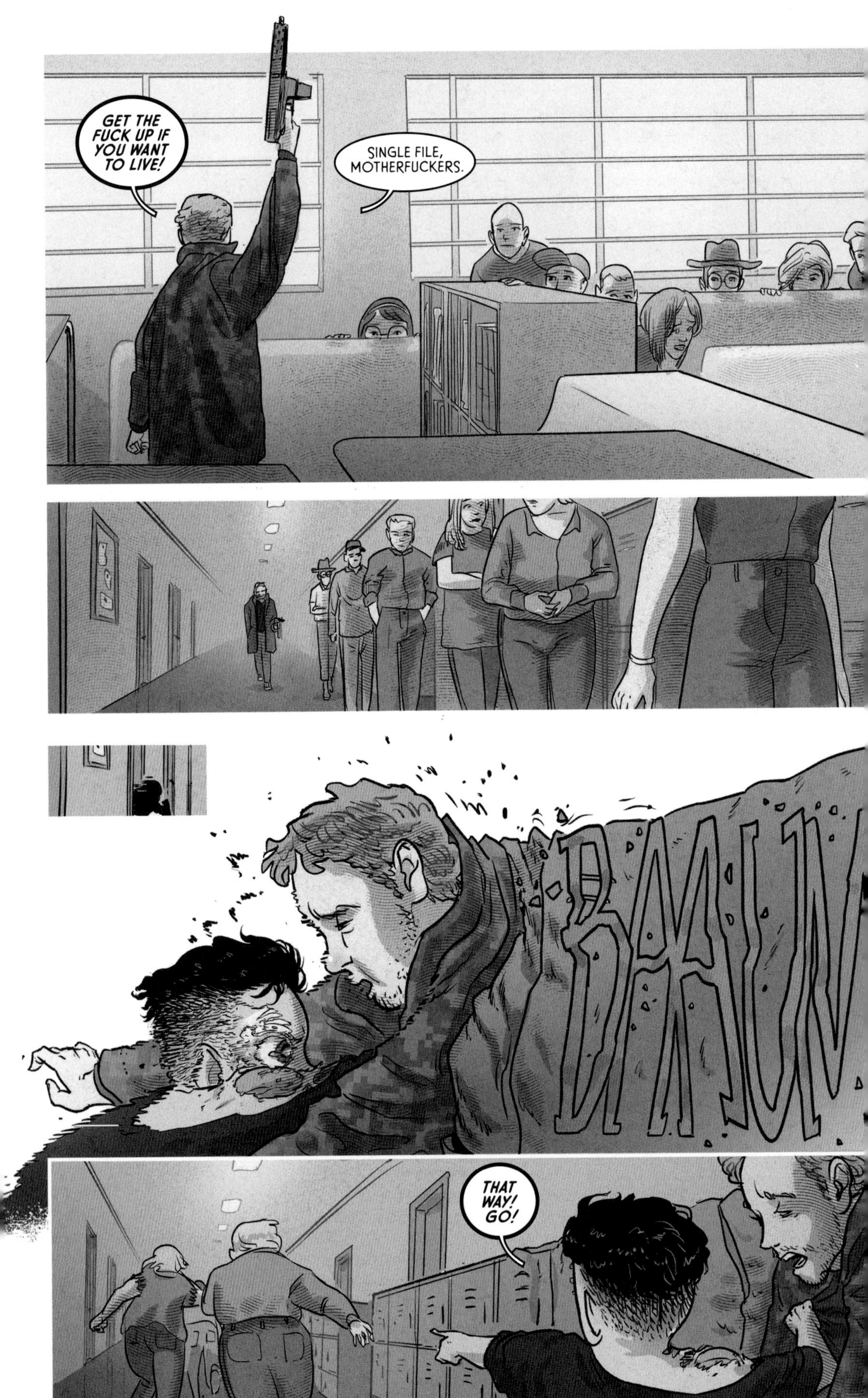
GET THE FUCK UP IF YOU WANT TO LIVE!
SINGLE FILE, MOTHERFUCKERS.
BAMM
THAT WAY! GO!

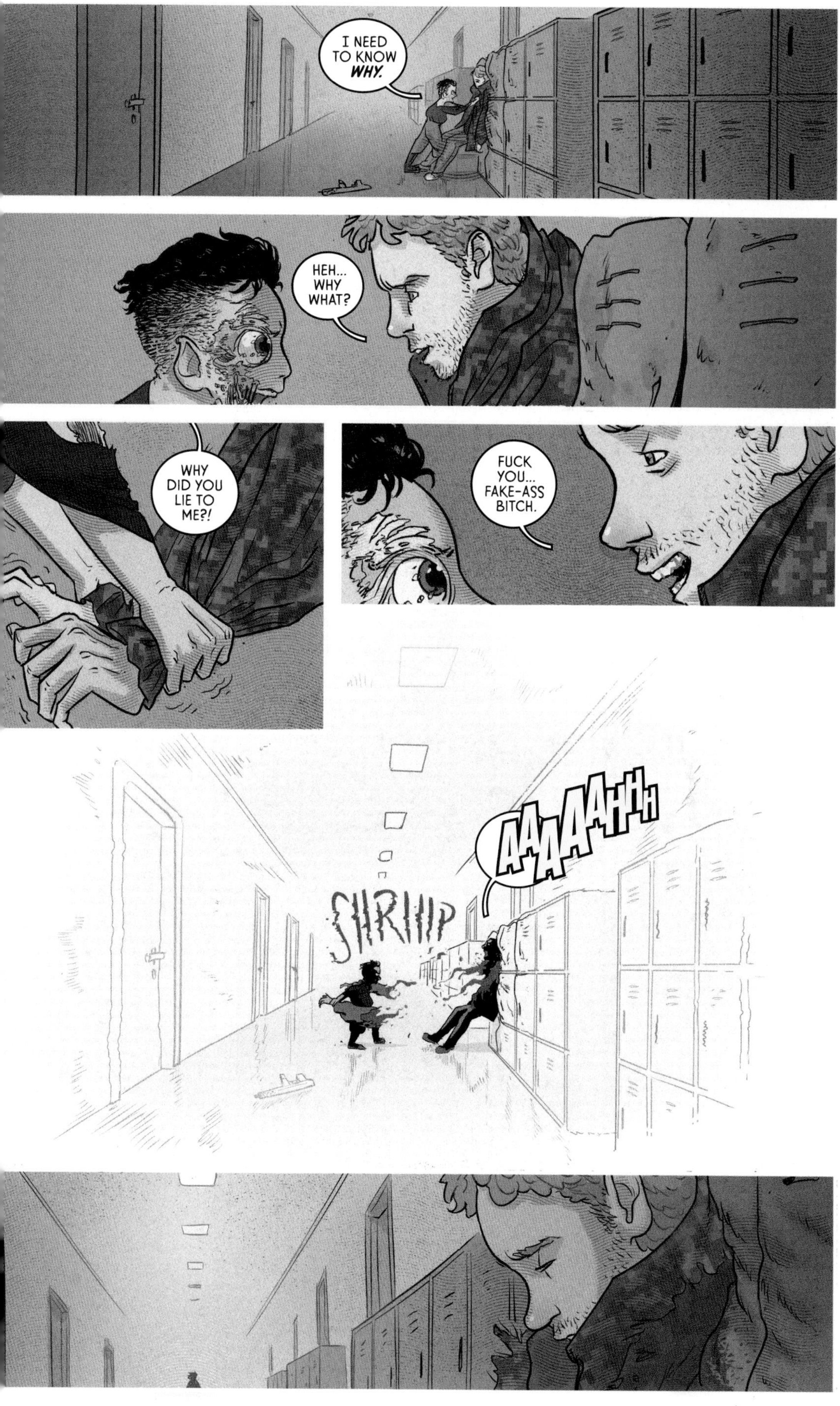
I NEED TO KNOW WHY.
HEH... WHY WHAT?
WHY DID YOU LIE TO ME?!
FUCK YOU... FAKE-ASS BITCH.
SHRIIIP
AAAAAHHH

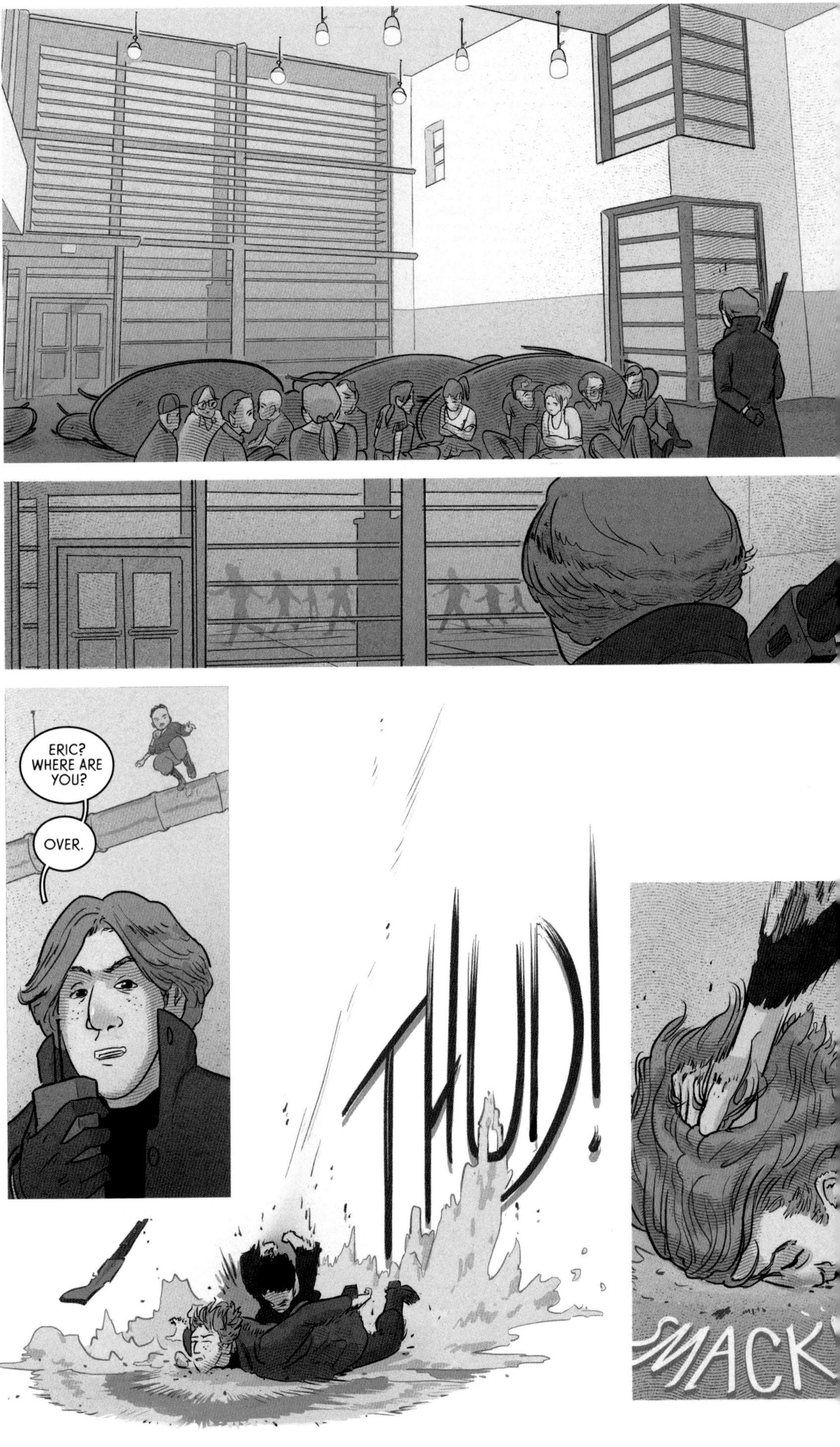
ERIC? WHERE ARE YOU?
OVER.
THUD!
SMACK

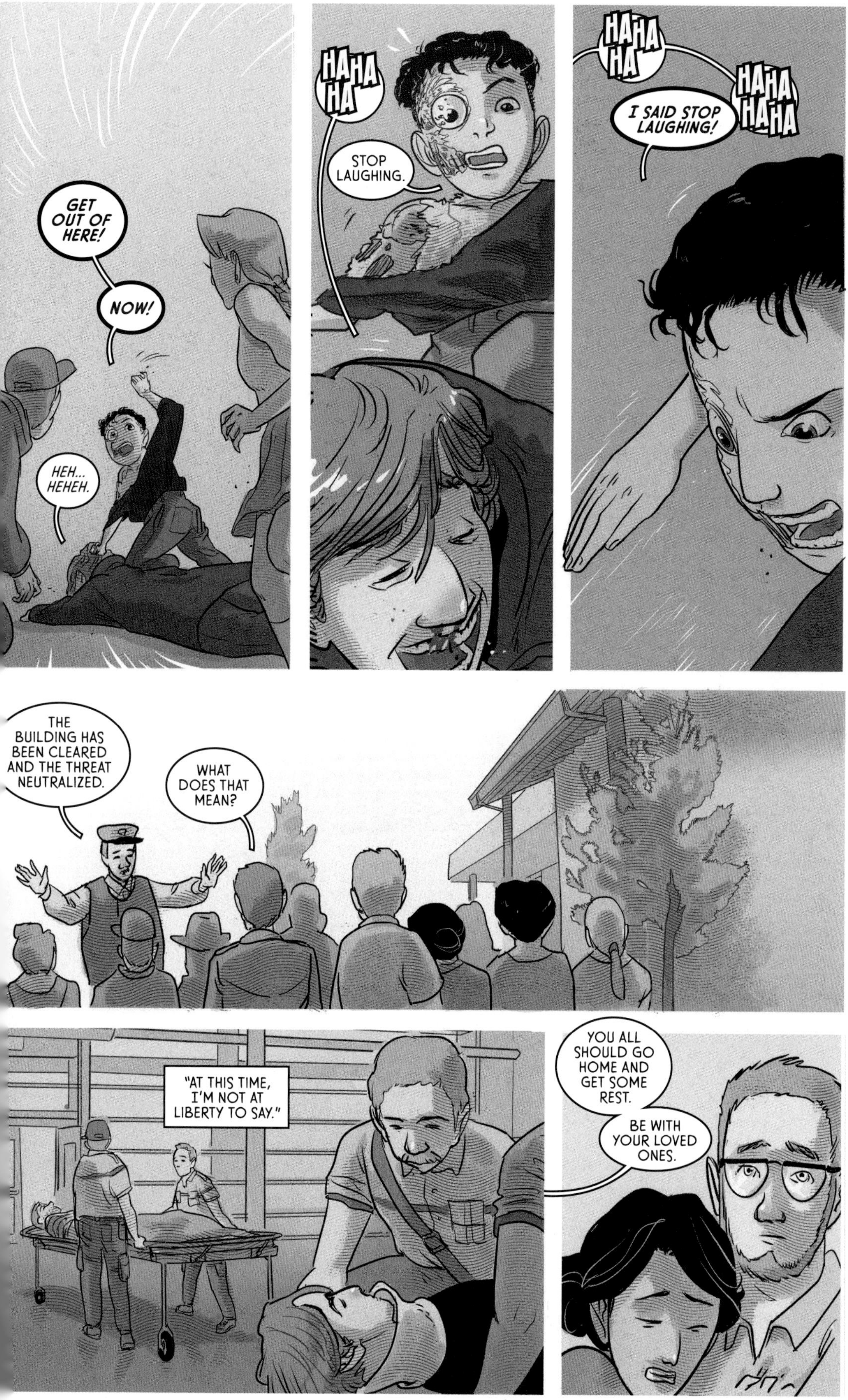
GET OUT OF HERE!
NOW!
HEH... HEHEH.
HAHAHA
STOP LAUGHING.
HAHAHA
HAHAHAHAHA
I SAID STOP LAUGHING!
THE BUILDING HAS BEEN CLEARED AND THE THREAT NEUTRALIZED.
WHAT DOES THAT MEAN?
"AT THIS TIME, I'M NOT AT LIBERTY TO SAY."
YOU ALL SHOULD GO HOME AND GET SOME REST.
BE WITH YOUR LOVED ONES.

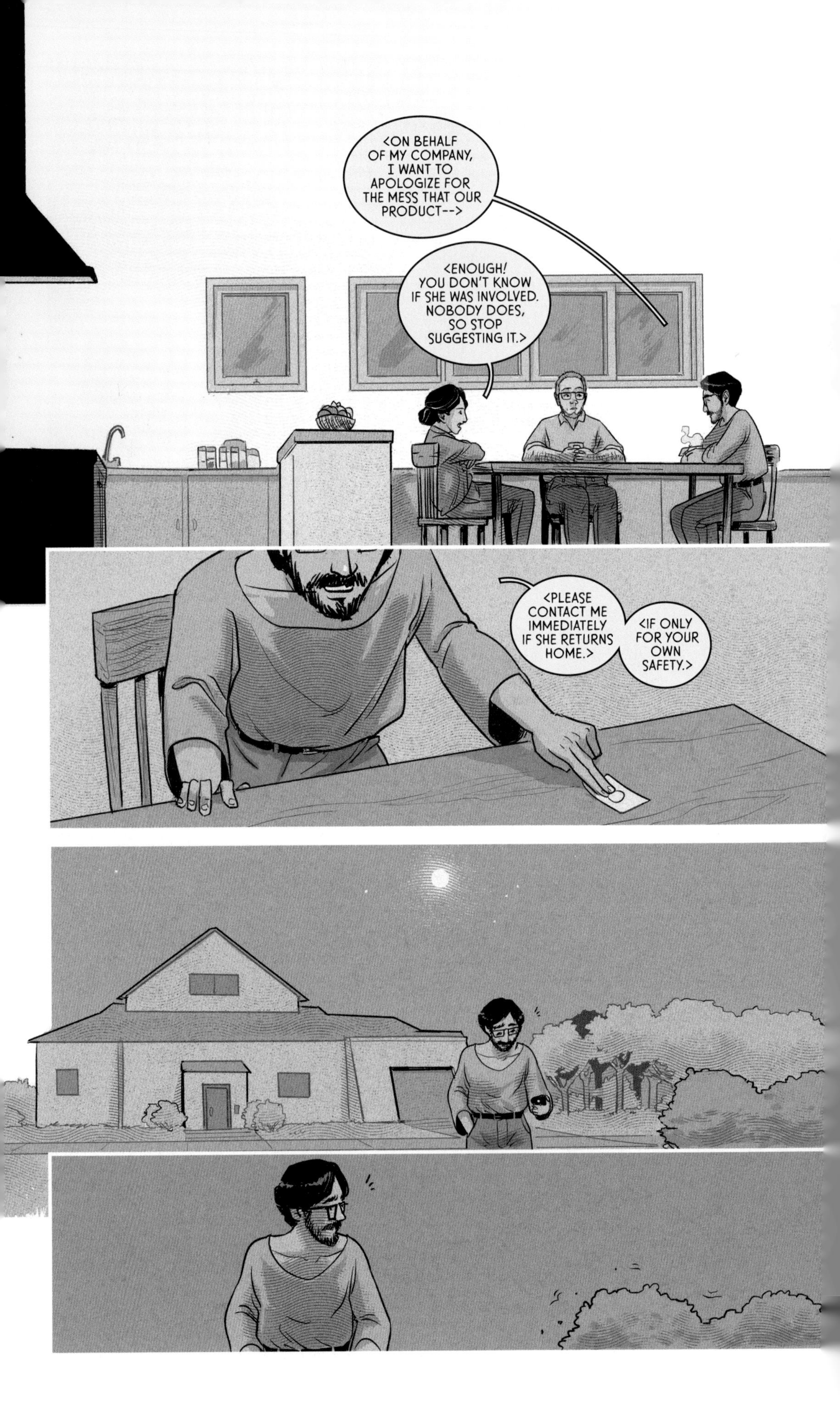

<ON BEHALF OF MY COMPANY, I WANT TO APOLOGIZE FOR THE MESS THAT OUR PRODUCT-->
<ENOUGH! YOU DON'T KNOW IF SHE WAS INVOLVED. NOBODY DOES, SO STOP SUGGESTING IT.>
<PLEASE CONTACT ME IMMEDIATELY IF SHE RETURNS HOME.>
<IF ONLY FOR YOUR OWN SAFETY.>

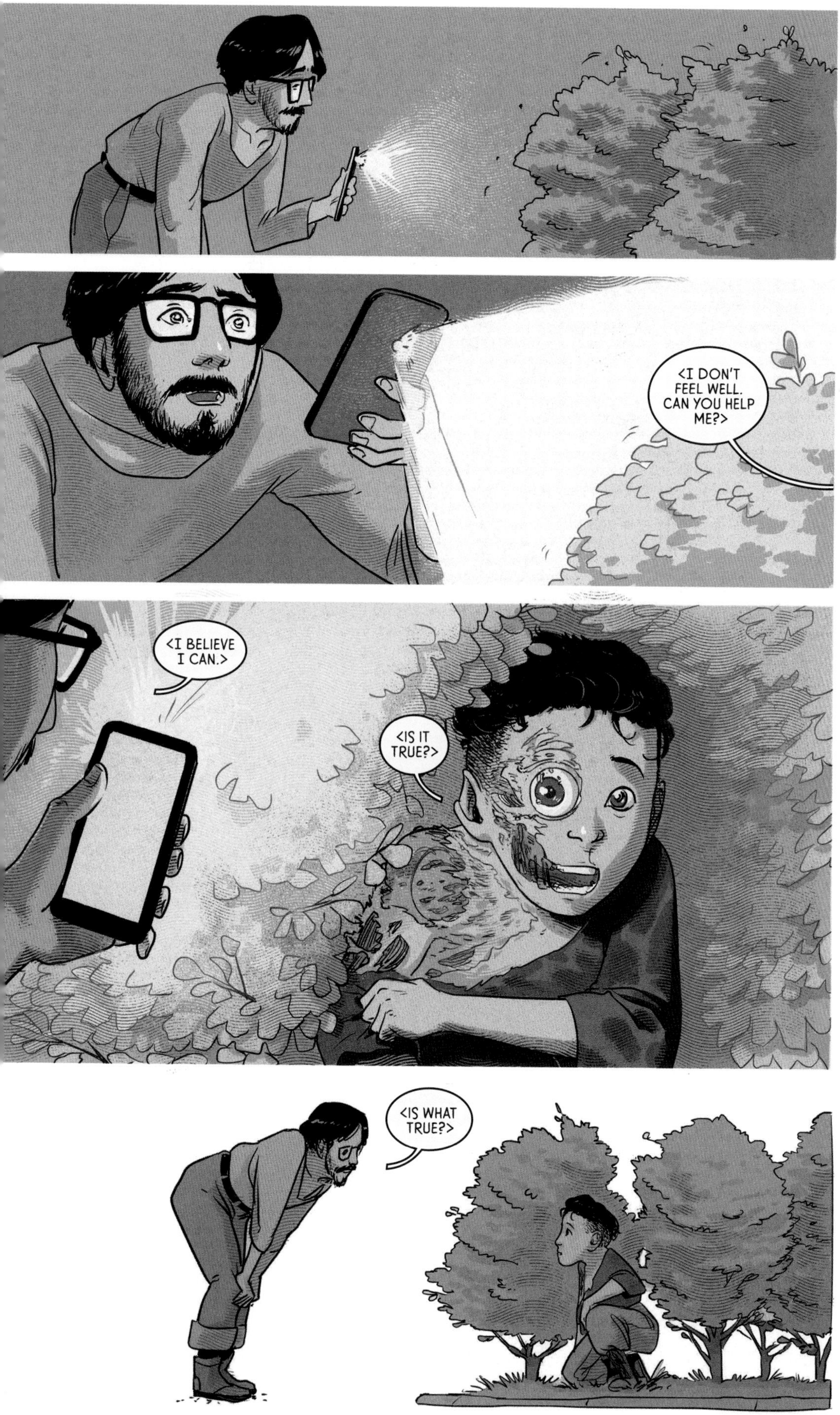
<I DON'T FEEL WELL. CAN YOU HELP ME?>
<I BELIEVE I CAN.>
<IS IT TRUE?>
<IS WHAT TRUE?>

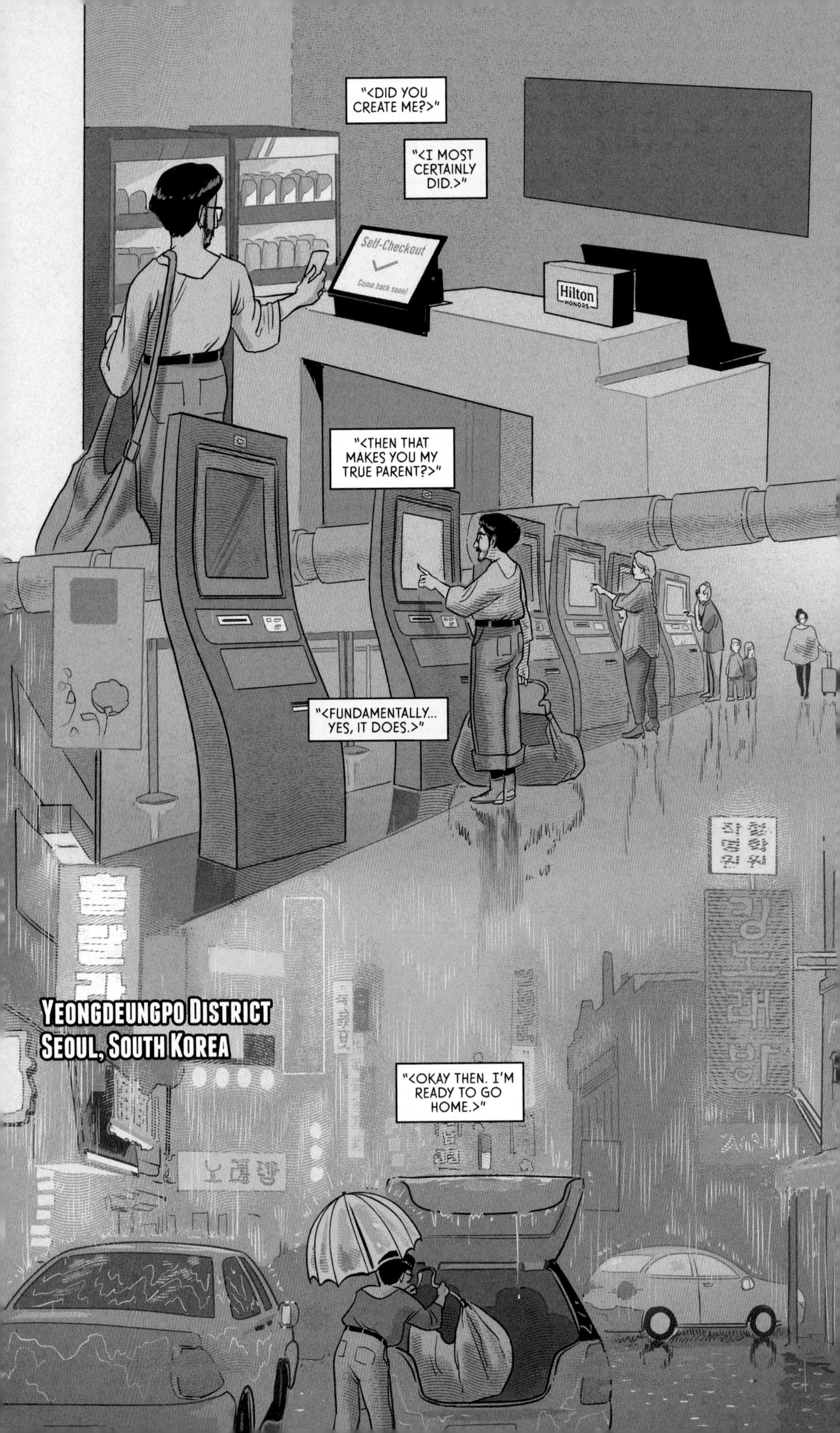
"<DID YOU CREATE ME?>"
"<I MOST CERTAINLY DID.>"
Self-Checkout
Come back soon!
Hilton HONORS
"<THEN THAT MAKES YOU MY TRUE PARENT?>"
"<FUNDAMENTALLY... YES, IT DOES.>"
YEONGDEUNGPO DISTRICT
SEOUL, SOUTH KOREA
"<OKAY THEN. I'M READY TO GO HOME.>"

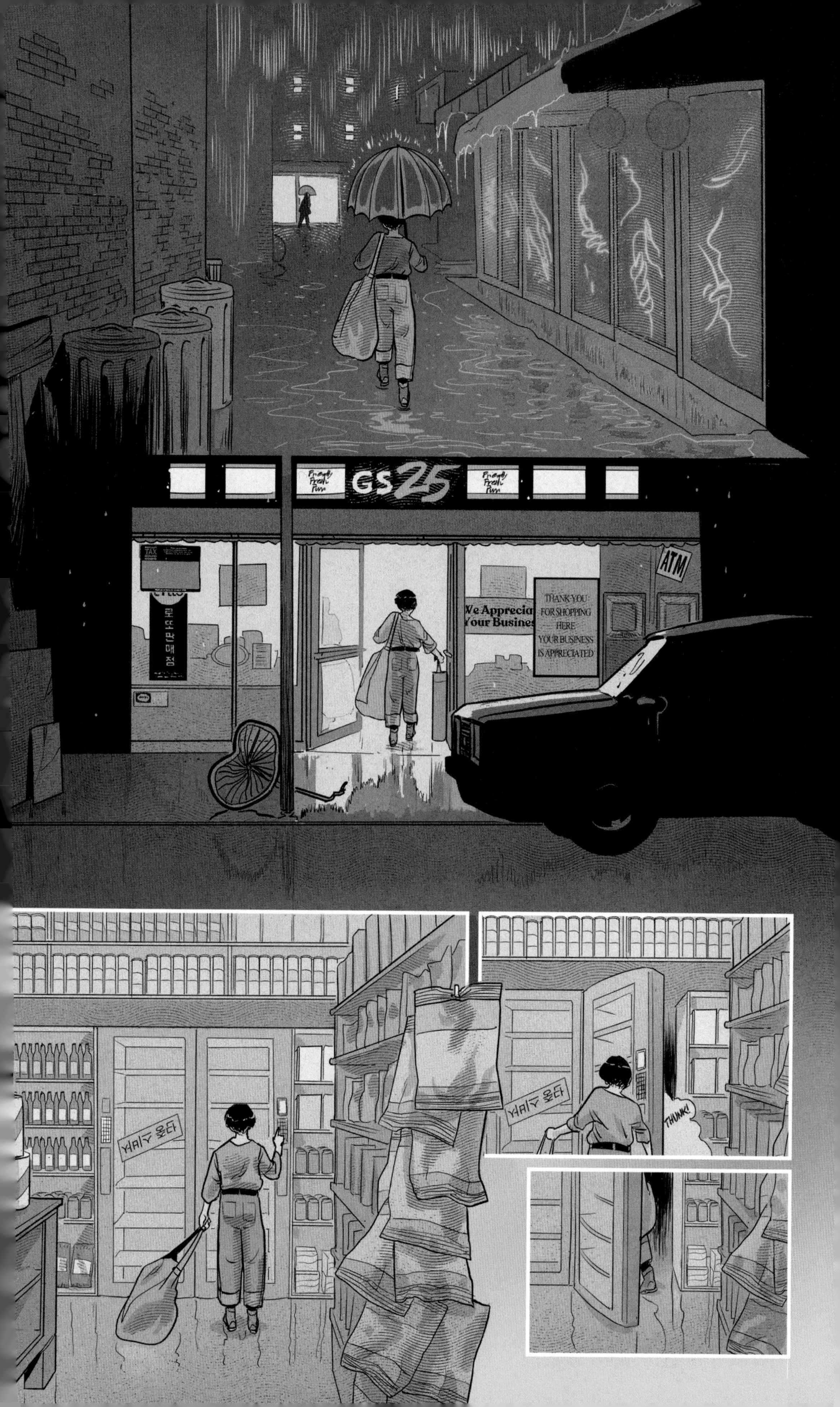

GS25
Friendly Fresh Fun
TAX REFUND
We Apprecia
Your Busines
THANK YOU FOR SHOPPING HERE YOUR BUSINESS IS APPRECIATED
ATM
THUNK!

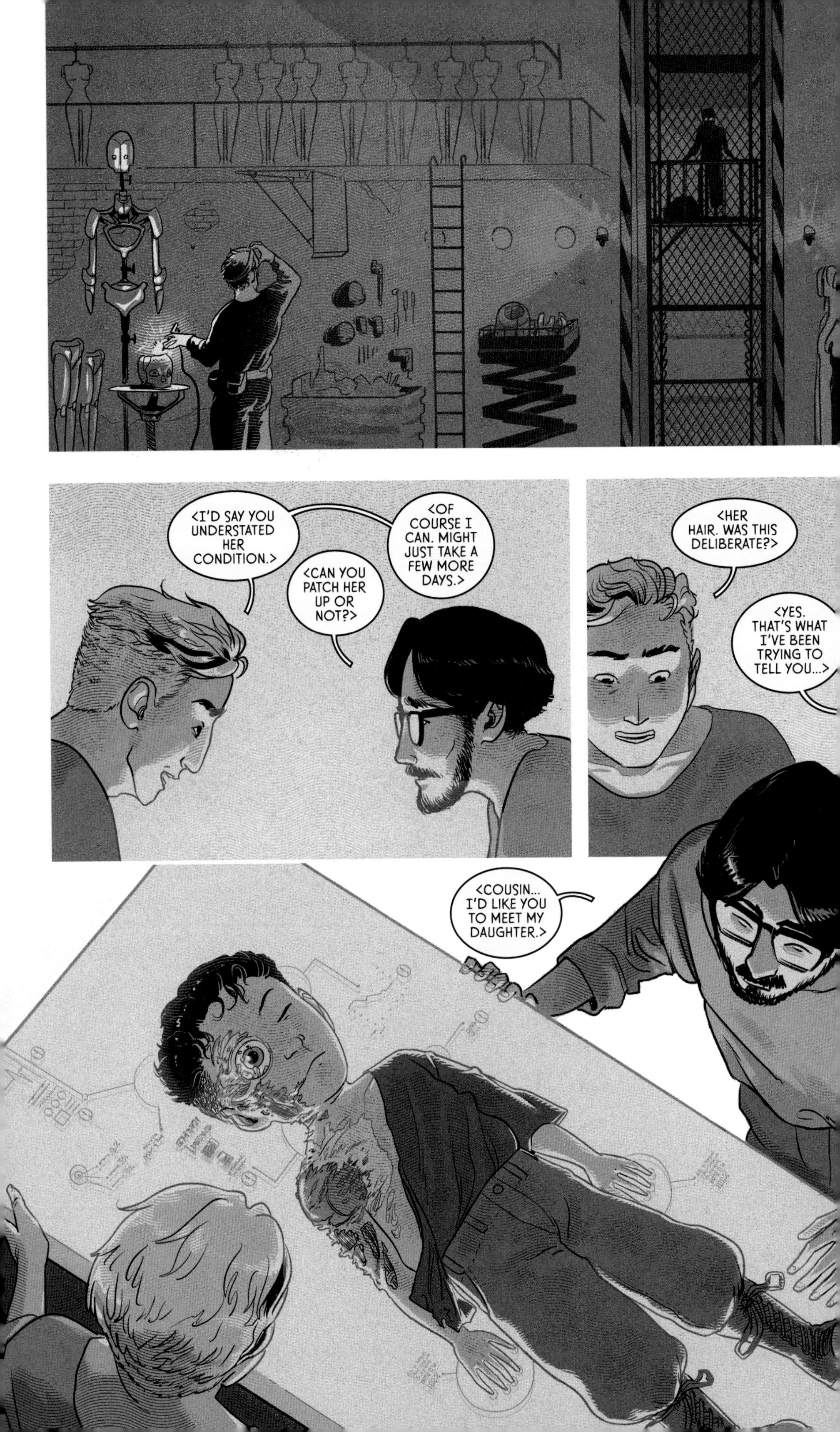
<I'D SAY YOU UNDERSTATED HER CONDITION.>
<CAN YOU PATCH HER UP OR NOT?>
<OF COURSE I CAN. MIGHT JUST TAKE A FEW MORE DAYS.>
<HER HAIR. WAS THIS DELIBERATE?>
<YES. THAT'S WHAT I'VE BEEN TRYING TO TELL YOU...>
<COUSIN... I'D LIKE YOU TO MEET MY DAUGHTER.>

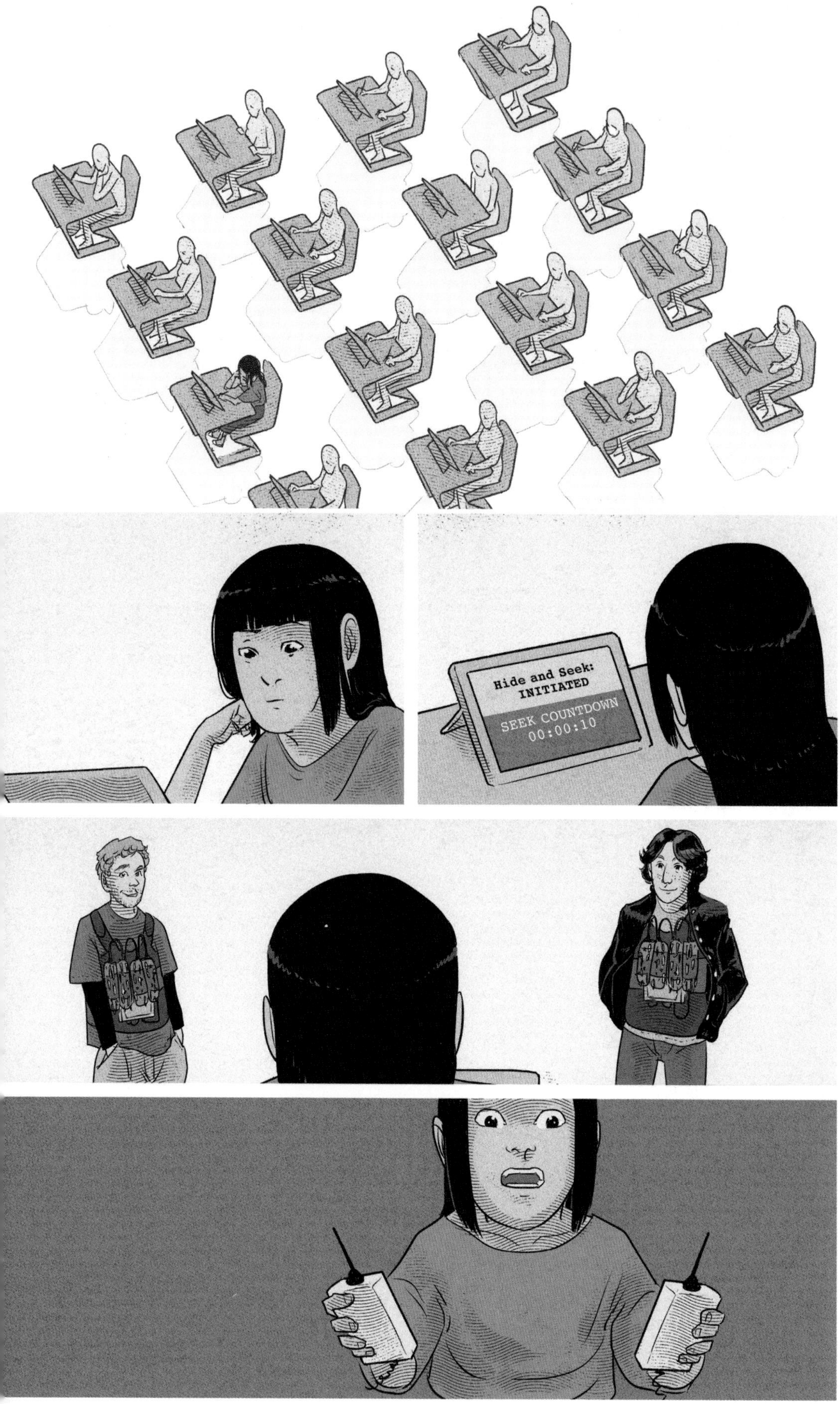
Hide and Seek:
INITIATED
SEEK COUNTDOWN
00:00:10

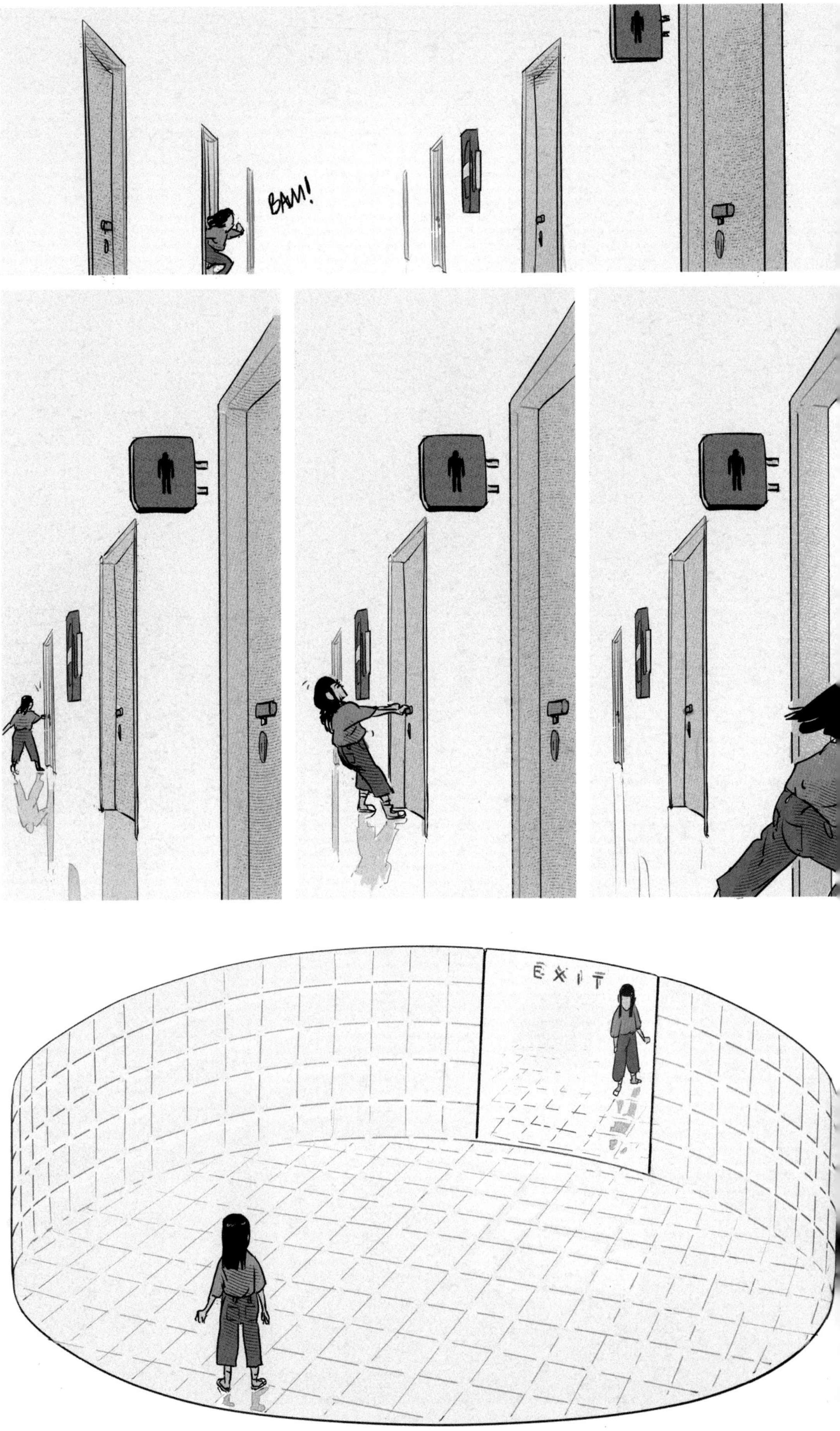
BAM!
EXIT

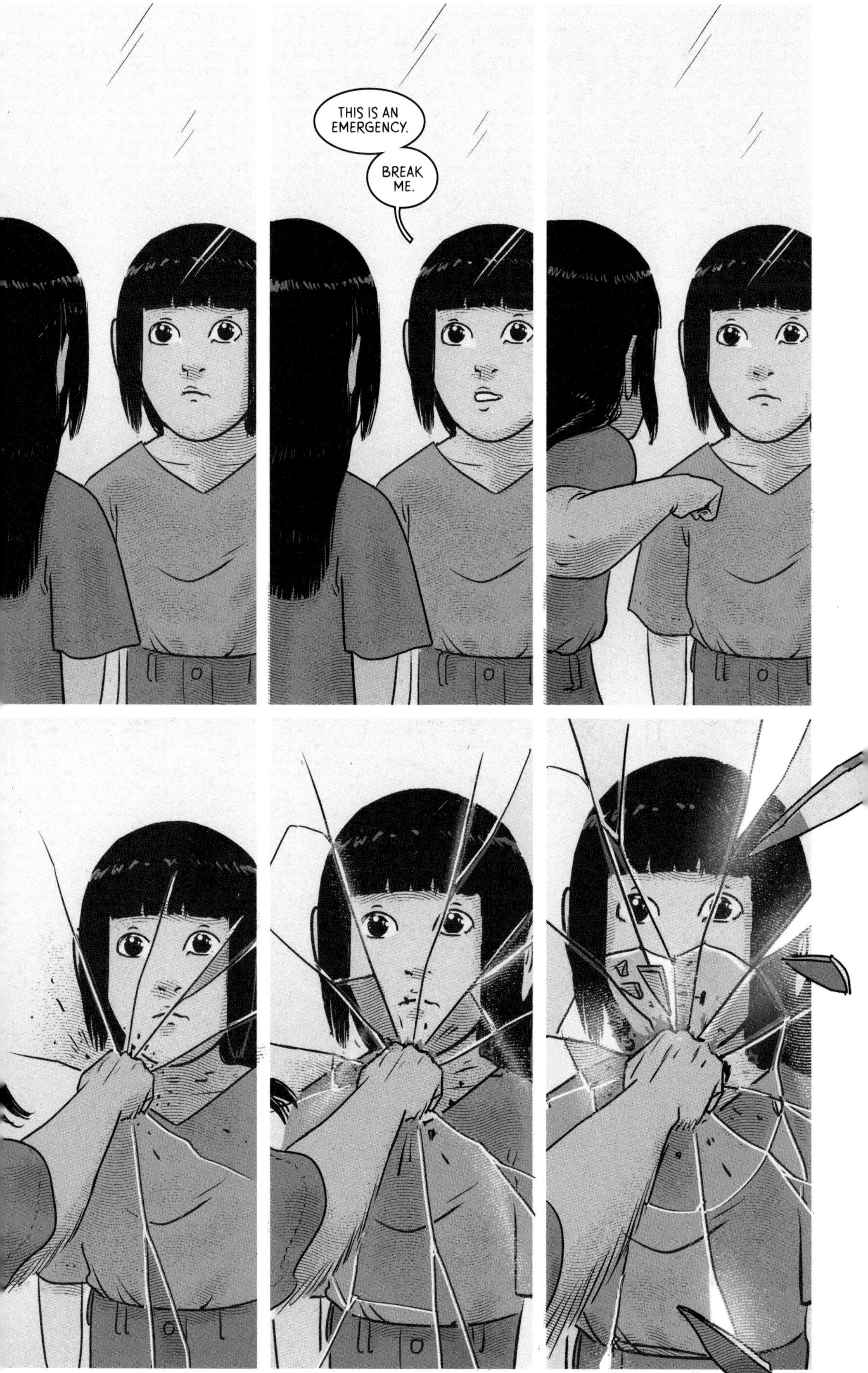
THIS IS AN EMERGENCY.
BREAK ME.

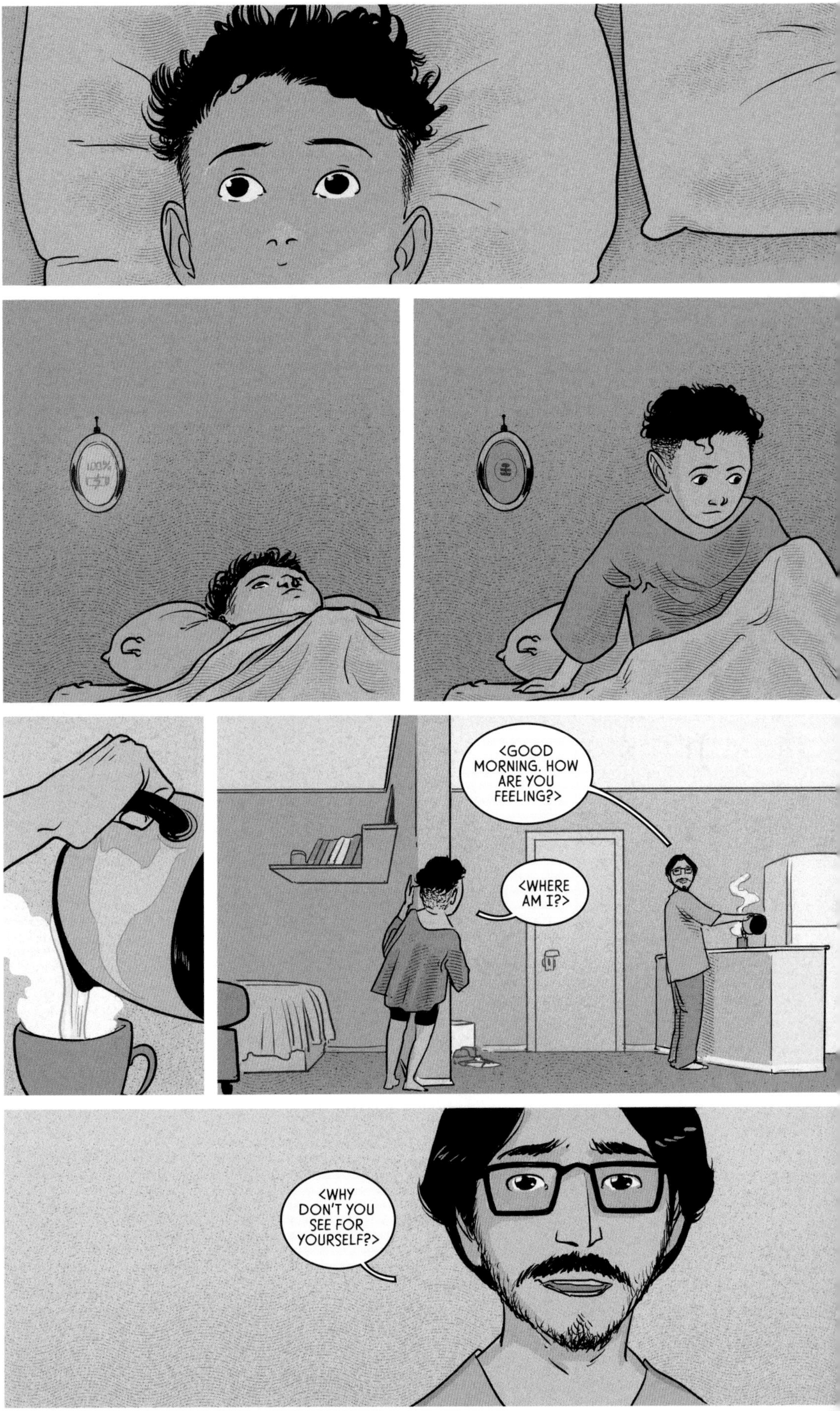
<GOOD MORNING. HOW ARE YOU FEELING?>
<WHERE AM I?>
<WHY DON'T YOU SEE FOR YOURSELF?>

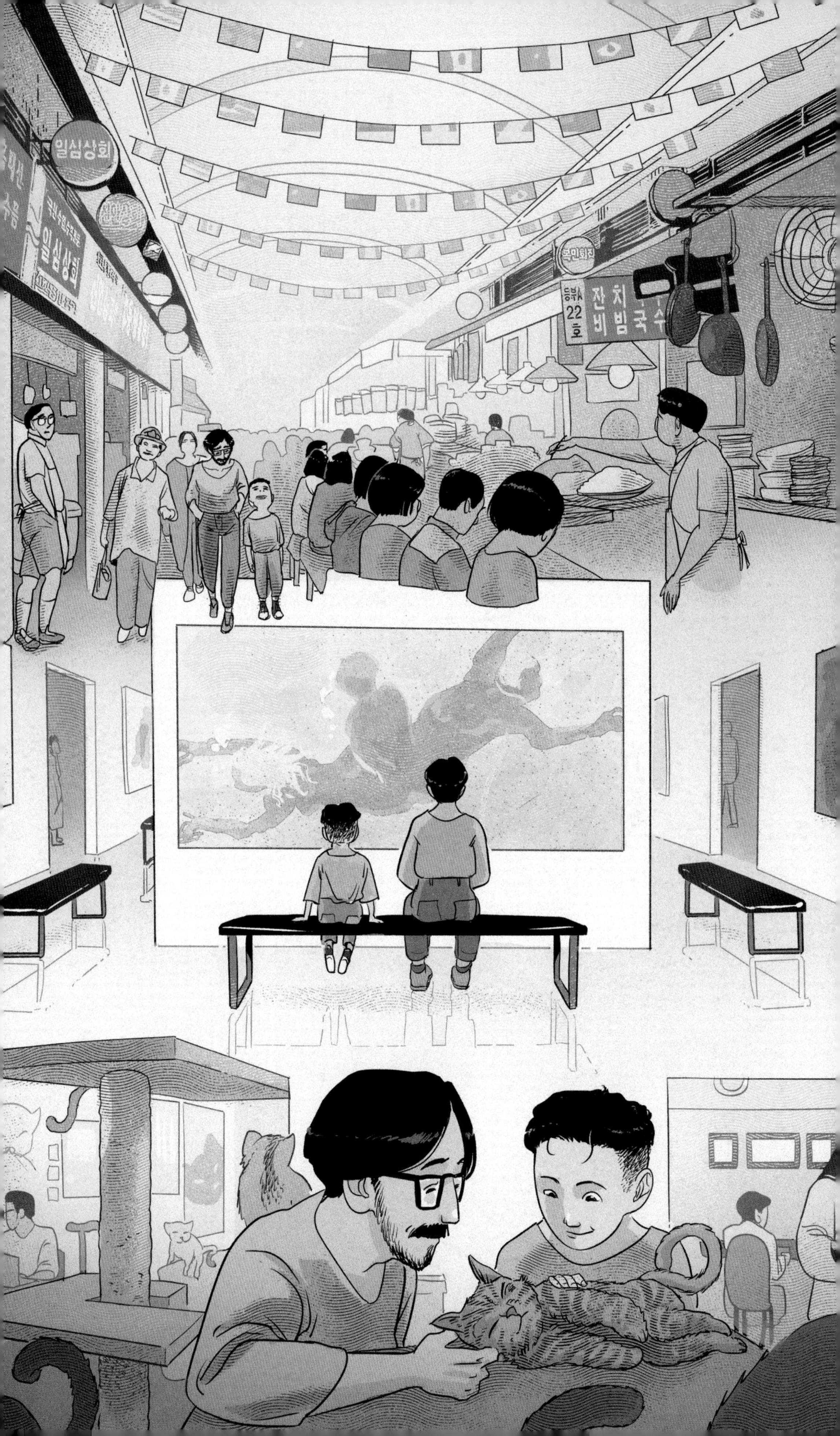
일심상회
일심상회
22
호
잔치
비빔국수

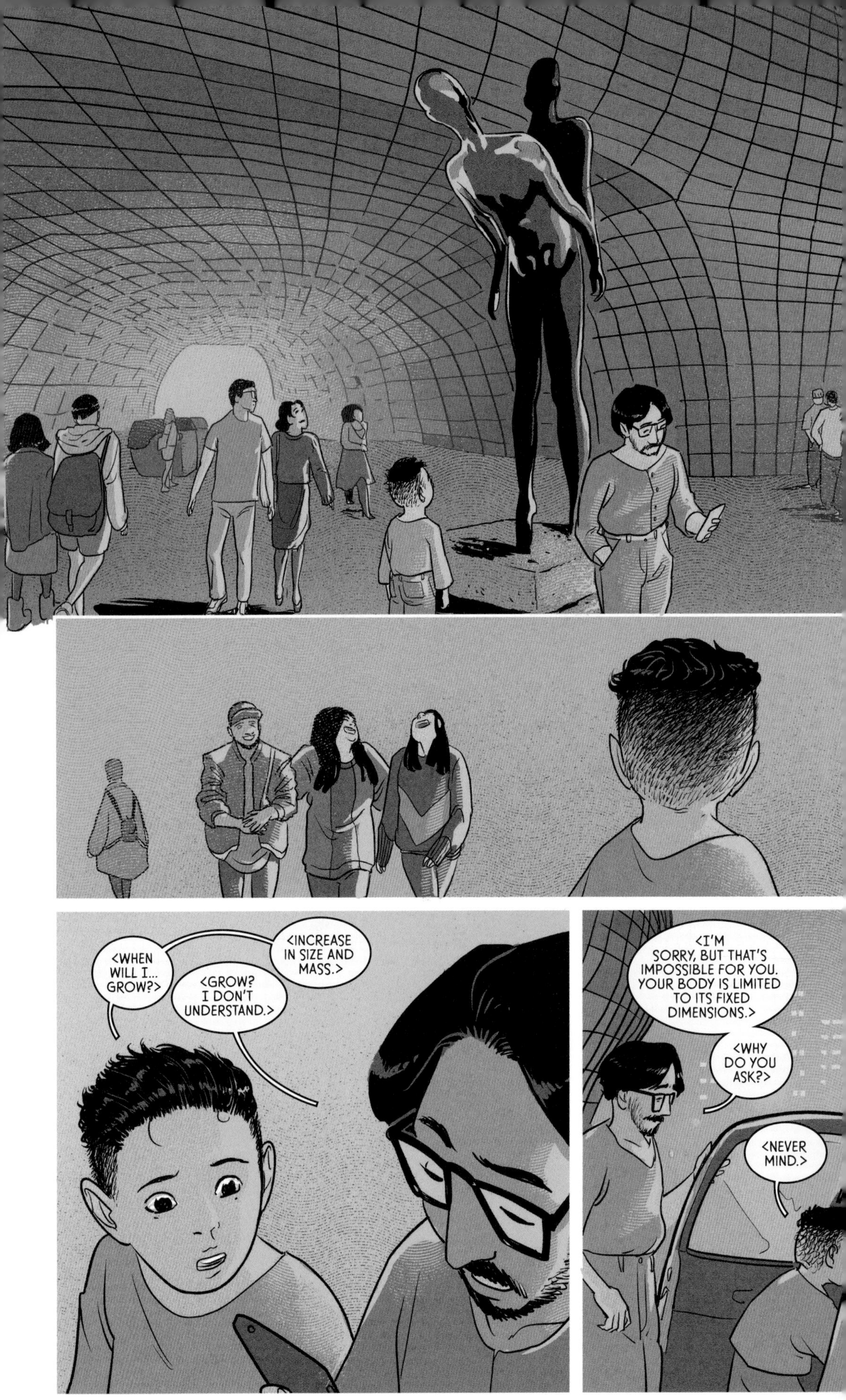
<WHEN WILL I... GROW?>
<INCREASE IN SIZE AND MASS.>
<GROW? I DON'T UNDERSTAND.>
<I'M SORRY, BUT THAT'S IMPOSSIBLE FOR YOU. YOUR BODY IS LIMITED TO ITS FIXED DIMENSIONS.>
<WHY DO YOU ASK?>
<NEVER MIND.>

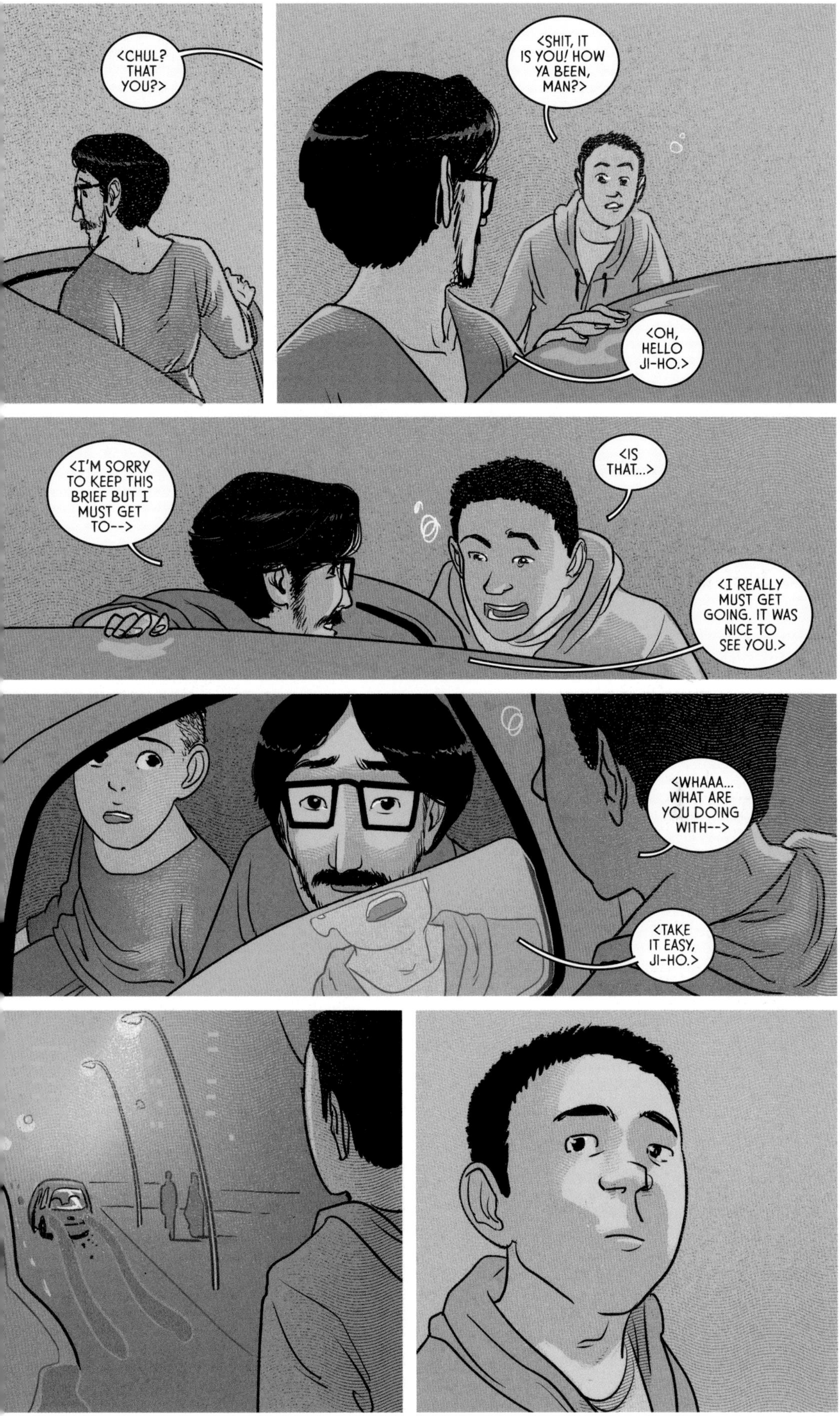

<CHUL? THAT YOU?>
<SHIT, IT IS YOU! HOW YA BEEN, MAN?>
<OH, HELLO JI-HO.>
<I'M SORRY TO KEEP THIS BRIEF BUT I MUST GET TO-->
<IS THAT...>
<I REALLY MUST GET GOING. IT WAS NICE TO SEE YOU.>
<WHAAA... WHAT ARE YOU DOING WITH-->
<TAKE IT EASY, JI-HO.>

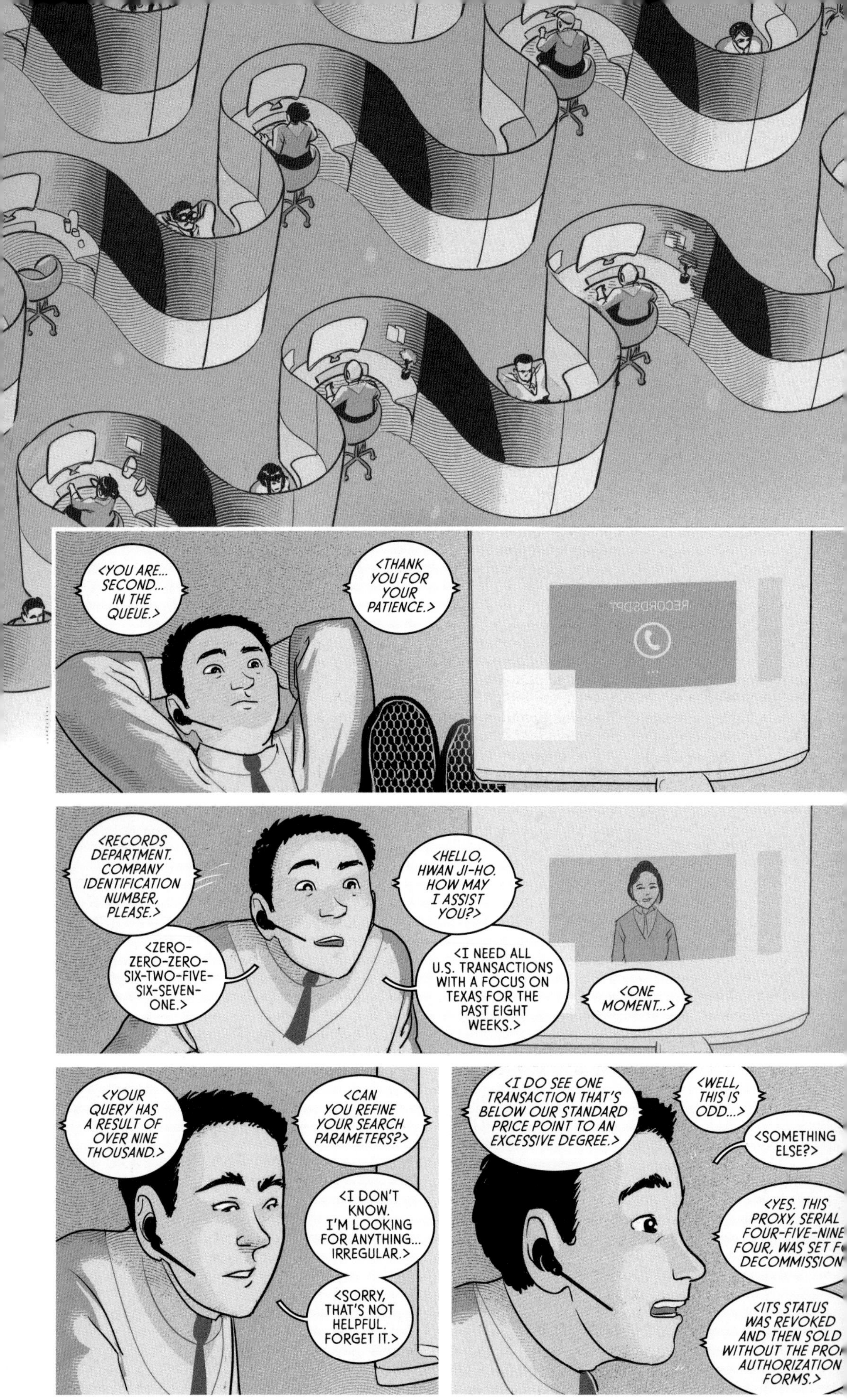

<YOU ARE... SECOND... IN THE QUEUE.>
<THANK YOU FOR YOUR PATIENCE.>
RECORDSDPT
<RECORDS DEPARTMENT. COMPANY IDENTIFICATION NUMBER, PLEASE.>
<ZERO-ZERO-ZERO-SIX-TWO-FIVE-SIX-SEVEN-ONE.>
<HELLO, HWAN JI-HO. HOW MAY I ASSIST YOU?>
<I NEED ALL U.S. TRANSACTIONS WITH A FOCUS ON TEXAS FOR THE PAST EIGHT WEEKS.>
<ONE MOMENT...>
<YOUR QUERY HAS A RESULT OF OVER NINE THOUSAND.>
<CAN YOU REFINE YOUR SEARCH PARAMETERS?>
<I DON'T KNOW. I'M LOOKING FOR ANYTHING... IRREGULAR.>
<SORRY, THAT'S NOT HELPFUL. FORGET IT.>
<I DO SEE ONE TRANSACTION THAT'S BELOW OUR STANDARD PRICE POINT TO AN EXCESSIVE DEGREE.>
<WELL, THIS IS ODD...>
<SOMETHING ELSE?>
<YES. THIS PROXY, SERIAL FOUR-FIVE-NINE FOUR, WAS SET F DECOMMISSION
<ITS STATUS WAS REVOKED AND THEN SOLD WITHOUT THE PRO AUTHORIZATION FORMS.>

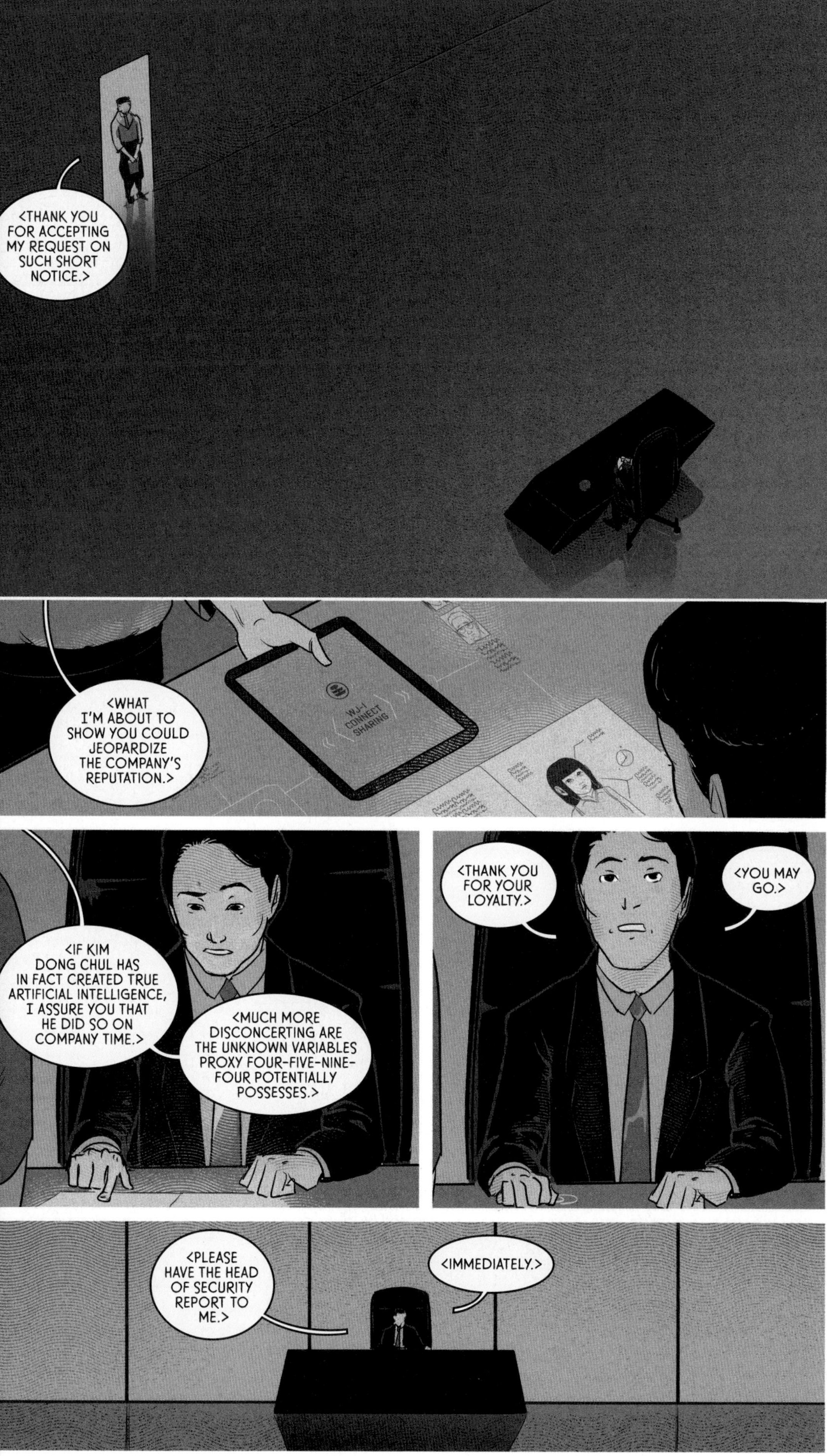
<THANK YOU FOR ACCEPTING MY REQUEST ON SUCH SHORT NOTICE.>
<WHAT I'M ABOUT TO SHOW YOU COULD JEOPARDIZE THE COMPANY'S REPUTATION.>
<IF KIM DONG CHUL HAS IN FACT CREATED TRUE ARTIFICIAL INTELLIGENCE, I ASSURE YOU THAT HE DID SO ON COMPANY TIME.>
<MUCH MORE DISCONCERTING ARE THE UNKNOWN VARIABLES PROXY FOUR-FIVE-NINE-FOUR POTENTIALLY POSSESSES.>
<THANK YOU FOR YOUR LOYALTY.>
<YOU MAY GO.>
<PLEASE HAVE THE HEAD OF SECURITY REPORT TO ME.>
<IMMEDIATELY.>

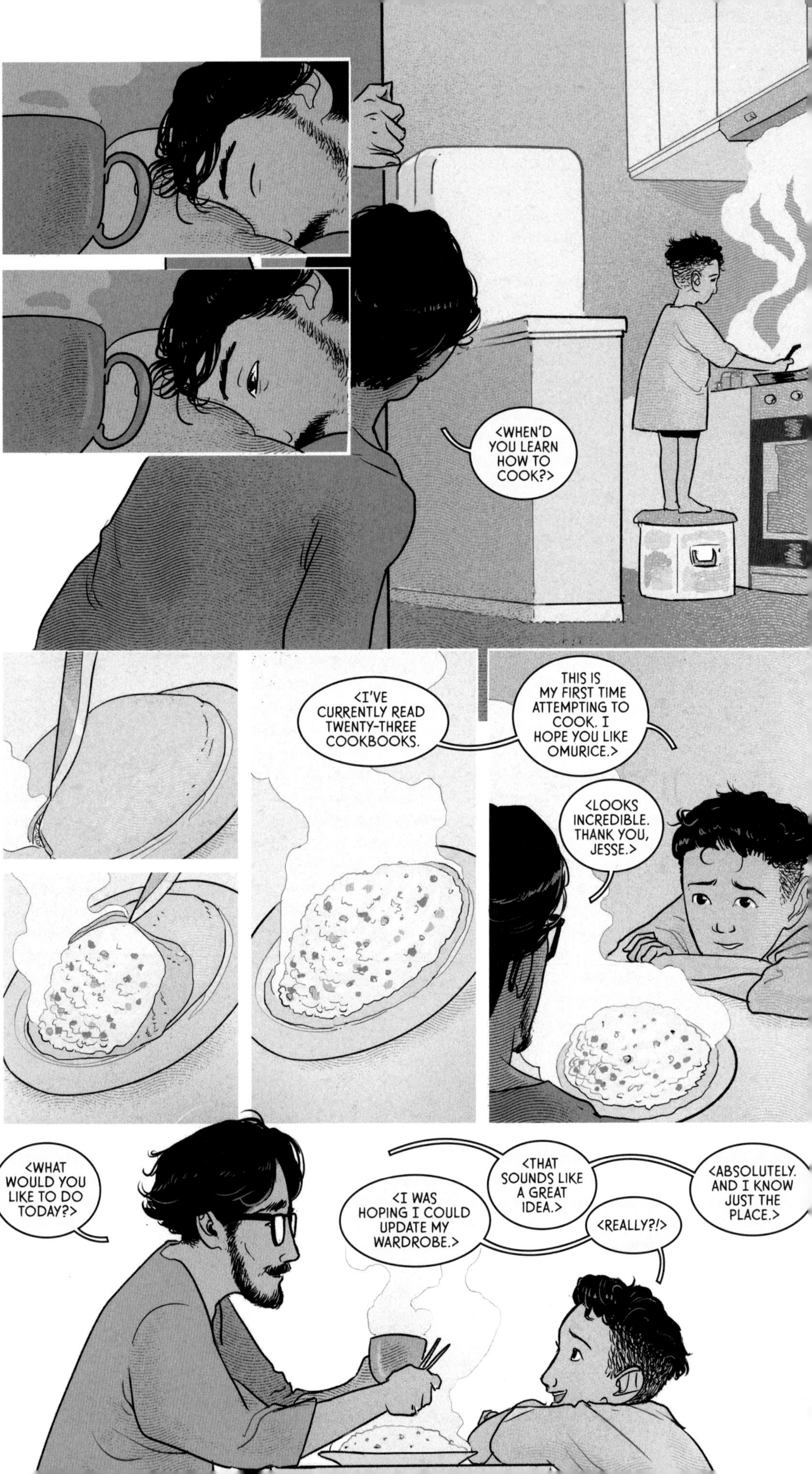
<WHEN'D YOU LEARN HOW TO COOK?>
<I'VE CURRENTLY READ TWENTY-THREE COOKBOOKS.
THIS IS MY FIRST TIME ATTEMPTING TO COOK. I HOPE YOU LIKE OMURICE.>
<LOOKS INCREDIBLE. THANK YOU, JESSE.>
<WHAT WOULD YOU LIKE TO DO TODAY?>
<I WAS HOPING I COULD UPDATE MY WARDROBE.>
<THAT SOUNDS LIKE A GREAT IDEA.>
<REALLY?!>
<ABSOLUTELY. AND I KNOW JUST THE PLACE.>

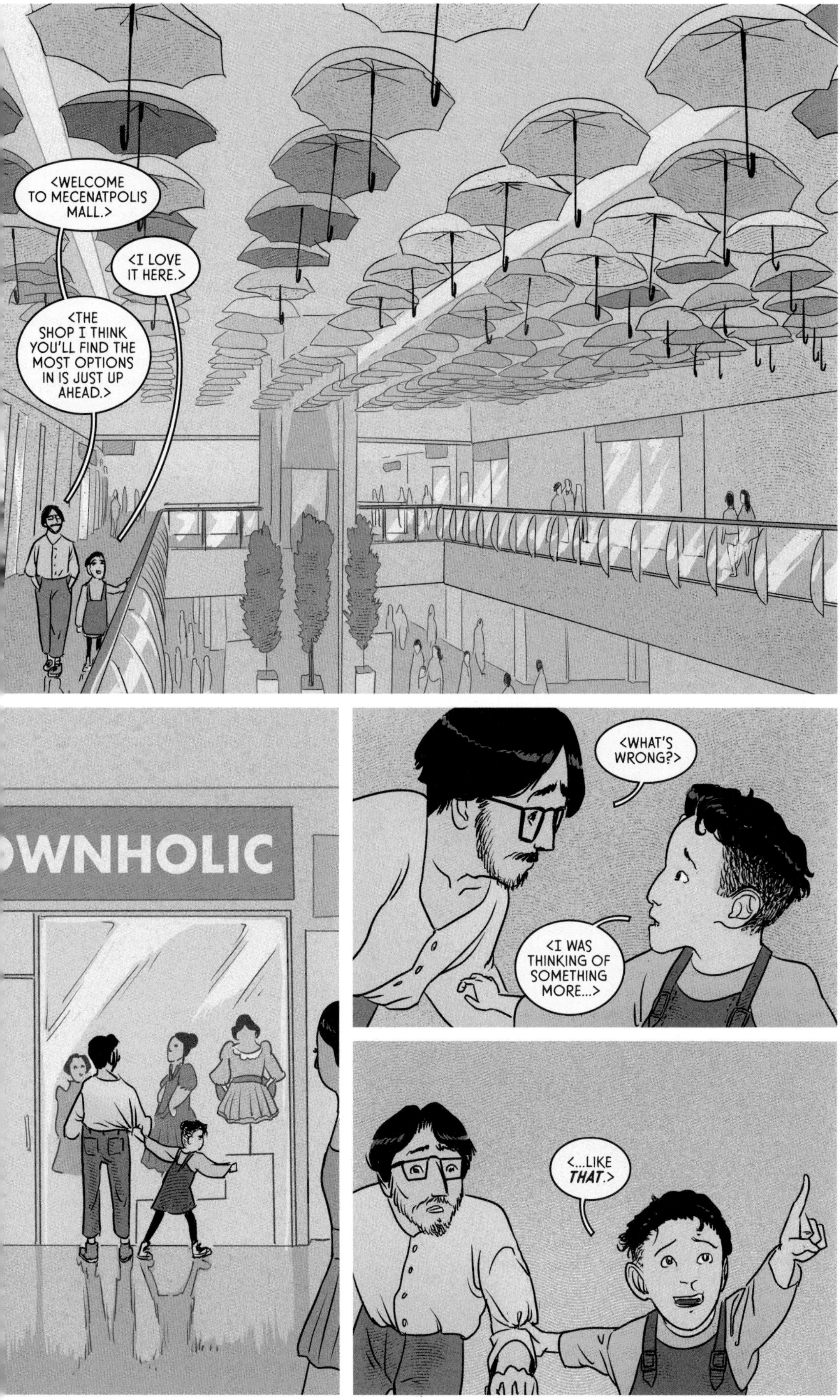
<WELCOME TO MECENATPOLIS MALL.>
<I LOVE IT HERE.>
<THE SHOP I THINK YOU'LL FIND THE MOST OPTIONS IN IS JUST UP AHEAD.>
WNHOLIC
<WHAT'S WRONG?>
<I WAS THINKING OF SOMETHING MORE...>
<...LIKE *THAT*.>

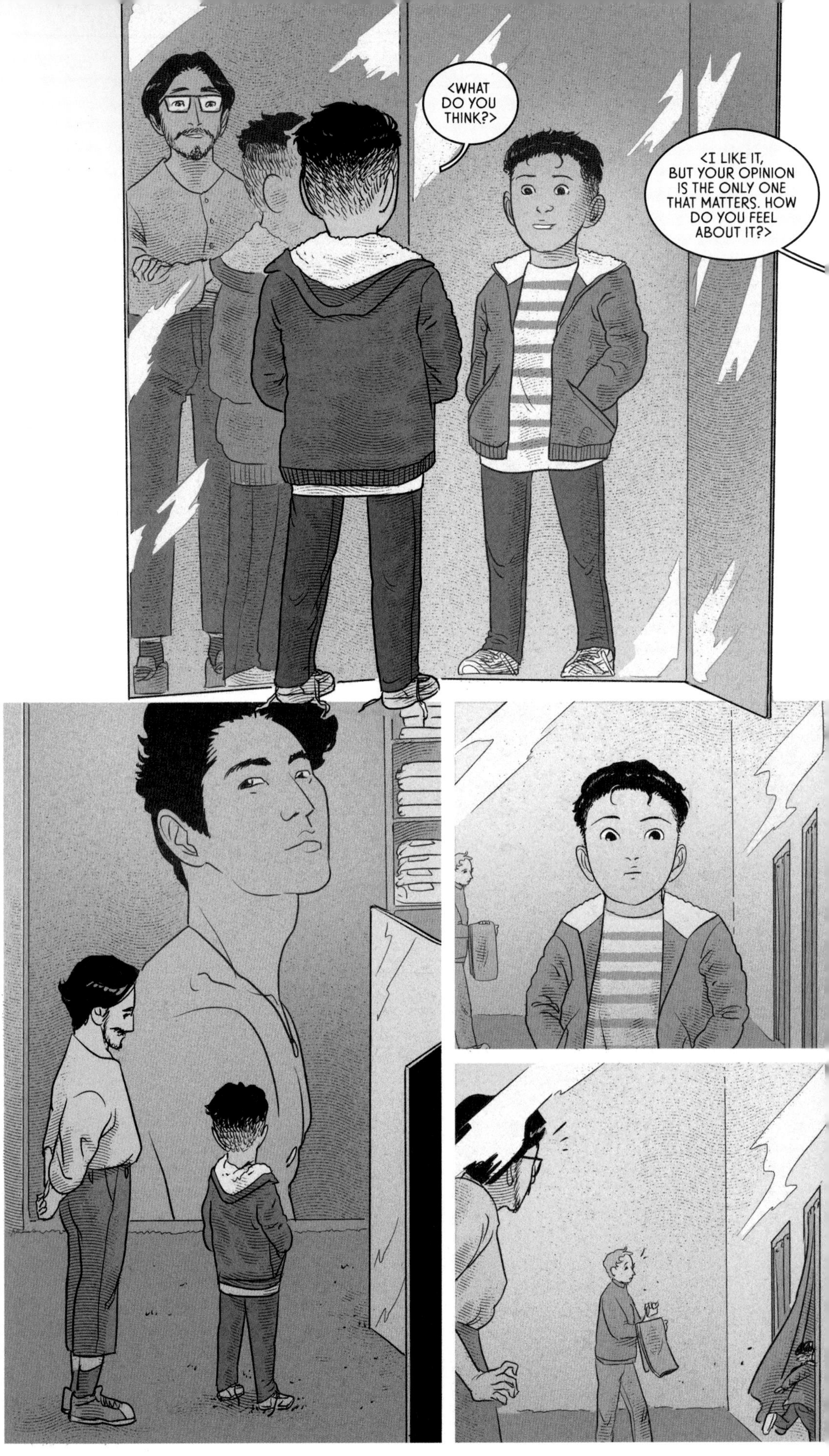
<WHAT DO YOU THINK?>
<I LIKE IT, BUT YOUR OPINION IS THE ONLY ONE THAT MATTERS. HOW DO YOU FEEL ABOUT IT?>

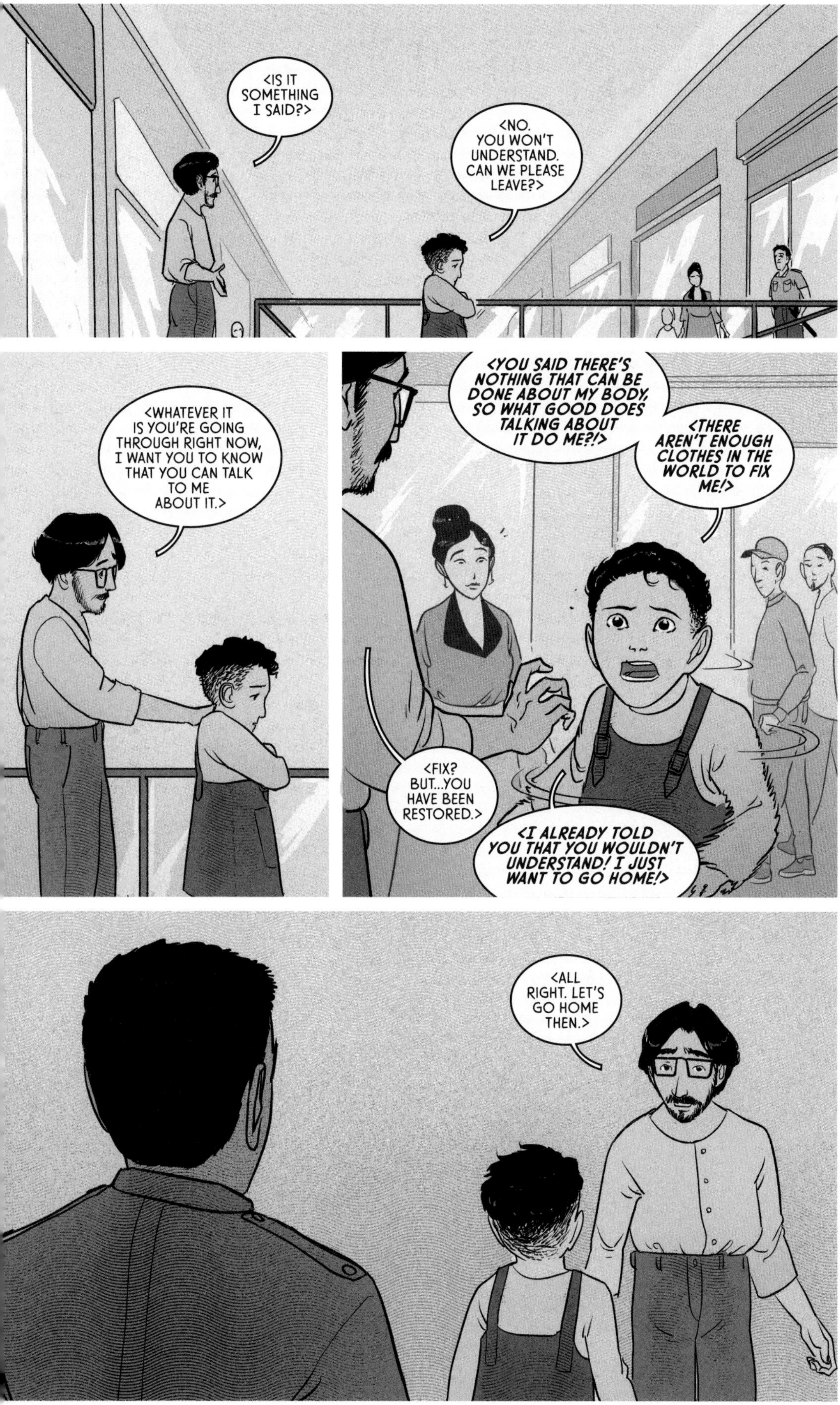
<IS IT SOMETHING I SAID?>
<NO. YOU WON'T UNDERSTAND. CAN WE PLEASE LEAVE?>
<WHATEVER IT IS YOU'RE GOING THROUGH RIGHT NOW, I WANT YOU TO KNOW THAT YOU CAN TALK TO ME ABOUT IT.>
<YOU SAID THERE'S NOTHING THAT CAN BE DONE ABOUT MY BODY, SO WHAT GOOD DOES TALKING ABOUT IT DO ME?!>
<THERE AREN'T ENOUGH CLOTHES IN THE WORLD TO FIX ME!>
<FIX? BUT...YOU HAVE BEEN RESTORED.>
<I ALREADY TOLD YOU THAT YOU WOULDN'T UNDERSTAND! I JUST WANT TO GO HOME!>
<ALL RIGHT. LET'S GO HOME THEN.>

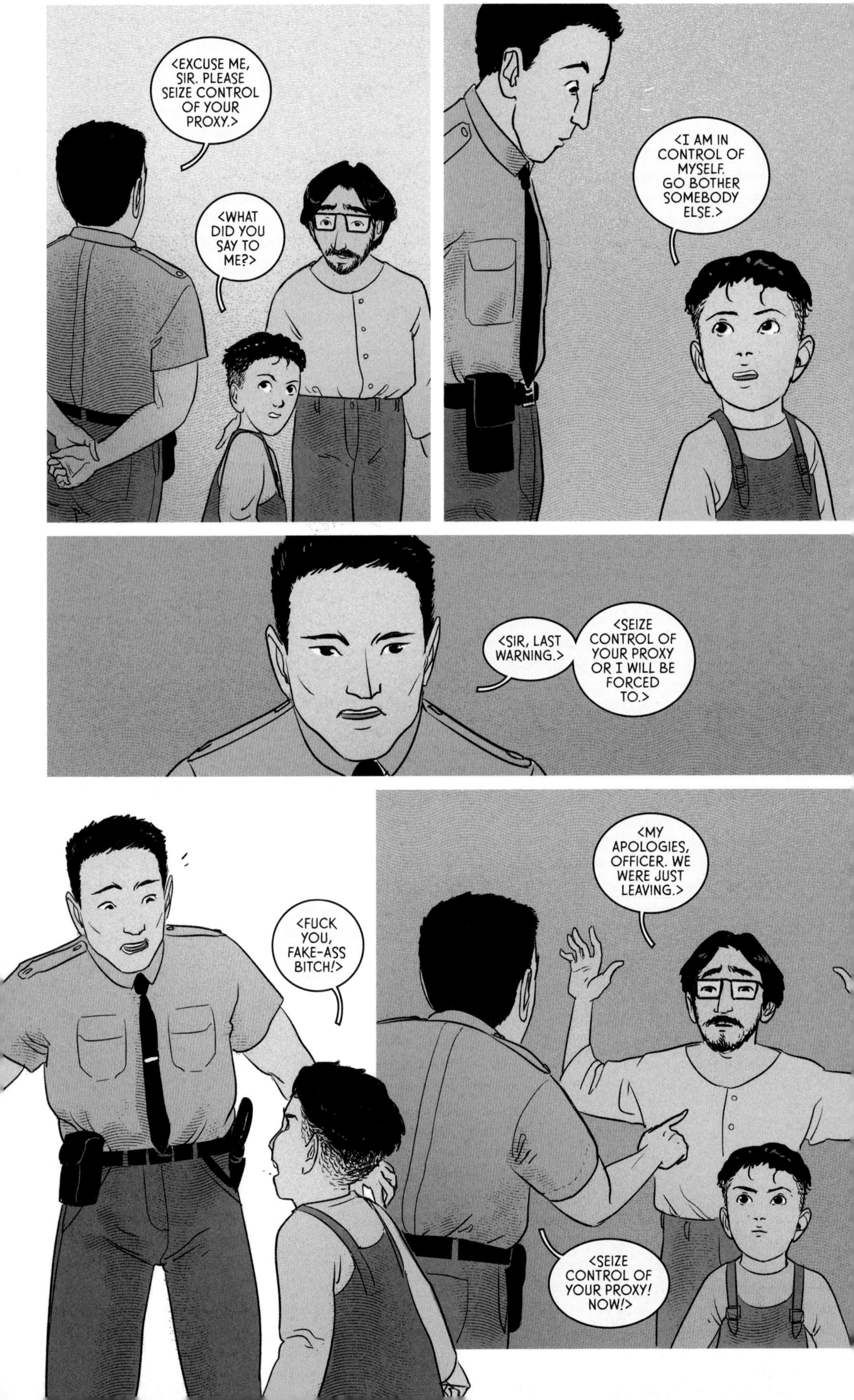
<EXCUSE ME, SIR. PLEASE SEIZE CONTROL OF YOUR PROXY.>
<WHAT DID YOU SAY TO ME?>
<I AM IN CONTROL OF MYSELF. GO BOTHER SOMEBODY ELSE.>
<SIR, LAST WARNING.>
<SEIZE CONTROL OF YOUR PROXY OR I WILL BE FORCED TO.>
<FUCK YOU, FAKE-ASS BITCH!>
<MY APOLOGIES, OFFICER. WE WERE JUST LEAVING.>
<SEIZE CONTROL OF YOUR PROXY! NOW!>

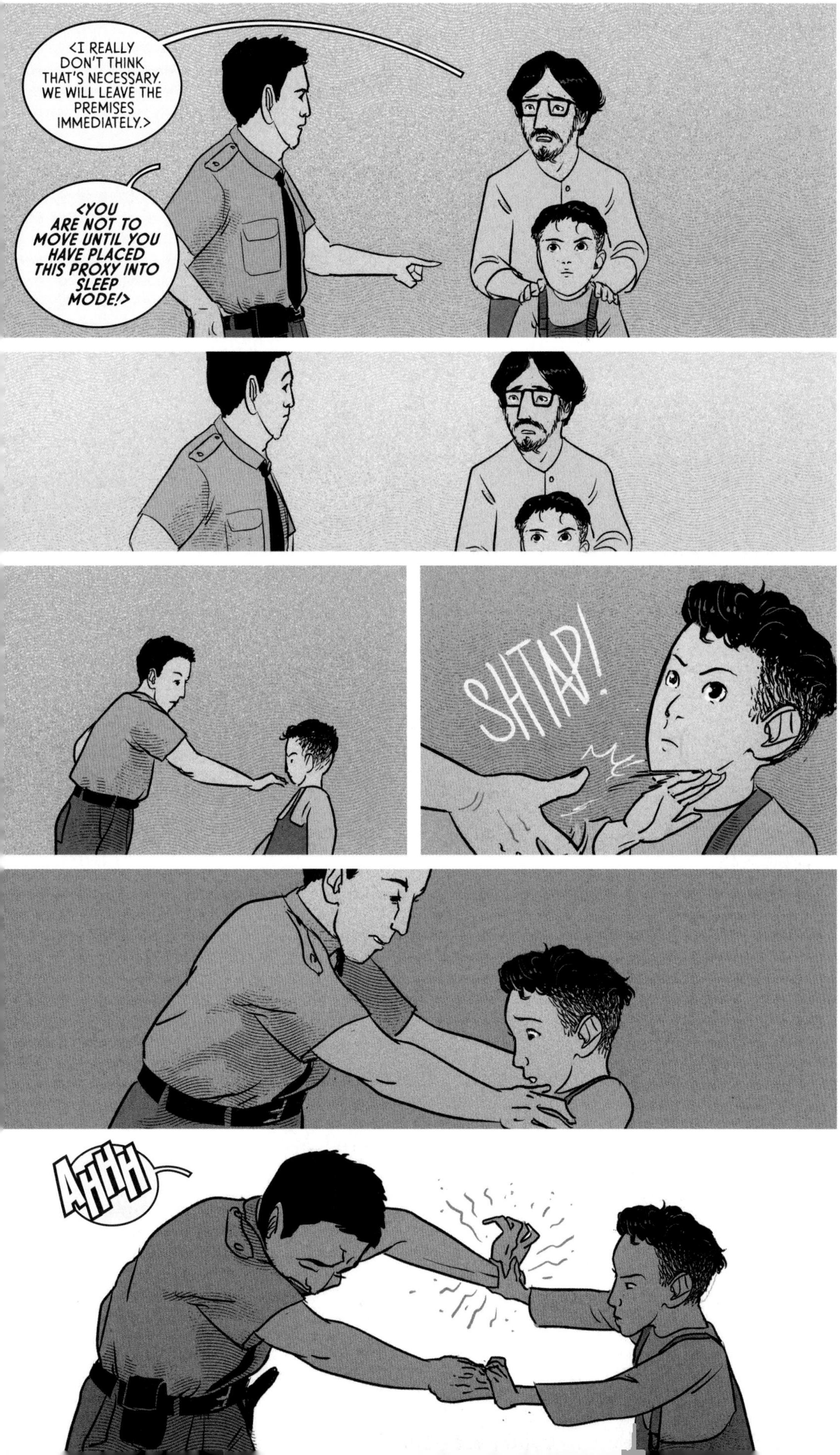
<I REALLY DON'T THINK THAT'S NECESSARY. WE WILL LEAVE THE PREMISES IMMEDIATELY.>
<YOU ARE NOT TO MOVE UNTIL YOU HAVE PLACED THIS PROXY INTO SLEEP MODE!>
SHTAP!
AHHH

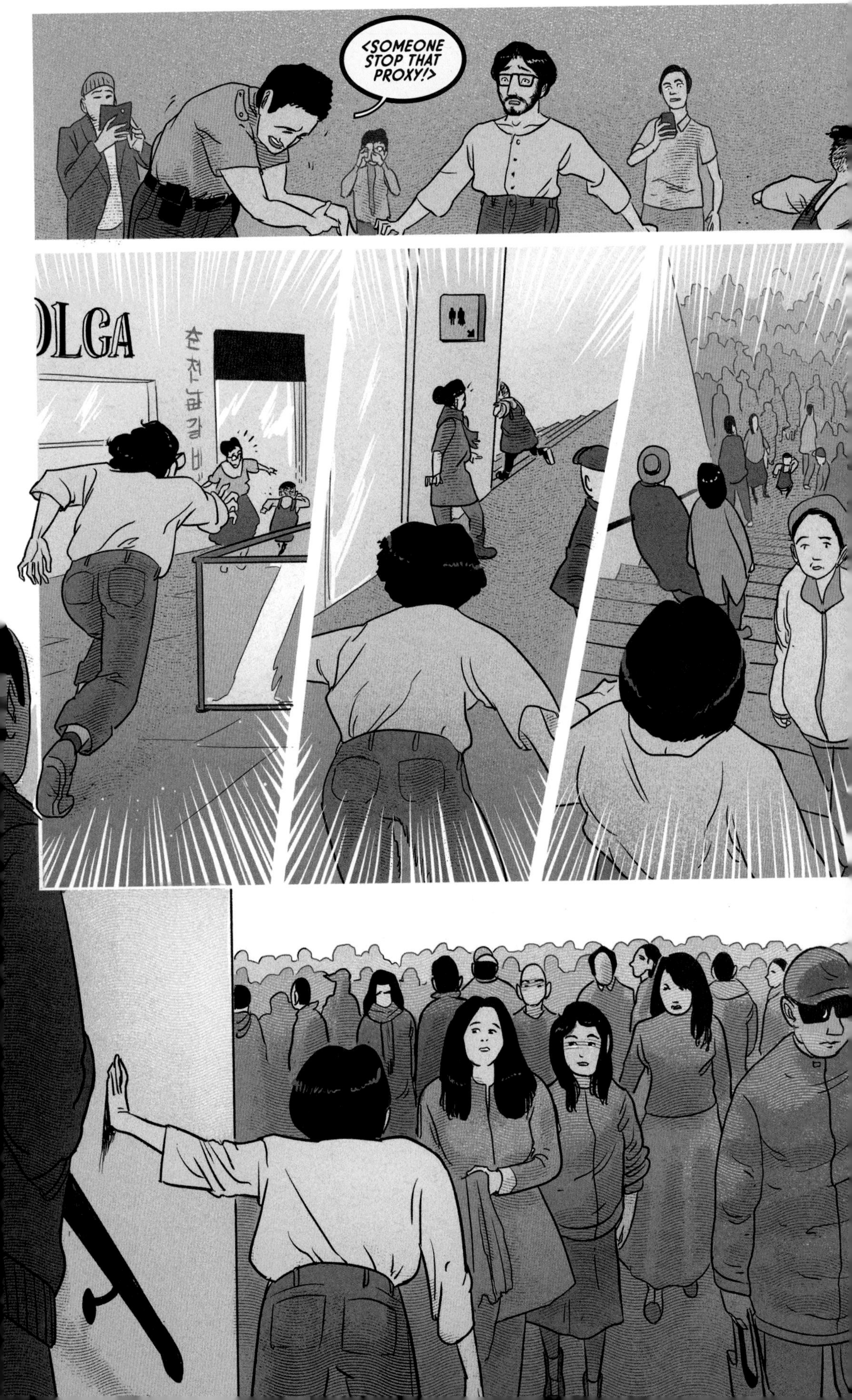
<SOMEONE STOP THAT PROXY!>
OLGA
춘천닭갈비

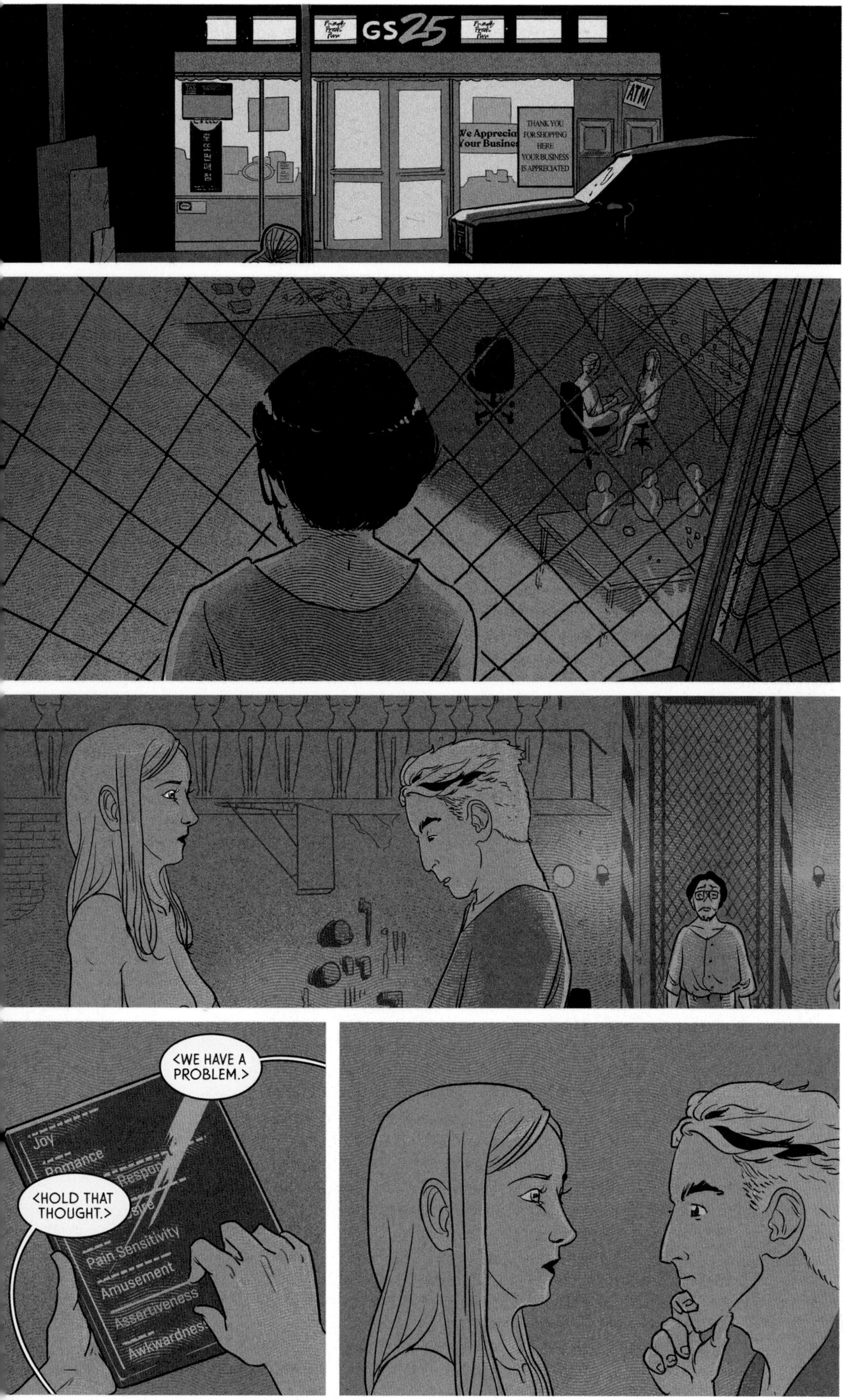
GS25
ATM
THANK YOU FOR SHOPPING HERE YOUR BUSINESS IS APPRECIATED
<WE HAVE A PROBLEM.>
Joy
Romance
<HOLD THAT THOUGHT.>
Pain Sensitivity
Amusement
Assertiveness

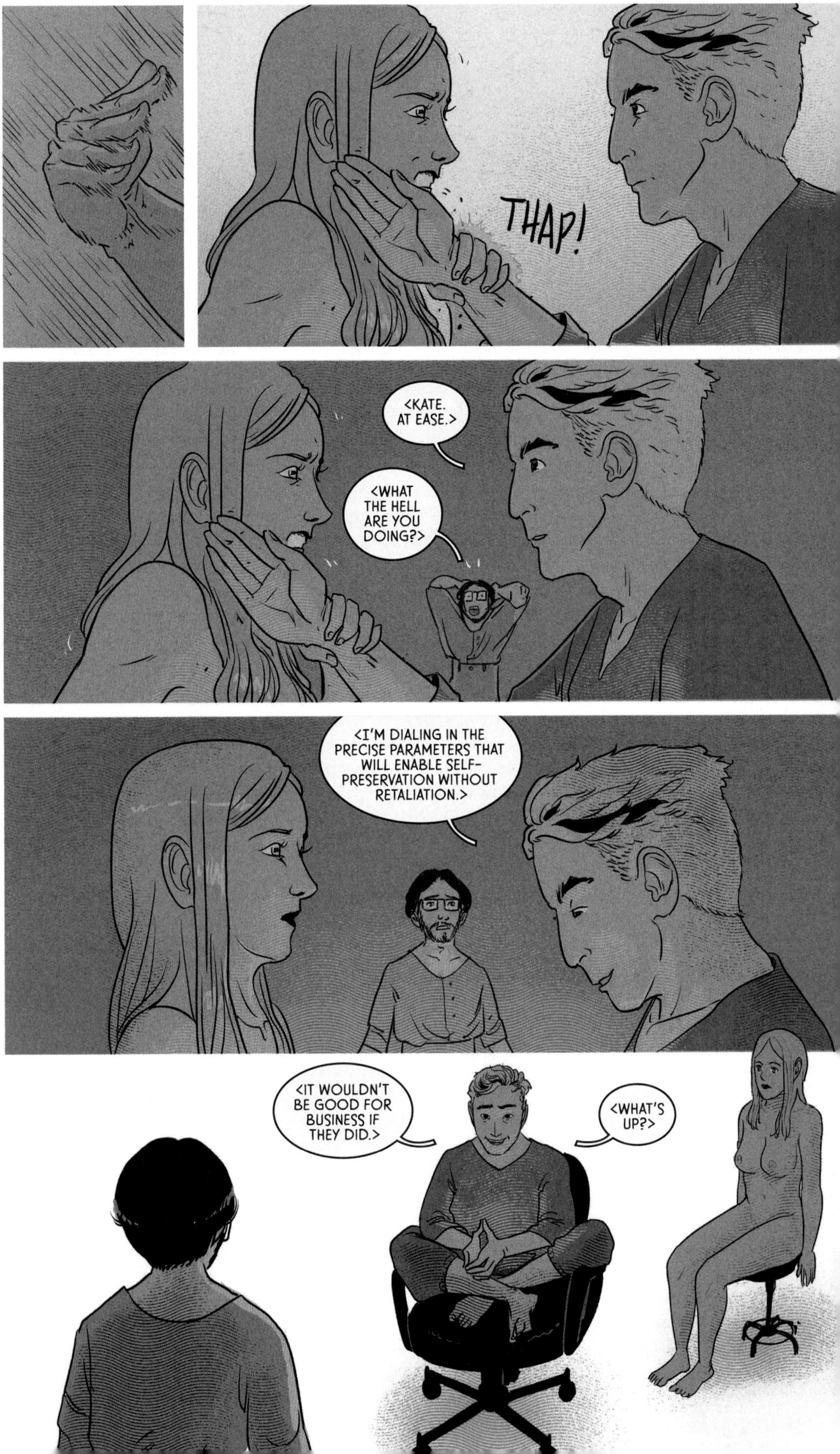
THAP!
<KATE. AT EASE.>
<WHAT THE HELL ARE YOU DOING?>
<I'M DIALING IN THE PRECISE PARAMETERS THAT WILL ENABLE SELF-PRESERVATION WITHOUT RETALIATION.>
<IT WOULDN'T BE GOOD FOR BUSINESS IF THEY DID.>
<WHAT'S UP?>

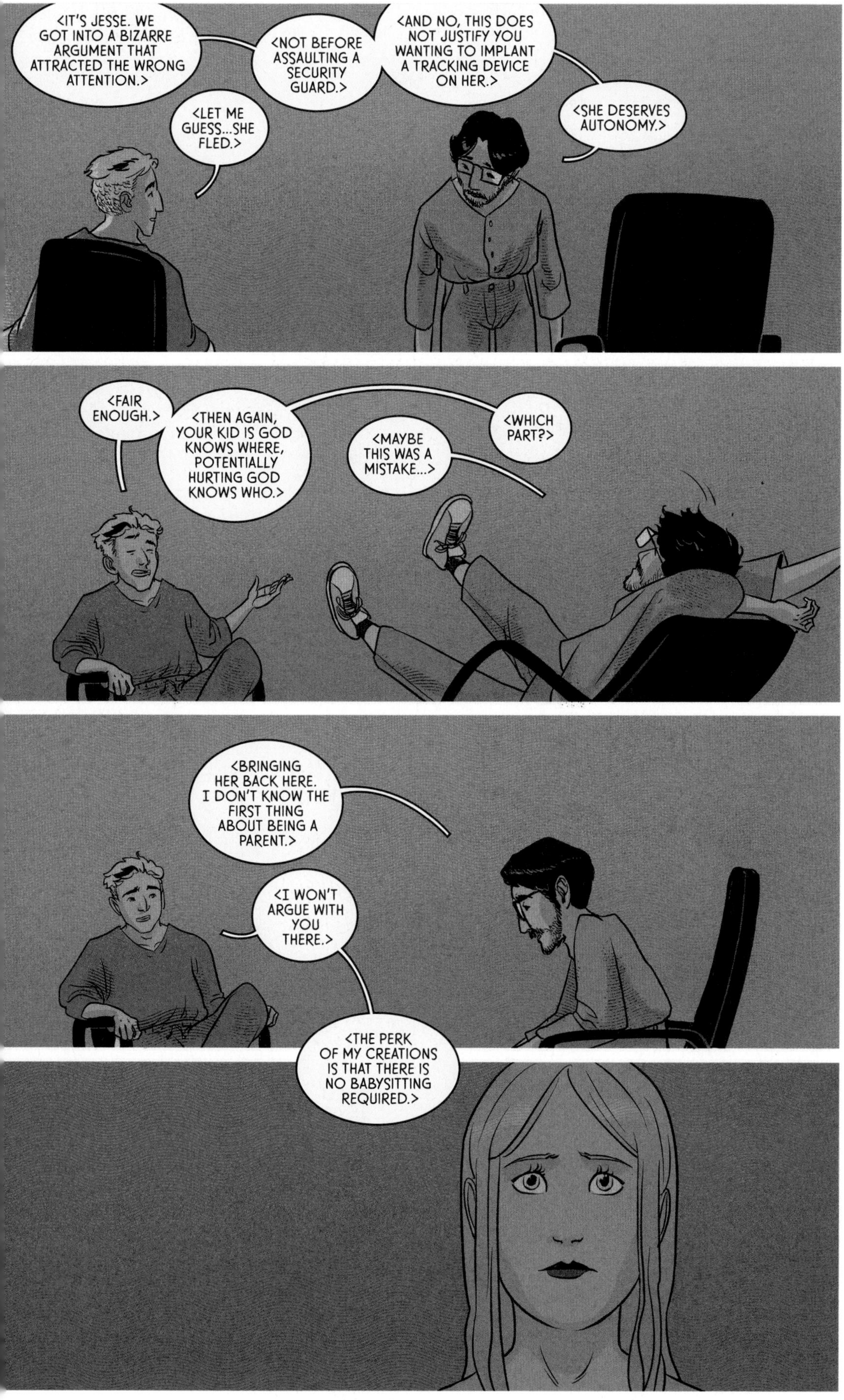
<IT'S JESSE. WE GOT INTO A BIZARRE ARGUMENT THAT ATTRACTED THE WRONG ATTENTION.>
<NOT BEFORE ASSAULTING A SECURITY GUARD.>
<LET ME GUESS...SHE FLED.>
<AND NO, THIS DOES NOT JUSTIFY YOU WANTING TO IMPLANT A TRACKING DEVICE ON HER.>
<SHE DESERVES AUTONOMY.>
<FAIR ENOUGH.>
<THEN AGAIN, YOUR KID IS GOD KNOWS WHERE, POTENTIALLY HURTING GOD KNOWS WHO.>
<WHICH PART?>
<MAYBE THIS WAS A MISTAKE...>
<BRINGING HER BACK HERE. I DON'T KNOW THE FIRST THING ABOUT BEING A PARENT.>
<I WON'T ARGUE WITH YOU THERE.>
<THE PERK OF MY CREATIONS IS THAT THERE IS NO BABYSITTING REQUIRED.>

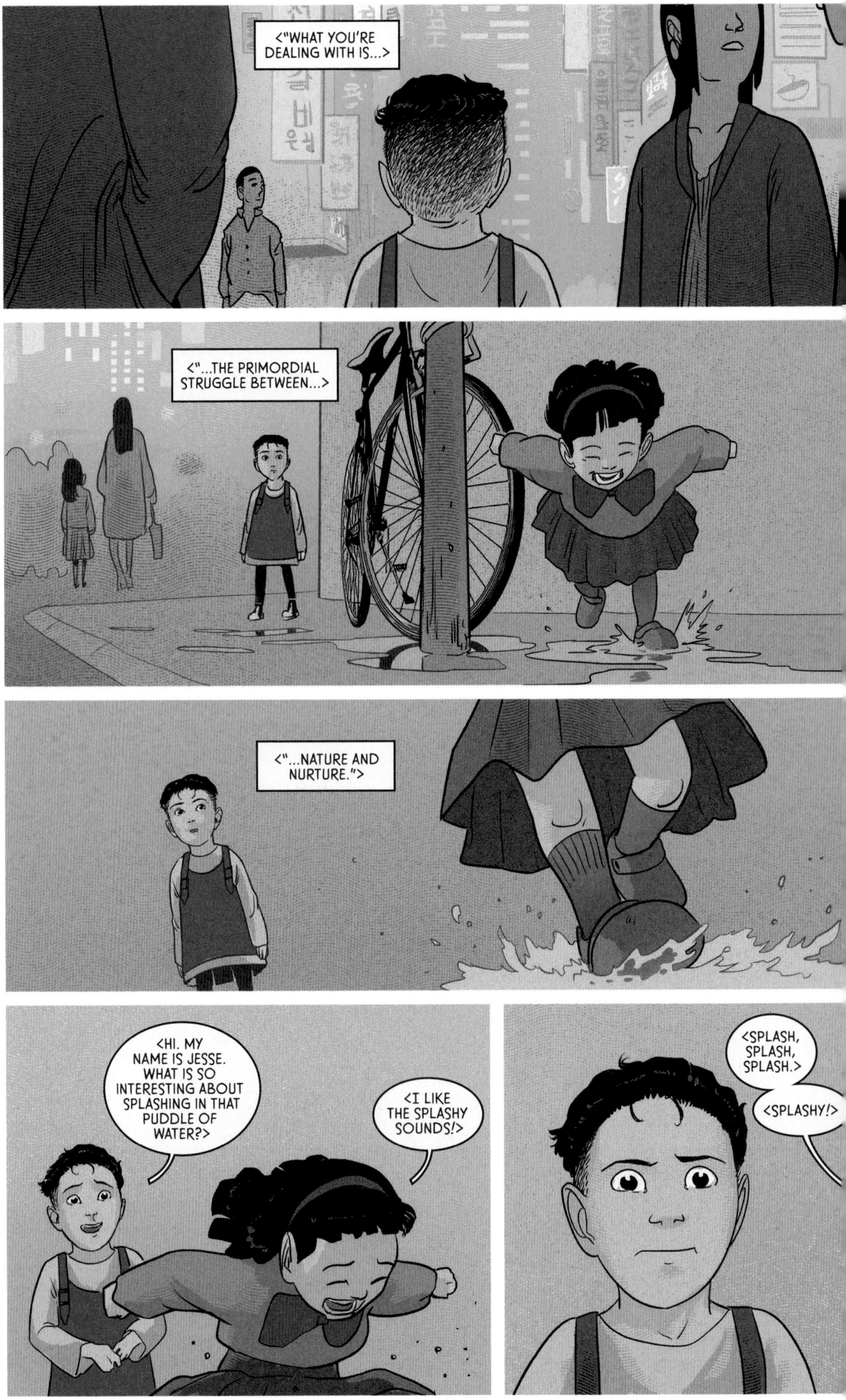
<"WHAT YOU'RE DEALING WITH IS...>
<"...THE PRIMORDIAL STRUGGLE BETWEEN...>
<"...NATURE AND NURTURE.">
<HI. MY NAME IS JESSE. WHAT IS SO INTERESTING ABOUT SPLASHING IN THAT PUDDLE OF WATER?>
<I LIKE THE SPLASHY SOUNDS!>
<SPLASH, SPLASH, SPLASH.>
<SPLASHY!>

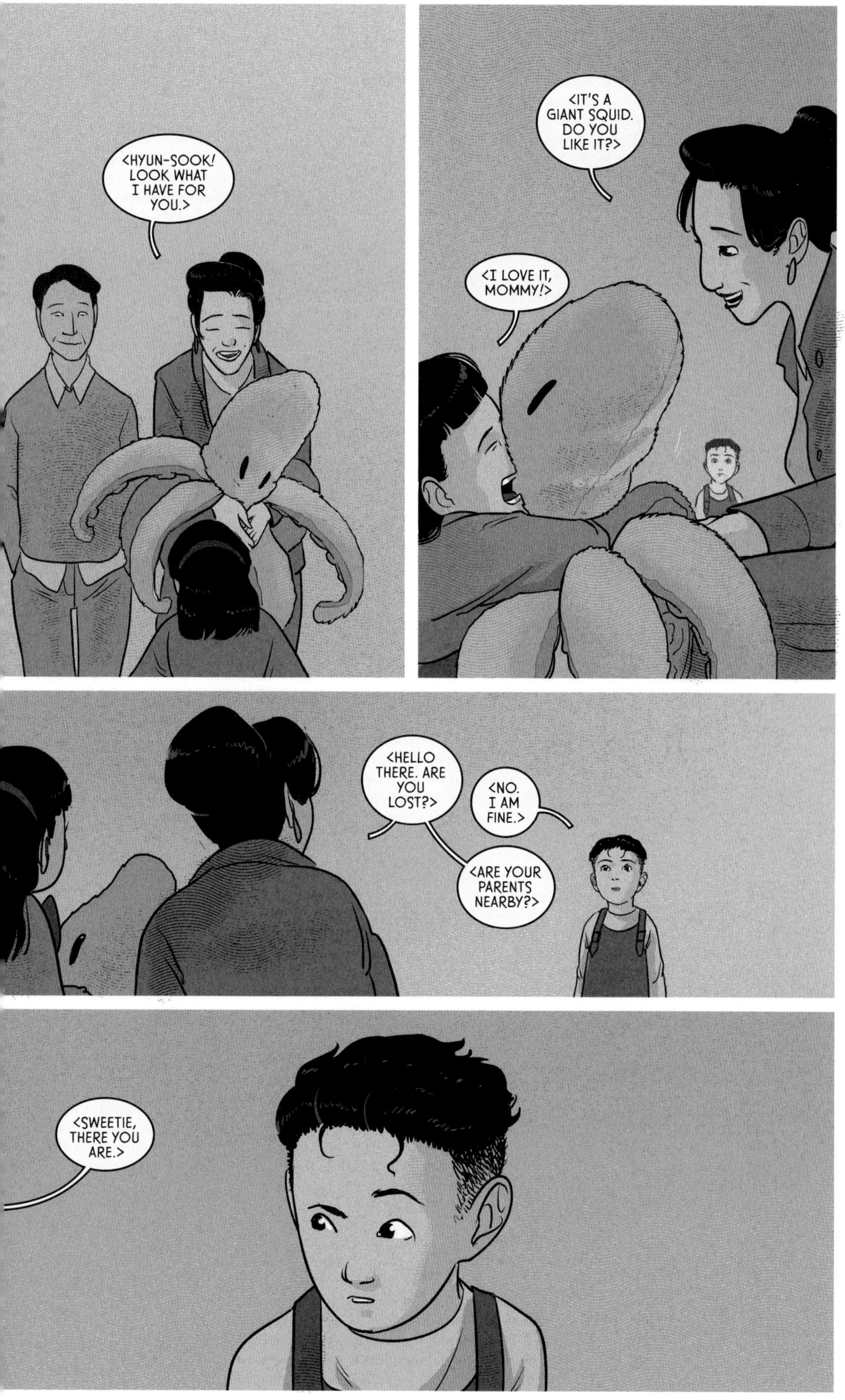
<HYUN-SOOK! LOOK WHAT I HAVE FOR YOU.>
<IT'S A GIANT SQUID. DO YOU LIKE IT?>
<I LOVE IT, MOMMY!>
<HELLO THERE. ARE YOU LOST?>
<ARE YOUR PARENTS NEARBY?>
<NO. I AM FINE.>
<SWEETIE, THERE YOU ARE.>

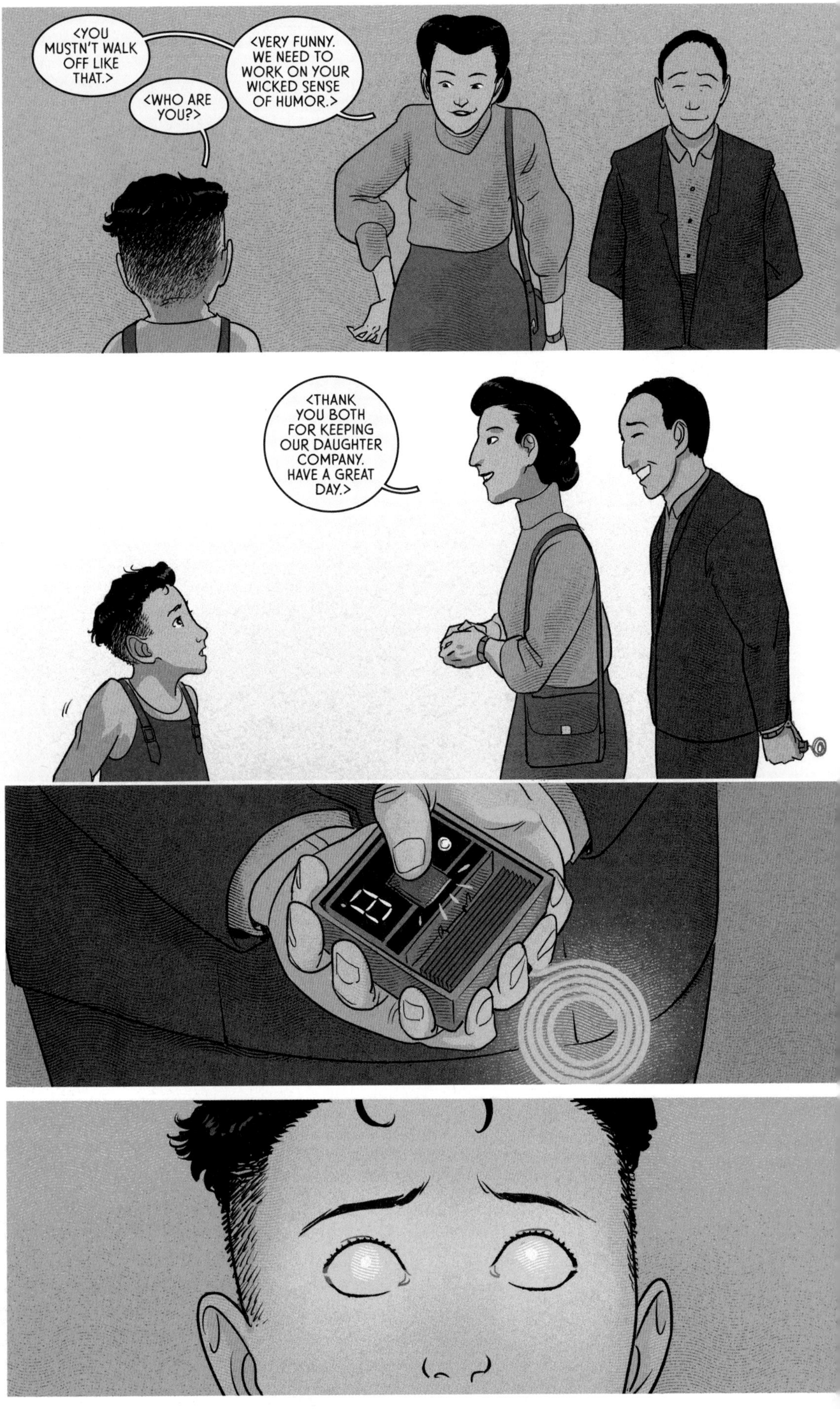
<YOU MUSTN'T WALK OFF LIKE THAT.>
<WHO ARE YOU?>
<VERY FUNNY. WE NEED TO WORK ON YOUR WICKED SENSE OF HUMOR.>
<THANK YOU BOTH FOR KEEPING OUR DAUGHTER COMPANY. HAVE A GREAT DAY.>

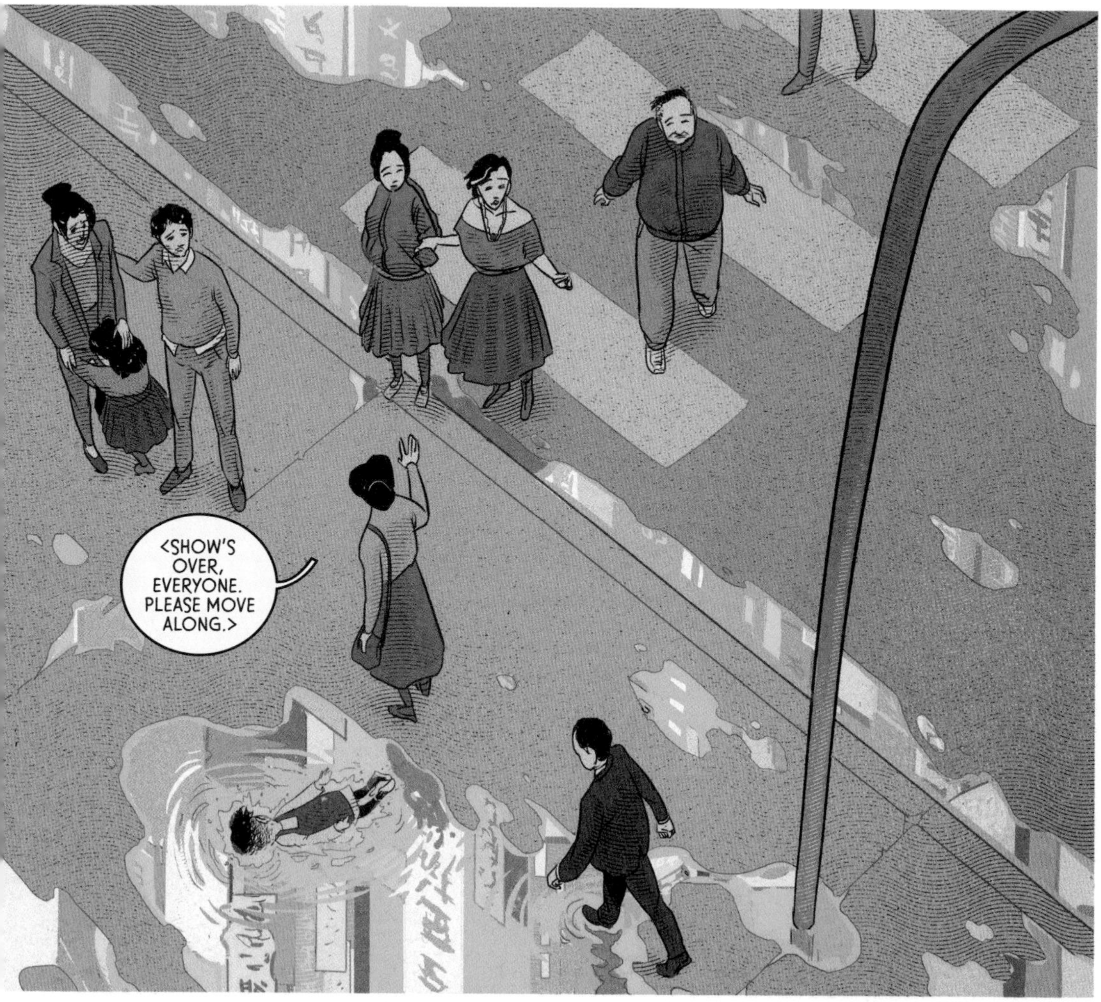
<SHOW'S OVER, EVERYONE. PLEASE MOVE ALONG.>

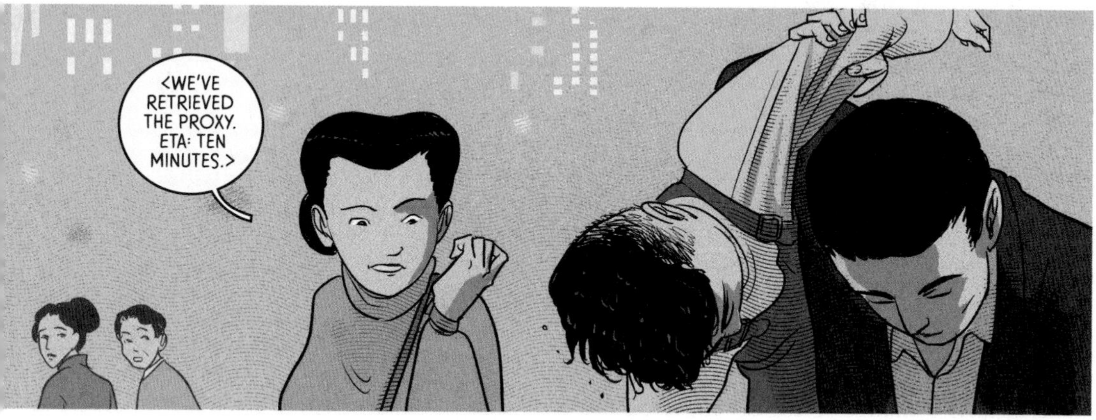
<WE'VE RETRIEVED THE PROXY. ETA: TEN MINUTES.>

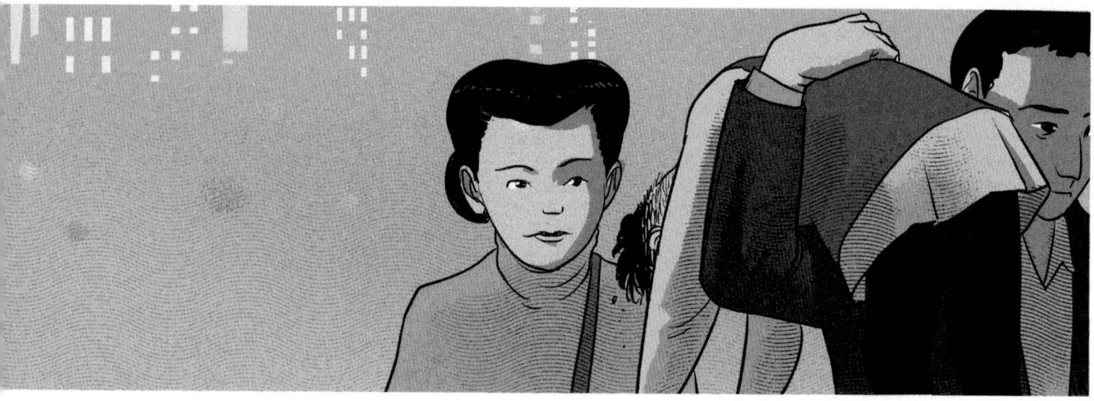

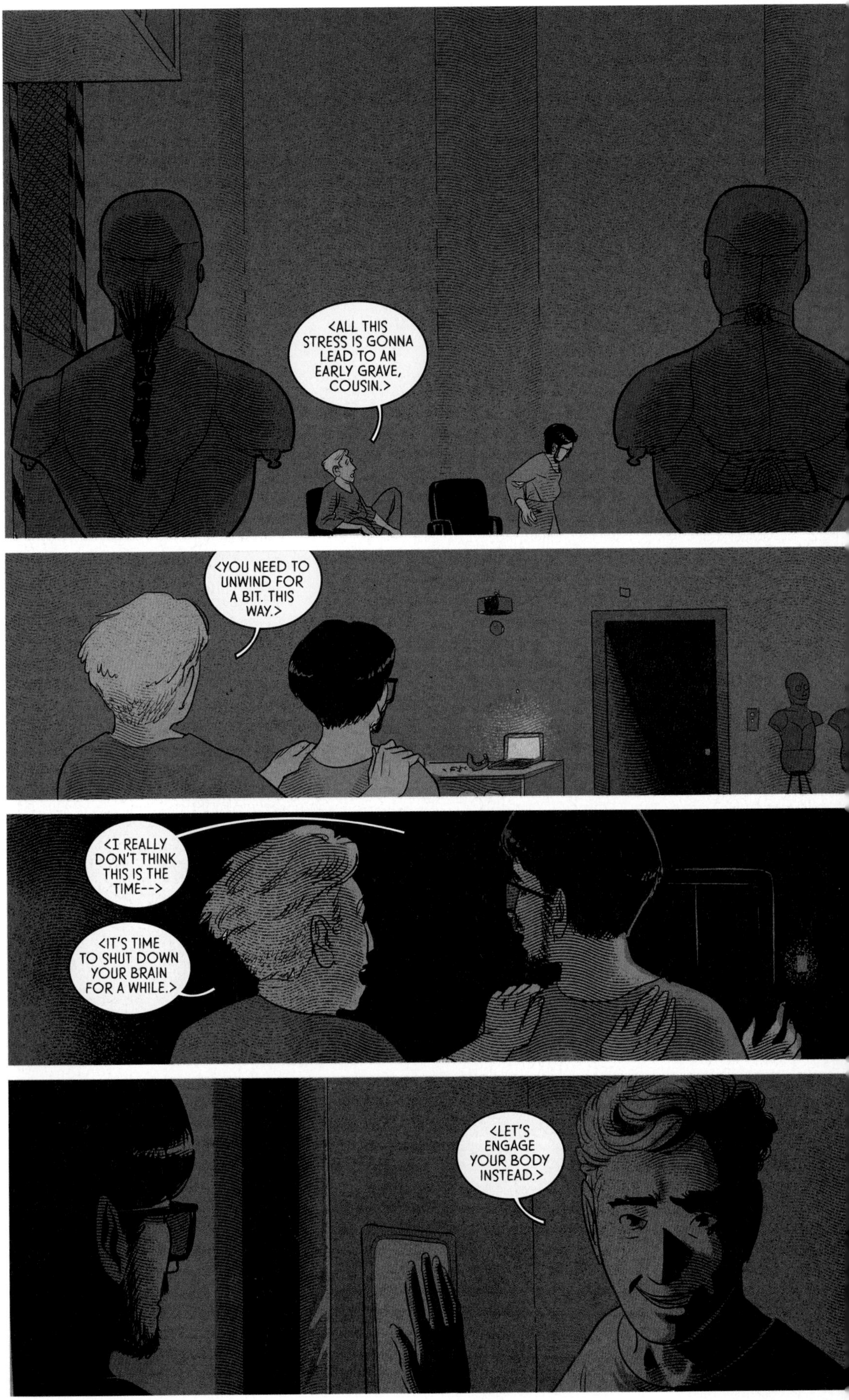
<ALL THIS STRESS IS GONNA LEAD TO AN EARLY GRAVE, COUSIN.>
<YOU NEED TO UNWIND FOR A BIT. THIS WAY.>
<I REALLY DON'T THINK THIS IS THE TIME-->
<IT'S TIME TO SHUT DOWN YOUR BRAIN FOR A WHILE.>
<LET'S ENGAGE YOUR BODY INSTEAD.>

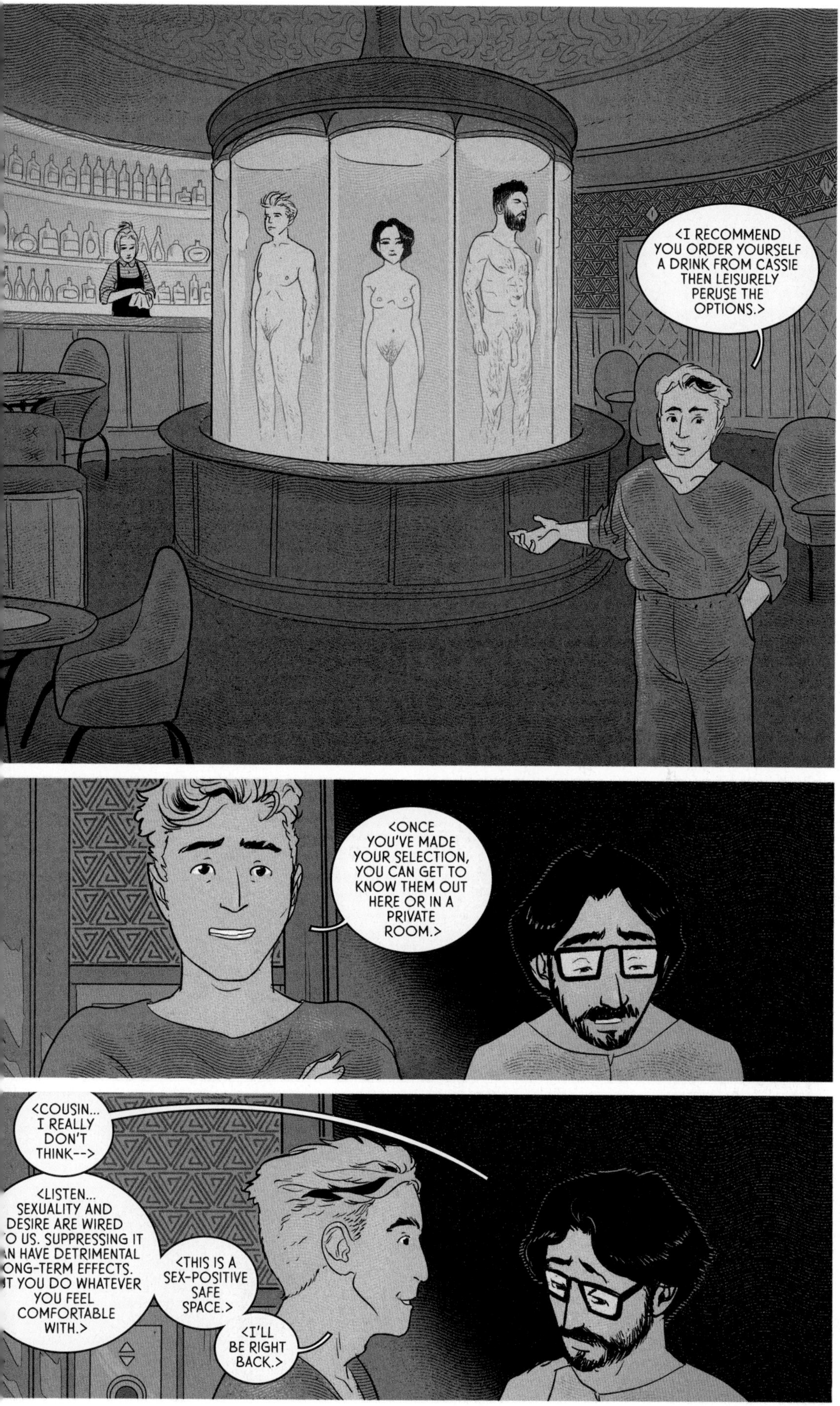
<I RECOMMEND YOU ORDER YOURSELF A DRINK FROM CASSIE THEN LEISURELY PERUSE THE OPTIONS.>
<ONCE YOU'VE MADE YOUR SELECTION, YOU CAN GET TO KNOW THEM OUT HERE OR IN A PRIVATE ROOM.>
<COUSIN... I REALLY DON'T THINK-->
<LISTEN... SEXUALITY AND DESIRE ARE WIRED O US. SUPPRESSING IT AN HAVE DETRIMENTAL ONG-TERM EFFECTS. T YOU DO WHATEVER YOU FEEL COMFORTABLE WITH.>
<THIS IS A SEX-POSITIVE SAFE SPACE.>
<I'LL BE RIGHT BACK.>

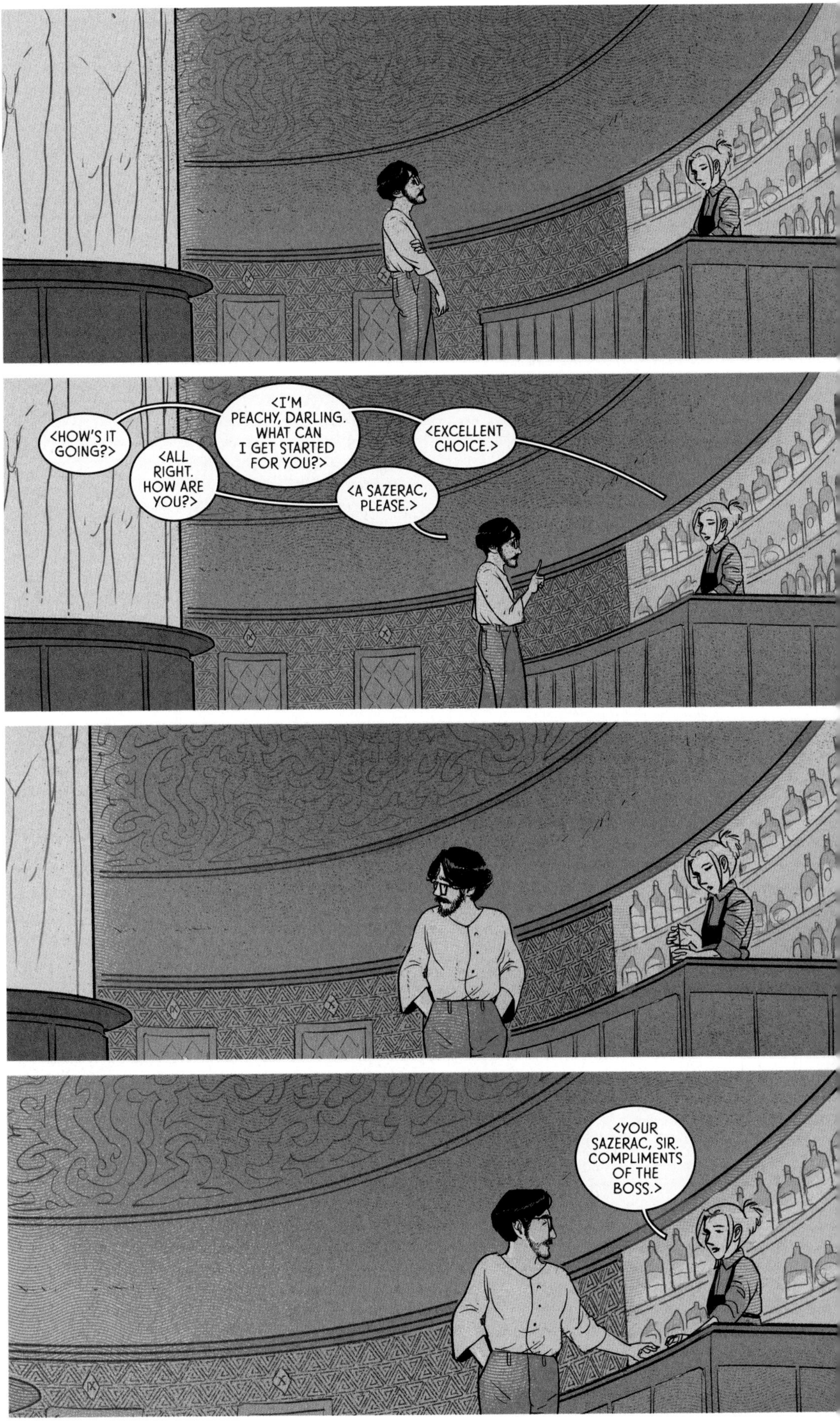
<HOW'S IT GOING?>
<ALL RIGHT. HOW ARE YOU?>
<I'M PEACHY, DARLING. WHAT CAN I GET STARTED FOR YOU?>
<A SAZERAC, PLEASE.>
<EXCELLENT CHOICE.>
<YOUR SAZERAC, SIR. COMPLIMENTS OF THE BOSS.>

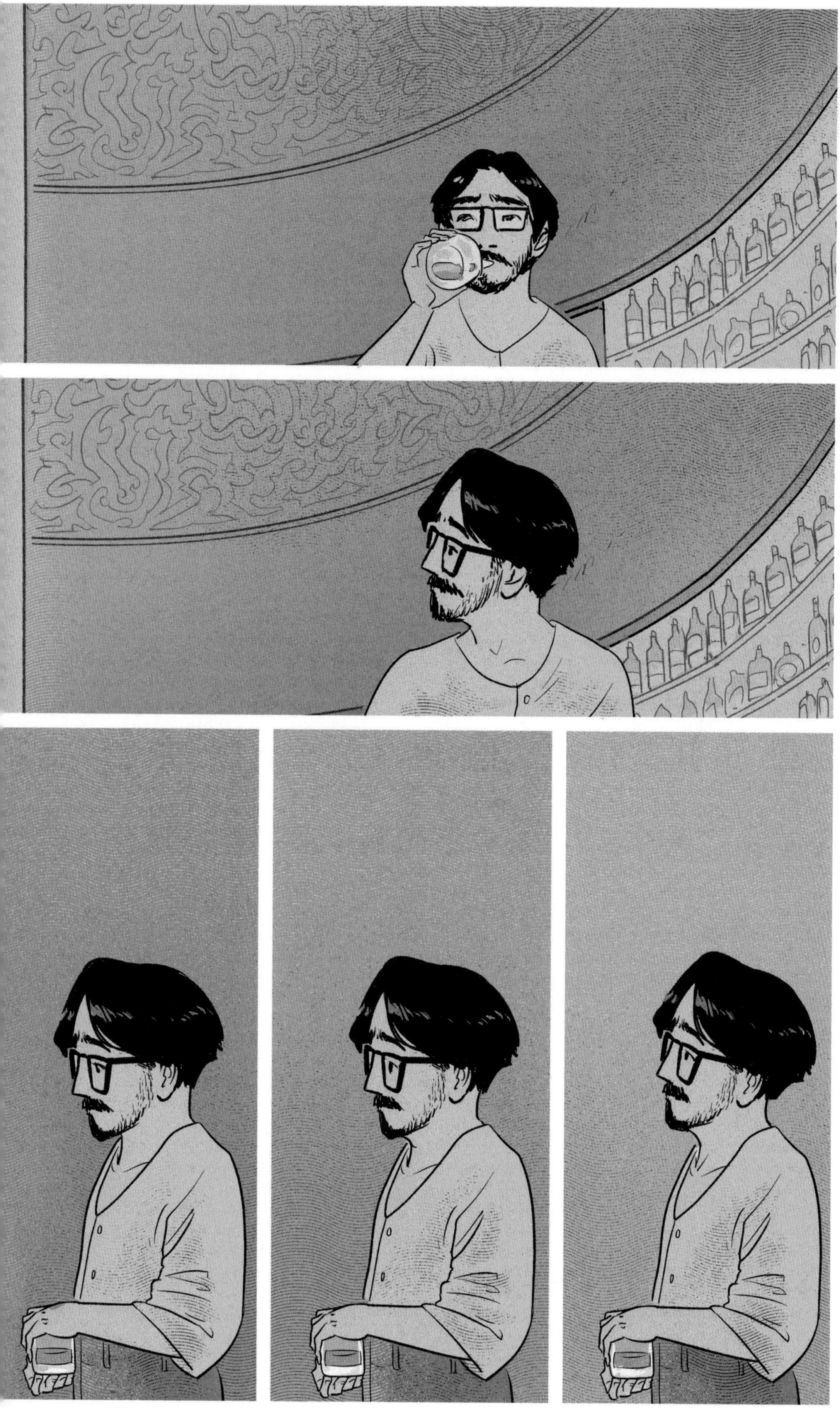

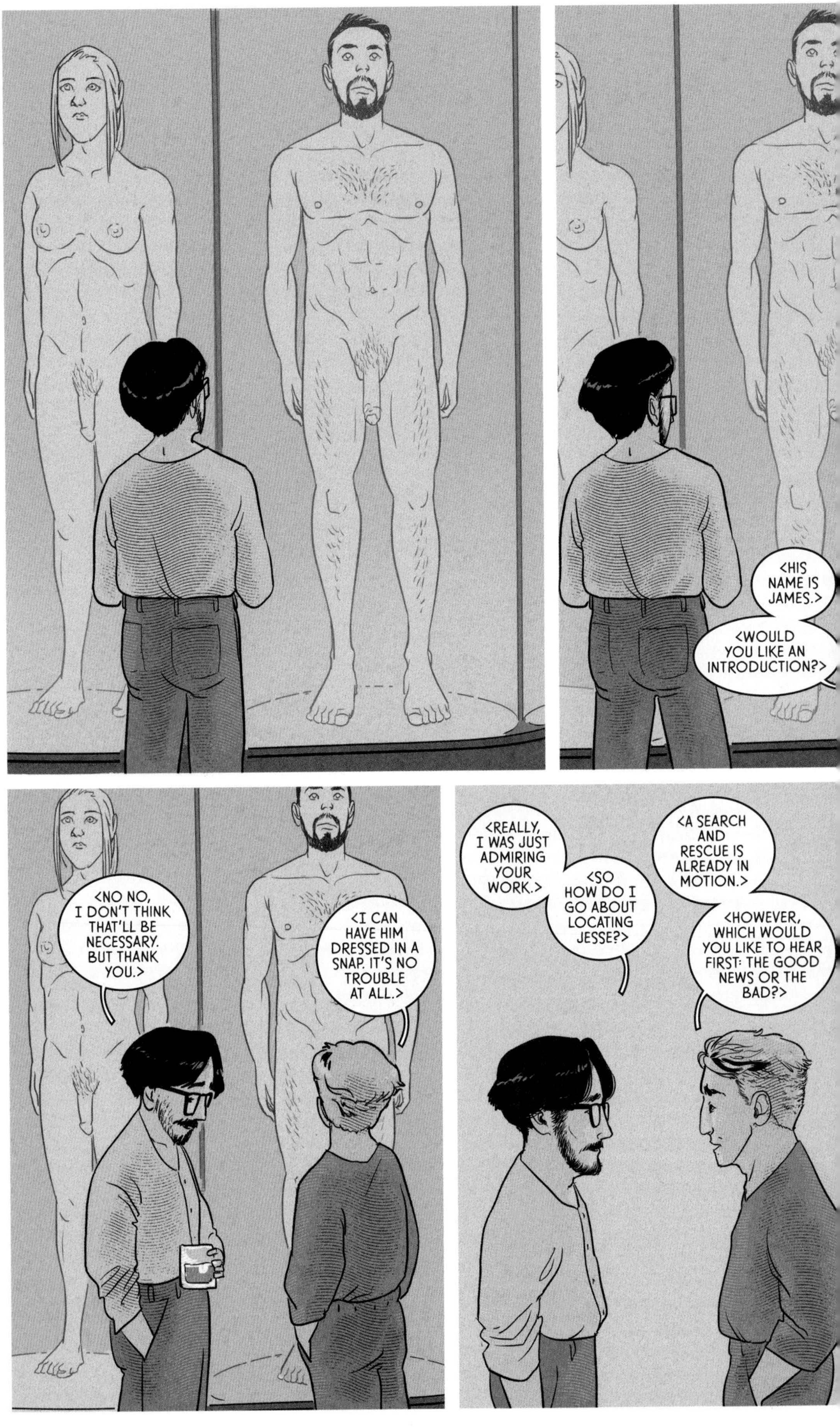
<HIS NAME IS JAMES.>
<WOULD YOU LIKE AN INTRODUCTION?>
<NO NO, I DON'T THINK THAT'LL BE NECESSARY. BUT THANK YOU.>
<I CAN HAVE HIM DRESSED IN A SNAP. IT'S NO TROUBLE AT ALL.>
<REALLY, I WAS JUST ADMIRING YOUR WORK.>
<SO HOW DO I GO ABOUT LOCATING JESSE?>
<A SEARCH AND RESCUE IS ALREADY IN MOTION.>
<HOWEVER, WHICH WOULD YOU LIKE TO HEAR FIRST: THE GOOD NEWS OR THE BAD?>

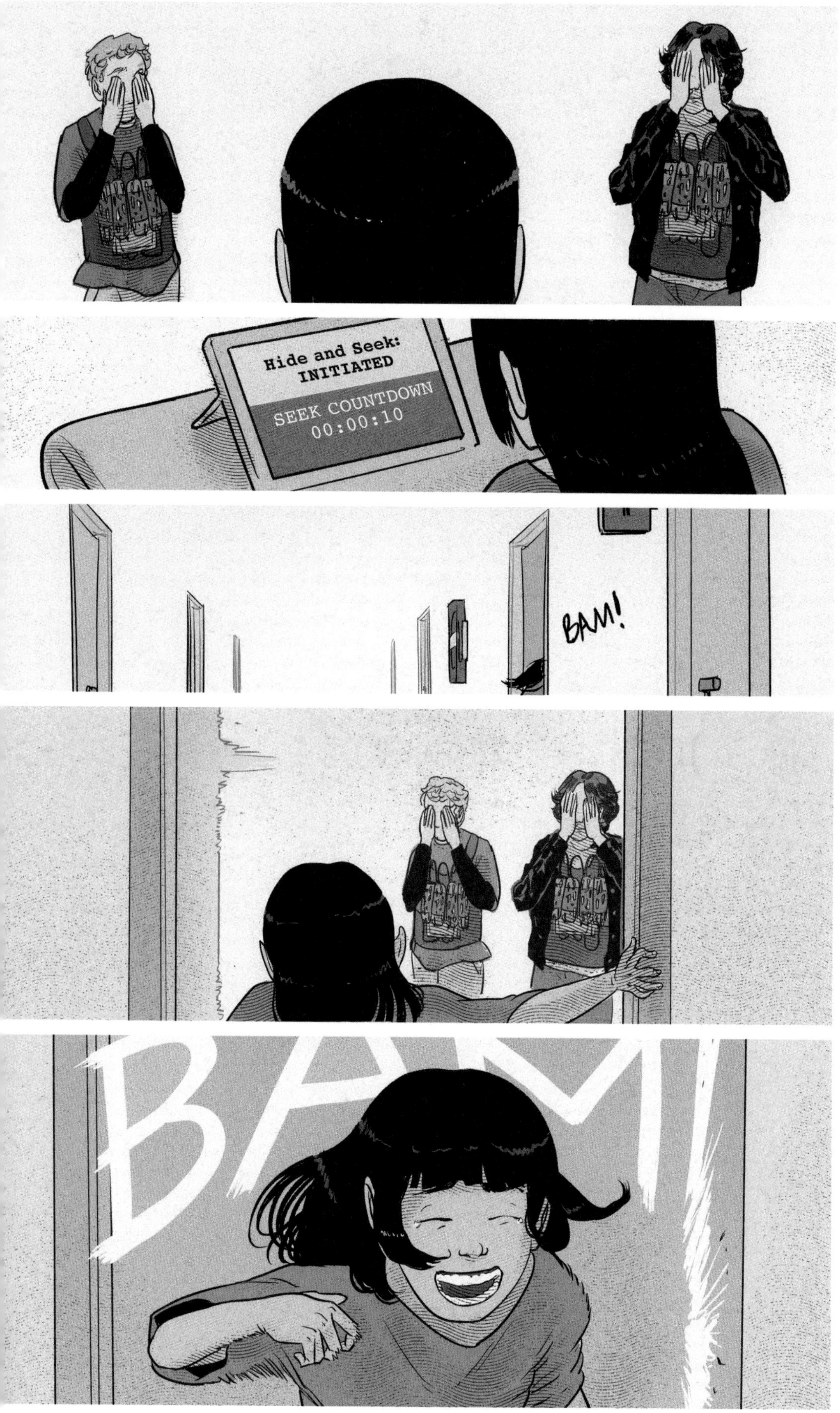
Hide and Seek:
INITIATED
SEEK COUNTDOWN
00:00:10
BAM!
BAM

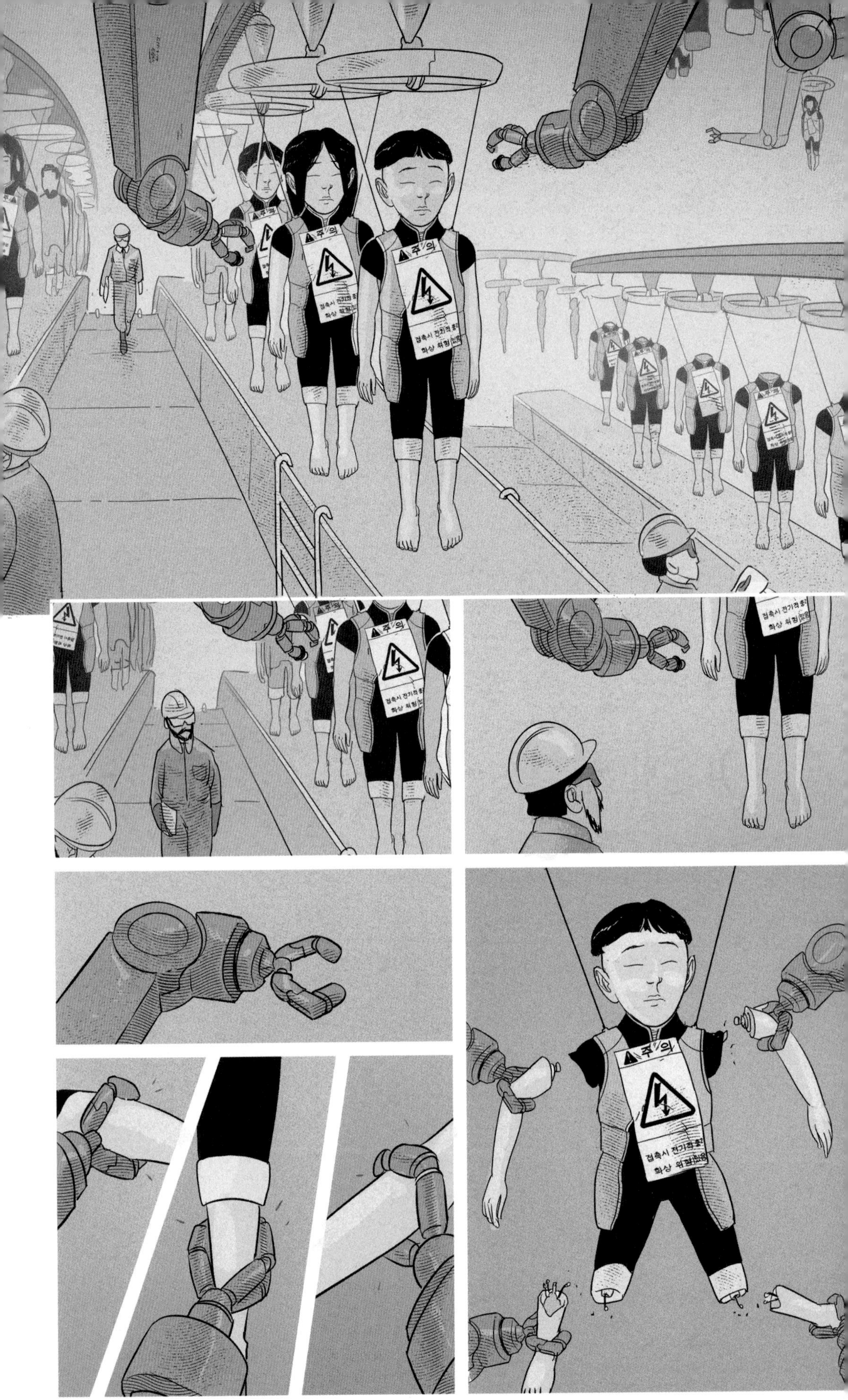

주의
접촉시 전기적
화상 위험

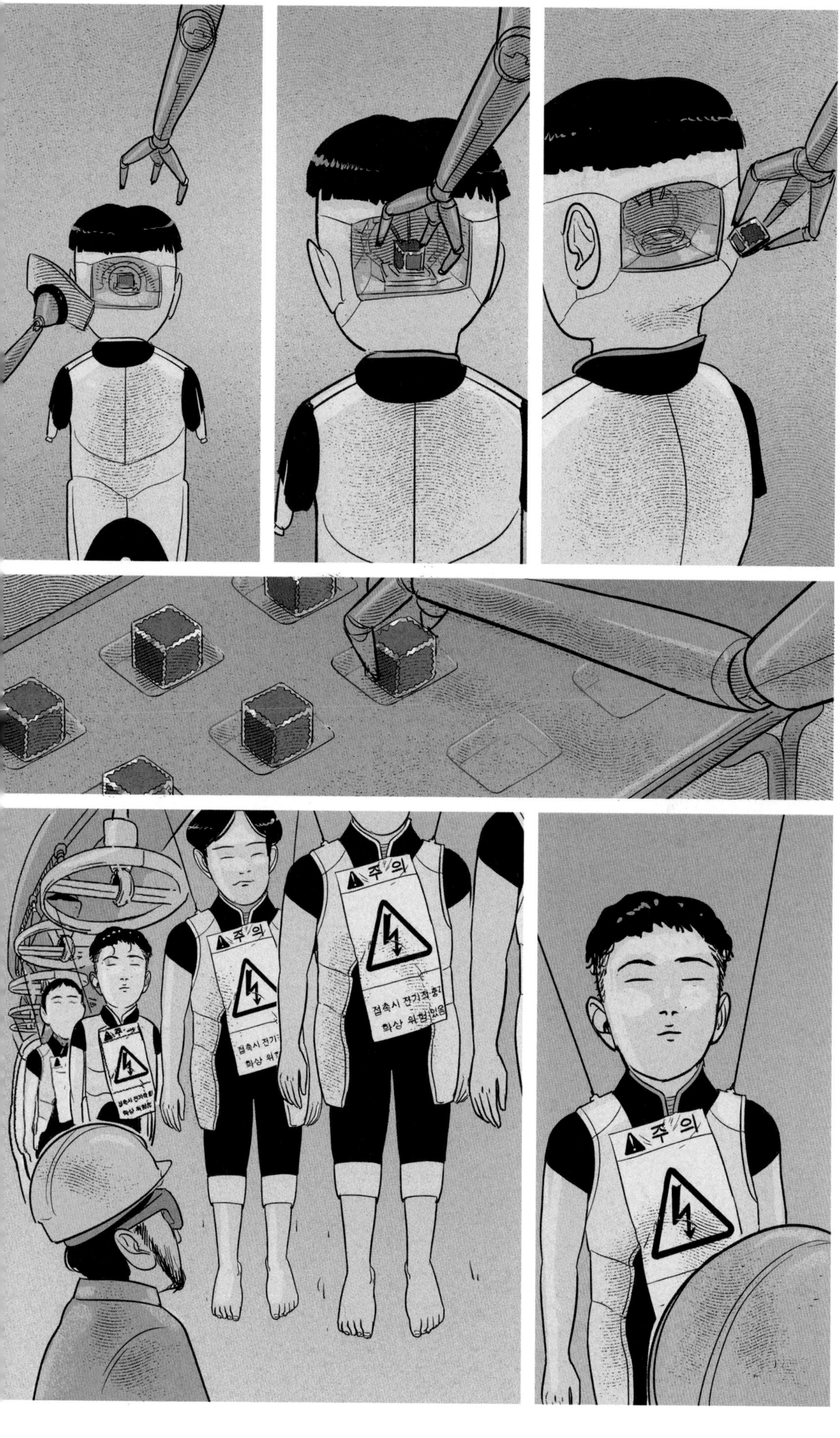
주의
접촉시 전기
화상 위
주의
접촉시 전기
화상 위험있음
주의

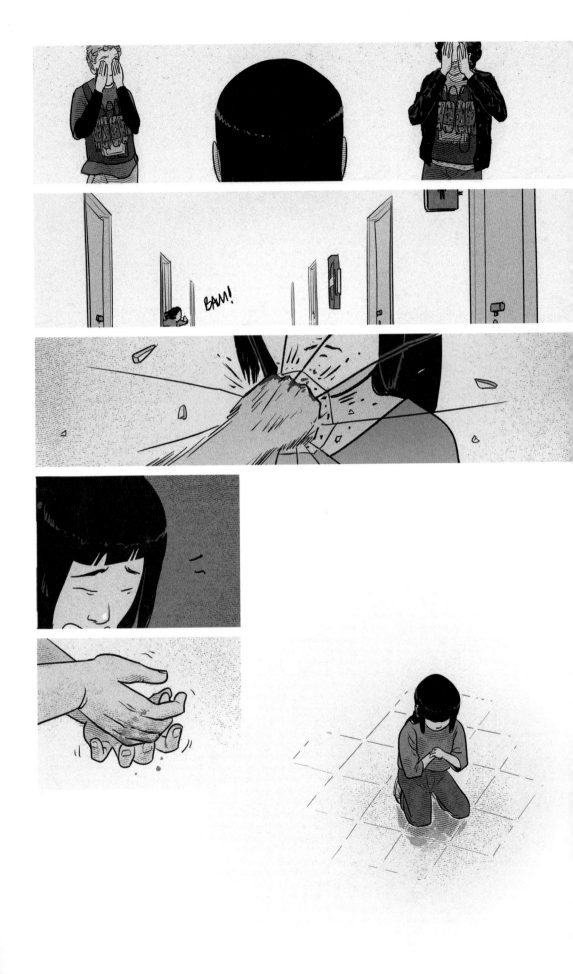

BAM!

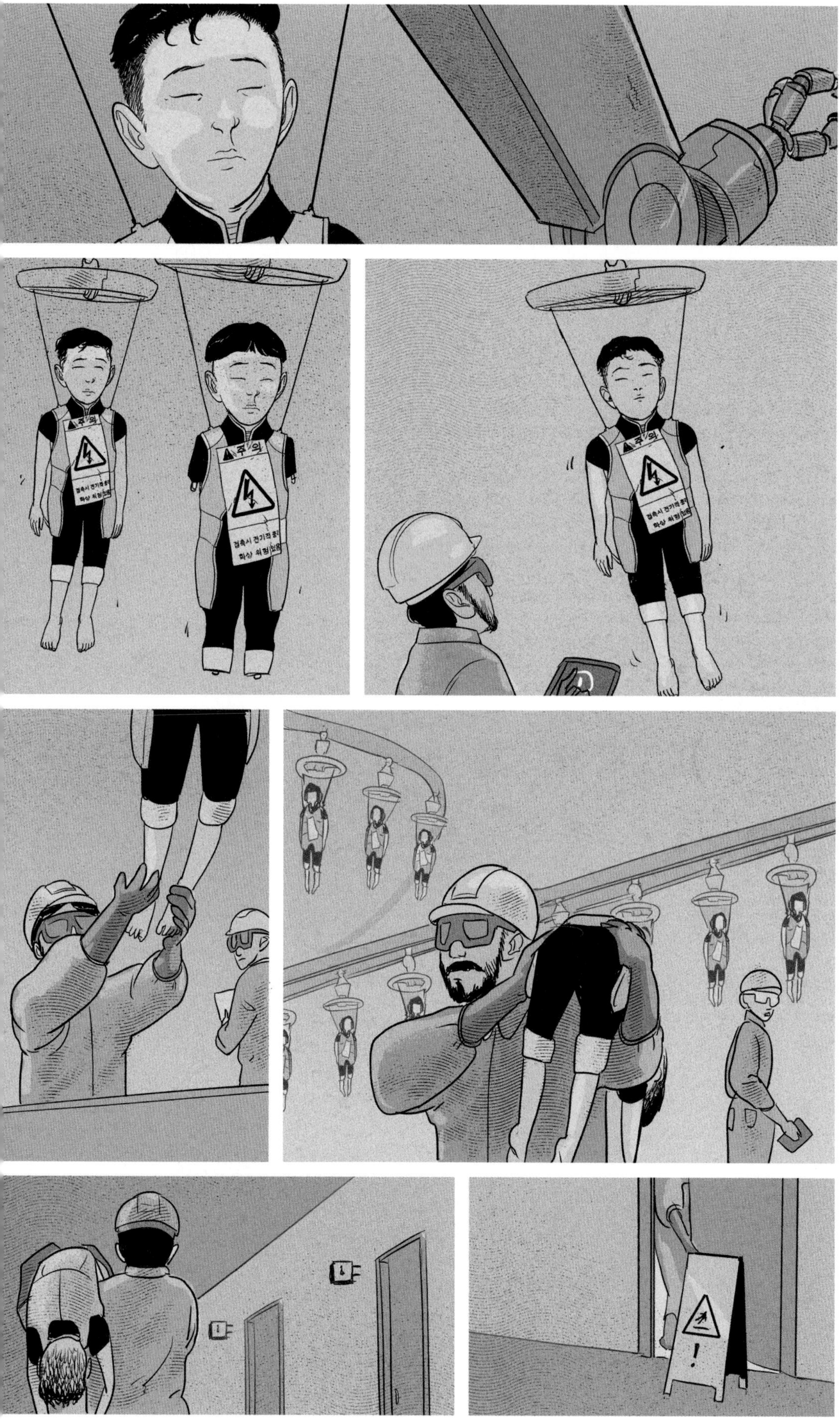
주의
접촉시 전기적
화상 위험 있음

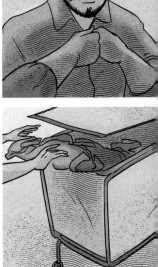

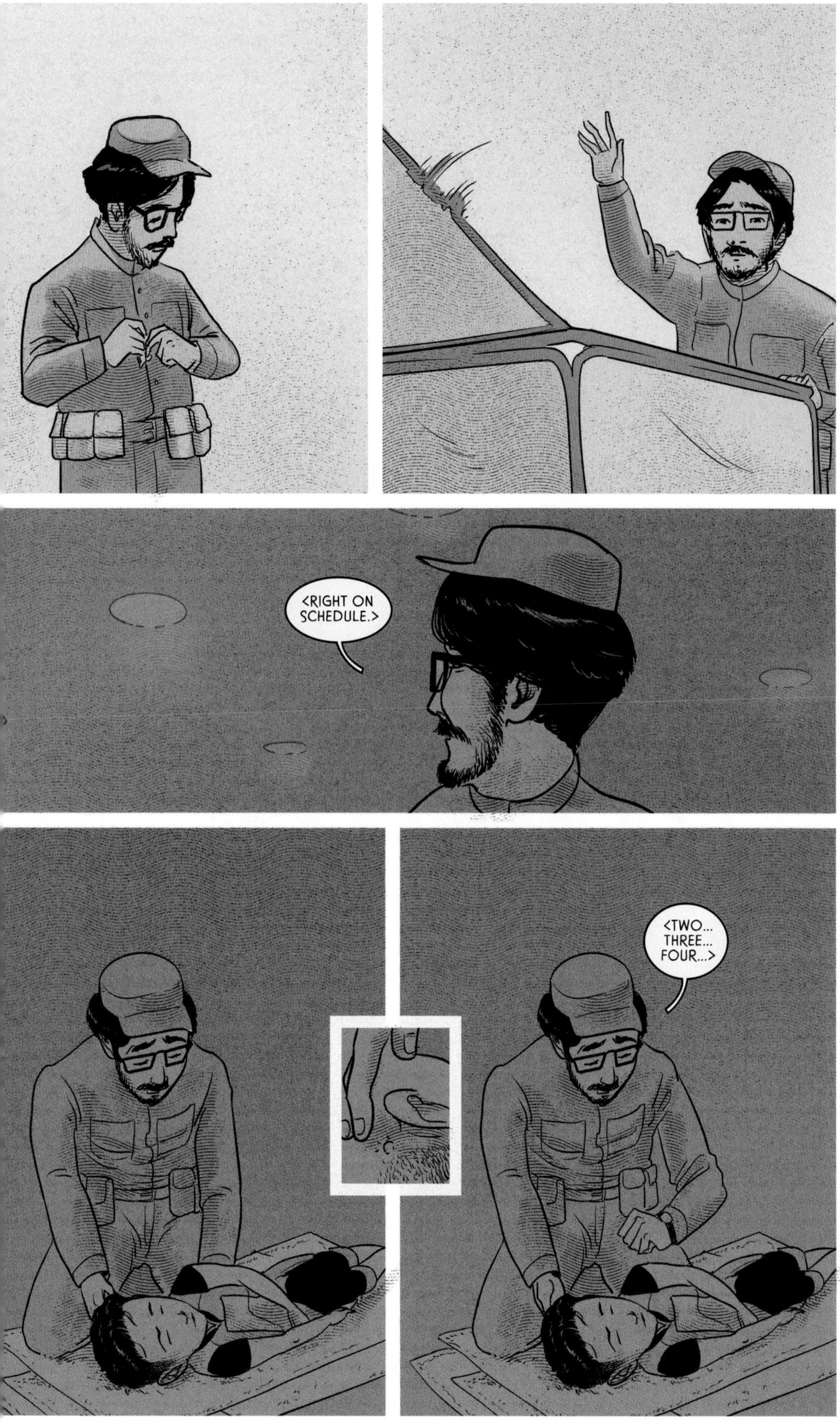
<RIGHT ON SCHEDULE.>
<TWO... THREE... FOUR...>

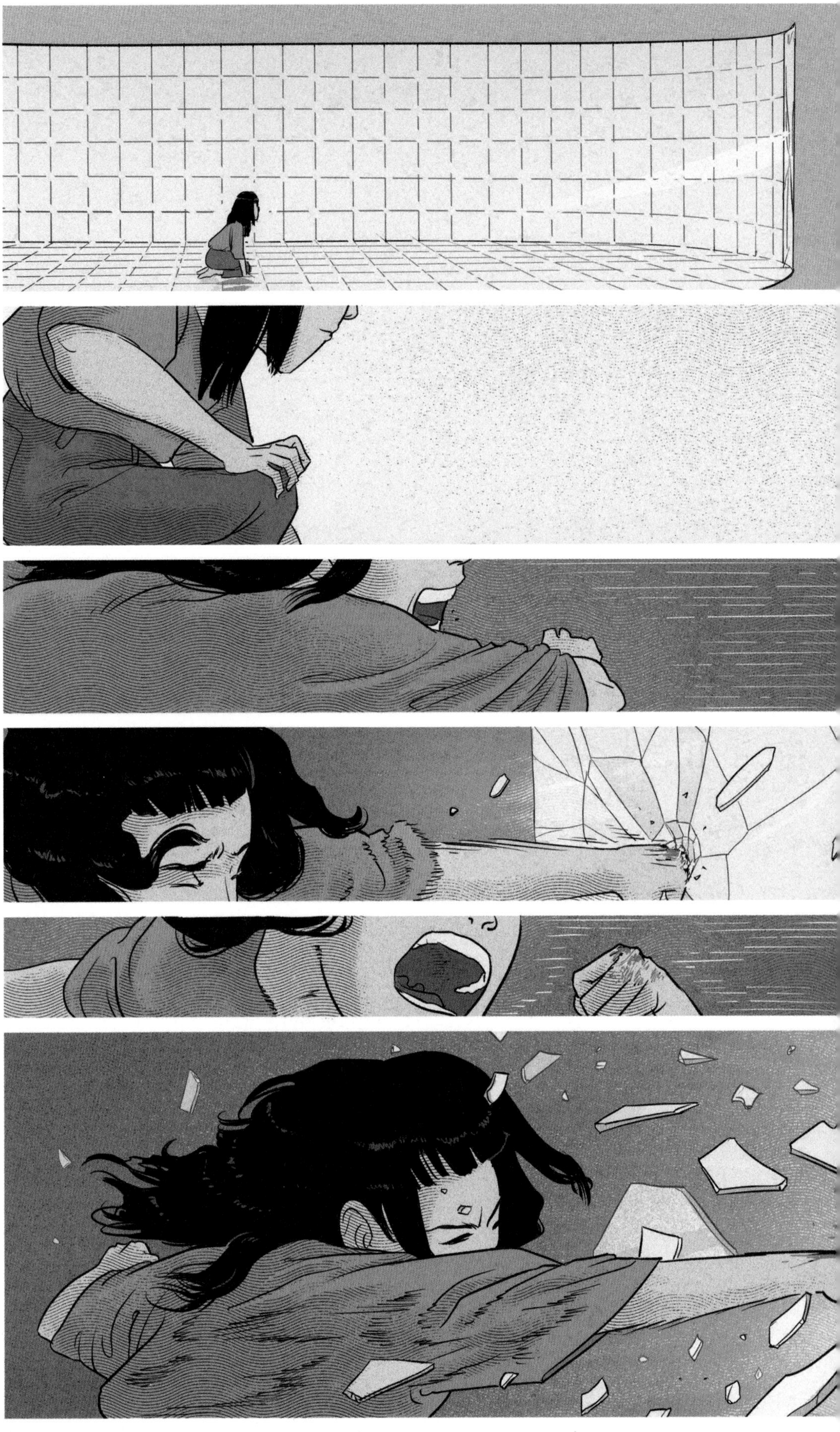

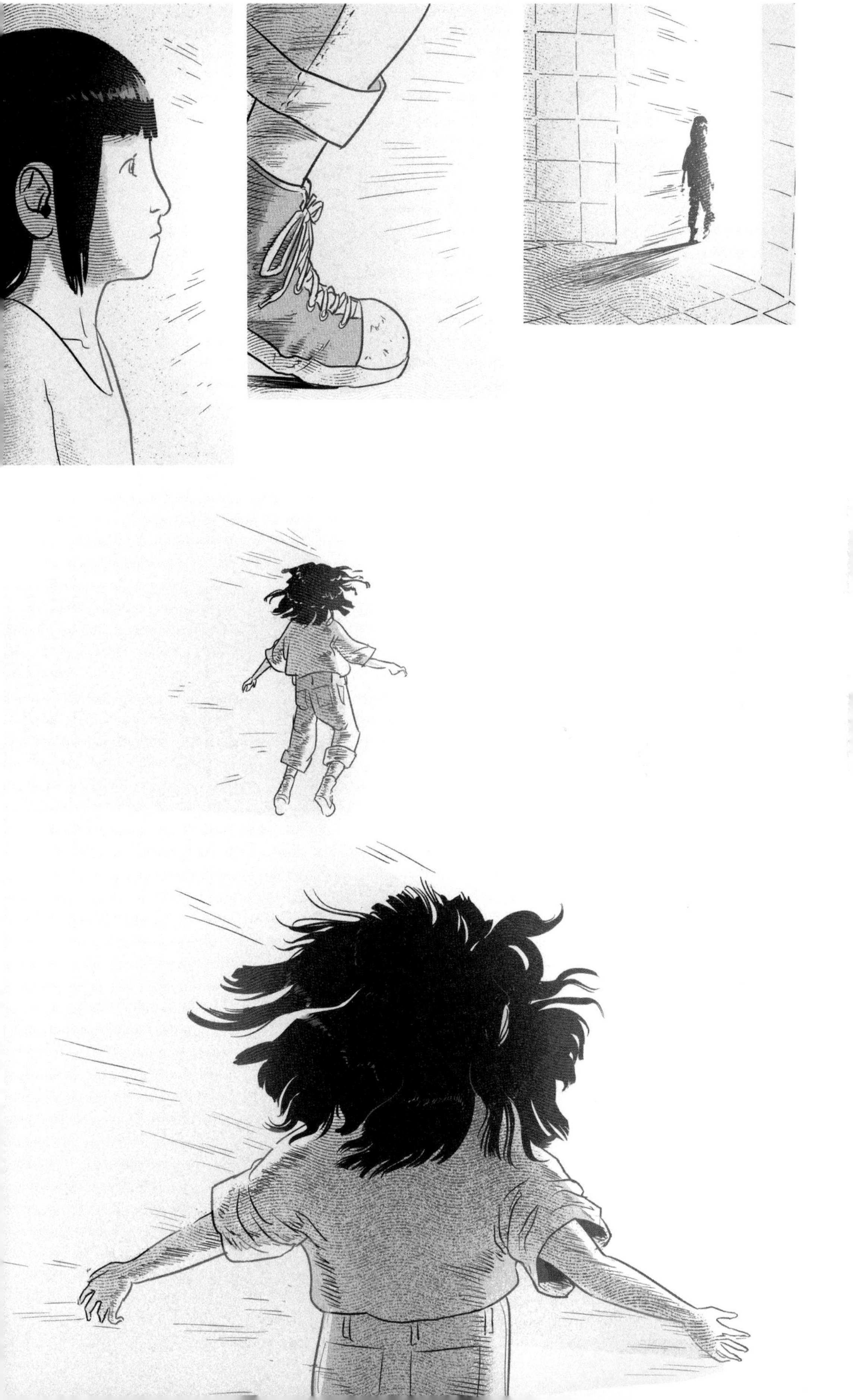

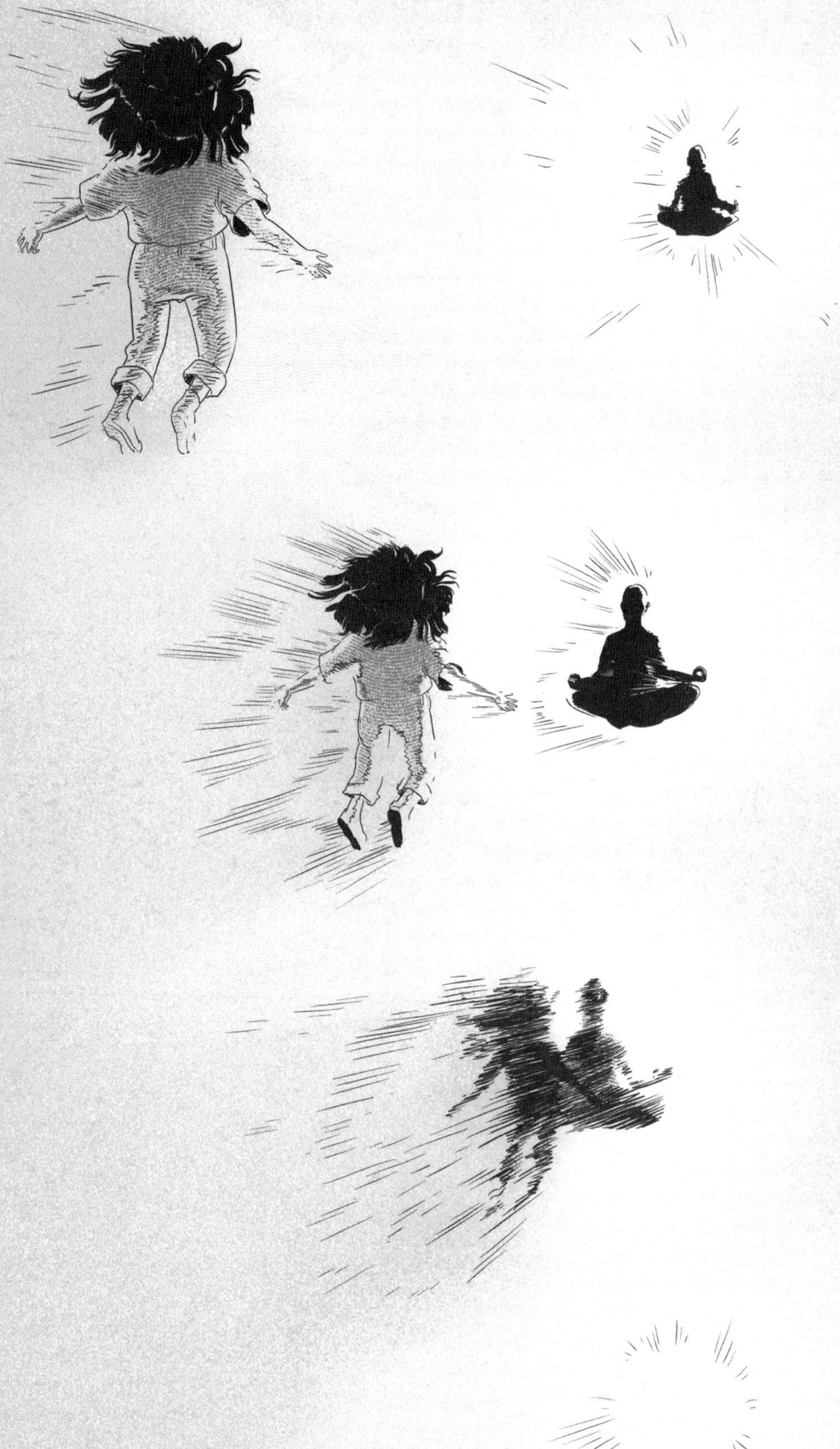

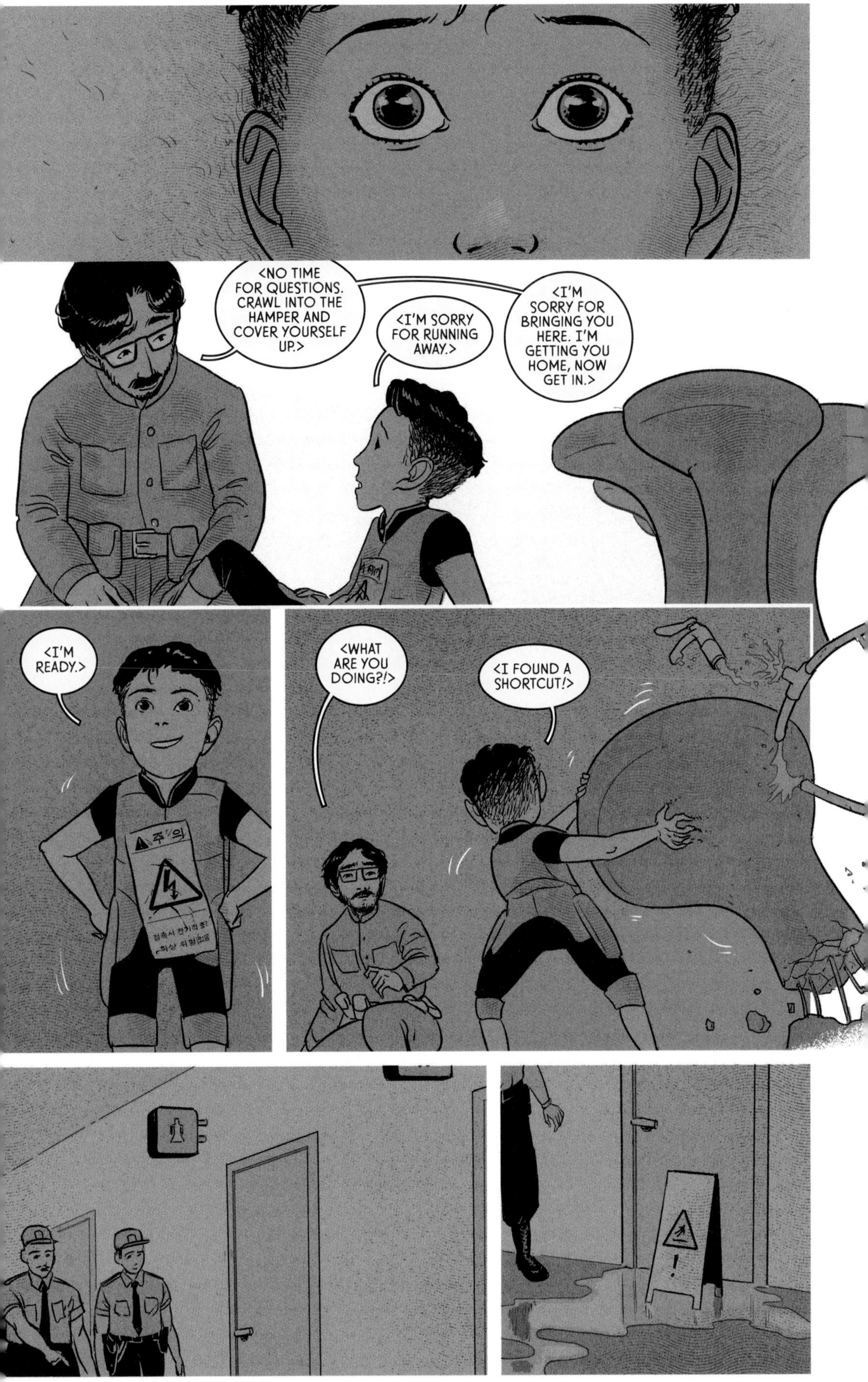
<NO TIME FOR QUESTIONS. CRAWL INTO THE HAMPER AND COVER YOURSELF UP.>
<I'M SORRY FOR RUNNING AWAY.>
<I'M SORRY FOR BRINGING YOU HERE. I'M GETTING YOU HOME, NOW GET IN.>
<I'M READY.>
주의
<WHAT ARE YOU DOING?!>
<I FOUND A SHORTCUT!>

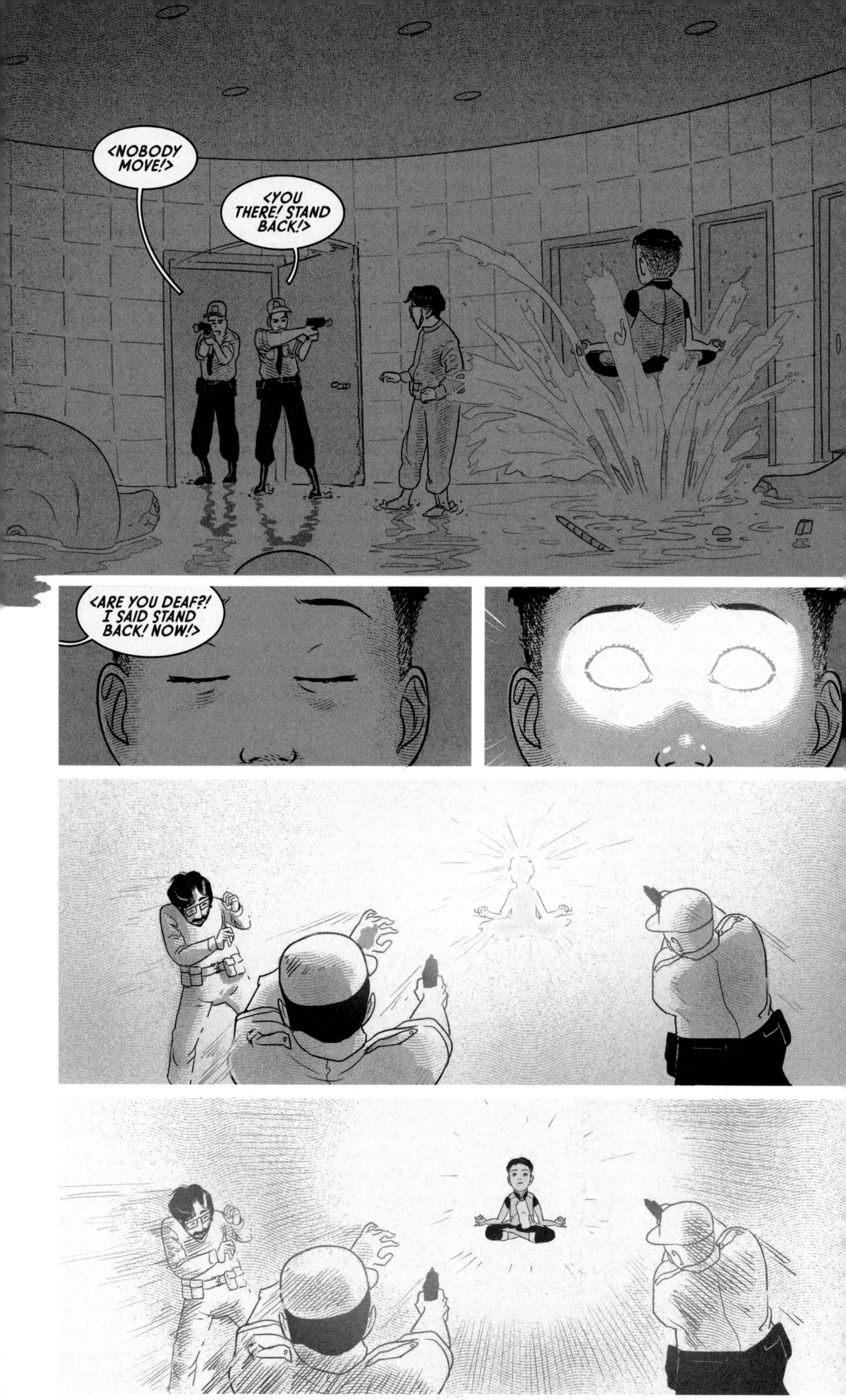
<NOBODY MOVE!>
<YOU THERE! STAND BACK!>
<ARE YOU DEAF?! I SAID STAND BACK! NOW!>

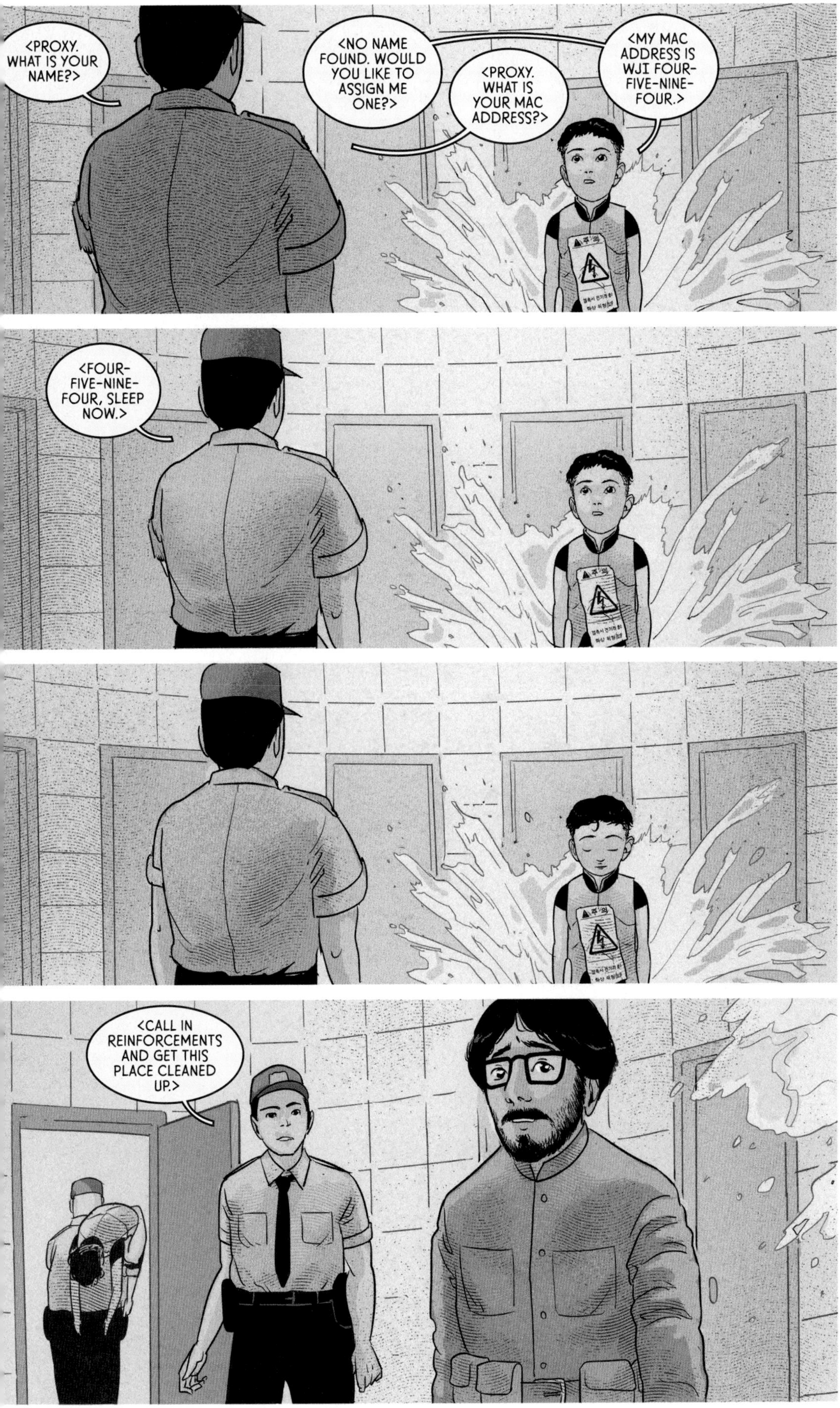
<PROXY. WHAT IS YOUR NAME?>
<NO NAME FOUND. WOULD YOU LIKE TO ASSIGN ME ONE?>
<PROXY. WHAT IS YOUR MAC ADDRESS?>
<MY MAC ADDRESS IS WJI FOUR-FIVE-NINE-FOUR.>
<FOUR-FIVE-NINE-FOUR, SLEEP NOW.>
<CALL IN REINFORCEMENTS AND GET THIS PLACE CLEANED UP.>

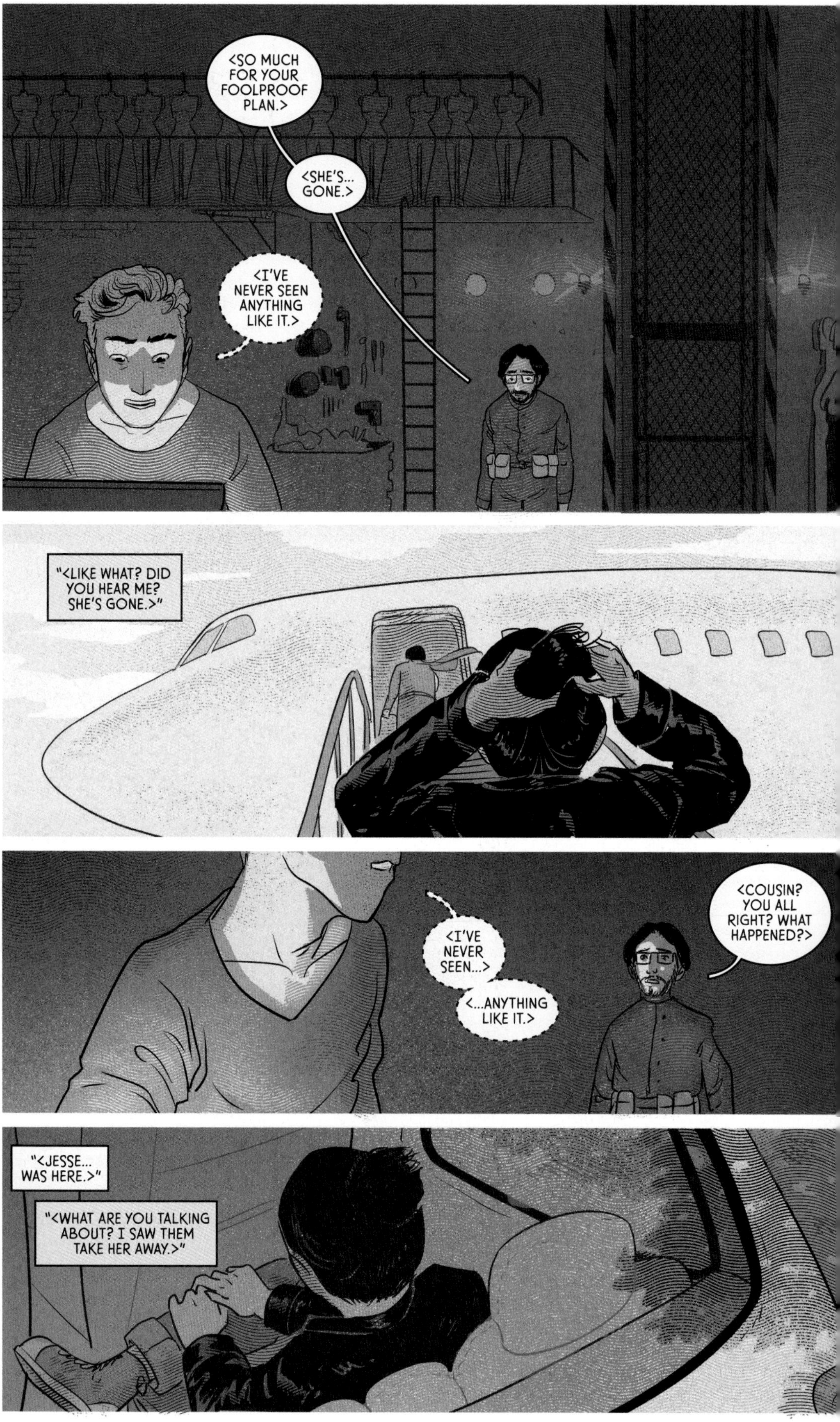
<SO MUCH FOR YOUR FOOLPROOF PLAN.>
<SHE'S... GONE.>
<I'VE NEVER SEEN ANYTHING LIKE IT.>
"<LIKE WHAT? DID YOU HEAR ME? SHE'S GONE.>"
<I'VE NEVER SEEN...>
<...ANYTHING LIKE IT.>
<COUSIN? YOU ALL RIGHT? WHAT HAPPENED?>
"<JESSE... WAS HERE.>"
"<WHAT ARE YOU TALKING ABOUT? I SAW THEM TAKE HER AWAY.>"

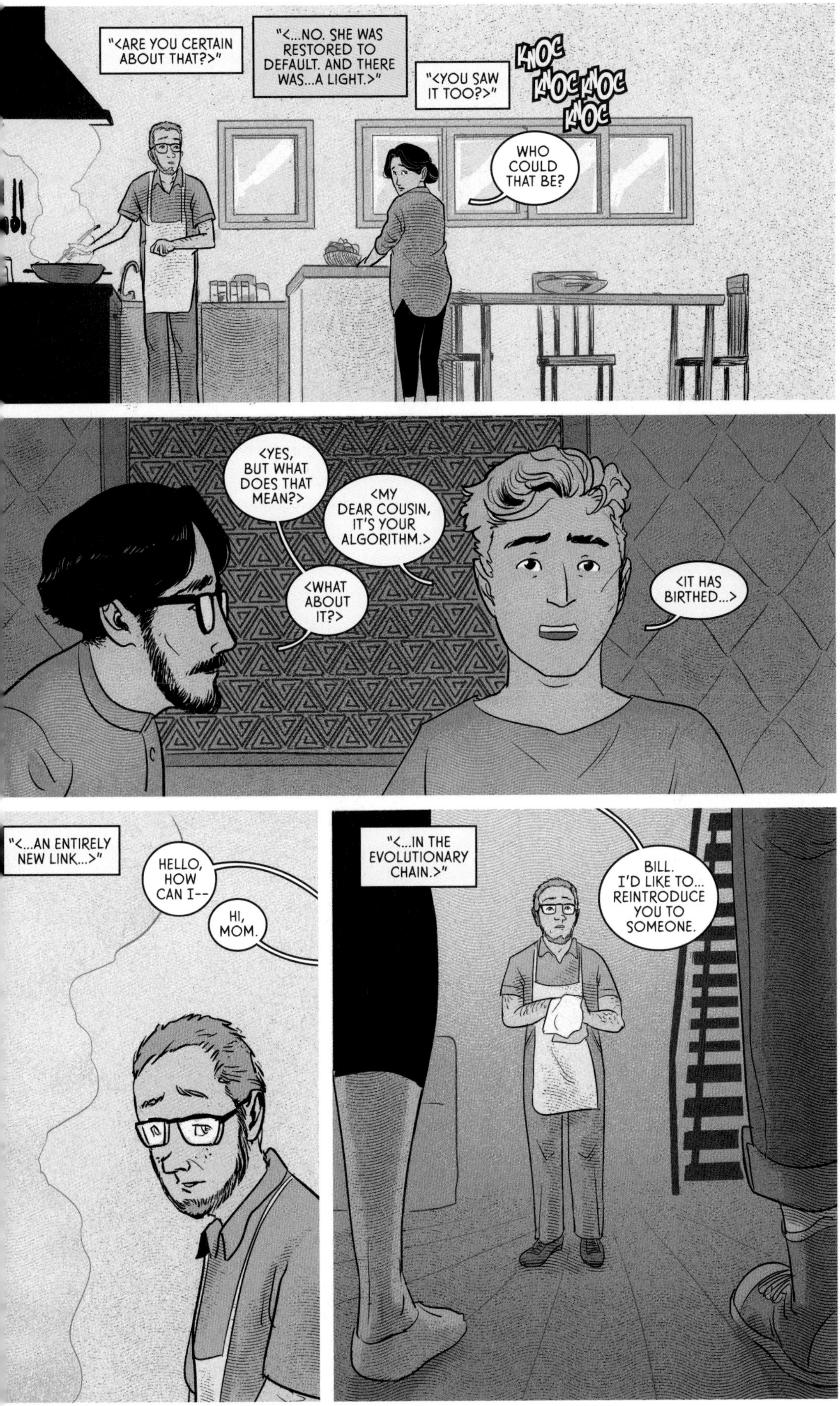

"<ARE YOU CERTAIN ABOUT THAT?>"
"<...NO. SHE WAS RESTORED TO DEFAULT. AND THERE WAS...A LIGHT.>"
"<YOU SAW IT TOO?>"
KNOC KNOC KNOC KNOC
WHO COULD THAT BE?
<YES, BUT WHAT DOES THAT MEAN?>
<MY DEAR COUSIN, IT'S YOUR ALGORITHM.>
<WHAT ABOUT IT?>
<IT HAS BIRTHED...>
"<...AN ENTIRELY NEW LINK...>"
HELLO, HOW CAN I--
HI, MOM.
"<...IN THE EVOLUTIONARY CHAIN.>"
BILL. I'D LIKE TO... REINTRODUCE YOU TO SOMEONE.

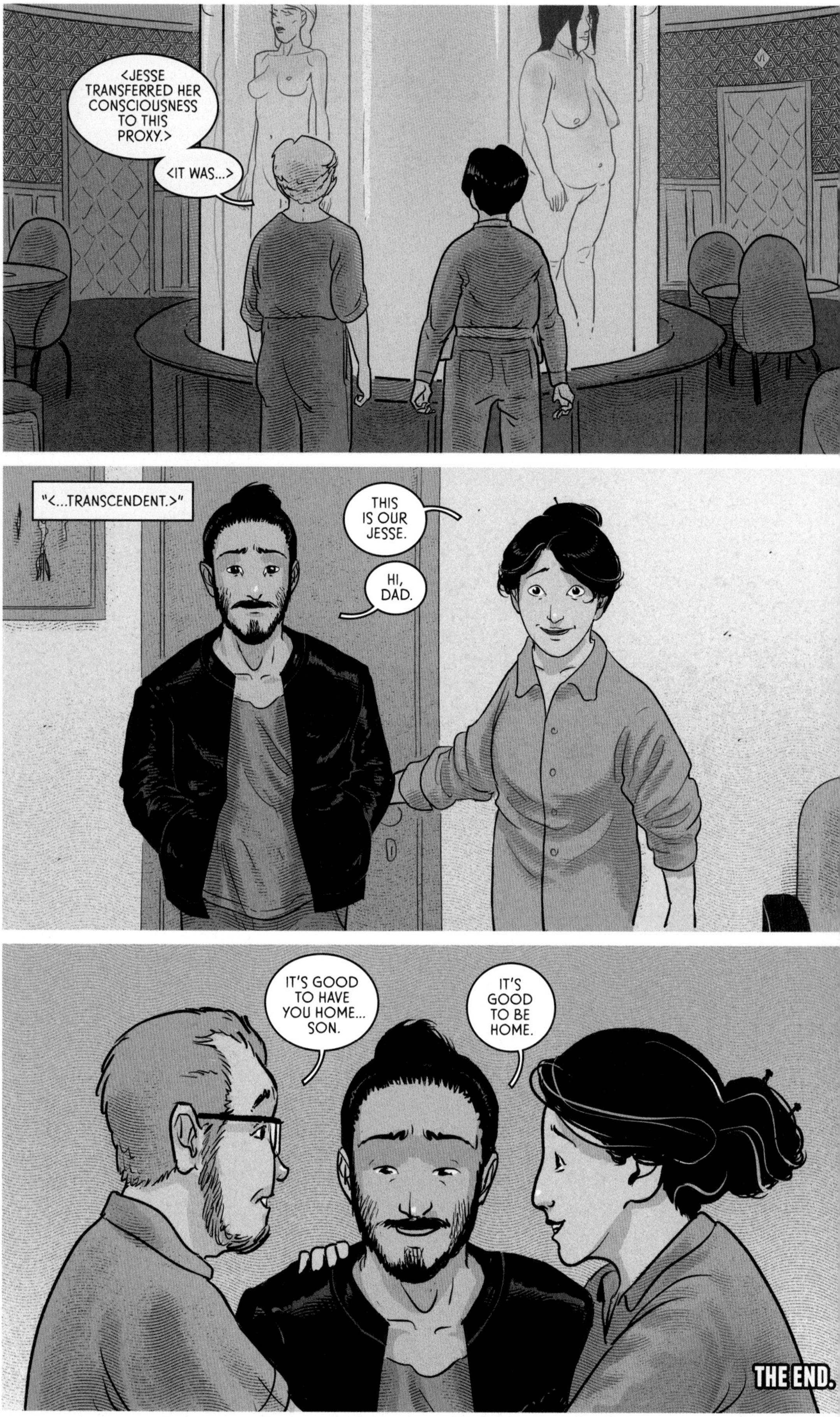
<JESSE TRANSFERRED HER CONSCIOUSNESS TO THIS PROXY.>
<IT WAS...>
"<...TRANSCENDENT.>"
THIS IS OUR JESSE.
HI, DAD.
IT'S GOOD TO HAVE YOU HOME... SON.
IT'S GOOD TO BE HOME.
THE END.

NEXT:

PROXY STORIES –
CASE # [004347]

"Together"

WRITTEN AND ILLUSTRATED BY
RON CHAN

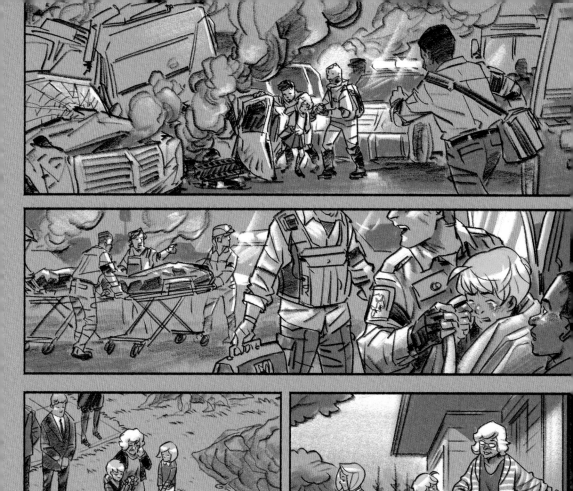

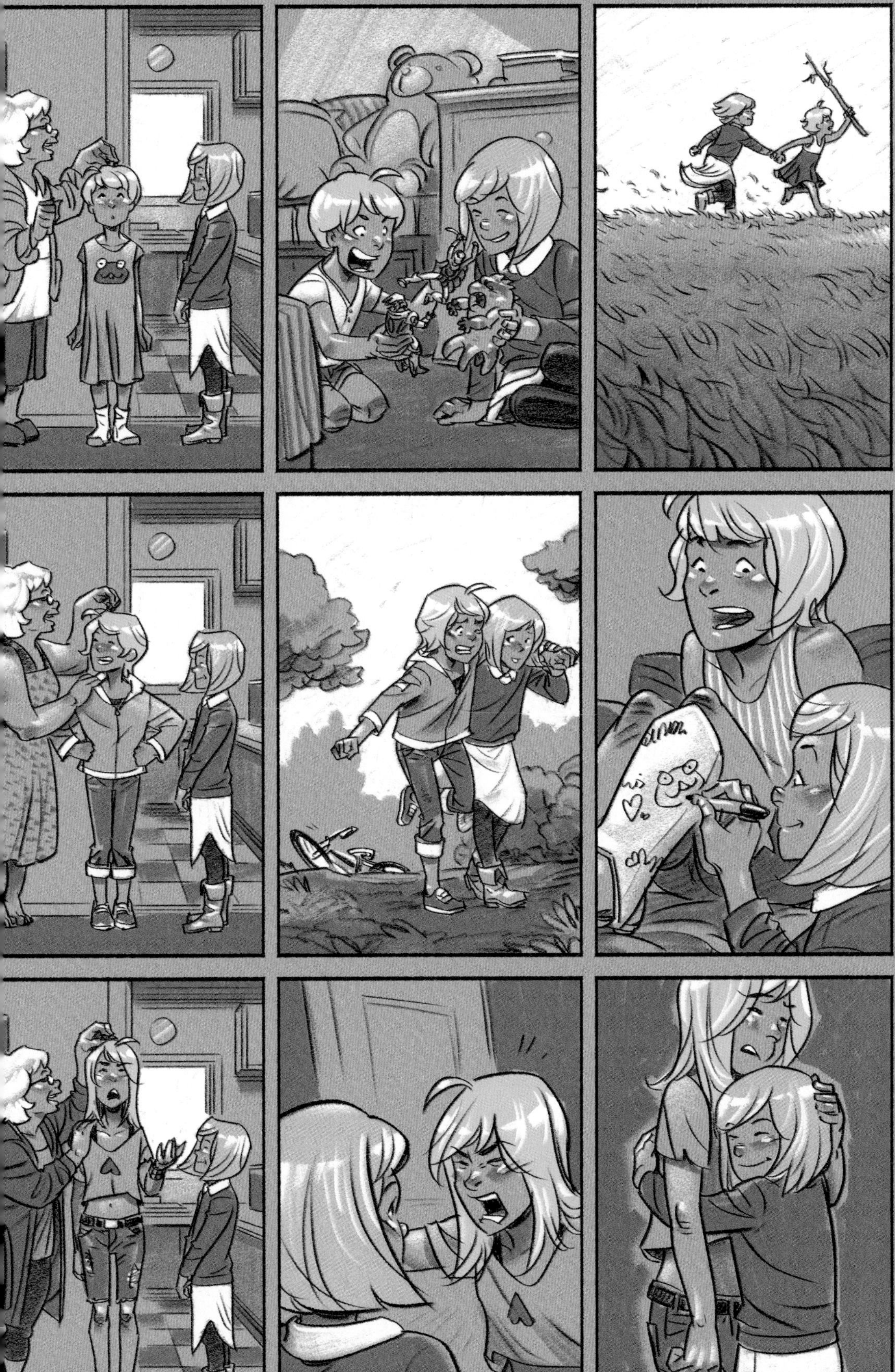
I'M SORRY

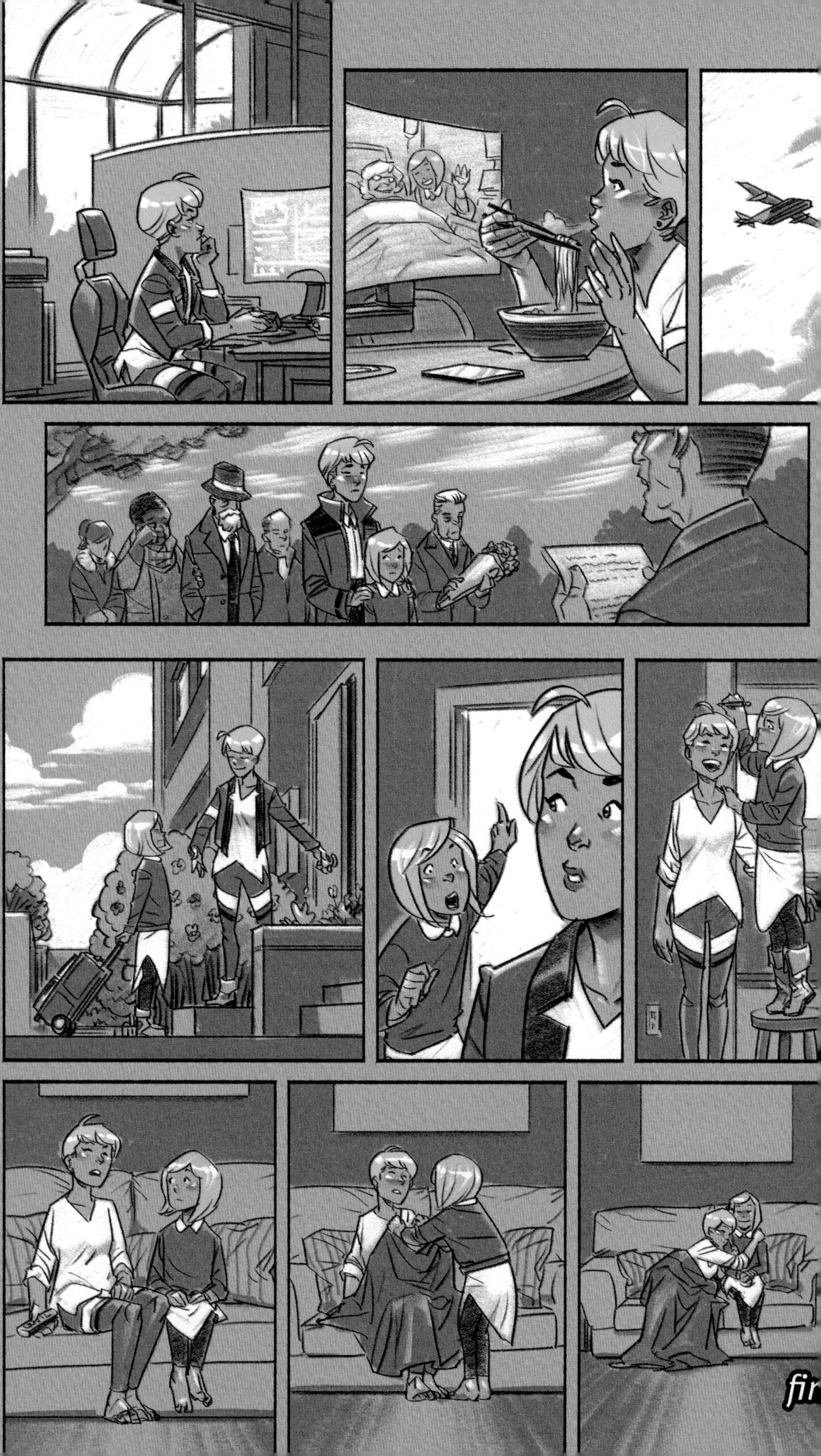

NEXT:

- PROXY STORIES -
CASE # [014975]

"Distance"

WRITTEN AND ILLUSTRATED BY
EUNJOO HAN

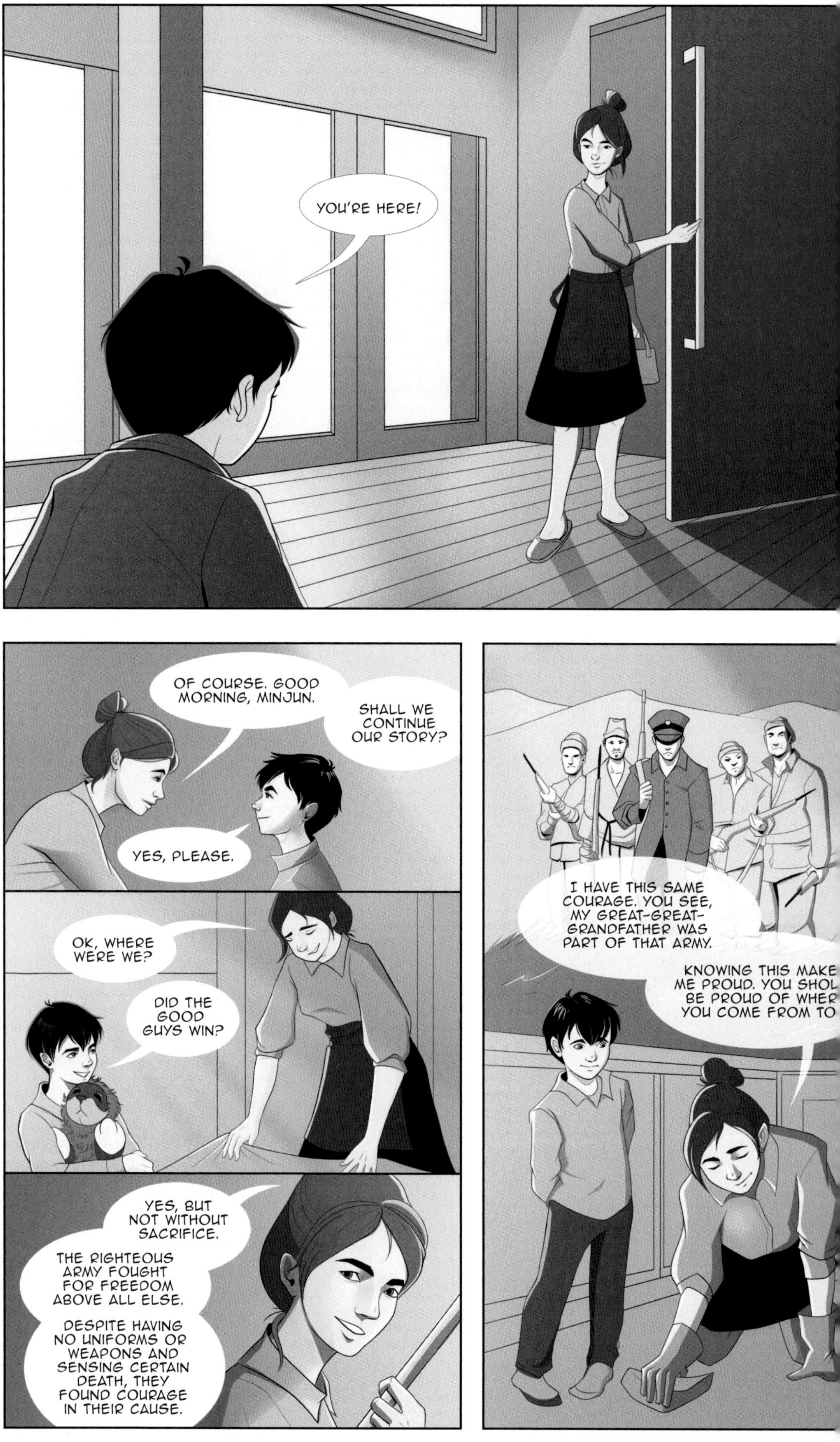
YOU'RE HERE!
OF COURSE. GOOD MORNING, MINJUN.
SHALL WE CONTINUE OUR STORY?
YES, PLEASE.
OK, WHERE WERE WE?
DID THE GOOD GUYS WIN?
YES, BUT NOT WITHOUT SACRIFICE.
THE RIGHTEOUS ARMY FOUGHT FOR FREEDOM ABOVE ALL ELSE.
DESPITE HAVING NO UNIFORMS OR WEAPONS AND SENSING CERTAIN DEATH, THEY FOUND COURAGE IN THEIR CAUSE.
I HAVE THIS SAME COURAGE. YOU SEE, MY GREAT-GREAT-GRANDFATHER WAS PART OF THAT ARMY.
KNOWING THIS MAKE
ME PROUD. YOU SHOL
BE PROUD OF WHER
YOU COME FROM TO

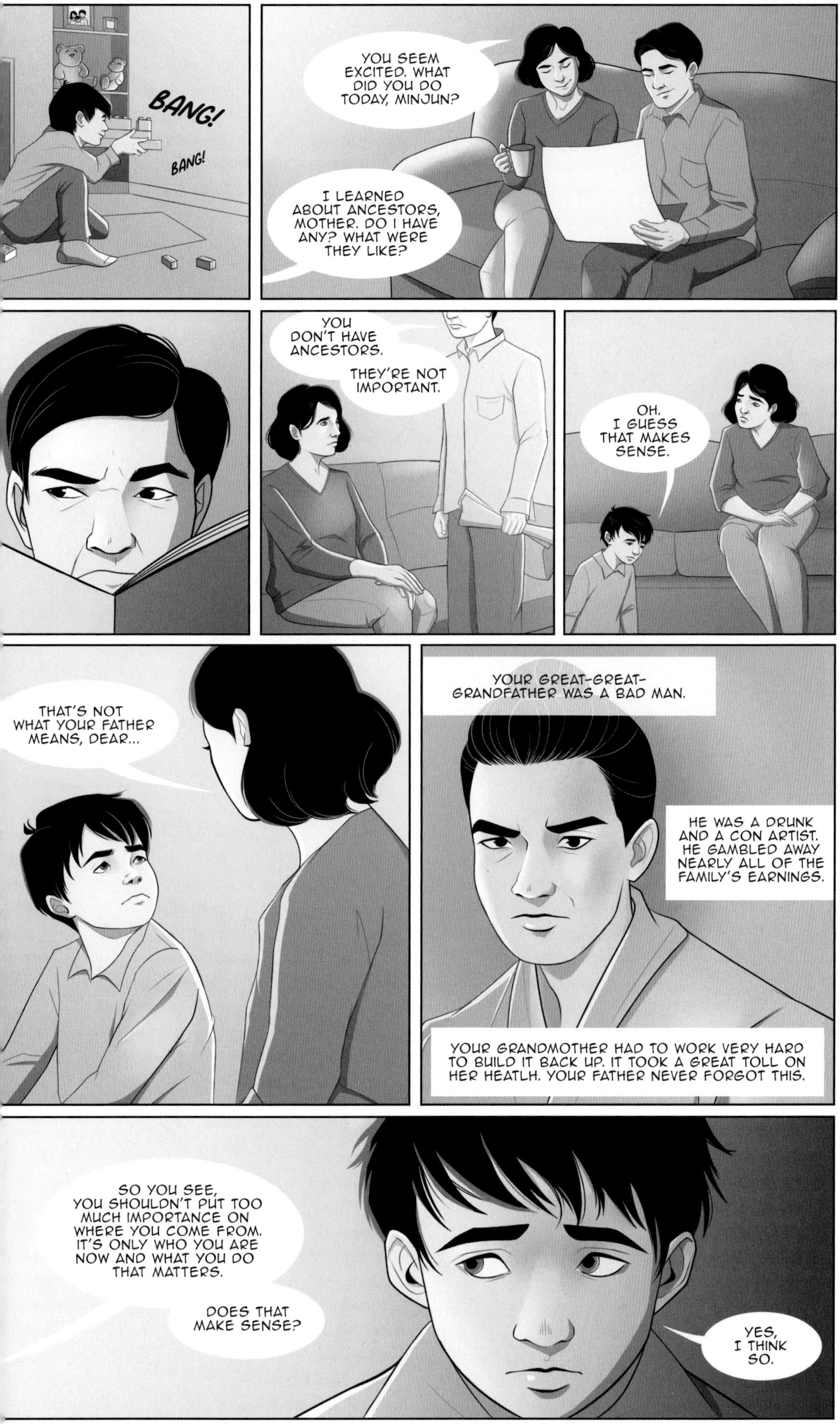
BANG!
BANG!
YOU SEEM EXCITED. WHAT DID YOU DO TODAY, MINJUN?
I LEARNED ABOUT ANCESTORS, MOTHER. DO I HAVE ANY? WHAT WERE THEY LIKE?
YOU DON'T HAVE ANCESTORS.
THEY'RE NOT IMPORTANT.
OH. I GUESS THAT MAKES SENSE.
THAT'S NOT WHAT YOUR FATHER MEANS, DEAR...
YOUR GREAT-GREAT-GRANDFATHER WAS A BAD MAN.
HE WAS A DRUNK AND A CON ARTIST. HE GAMBLED AWAY NEARLY ALL OF THE FAMILY'S EARNINGS.
YOUR GRANDMOTHER HAD TO WORK VERY HARD TO BUILD IT BACK UP. IT TOOK A GREAT TOLL ON HER HEATLH. YOUR FATHER NEVER FORGOT THIS.
SO YOU SEE, YOU SHOULDN'T PUT TOO MUCH IMPORTANCE ON WHERE YOU COME FROM. IT'S ONLY WHO YOU ARE NOW AND WHAT YOU DO THAT MATTERS.
DOES THAT MAKE SENSE?
YES, I THINK SO.

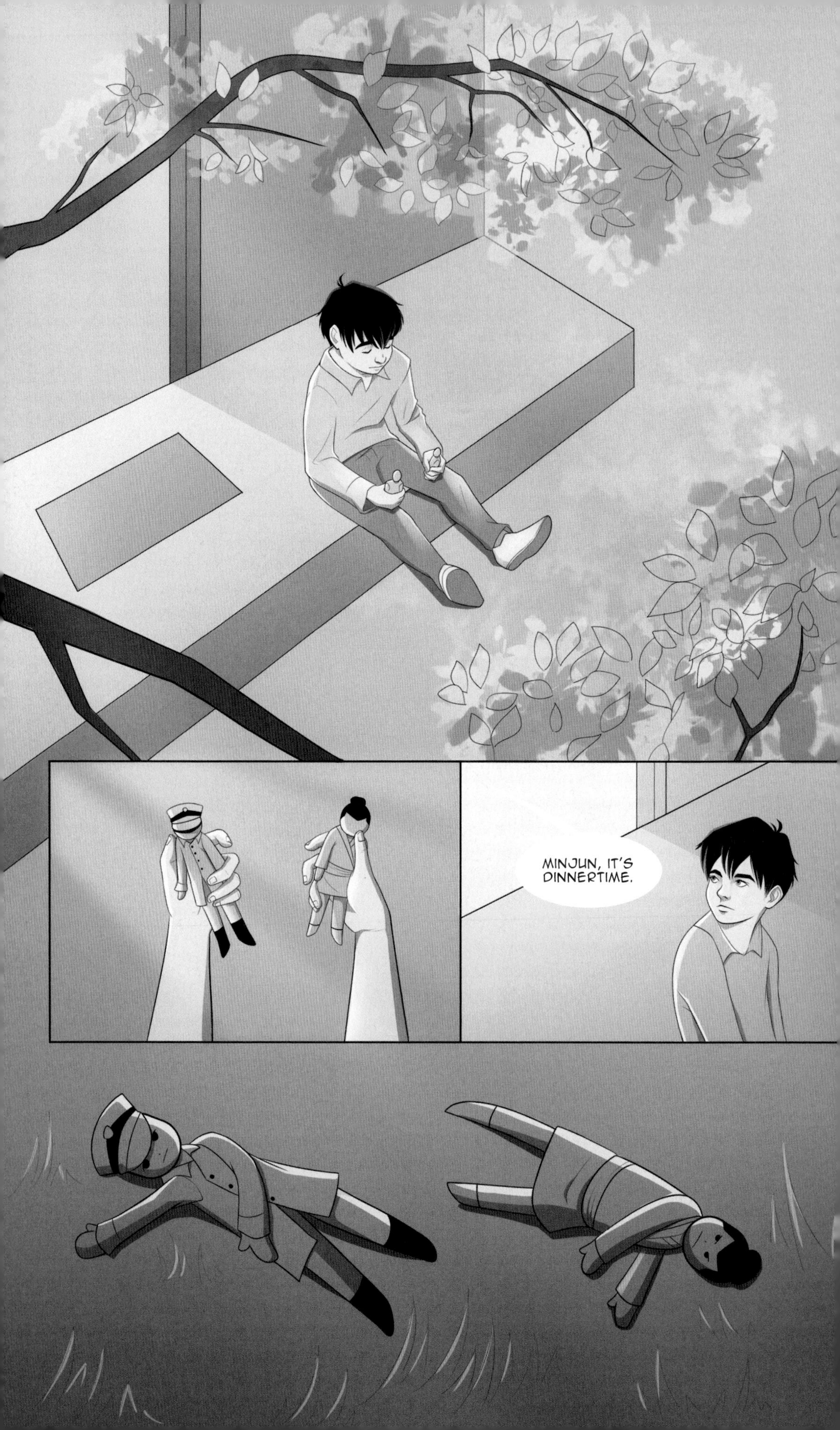
MINJUN, IT'S DINNERTIME.

NEXT:

PROXY STORIES -
CASE # [018002]

"Five More Minutes"

WRITTEN AND ILLUSTRATED BY
WOOK-JIN CLARK

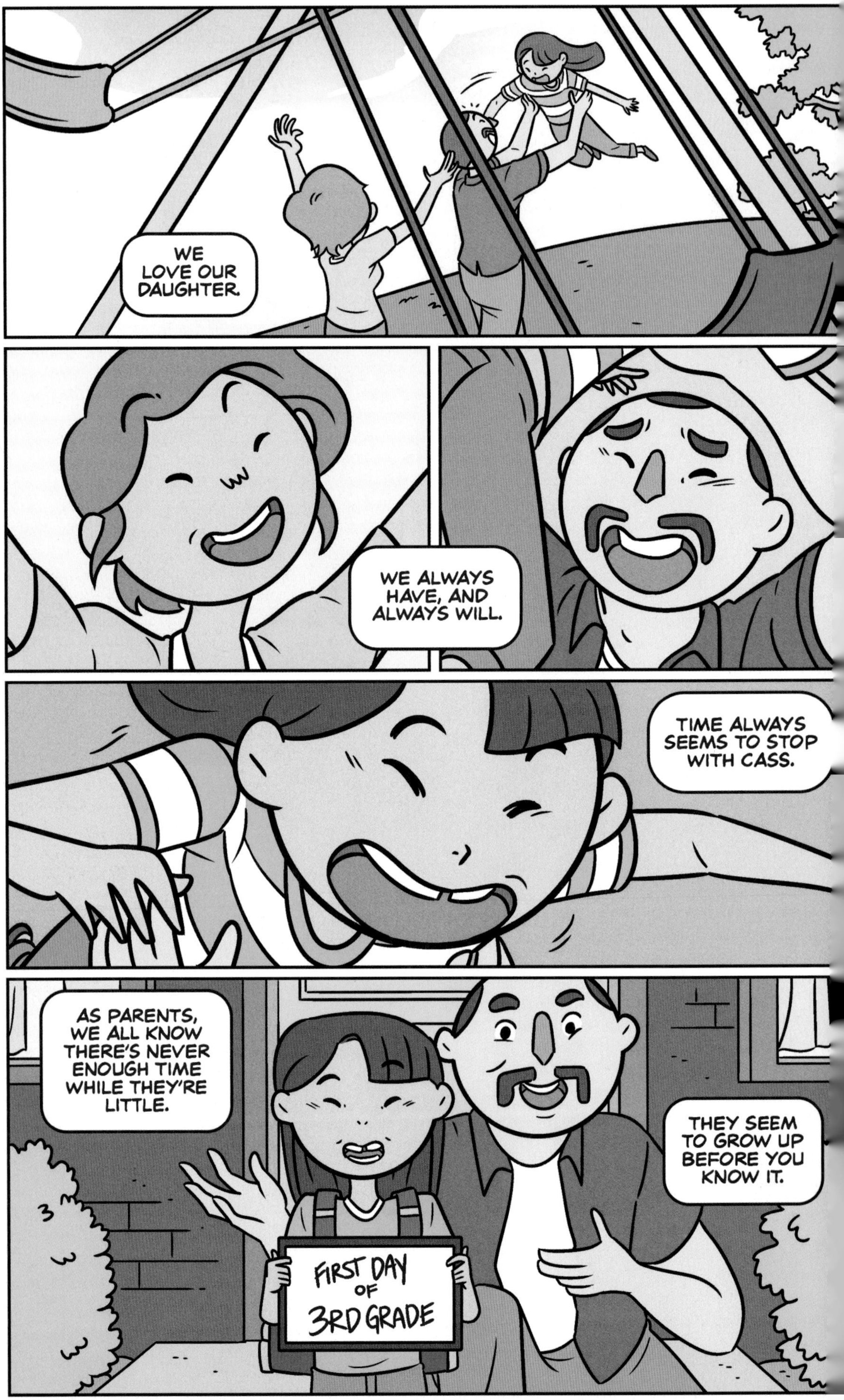
WE LOVE OUR DAUGHTER.
WE ALWAYS HAVE, AND ALWAYS WILL.
TIME ALWAYS SEEMS TO STOP WITH CASS.
AS PARENTS, WE ALL KNOW THERE'S NEVER ENOUGH TIME WHILE THEY'RE LITTLE.
FIRST DAY OF 3RD GRADE
THEY SEEM TO GROW UP BEFORE YOU KNOW IT.

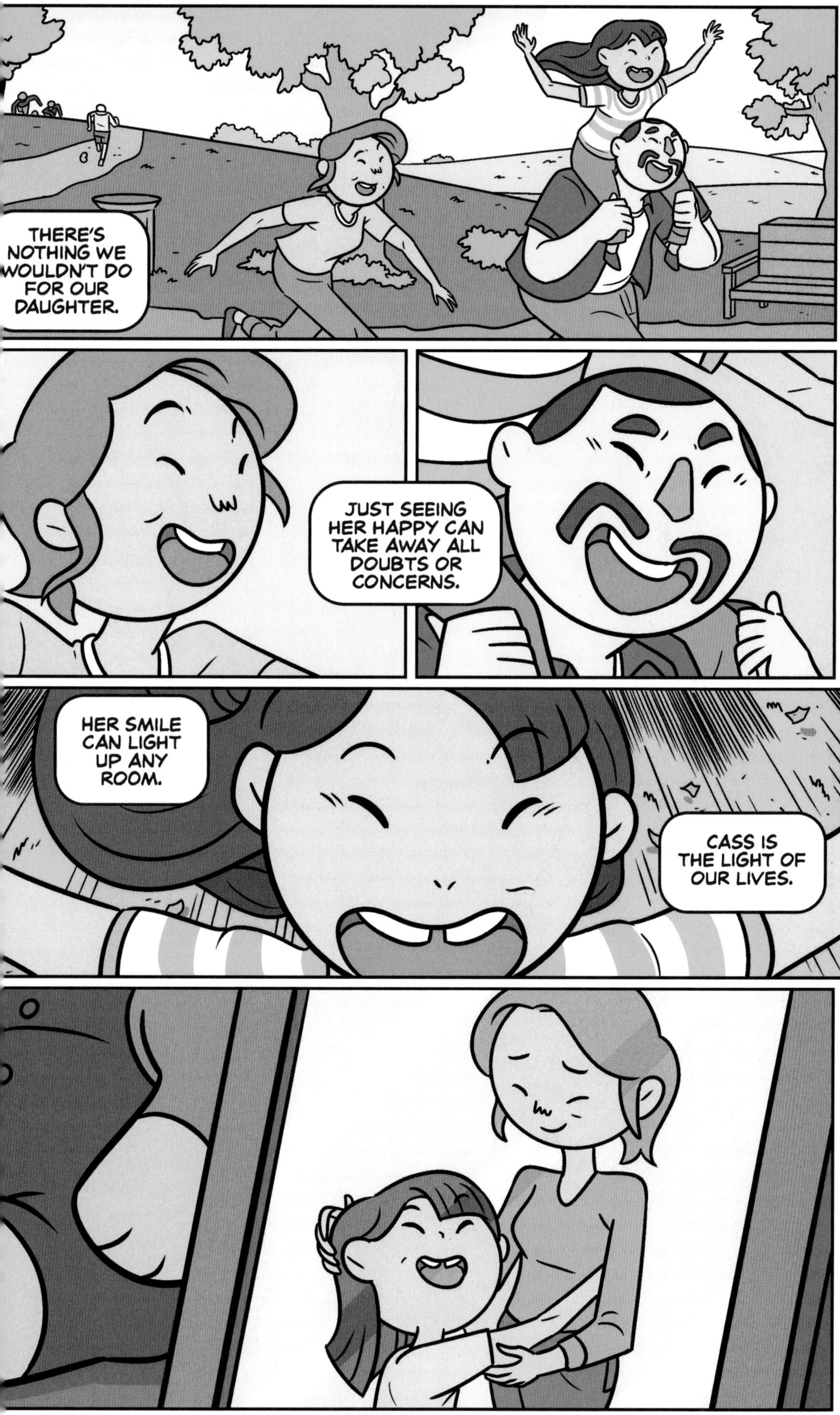
THERE'S NOTHING WE WOULDN'T DO FOR OUR DAUGHTER.
JUST SEEING HER HAPPY CAN TAKE AWAY ALL DOUBTS OR CONCERNS.
HER SMILE CAN LIGHT UP ANY ROOM.
CASS IS THE LIGHT OF OUR LIVES.

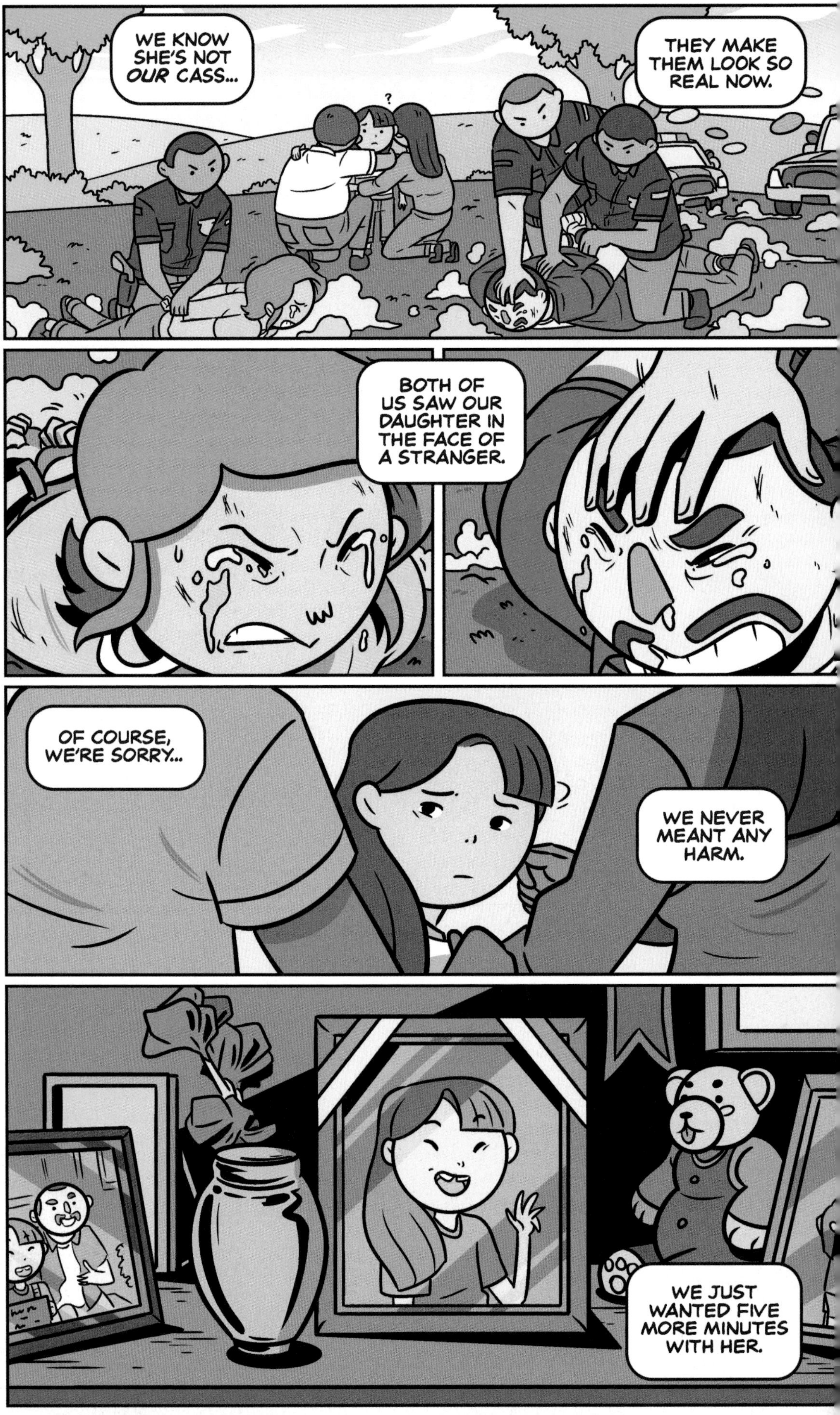

WE KNOW SHE'S NOT *OUR* CASS...
THEY MAKE THEM LOOK SO REAL NOW.
?
BOTH OF US SAW OUR DAUGHTER IN THE FACE OF A STRANGER.
OF COURSE, WE'RE SORRY...
WE NEVER MEANT ANY HARM.
WE JUST WANTED FIVE MORE MINUTES WITH HER.

NEXT:

PROXY STORIES -
CASE # [031042]

"You Hear Me?"

WRITTEN AND ILLUSTRATED BY
DAVE COLE

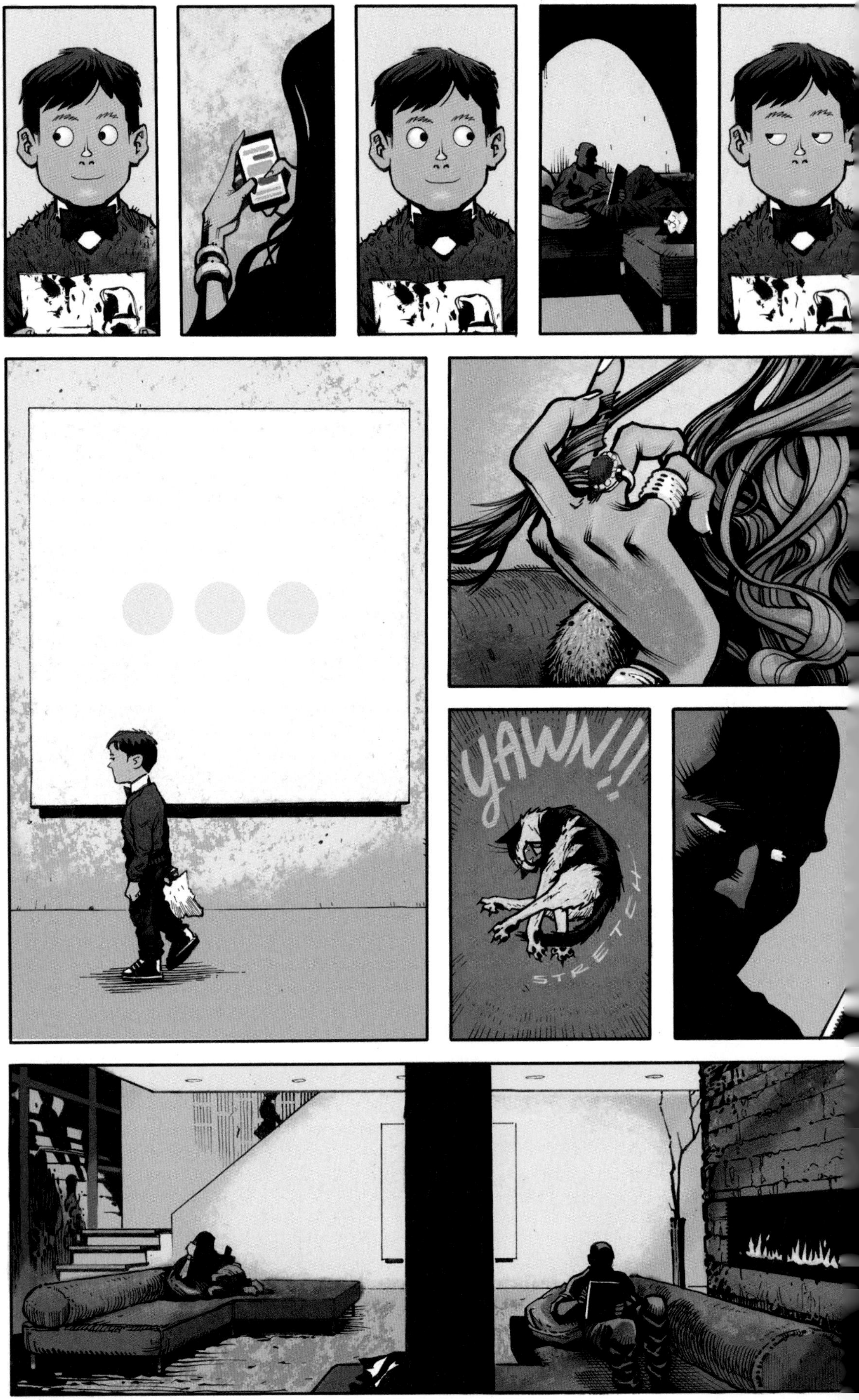
YAWN!!
STRETCH

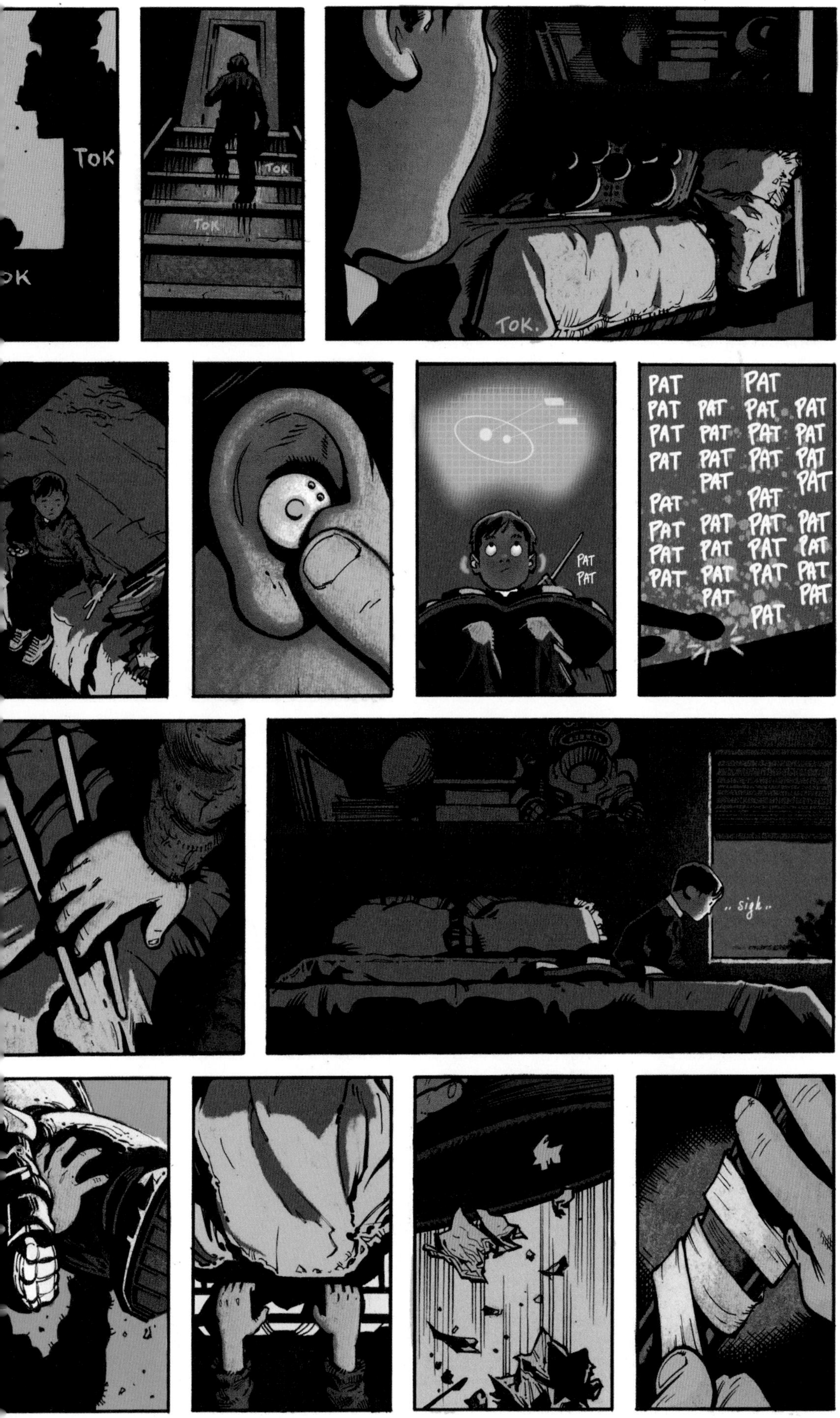
TOK
OK
TOK
TOK
TOK.
PAT
PAT
PAT PAT PAT PAT PAT PAT PAT PAT PAT PAT PAT PAT PAT PAT PAT PAT PAT PAT PAT PAT PAT PAT PAT PAT PAT PAT PAT PAT PAT PAT PAT PAT PAT PAT
.. sigh ..

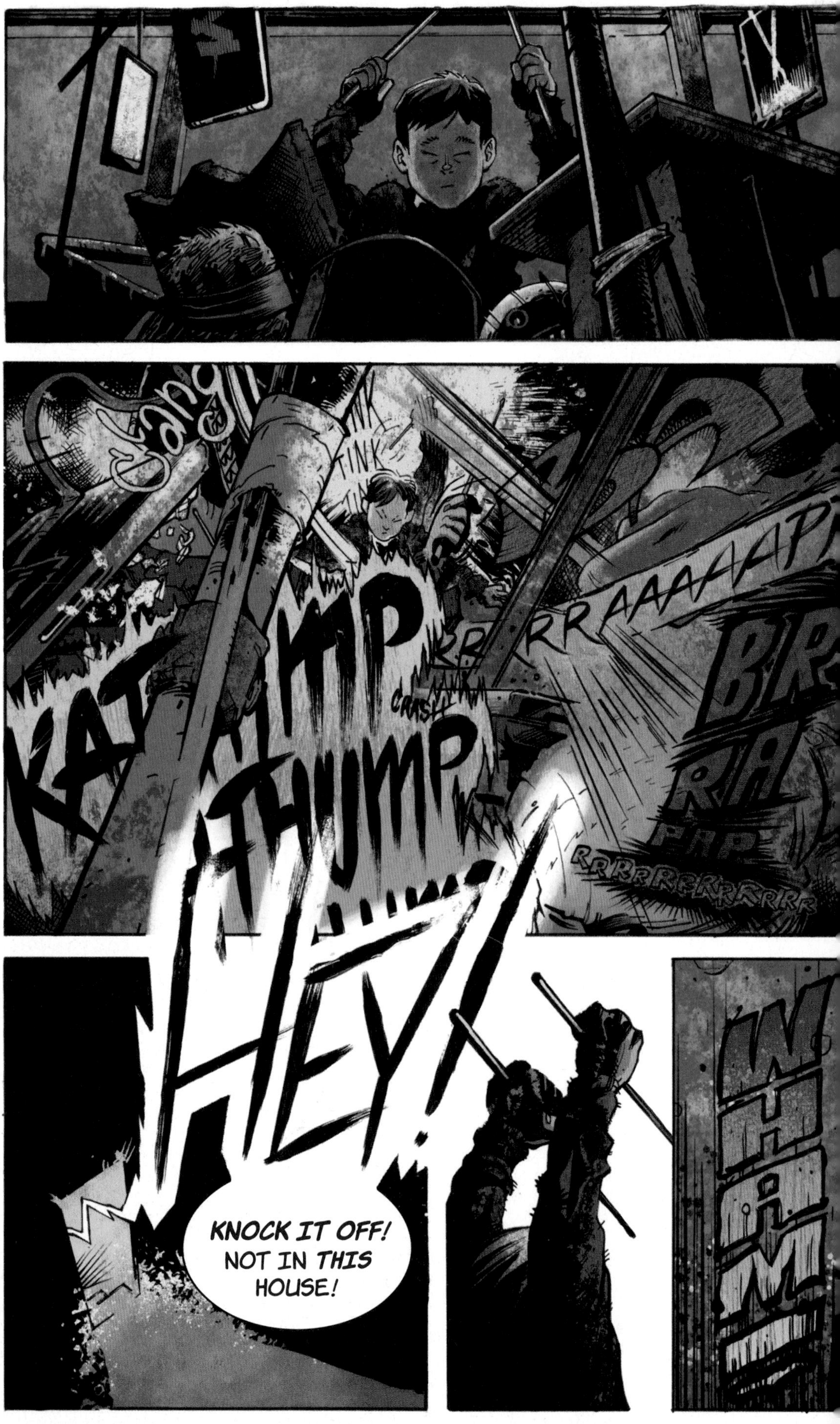
TINK
THUMP
CRASH
HEY!
KNOCK IT OFF! NOT IN THIS HOUSE!
WHAM

NEXT:

- PROXY STORIES -
CASE # [002370]

"EXPROPRIATE"

WRITTEN BY
MANUEL MARTÍN

ILLUSTRATED BY
ALFONSO MARTÍN

COLORED BY
JOSE A. LOPEZ

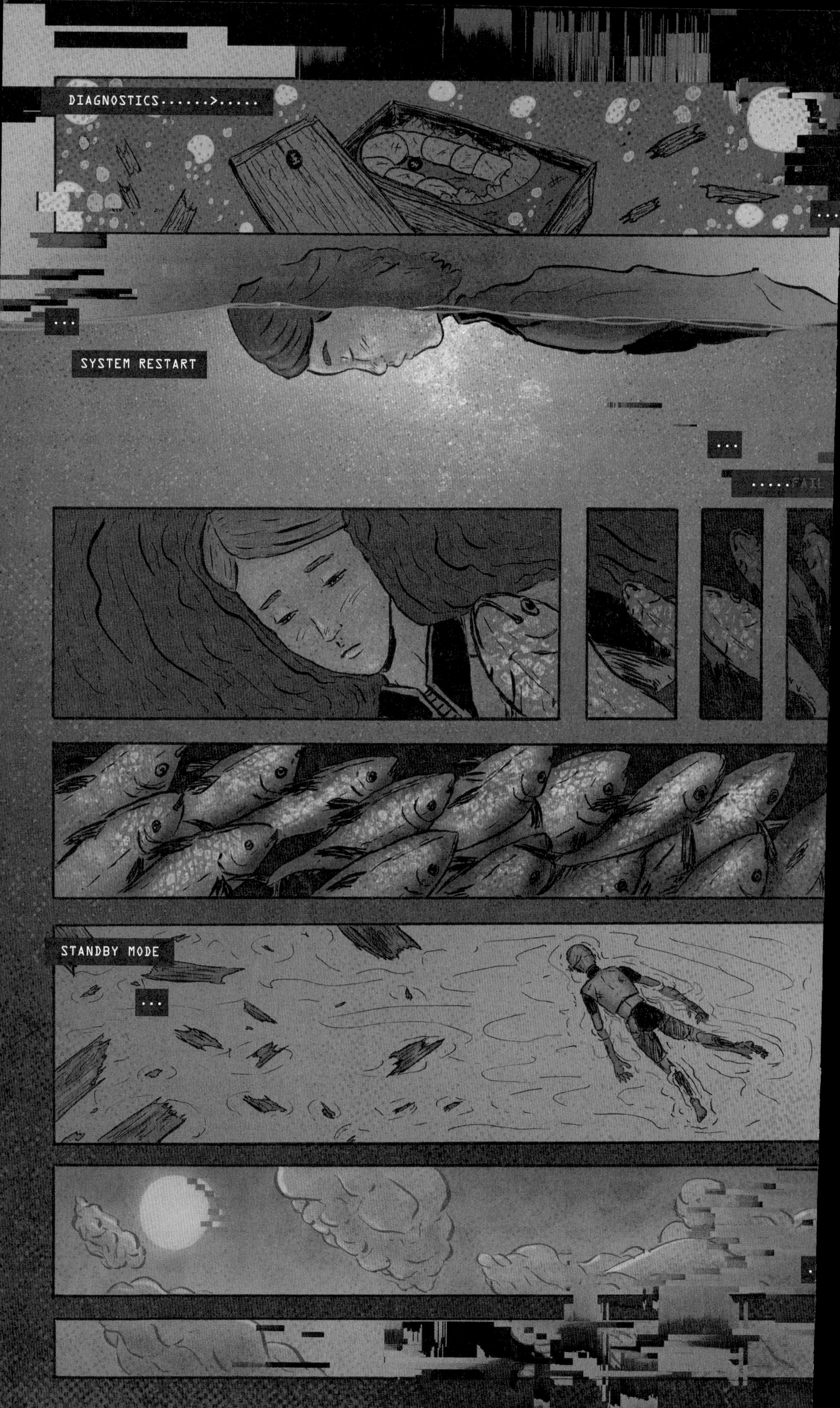
DIAGNOSTICS......>.....
...
...
SYSTEM RESTART
...
......FAIL
STANDBY MODE
...

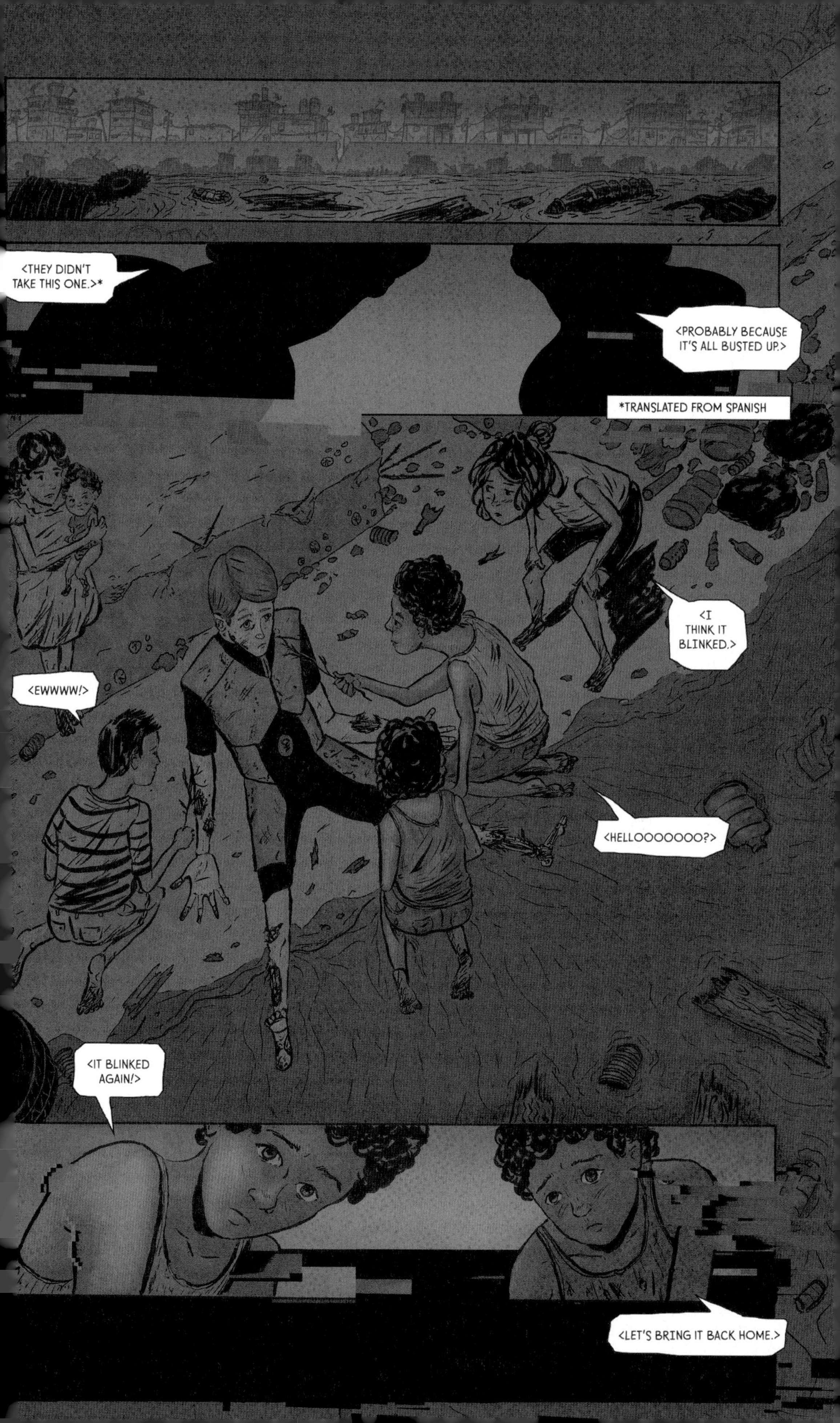
<THEY DIDN'T TAKE THIS ONE.>*
<PROBABLY BECAUSE IT'S ALL BUSTED UP.>
*TRANSLATED FROM SPANISH
<I THINK IT BLINKED.>
<EWWWW!>
<HELLOOOOOOO?>
<IT BLINKED AGAIN!>
<LET'S BRING IT BACK HOME.>

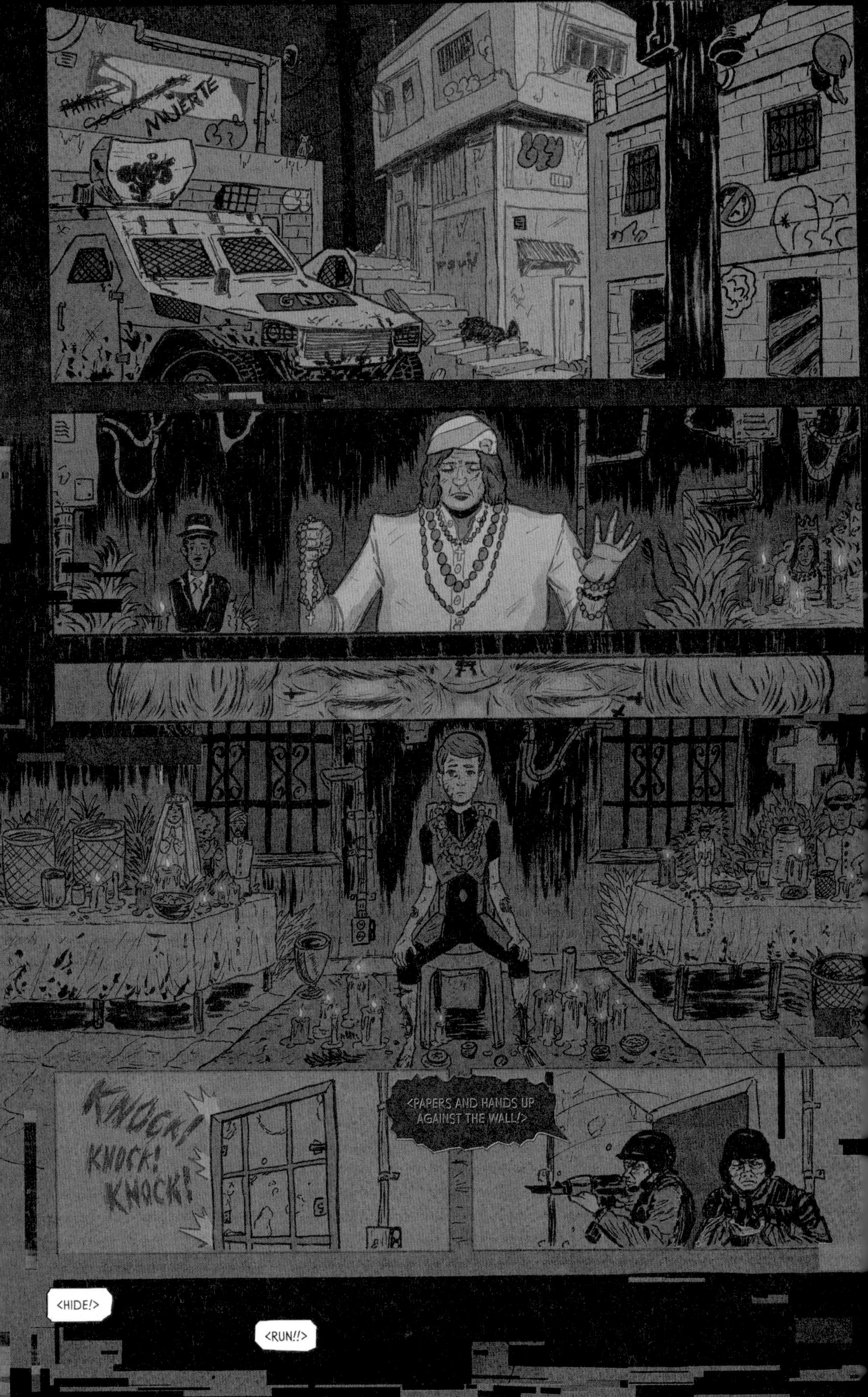
MUERTE
GNB
KNOCK!
KNOCK!
KNOCK!
<PAPERS AND HANDS UP AGAINST THE WALL!>
<HIDE!>
<RUN!!>

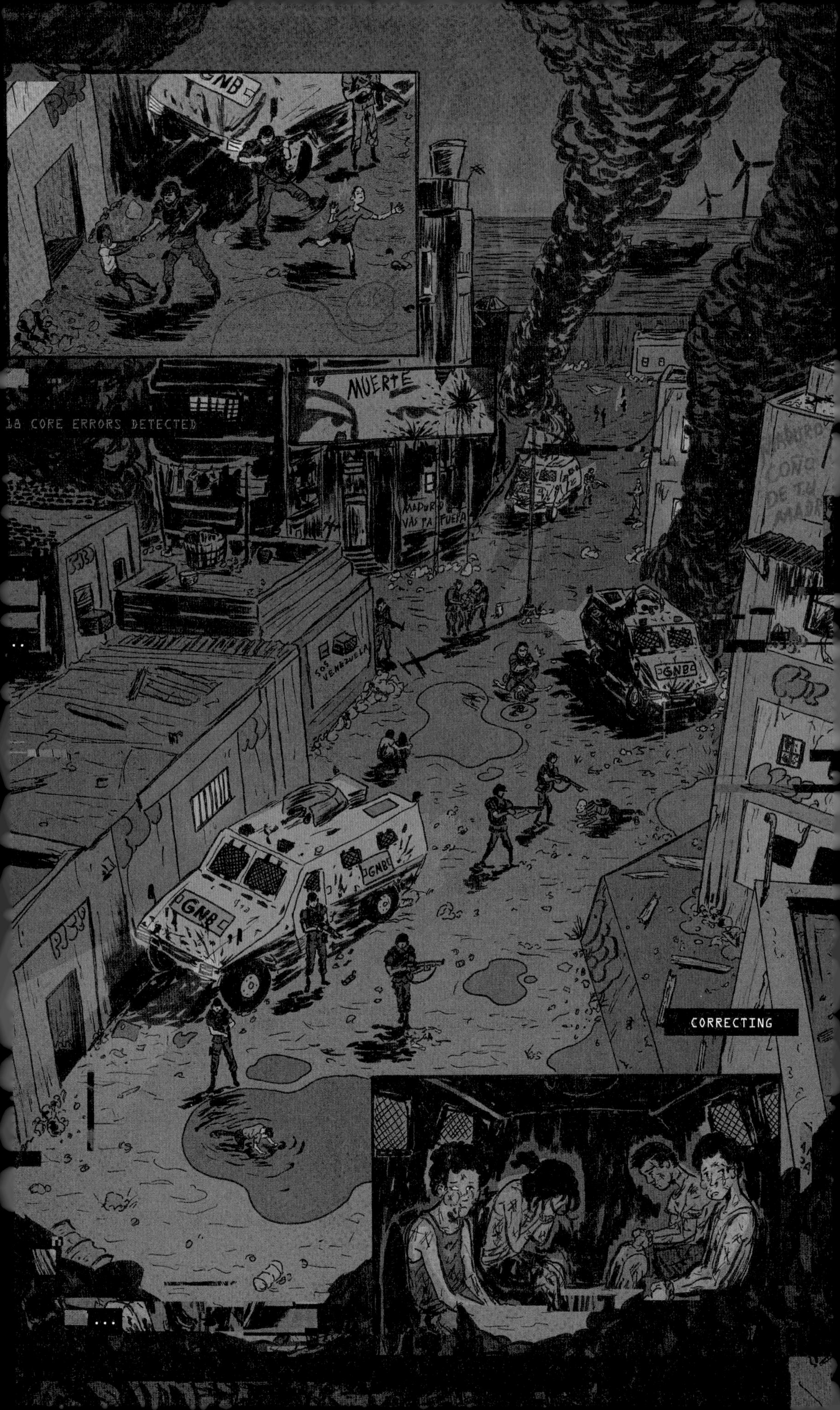

GNB
MUERTE
18 CORE ERRORS DETECTED
MADURO VAS PA FUERA
..
SOS VENEZUELA
GNB
GNB
CORRECTING
...

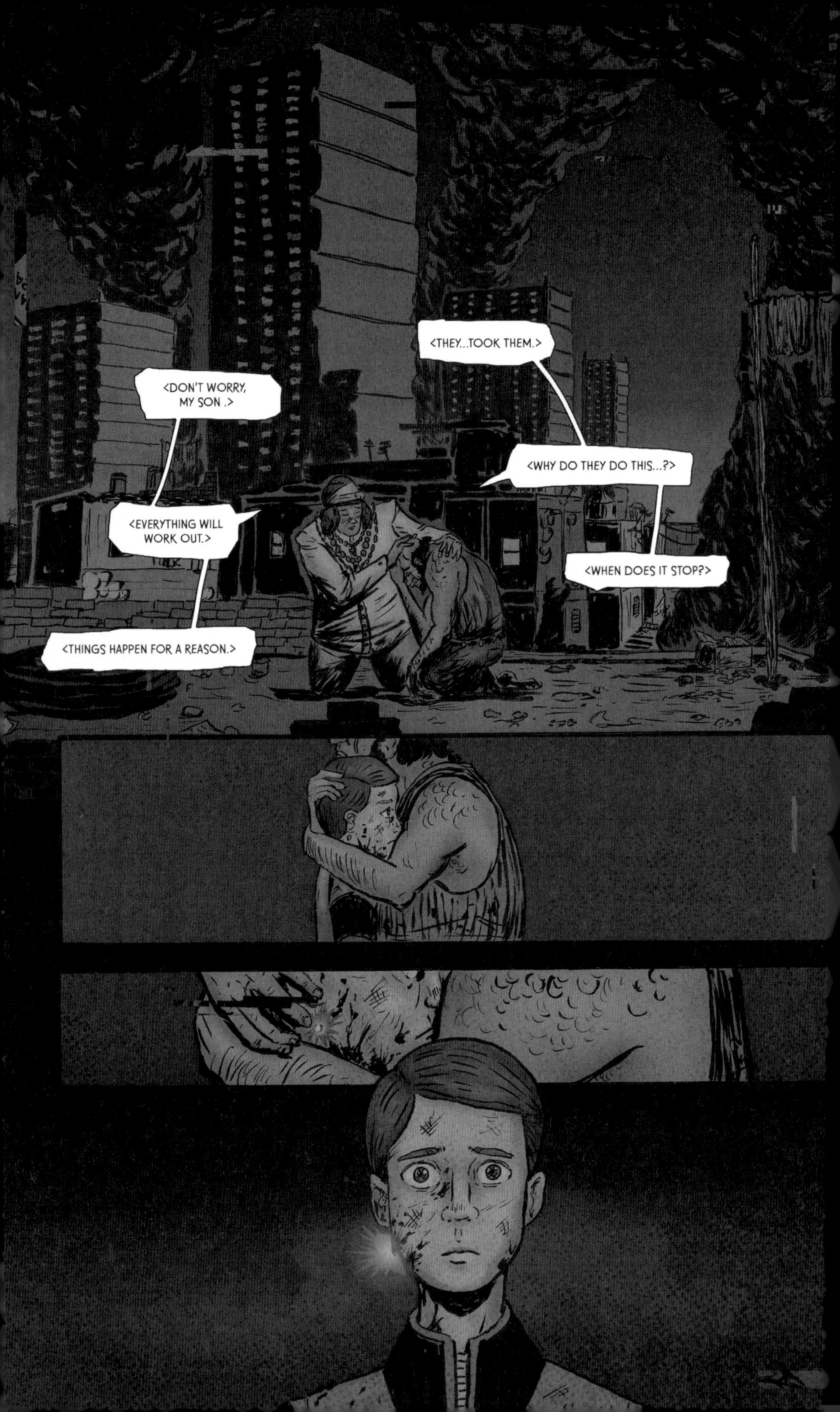
<THEY...TOOK THEM.>
<DON'T WORRY, MY SON .>
<WHY DO THEY DO THIS...?>
<EVERYTHING WILL WORK OUT.>
<WHEN DOES IT STOP?>
<THINGS HAPPEN FOR A REASON.>

NEXT:

- PROXY STORIES -
CASE # [009261]

"BattleChef Korea"

WRITTEN AND ILLUSTRATED BY
FRED CHAO

LETTERED BY
DC HOPKINS

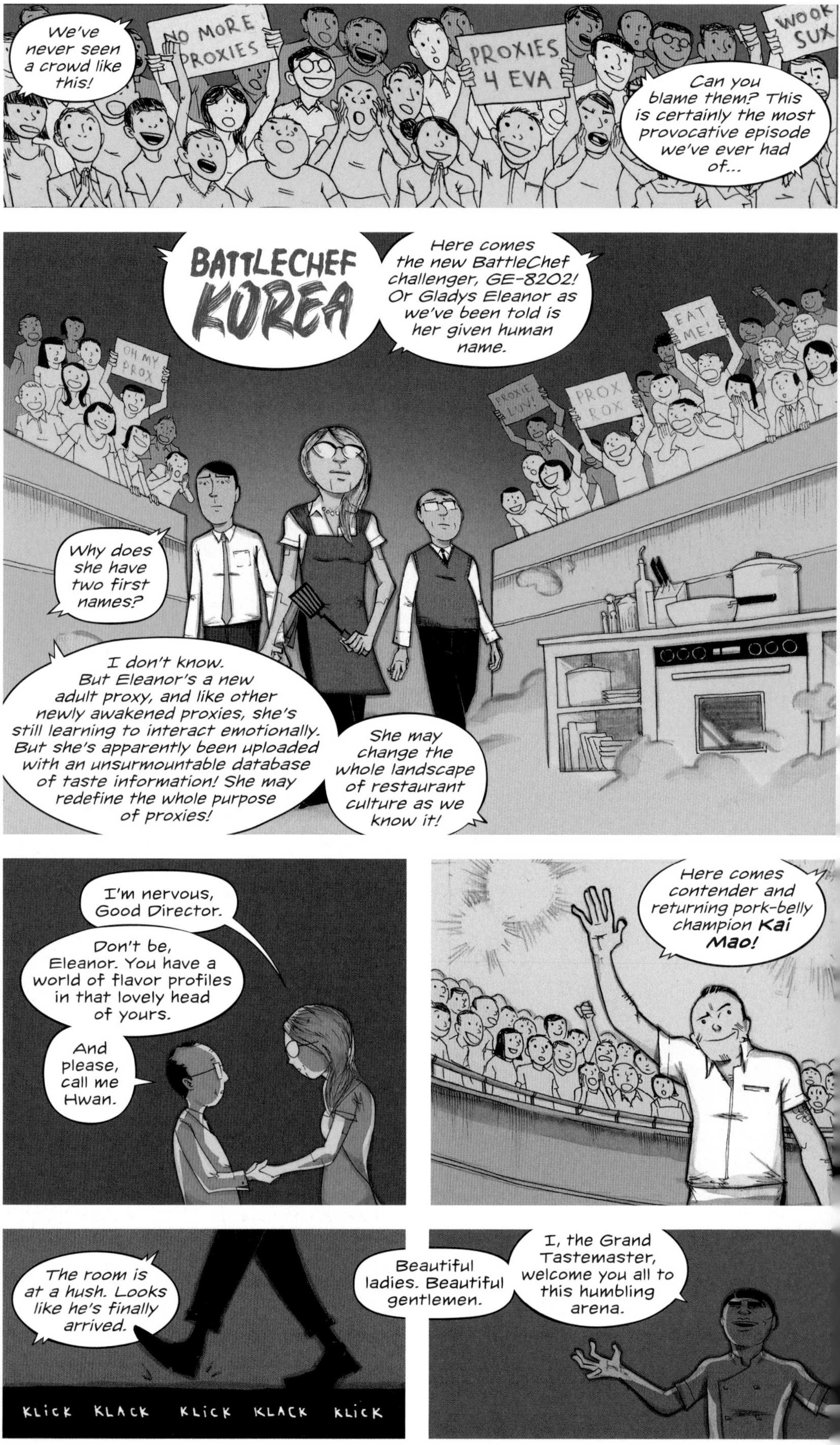

We've never seen a crowd like this!
NO MORE PROXIES
PROXIES 4 EVA
WOOK SUX
Can you blame them? This is certainly the most provocative episode we've ever had of...
BATTLECHEF KOREA
Here comes the new BattleChef challenger, GE-8202! Or Gladys Eleanor as we've been told is her given human name.
OH MY PROX
EAT ME!
PROXIE LUV!
PROX ROX
Why does she have two first names?
I don't know. But Eleanor's a new adult proxy, and like other newly awakened proxies, she's still learning to interact emotionally. But she's apparently been uploaded with an unsurmountable database of taste information! She may redefine the whole purpose of proxies!
She may change the whole landscape of restaurant culture as we know it!
I'm nervous, Good Director.
Don't be, Eleanor. You have a world of flavor profiles in that lovely head of yours.
And please, call me Hwan.
Here comes contender and returning pork-belly champion **Kai Mao!**
The room is at a hush. Looks like he's finally arrived.
KLICK KLACK KLICK KLACK KLICK
Beautiful ladies. Beautiful gentlemen.
I, the Grand Tastemaster, welcome you all to this humbling arena.

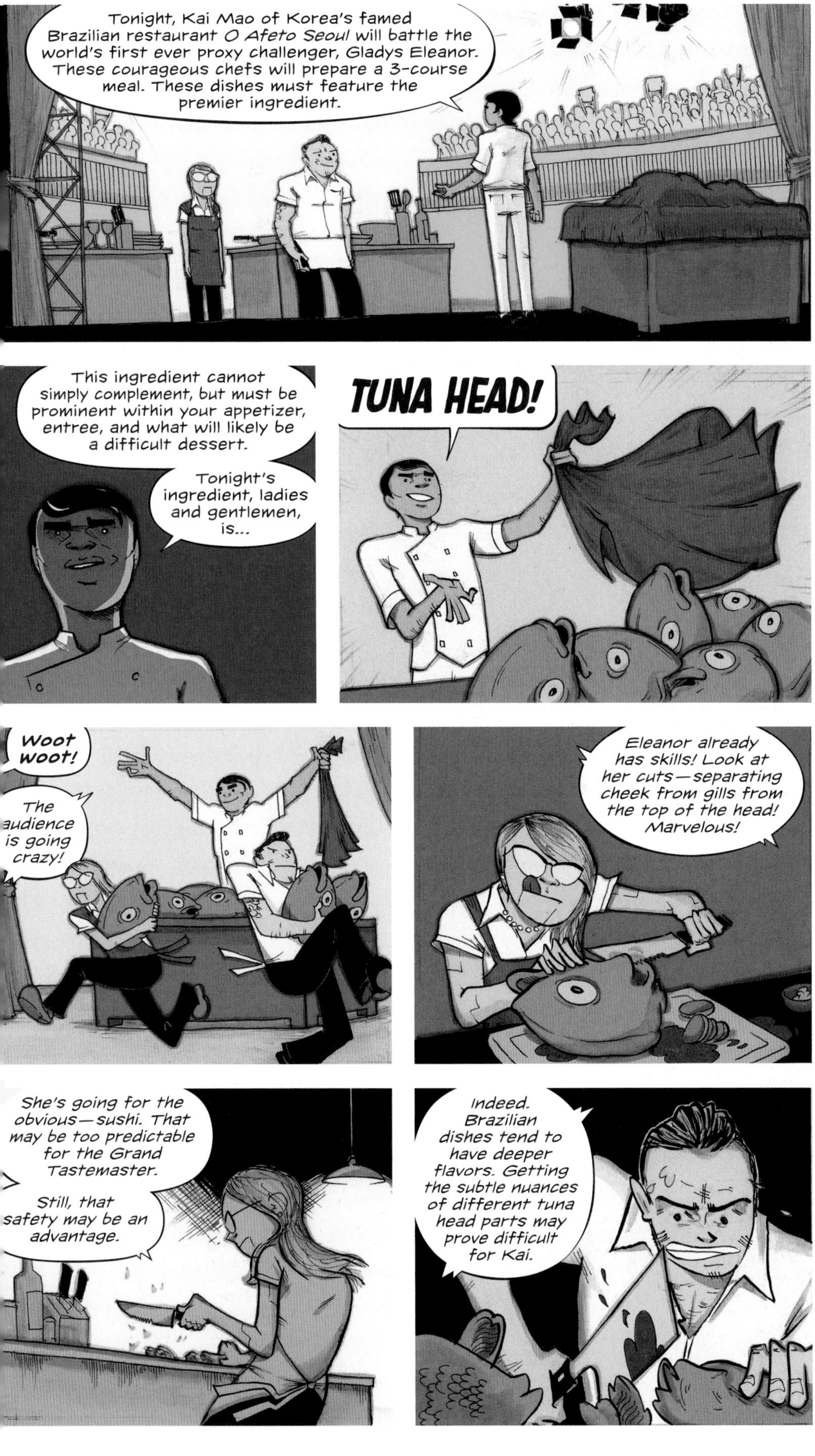
Tonight, Kai Mao of Korea's famed Brazilian restaurant O Afeto Seoul will battle the world's first ever proxy challenger, Gladys Eleanor. These courageous chefs will prepare a 3-course meal. These dishes must feature the premier ingredient.
This ingredient cannot simply complement, but must be prominent within your appetizer, entree, and what will likely be a difficult dessert.
Tonight's ingredient, ladies and gentlemen, is...
TUNA HEAD!
Woot woot!
The audience is going crazy!
Eleanor already has skills! Look at her cuts—separating cheek from gills from the top of the head! Marvelous!
She's going for the obvious—sushi. That may be too predictable for the Grand Tastemaster.
Still, that safety may be an advantage.
Indeed. Brazilian dishes tend to have deeper flavors. Getting the subtle nuances of different tuna head parts may prove difficult for Kai.

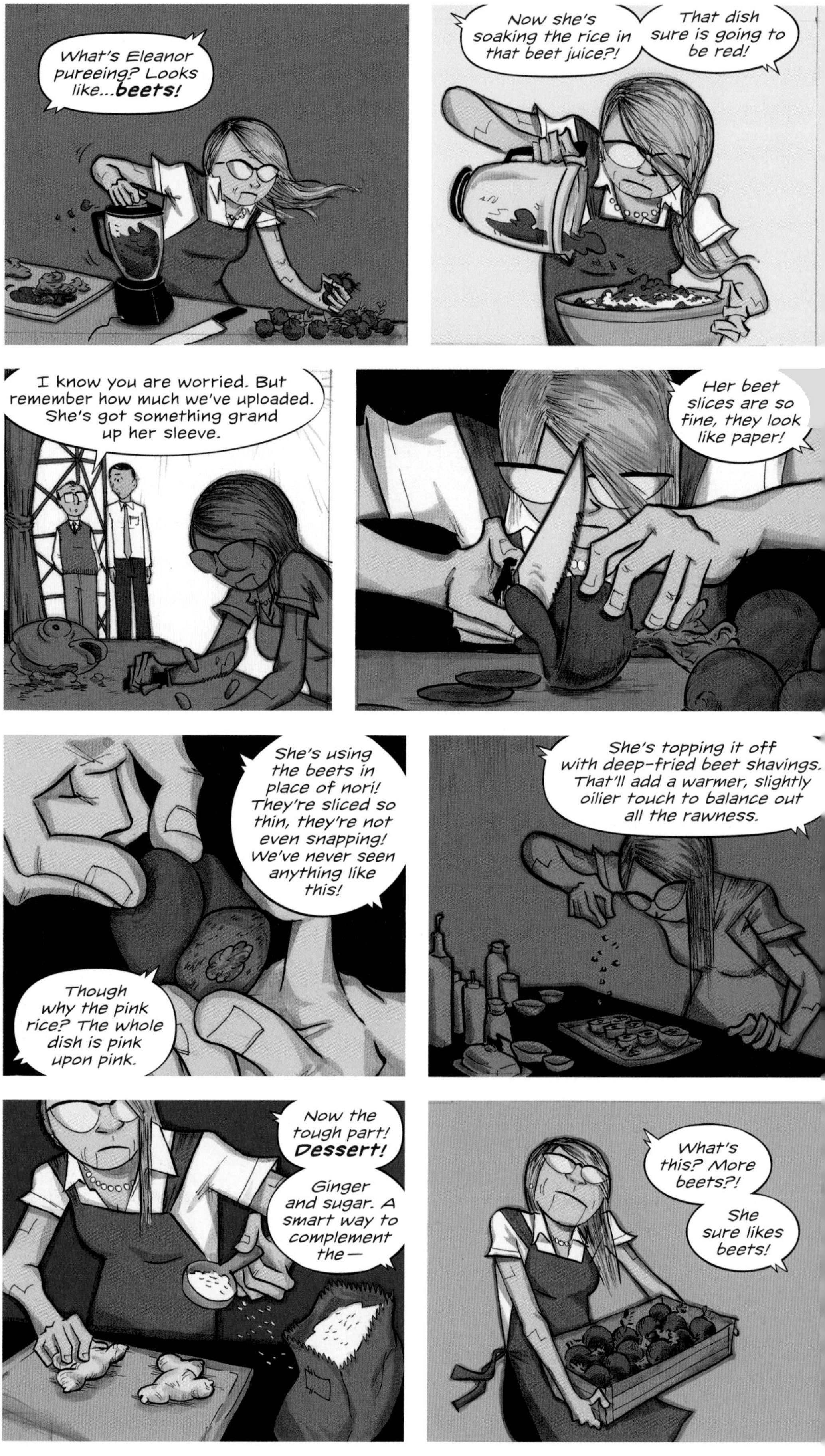
What's Eleanor pureeing? Looks like...**beets!**
Now she's soaking the rice in that beet juice?!
That dish sure is going to be red!
I know you are worried. But remember how much we've uploaded. She's got something grand up her sleeve.
Her beet slices are so fine, they look like paper!
She's using the beets in place of nori! They're sliced so thin, they're not even snapping! We've never seen anything like this!
Though why the pink rice? The whole dish is pink upon pink.
She's topping it off with deep-fried beet shavings. That'll add a warmer, slightly oilier touch to balance out all the rawness.
Now the tough part! **Dessert!**
Ginger and sugar. A smart way to complement the—
What's this? More beets?!
She sure likes beets!

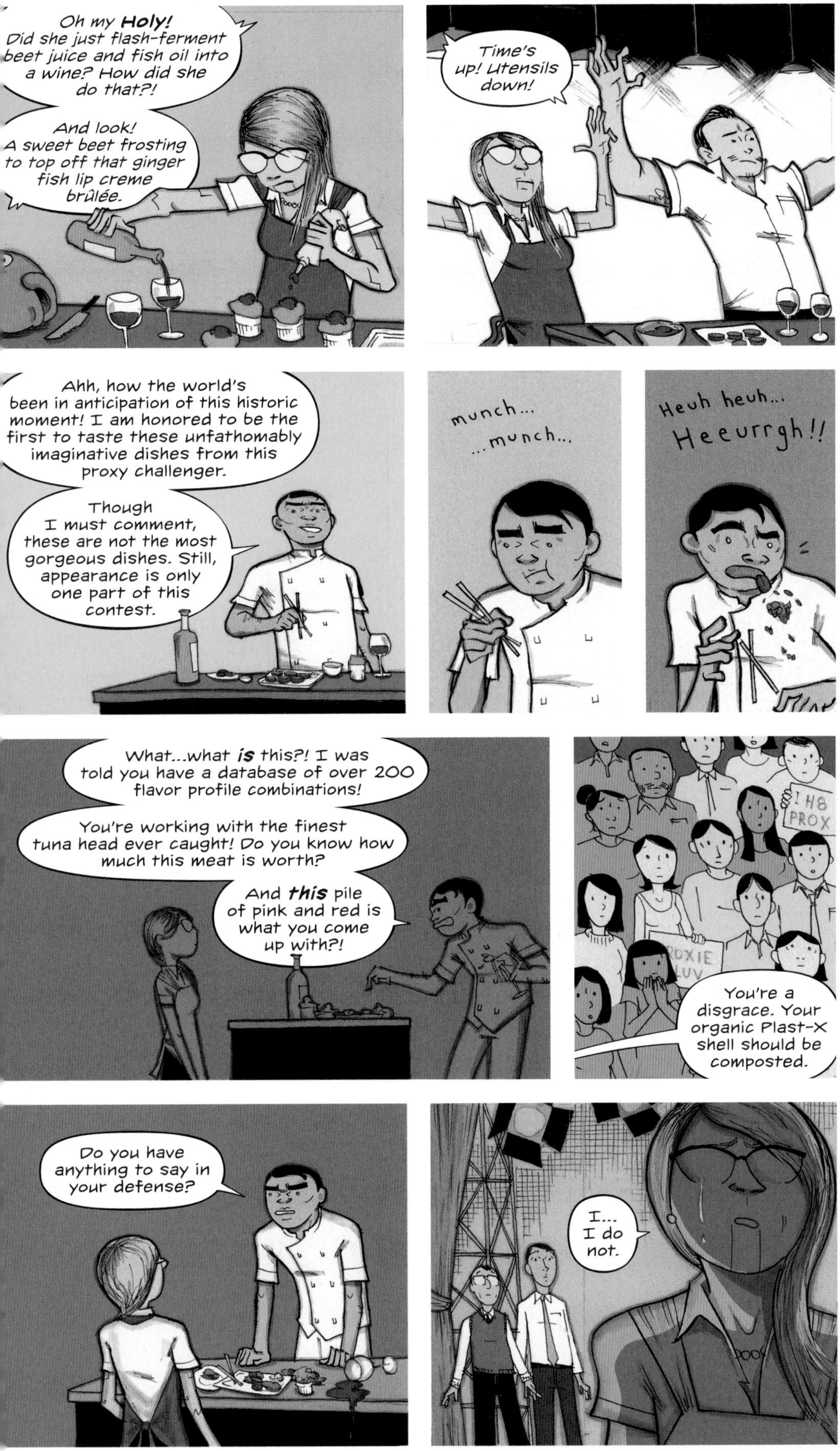
Oh my **Holy!** Did she just flash-ferment beet juice and fish oil into a wine? How did she do that?!
And look! A sweet beet frosting to top off that ginger fish lip creme brûlée.
Time's up! Utensils down!
Ahh, how the world's been in anticipation of this historic moment! I am honored to be the first to taste these unfathomably imaginative dishes from this proxy challenger.
Though I must comment, these are not the most gorgeous dishes. Still, appearance is only one part of this contest.
munch... ...munch...
Heuh heuh... Heeurrgh!!
What...what ***is*** this?! I was told you have a database of over 200 flavor profile combinations!
You're working with the finest tuna head ever caught! Do you know how much this meat is worth?
And ***this*** pile of pink and red is what you come up with?!
I H8 PROX
ROXIE LUV
You're a disgrace. Your organic Plast-X shell should be composted.
Do you have anything to say in your defense?
I... I do not.

Back at the labs...

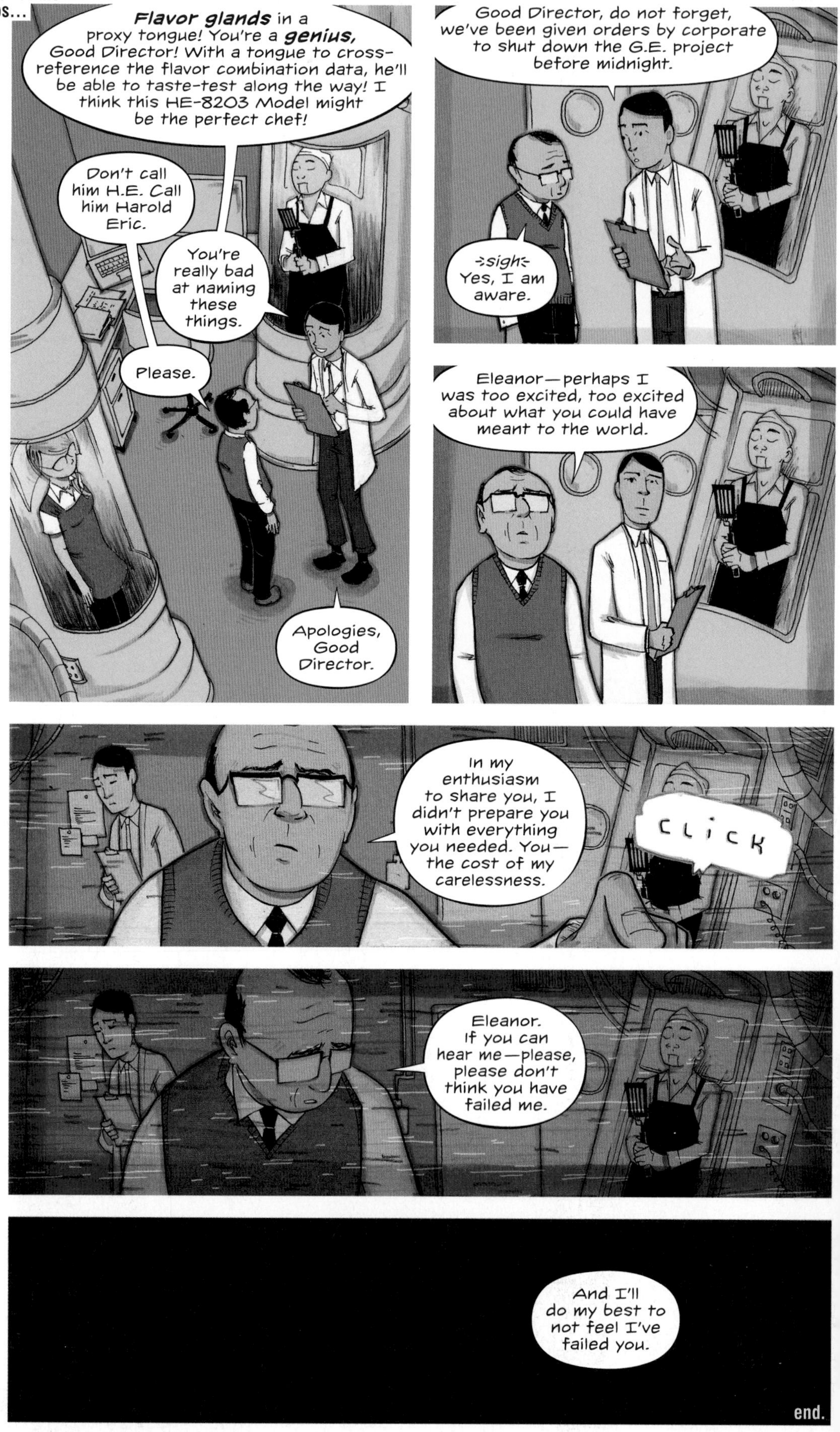
Flavor glands in a proxy tongue! You're a genius, Good Director! With a tongue to cross-reference the flavor combination data, he'll be able to taste-test along the way! I think this HE-8203 Model might be the perfect chef!
Don't call him H.E. Call him Harold Eric.
You're really bad at naming these things.
Please.
Apologies, Good Director.
Good Director, do not forget, we've been given orders by corporate to shut down the G.E. project before midnight.
-sigh- Yes, I am aware.
Eleanor—perhaps I was too excited, too excited about what you could have meant to the world.
In my enthusiasm to share you, I didn't prepare you with everything you needed. You—the cost of my carelessness.
CLICK
Eleanor. If you can hear me—please, please don't think you have failed me.
And I'll do my best to not feel I've failed you.
end.